HARD MAGIC

Book I of the Grimnoir Chronicles

Baen Books by Larry Correia

The Monster Hunter International Series
Monster Hunter International
Monster Hunter Vendetta
Monster Hunter Alpha (forthcoming)

The Grimnoir Chronicles
Hard Magic
Spellbound (forthcoming)
Dead Six (forthcoming)

HARD MAGIC

Book I of the Grimnoir Chronicles

LARRY CORREIA

Hard Magic: Book I of the Grimnoir Chronicles

This is a work of fiction. All the characters and events portrayed in this book are fictional, and any resemblance to real people or incidents is purely coincidental.

A Baen Book Original

Baen Publishing Enterprises
P.O. Box 1403
Riverdale, NY 10471
www.baen.com

ISBN: 978-1-4391-3434-4

Cover art by Alan Pollack
Interior art by Justin Otis, Aura Farwell, and Zachary Hill

First Baen printing, May 2011

Distributed by Simon & Schuster
1230 Avenue of the Americas
New York, NY 10020

Library of Congress Cataloging-in-Publication Data

Correia, Larry.
Hard magic / Larry Correia.
p. cm. -- (The Grimnoir chronicles ; bk. 1)
ISBN 978-1-4391-3434-4 (trade pbk.)
I. Title.
PS3603.O7723H37 2011
813'.6--dc22

2011004663

Printed in the United States of America

10 9 8 7 6 5 4 3 2 1

To Jackie

Acknowledgments

Thanks to the members of Reader Force Alpha, who keep me from making a fool of myself; the awesome crew at Baen Books; and Mike Kupari, for helping brainstorm the Grimnoir world into existence. Specials thanks go the talented artists whose work appears in these pages: Justin Otis and Aura Farwell for the glossary art, and Zachary Hill for the interior drawings.

Prologue

One general law, leading to the advancement of all organic beings, namely, multiply, vary, let the strongest live and the weakest die. The appearance of esoteric and etheral abiliites, magical fires and feats of strength, in recent decades are the purest demonstration of natural selection. Surely, in time, that general law will require the extinction of traditional man.

—Charles Darwin,
On the Origin of Man and Selection of Human Magical Abilities, 1879

El Nido, California

"OKIES." The Portuguese farmer spat on the ground, giving the evil eye to the passing automobiles weighed down with baskets, bushels, and crates. The cars just kept coming up the dusty San Joaquin Valley road like some kind of Okie wagon train. He left to make sure all his valuables were locked up and his Sears & Roebuck single-shot 12 gauge was loaded.

The tool shed was locked and the shotgun was in his hands when the short little farmer returned to watch.

One of the Ford Model Ts rattled to a stop in front of the farmhouse fence. The old farmer leaned on his shotgun and waited. His son would talk to the visitors. The boy spoke English. So did he, but not as well, just good enough to take the Dodge truck into Merced to buy supplies, and it wasn't like the mangled inbred garbage dialect the Okies spoke was English anyway.

The farmer watched the transients carefully as his son approached the automobile. They were asking for work. They were always asking for work. Ever since the dusts had blown up and cursed their stupid land, they'd all driven west in some Okie exodus until they ran out of farmland and stopped to harass the Portuguese, who had gotten here first.

Of course they'd been here first. Like he gave a shit if these people were homeless or hungry. He'd been born in a hut on the tiny island of Terceira and had milked cows every single day of his life until his hands were leather bags so strong he could bend pipe. The San Joaquin Valley had been a hole until his people had shown up, covered the place in Holsteins, and put the Mexicans to work. Now these Okies show up, build tent cities, bitch about how the government should save them, and sneak out at night to rob the Catholics. It really pissed him off.

It always amazed him how much the Okies could fit onto an old Model T. He'd come from Terceira on a steamship, spending weeks in a steel hole between hot steam pipes. He'd owned a blanket, one pair of pants, a hat, and a pair of shoes with holes in them. He'd worked his ass off in a Portuguese town in Rhode Island, neck deep in fish guts, married a nice Portuguese girl, even if she was from the screwed up island of St. George, which everybody from Terceira knew was the ass crack of the Azores, and saved up enough money doing odd jobs to come out here to another Portuguese town and buy some scrawny Holsteins. Five cows, a bull, and twenty years of backbreaking labor had turned into a hundred and twenty cows, fifty acres, a Ford tractor, a Dodge pickup, a good milk barn, and a house with six whole rooms. By Portuguese standards, he was living like a king.

So he wasn't going to give these Okies shit. They weren't even Catholic. They should have to work like he did. He watched the Okie father talking to his son as his son patiently explained for the hundredth time that there wasn't any work, and that they needed to head toward Los Banos or maybe Chowchilla, not that they were going to work anyway when they could just break into his milk barn and steal his tools to sell for rotgut moonshine again. His grandkids were poking their heads around the house, checking out the Model T, but he'd warned them enough times about the dangers of outsiders, and they stayed safely away. He wasn't about to have his family corrupted from their good Catholic work ethic by being exposed to bums.

Then he noticed the girl.

She was just another scrawny Okie kid. Barely even a woman yet, so it was surprising that she hadn't already had three kids from her brothers. But there was something strange about this one . . . something he'd seen before.

The girl glanced his way, and he knew then what had set him off. She had grey eyes.

"Mary, mother of God," the old farmer muttered, fingering the crucifix at his neck. "Not this shit again . . ." His first reaction was to walk away, leave it alone. It wasn't any of his business, and the girl would probably be dead soon enough, impaled through her guts by some random tree branch or a flying bug stuck in an artery. And he didn't even know if the grey eyes meant the same thing to an Okie as it did to the Portuguese. For all he knew she was a normal girl who just looked funny, and she'd go have a long and stupid life in an Okie tent city popping out fifteen kids who'd also break into his milk barn and steal his tools.

The girl was studying him, dirty hair whipping in the wind, and he could just tell . . .

"Fooking shit damn," he said in English, which was the first English any immigrant who worked with cows learned. He'd seen what happened to the grey eyes when they weren't taught correctly, and as much as he despised Okies, he didn't want to see one of their kids with their brains spread all over the road because they'd magically appeared in front of a speeding truck.

Leaning the shotgun against the tractor tire, he approached the Model T. The Okie parents looked at him with mild belligerence as he approached their daughter. The old farmer stopped next to the girl's window. There were half a dozen other kids crammed in there, but they were just regular desperate and starving Okies. This one was special.

He lifted his hat so she could see that his eyes were the same color as hers. He tried his best English. "You . . . girl. Grey eyes." She pointed at herself, curious, but didn't speak. He nodded. "You . . . Jump? Travel?" She didn't understand, and now her idiot parents were staring at him in slack jawed ignorance. The old farmer took one hand and held it out in a fist. He suddenly opened it. "Poof!" Then he raised his other hand as far away as possible, "Poof!" and made a fist.

She smiled and nodded her head vigorously. He grinned. She was a Traveler all right.

"You know about what she does?" the Okie father asked.

The old farmer nodded, finding his own magic inside and poking it to wake it up. Then he was gone, and instantly he was on the other side of the Model T. He tapped the Okie mother on the arm through the open window and she shrieked. All his grandkids cheered. They loved when he did that. His son just rolled his eyes.

The Okie father looked at the Portuguese farmer, back at his daughter, and then back to the farmer. The grey eyed girl was happy as could be that she'd found somebody just like her. The father scowled for a long time, glancing again at his strange child that had caused them so much grief, and then at all the other starving mouths he had to find a way to feed. Finally he spoke. "I'll sell you her for twenty dollars."

The old farmer thought about it. He didn't need any more people eating up his food, but his brother and sisters had all ended up dead before they had mastered Traveling, and this was the first other person like him he'd seen in twenty years, but he also hadn't gotten where he was by getting robbed by Okies. "Make it ten."

The girl giggled and clapped.

New York City, New York

THE RICHEST MAN IN THE WORLD stepped into the elevator lift and looked in distaste at the gleaming silver buttons. The message had said to come alone, so he did not even have one of his usual functionaries to perform the service of requesting the correct floor. Rather than soiling his hands or a perfectly good handkerchief, he sighed, tapped into the lowest level of his Power, and pushed the button for the penthouse suite with his mind. Cornelius Gould Stuyvesant, billionaire industrialist, could not tolerate filth. A man of his stature simply did not get his hands dirty.

He had people for that.

The steel doors closed. They were carved with golden figures of muscular workers creating the American dream through their sweat and industry under a rising sun emitting rays as straight as a Tesla cannon. He sniffed the air. The elevator car *seemed* clean. The hotel was considered a five-star luxury establishment, but Cornelius just *knew* that there were germs everywhere, disgusting, diseased, tiny plague nodules just itching to get on his skin. Cornelius understood the true nature of the man who was staying in this hotel, and he must have ridden in this very car. Cornelius shuddered as he squeezed his arms and briefcase closer to his sides, careful not to touch the walls.

He could afford the finest Healers. In fact, he was one of the only men in the world that had an actual Mender on his personal staff, but nothing could stop the blight of a Pale Horse, and it was that foul Power that brought him here today, reduced to a mere caller. Cornelius had tried to seek out others, once under a gypsy tent on Coney Island, again in a tiny shack in the Louisiana Bayou, but those had been frauds, charlatans, wastes of his valuable time. He tapped his foot impatiently. After what seemed like an eternity, the doors whisked open.

A tuxedoed servant was waiting for him, an older negro with stark white hair. The servant bowed his head. "Good evening, Mr. Stuyvesant. Mr. Harkeness is waiting on the balcony. May I take your coat, sir?"

"Not necessary. My business will not take long."

The servant studied him with cunning eyes. "Of course, sir. Would you care for a drink? Mr. Harkeness has a selection of the finest."

"As if I would drink anything *here*," Cornelius sputtered. The notion of ingesting something from the household of a Pale Horse was madness. "Take me to him immediately."

"Of course, sir." The servant led the way down the marble hall. Carved busts of long-dead Greeks watched him from pedestals, judging. Cornelius hated statues. Statues made him prickly. Even the giant idolized bronze of himself at the new super-dirigible dock bearing his name atop the new Empire State Building bothered him.

Lots of things made Cornelius Gould Stuyvesant uncomfortable, including this servant. He did not like the way he had examined him, like he was being sized up. The information he'd gathered on Harkeness indicated that the man surrounded himself with other like-minded Actives. There were many who would kill a Pale Horse on basic principle, so it made sense to have loyal staff with Power for security. He idly wondered what kind of Active the old servant was. Probably something barbaric, like a Brute, or even worse, a Torch. That would seem to suit a race that was so easily inflamed by its passions.

"Mr. Harkeness is through here, sir." The servant paused at the fine wood and thick glass door leading to the balcony. He turned the knob and opened it. "He prefers the fresh air. Will there be anything else?"

Cornelius did not bother to respond as he stepped onto the balcony. His time was valuable, more valuable than any man in the world, more valuable than emperors, kings, tsars, kaisers, and especially that imbecile, Herbert Hoover, and the very idea that he was reduced to having to take time from his busy schedule to meet someone on their terms rather than his own was blatantly offensive.

To further the sleight, Harkeness was leaning on the balcony, overlooking the city, placing his back toward the richest man in the world, as if Manhattan were somehow more important than Cornelius Gould Stuyvesant himself. The balcony lights had been extinguished, so as not to hamper the view. The city was illuminated forty stories below by electric lights and flashing marquees. Thousands of automobiles filled the streets, bustling even at this hour, and overhead a passing dirigible train floated in the amber spotlights like a herd of sea cows. Cornelius snorted in greeting.

"Mr. Stuyvesant." The Pale Horse didn't bother to turn around. His voice was neutral, flat. "I was just admiring your marvelous city. Have a seat."

Cornelius felt a single drop of sweat roll down his neck. It was shameful, but he found that he was actually frightened. He glanced at the pair of chairs, fine, stuffed leather things that in any other scenario would be inviting to rest his ponderous bulk, but at that moment, all he could imagine were the horrible diseases crawling on the cushions.

"I said have a seat," Harkeness repeated, still not turning around. His accent was indeterminate, his pronunciation awkward. "You are a guest of mine. I would not harm a guest. I am a civilized man, Mr. Stuyvesant."

Cornelius sat, vowing that he would throw this suit into the fireplace as soon as he got home, then he would have his personal

Healer expend a month's worth of Power checking his health. He would probably burn the Cadillac car he had traveled in, maybe the driver too, just to be on the safe side.

Harkeness left the railing and took the other seat. He did not offer his hand. He was older than Cornelius had expected, tall and thin, face lined with creases, and blue eyes that sparked with an unnerving energy. His hair was receding, and what remained was artificially blackened. His tailored suit was as fine as could be had, and his tie was made of silk as red as fresh blood. He smiled, and his teeth were slightly yellow in the dim city light. "Smoke?"

Cornelius looked down at the wooden humidor on the table between them. The cigars were sorely tempting, but the very thought of touching his lips with an item tainted by Harkeness's evil made his stomach roil. "No, thank you."

Harkeness nodded in understanding as he puffed on his own Cuban. "Straight to the chase then. I was informed that you were looking for me."

"Nobody can ever know we spoke," Cornelius insisted. He was the founder and owner of United Blimp & Freight, the primary shareholder in Federal Steel, and the man that bankrolled the development of the Peace Ray. He'd sired children who had gone on to be ambassadors to powerful nations, senators, congressmen, and even a governor. A Stuyvesant could not be seen consorting with such sordid types.

"I assure you, I am a man of discretion." Harkeness exhaled a pungent tobacco cloud, not seeming to notice his guest's discomfort.

Cornelius cringed, trying not to inhale smoke that had actually been inside the very lungs of such a pestilent creature. "You are a hard man to find, Mr. Harkeness," the billionaire said, aware that he had to tread carefully. Even with eight decades of mankind dealing with the presence of Powers, of actual magic, to the point that they were just an accepted part of life in most of the world, the Pale Horse was such a rarity that most still considered it to be a myth, crude antimagic propaganda created to sow fear and distrust in the hearts of the masses. "Men of your . . . skills . . . are especially rare."

"Yes . . . What is it you were told I am?" Harkeness asked rhetorically, examining the ash on the end of his cigar.

Cornelius hesitated, not sure if he should answer, but growing tired off the awkward silence, he finally spoke. "I was told you are a Pale Horse."

Harkeness laughed hard, slapping his knee. "I like that. So . . . biblical! So much nicer than plague bearer, or grim reaper, or angel of death. That title has gravitas. Pale Horse! You, sir, have made my day. Perhaps I shall add that to my business cards." His pronunciation was stilted, with pauses between random words. Cornelius found it almost hypnotic, and realized he was nervously smiling along with the other man's mirth. Then Harkeness abruptly quit laughing and his voice turned deadly serious. "So, who must die?"

"You presume much," Cornelius said defensively.

"If you just wanted to merely curse someone and make their hair fall out, or to give them boils, fits, or incontinence, there are far easier Actives to reach than I." Harkeness's smile was unnerving. "People come to me when they desire something . . . epic."

The industrialist swallowed and placed his briefcase on the table. He unlocked it, then turned it so that Harkeness could see inside. It was filled with neatly stacked and meticulously counted bank notes and a single newspaper clipping. Cornelius quickly snatched his hand away before the Pale Horse could touch the contents, as if his Power might somehow be transmitted through the leather.

The Pale Horse did not seem to notice the money. He gently removed the yellowed clipping, took a pair of spectacles from his breast pocket, set them atop his hawklike nose and began reading. After a moment he removed the glasses and returned them and the clipping to his pocket. "An important man. Very well . . . What will it be? Bone rot? Consumption? Cancers of the brain or bowel? Syphilis? Leprosy? I can do anything from a minor vapor to turn his joints to sand while his skin boils off in a cancerous sludge. I am an encyclopedia of affliction, sir."

Cornelius bobbed his head in time with the litany of diseases. "All of them."

"I see . . ." Harkeness seemed to approve. "Very well, but first, I must know . . ."

"Yes," Cornelius answered hesitantly. The hairs on the back of his neck were standing up.

"Why? A man such as you has no shortage of killers to choose from. Why not a knife in the back? A bullet in the head? You yourself are a Mover, why not just invite him to a balcony such as this and shove him off? It would even look like a suicide, which would be particularly scandalous in the papers."

"How—" Cornelius sputtered. His Power was a secret. "Me? A Magical? Who told you such slanderous lies?"

Harkeness shrugged. "I have a trained eye, Mr. Stuyvesant. Now answer my question. Why do you need me to curse this man?"

Cornelius felt his face flush with anger. No matter how dangerous Harkeness was, Cornelius Gould Stuyvesant was not about to have his motives questioned by a mere hireling. He pushed himself away from the table and rose, bellowing, "Why you? I do not want him dead. That is far too good a fate for one such as he! I want him to suffer first. I want him to know he's dying and I want him to pray to his ineffectual God to save him as his body rots and stinks and melts to the blackest filth. I want it to hurt and I want it to be embarrassing. I want his lungs to fill with pus. I want his balls to fall off and I want him to piss fire! I want his loved ones to look away in disgust, and I want it to take a very, very *long* time."

Harkeness nodded, his face now an emotionless mask. "I can do this thing for you, but first, I must ask, what terrible thing did this man do to deserve such a fate?"

The billionaire paused, pudgy hands curled into fists. He lowered his voice before continuing. He had planned this revenge for years. It was only the purity of the hate for his enemy that drove him to this place. "He took something . . . *someone* . . . from me. Leave it at that." Cornelius tried to calm himself. He was not a man given to such unseemly outbursts. "Will that do?"

"It is enough."

Cornelius realized he was standing, but it did make him feel more in control, more in his element. He gestured at the open briefcase. "I was given your name by an associate. I believe that this is the same amount that he paid for your services." Rockefeller had warned Cornelius about how expensive the Pale Horse would be, but it would be so very worth the money. "Take it."

The other man shook his head. "No. I don't think so."

"What!" Cornelius objected. Was he going to try and shake him down for more money than Rockefeller? The *nerve*. "How dare you!"

Harkeness leaned back in his chair, puffing on the cigar. He took it away from his mouth and smiled without any joy. "I don't want your money, Mr. Stuyvesant. I want something *else*."

Cornelius trembled. Of course, he'd heard the odder stories about the Pale Horses, the rarest of the Actives, but he had paid them no heed. He was a man of science, not superstition. Sure, he had magic himself, nowadays one in a hundred Americans had some small measure, but it didn't mean he understood how it actually worked. One in a thousand had access to greater Power, being actual Actives, but men like Harkeness were something different, something rare and strange, themselves oddities in an odd bunch. Hesitantly he spoke. "Do . . . do you want . . . my *soul*?"

This time Harkeness really did laugh, almost choking on his cigar. "Now that's funny! Do I look like a spiritualist? I'm certainly not the devil, Mr. Stuyvesant. I do not even know if I believe in such preposterous things. What would I even do with your soul if I had it?"

That was a relief, even if Cornelius wasn't particularly sure that he had a soul, he didn't want to deed it over to a man like Harkeness. "I don't know," Cornelius shrugged. "I just thought . . ."

Harkeness was still chuckling. "No, nothing so mysterious. All I want is a *favor*."

That caused Cornelius to pause. "A favor?"

Harkeness was done laughing. "Yes, a favor. Not today. But someday in the future I will call and ask for a favor. You will remember this service performed, and you will grant me that favor without hesitation or question. Is that understood?"

"What manner of favor?"

The Pale Horse shrugged. "I do not yet know this thing. But I do know that if you fail to honor our bargain at that particular time, I will be greatly displeased."

He was not, by nature, a man who intimidated easily, but Cornelius Gould Stuyvesant was truly unnerved. The threat went unsaid, but who would want to cross such a man? The industrialist almost walked out on the absurd and frightening proposal, but he had been planning his revenge for far too long to turn back now. If the favor was too large, Cornelius knew he always had other options. Harkeness was deadly, but he wasn't immortal. It would not be the first time he had used murder to get out of an inequitable contract.

"Very well," Cornelius said. "You have a deal. When will he get sick?"

Harkeness closed his eyes for a few seconds, as if pondering a difficult question. "It is already done," the Pale Horse said, opening his eyes. "Isaiah will see you out."

Isaiah joined his employer on the balcony a few minutes later. Harkeness had gone back to admiring the view. "Could you Read him?"

"He's very intelligent. I had to be gentle or he would've known. He's got a bad tendency to shout his thoughts when he gets riled up." The servant leaned against the concrete wall and folded his arms. "He even thought I might be a Torch. Can you believe that?"

Harkeness chuckled, knowing that Isaiah was far more dangerous than some mere human flame hurler. "Was he truthful?"

"Mostly. He absolutely despises this man."

"For what he did to him? Wouldn't you?"

Isaiah sounded disgusted. "Stuyvesant is utterly ruthless."

So am I, Harkeness thought, knowing full well that Isaiah would pick that up as clearly as a high-strength radio broadcast. "You don't get to such lofty positions without being dangerous. I'll have to curse him quickly. Arranging a meeting should be easy enough. Stuyvesant will be expecting immediate results now."

Isaiah left the wall and took one of the cigars from the table. "I liked your little show, with closing the eyes and just wishing for somebody to die and all that. That's good theater."

Of course, even he had his limits. He would actually have to touch the victim, and it took constant Power thereafter to keep up the onslaught against the ministrations of Menders, which he already knew this man would have. This would be an extremely draining assignment. "Whatever keeps Stuyvesant nervous," Harkeness shrugged. "I do like the new term though. It suits me."

Isaiah quoted from memory as he clipped the end from the Cuban. "And I heard a voice in the midst of the four beasts, and I looked and beheld a pale horse, and the name that sat upon him was death . . ."

"And hell followed with him," Harkeness finished, smiling. "Appropriate . . ."

"If the favor you ask of him is too difficult, he'll have you killed."

Harkeness had suspected as much. "He could try. Wouldn't be the first."

"The man's got a phobia about sickness. The Spanish flu near did him when it came through, been worrying him ever since." Isaiah said as he lit the cigar. "He's scared of you."

"Good," the Pale Horse muttered, watching the people moving below, scuttling about like ants, ignorant little creatures, unaware of the truth of the world in which they lived. The Chairman was about to change the world, whether any of the ants liked it or not, and that meant war. Many ants would be stepped on, but that was just too bad. It was unfortunate to be born an ant. "He should be . . ."

Billings, Montana

EVERY DAY WAS THE SAME. Every prisoner in the Special Prisoners' Wing of the Rockville State Penitentiary had the exact same schedule. You slept. You worked. You got put back in your cage. You slept. You worked. You got put back in your cage. Repeat until time served.

Working meant breaking rocks. Normal prisoners were put on work crews to be used by mayors trying to keep budgets low. They got to go outside. The convicts in Special Wing got to break rocks in a giant stone pit. Some of them were even issued tools. The name of the facility was just a coincidence.

One particular convict excelled at breaking rocks. He did a good job of it because he did a good job of everything he set his mind to. First he'd been good at war and now he was good at breaking rocks. It was just his nature. The convict had single-minded determination, and once he got to pushing something, he just couldn't find it in himself to stop. He was as constant as gravity. After a year, he was the finest rock breaker and mover in the history of Rockville State Penitentiary.

Occasionally some other prisoner would try to start trouble because he thought the convict was making the rest of them look bad, but even in a place dedicated to holding felons who could tap into all manner of magical affinities, most were smart enough not to cross this particular convict. After the first few left in bags, the rest understood that he just wanted to be left alone to do his time. Occasionally some new man, eager to show off his Power, would step up and challenge the convict, and he too would leave in a bag.

The warden did not blame the convict for the violence. He understood the type of men he had under his care, and knew that the convict was just defending himself. Between helping meet the quota for the gravel quarry that padded the warden's salary under the table, and for ridding the Special Wing of its most dangerous and troublesome men, the warden took a liking to the convict. He read the convict's records, and came to respect the convict as a man for the deeds he'd done before committing his crime. He was the first Special Prisoner ever granted access to the extremely well-stocked, but very dusty prison library.

So the convict's schedule changed. Sleep. Work. Read. Sleep. Work. Read. So now the time passed faster. The convict read books by the greatest minds of the day. He read the classics. He began to question his Power. Why did his Power work the way it did? What separated him from normal men? Why could he do the things he could do? Because of its relation to his own specific gifts, he started with Newton, then Einstein, finally Bohr and Heisenberg, and then every other mind that had pontificated on the science related to his magic. And when he had exhausted the books on science, he turned to the philosophers' musings on the nature of magic and the mystery of where it had suddenly come from and all of its short history. He read Darwin. He read Schuman, and Kelser, Reed, and Spengler. When that was done, he read *everything* that was left.

The convict began to experiment with his Power. He would sneak bits of rock back into his cell to toy with. Reaching deep inside himself, twisting, testing, always pushing with that same dogged determination that had made him the best rock breaker, and when he got tired of experimenting with rocks, he started to experiment on his own body. Eventually all those hours of testing and introspection enabled him to discover things about magic that very few other people would ever understand.

But he kept that to himself.

Then one day the warden offered the convict a deal . . .

Chapter One

We now have over a thousand confirmed cases of individuals with these so-called magical abilities on the continent alone. The faculty has descended into a terrible uproar over the proper nomenclature for such specimens. All manner of Latin phrases have been bandied about. Professor Gerard even suggested Grimnoir, *a combination of the old French Grimoire, or book of spells, with Noir, for Black, in the sense of the mysterious, for at this juncture the origin of said Powers remains unknown. He was laughed down. Personally, I've taken to calling them wizards, for the very idea of there being actual magic beyond the bounds of science causes my esteemed colleagues to sputter and choke.*

—Dr. L. Fulci,
Professor of Natural Science, University of Bern,
Personal Journal, 1852

THREE YEARS LATER

Springfield, Illinois

THERE WERE TWENTY LOCAL BULLS, ten state coppers, and half a dozen agents from the Bureau of Investigation, and every one of them was packing serious heat. Jake Sullivan approved. Purvis wasn't screwing around this time. Delilah Jones was going down.

The lead government man was pacing back and forth in front of the crew assembled in the warehouse. "You don't hesitate. None of you hesitate even for a second. She's a woman, but don't you dare underestimate her. She's robbed twenty banks in four states, and killed five people." He paused long enough to jerk a thumb at his men. "When you see her, nobody makes a move until me or Agent Cowley says the word."

A second government man raised his hand. Sam Cowley's suit was cheap, but his 1928 Thompson was meticulously maintained. Sullivan knew he was a man who kept his priorities in order, so at least he'd been roped into working with an experienced crew this time.

There was a wanted poster stuck to the wall. Sullivan had known Delilah back in New Orleans. She was a dish, a real looker. He had to admit that the ink drawing was actually realistic, unlike his old wanted poster, where they had uglied him up for dramatic effect, but in the sketch artists' defense, somebody that could crush every bone in your body should look scary.

"How many men in the gang?" one of the locals asked.

Melvin Purvis paused. "I'm not expecting a gang. Just her."

The room got quiet. It normally didn't take thirty-seven men with rifles and shotguns to take down a lone woman, bank robber or not. They all realized what that meant about the same time, but nobody wanted to say it. Finally the same local slowly raised his hand. "She got big Powers then?"

"Yes, McKee. She does," Purvis responded. "She's a Brute, and she's Active. Probably the toughest I've heard of." McKee lowered his hand. The sea of blue and brown uniforms all looked at each other, grumbling and swearing. "Yeah, yeah, I know. Listen, boys, when I got here, I asked your chiefs for hard men. I know you're all up to it, but if any of you want out, there's no shame in leaving."

"Is that why he's here?" McKee asked, since he'd somehow become the leader of the uniforms, gesturing to where Sullivan had been trying to remain unnoticed in the back of the room.

"He's with me," Purvis said. "We let Sullivan do his job, and none of you have to worry about dealing with a little lady who can toss automobiles at you. You got a problem with that?"

"He's a murderer," McKee pointed out.

"Manslaughter," Sullivan corrected, speaking for the first time. "And I done served my time. J. Edgar Hoover says I'm *reformed*."

There were no more questions forthcoming. Somebody coughed. Purvis folded his arms and waited until the count of ten. Nobody stood up to leave. "Good. We try to take her alive. My men go in first with Sullivan. The rest hang back outside and get the bystanders out of the way. Nobody shoots unless she goes Active."

"Then don't miss," Agent Cowley suggested.

They'd be moving out in a matter of minutes and Sullivan sensed the room was nervous, kind of bouncy and tense. It reminded him a little of the Great War, in those few awful seconds before the whistle blew and they'd jump out of the relative safety of their muddy trenches and run screaming into Maxim gunfire, barbed wire, and the Kaiser's zombies.

Jake Sullivan had gotten the call from Washington two weeks before, telling him to report to Special Agent Melvin Purvis in Chicago. The assignment came at a good time. His regular business as a private dick was floundering, and he had been reduced to pulling the occasional security gig, standing in as muscle during some of the labor strikes. He didn't like it, but just being special didn't pay the bills. At least he hadn't had to hurt anyone. Just his reputation kept the strikers peaceful. Nobody wanted to cross a Heavy, especially one that had served time in Rockville.

The government jobs barely paid a decent wage, but more importantly, this was the last of the five assignments he had agreed to upon his early release. The warden had appealed to his patriotism when he had transmitted the offer, telling Sullivan that it would be a chance to serve his country again. He had found that amusing, since his only desire at that point was to get out of that hellhole. He'd already served his country once, and had the scars to show for it.

As had been agreed upon, every single other Magical he had assisted in capturing had been a murderer. Jake still had some principles left.

And this one was no different, though he had been surprised to find out that he had known her once. Hearing the name of the target, and then the terrible crimes she'd committed had left him stunned. Sullivan still couldn't picture Delilah as a cold-blooded killer, but people could change a lot in six years. He certainly had.

Sullivan sat uncomfortably in the backseat of the Ford as they watched yet another dirigible drift into the station. Purvis and

Cowley were in the front seat. It was raining hard, pounding mist from the pavement and creating halos around every street lamp.

"This should be it," Cowley said from behind the steering wheel. His Thompson was on the seat next to him and he rhythmically tapped his fingers on the wooden stock.

"The informant said she would be on the eight-fifteen," Purvis said, checking his pocket watch. "Must be running late 'cause of the weather."

An informant? "So that's how you found her." Sullivan wasn't surprised. He'd been ratted out himself all those years ago. "Figures."

"I don't like this," Cowley said. "There's too many people around if she goes Active. It'd be safer to tail her to someplace quiet."

"We already talked about this. We can't risk losing her. She's supposed to be coming here to do a job for the Torrios. You want somebody like her working for Crazy Lenny?"

Sullivan just listened. Strategy wasn't his area. He just did what he was told. Nobody expected a Heavy to be smart, so Jake found life went easier if he just kept his mouth shut, but if it were up to him, he would have to go with Cowley's plan. It wasn't like Magicals didn't catch enough heat from a few bad apples as it was. The last thing they needed was stories in the papers about a Brute taking the heads off some G-men in public.

"You ready, Sullivan?" Purvis asked as he opened his door into the downpour.

"Yeah," he muttered. "This is the last time, you know. That was the deal. After this, I'm a free man. I ain't beholden to nobody."

"Over my pay grade," the senior agent responded before stepping out. He slammed the door behind him. All down the street other cops saw Purvis appear and the lawmen began to exit their cars as well.

"He better keep a leash on those bulls or this could get ugly," Sullivan said as he pulled a pack of smokes out of his coat. "Got a light, Sam?"

"You know I always do, Sullivan." Cowley turned around and snapped his fingers. A flame appeared from the end of his thumb. "Figures God would bless me with a little tiny Power, and he gives a magic lighter to somebody who doesn't smoke." He chuckled. Cowley was some religion that forbade smoking, a strange combination for a Torch.

Sullivan lit the fag. "Ironic." He took a long drag. Sullivan liked the agent. Cowley was homely and avoided the spotlight as much as Purvis sought it. They'd worked together before and Sullivan knew the agent was competent. "You know, you best not let your boss see you do that. I hear J. Edgar don't like magic."

"Lots of folks don't." Cowley turned around and opened his door. "We better go." He got out, pulling the Thompson with him.

Sullivan sighed. Cowley was the weakest kind of Magical, with just a flicker of natural Power, but even that could ruin a man's career in some circles. He tugged his hat down low and got ready, feeling the Power stored inside his chest. It took a lot of practice to build up that much and still keep it under control. He activated a small part and felt his body shift. For a brief moment the world around him seemed to flex. The springs on the Ford creaked. He cracked his knuckles, feeling the Spike, gently testing the tug of gravity around him.

Cigarette dangling from his lower lip, he opened the door and slowly unfolded himself from the backseat. Jake Sullivan was a big man, and he used a big gun. He reached back inside and maneuvered the long case from the backseat. The black canvas bag was enormous and he let it dangle from one hand.

Cowley looked over, rain running off his fedora, and pointed at the case. "I don't see how you can carry that thing around."

Sullivan took one last drag before tossing his smoke into a puddle. "Saved your life in Detroit, if I remember right."

"True, but it has to weigh a ton."

"Not to me," Sullivan said as he reached into the bag, grabbed the Lewis gun by its stock and withdrew it. Even twenty-six pounds empty didn't really concern somebody who could alter gravity. To him it was light as a feather and swung like a bird gun.

"Damn, is that a fence post?" Purvis asked, cradling a short barreled Browning Auto-5. "Put that thing back. This is an arrest, not a war."

"You don't know Delilah." Sullivan threw the sling over his shoulder and head so the massive machine gun could hang at his side. It wasn't exactly concealable, but his parole deal had specified he would help take down Active murderers, not that he had to be tactful about it. "You know, Purvis, I've never got in a gunfight and said afterwards, damn, I wish I hadn't brought all that extra ammo."

"Put it away, Sullivan. That's an order. I got lots of men who can shoot, and I've only got one that can do—" he waved his hands like a bad stage magician—"*whatever* it is you do."

"Where'd you get that monster anyway?" Cowley asked.

"Flea market," Sullivan answered as he unslung the mighty Lewis and put it back into its case. All the Spikers had been issued heavy weapons in Roosevelt's First Volunteer. He'd brought quite a few souvenirs back from France besides the shrapnel still lodged in his body. He might not be able to take the Lewis, but he still had a .45 auto riding his hip. Magic was great and all, but a lot of problems could still be solved faster the old-fashioned way, and Jake considered himself a practical man.

"Just do your job, and we'll keep you safe," Purvis promised. "I want this to go nice and clean. You just wrap her up."

At least Purvis seemed like the kind of agent who cared more about being effective than being popular in the papers, unlike the fiasco in Detroit six months ago. "Yeah, fine," he said, shoving the canvas case back into the Ford. He closed the door too hard. "You know, Agent Purvis, I know Delilah pretty good. The dame's had a tough run. She's not the kind that'll go down easy, and she ain't going quiet, that's for damn sure. She's a fighter, but I never knew her to be the murdering kind."

"You saw the same file I did. I've got five dead men that say different. Necks snapped, one arm torn clean off." Purvis scowled. "I've got my orders. We take her alive . . . But I'm more worried about the safety of these boys than I am about orders. You getting me, Heavy?"

Sullivan preferred the more dignified term Gravity Spiker. Heavy was what you called the Passives who were employed in factories as human forklifts. Cold water was slipping inside his trench coat as he shrugged. He just wanted to get this last job over with and finally get the Man off his back. "I get you, Agent Purvis." The street was clear of oncoming headlights, so he started across, big boots splashing through the puddles. The six G-men followed.

The wedge-shaped dirigible was gradually slowing between the towers, and when it came to a rest, the passengers would begin to debark. It was slow going in bad weather, and this particular balloon was just a little two-hundred-footer hybrid machine, so it was getting kicked around quite a bit by the wind. The Springfield dirigible station was relatively small, nothing like the enclosed behemoth just constructed in Chicago.

Ground crews were braving the rain and catching the security lines. One man was giving them orders with a bullhorn from the tower, probably a Crackler, redirecting lightning and static electricity to keep the airfield's workers safe at the ends of those cables, but it wasn't like Magicals like that got any credit in the press. No, everybody knew Hearst didn't care about working stiffs with Powers. He only wasted ink on people like Delilah. *And me . . .* Sullivan thought, *trouble makers*, but then shook his head, getting back to business.

He and the Bureau of Investigation men took cover beneath the overhang at the entrance to the waiting room. Through the glass he could see the room was nice, mosaic tile floor, all brass and glass on the walls, with lots of wood and iron benches for the commuters. There were a handful of people waiting. Purvis left two men outside, and the rest got out of the rain and entered the dry comfort of the lounge.

The lift was clearly visible. Sullivan noted that they'd be able to see the passengers before the passengers could see them, which was convenient for once. A United Blimp & Freight worker spotted the guns but Purvis flashed his badge and waved the man away. The G-men started ushering people out into the rain as fast as they could, and Purvis sent one to make sure nobody was loitering on the stairs. The uniformed bulls were out on the dark perimeter if Delilah somehow made it past or drew on her Power and turned it into a fight.

Most of the UBF employees didn't know what was going down, but word would spread quickly now. He stood with his back to the mirrored wall. The tower was four stories tall, and that was a lot of stairs, which meant that Delilah would probably come down in the elevator, especially if she had luggage. Either way, from this position he could watch both.

Everything in this place was mirrored and shiny—even the ceiling had mirrors—but the mighty UBF budget had been cut because of the recent downturns, and the place felt kind of grimy. The Twenties had been a huge economic boom time, but Sullivan had spent most of those happy years doing hard time. The papers were calling it a depression, but compared to Rockville, Jake thought the whole outside world seemed pretty damn nice.

The dirigible's cabin made a strange clanking noise as it mated with the docking platform through the roof above. Sullivan closed his eyes and used a little more of his Power to feel the world around him. The giant reserve of helium felt unnatural, being lighter than air, and that always made accurate Spiking a little difficult. He'd have to compensate for it. He was supposed to capture Delilah, not splatter her into red mush.

It wasn't even five minutes after the dirigible had docked that the elevator came down with its first load of passengers. UBF was the model of efficiency. Like the ads said, they were the *Convenient Way to Travel*. The agents tensed up, but there were only a few passengers, none of whom were Delilah Jones, and a young UBF employee pushing a cart full of suitcases. The passengers looked a little wobbly, which was understandable since blimping wasn't exactly a joyride during a storm. Two of the G-men flashed badges and converged on the car before the employee even had a chance to raise the gate. They started herding the passengers outside while Cowley grabbed the UBF and showed him the wanted poster. The kid nodded his head vigorously and Purvis smiled. "Got her."

Cowley came back. "She's in a red dress, black hat, black furs, and she's in line for the next ride."

The gate scissored closed, the elevator lift clanked back up, and it was just then Sullivan noticed a shadow moving on the stairs above. The grey shape was there for a second, but when he looked harder, it was gone. "I think we got somebody up there," he said, pointing.

"Hollis, Michaels, check the stairs," Purvis ordered and his two men immediately tromped up the brass capped steps, guns in hand. They were out of sight in a few seconds but their footfalls could still be heard. The agent in charge turned back to the elevator doors, nervously bouncing his shotgun. "I thought they'd already cleared those," he muttered.

"There's nobody up here," one of the G-men called from the stairs.

The elevator was coming down. Sullivan got ready. He had to be careful. He didn't want to damage any of the other passengers, so he would have to be very selective. If there were people in there with bad tickers or delicate constitutions, it was far too easy to hurt them by accident, and that still mattered to him. The safest thing to do for the bystanders would be to get nice and close, but getting close to a Brute was a game for suckers.

Guess I'm a sucker. He tilted his fedora down, stuck his hands in his suit pockets, and strolled to the elevator. When the doors opened, he'd just be loafing around, as if he were waiting for the next one up. Hopefully she wouldn't recognize him until it was too late. His best bet was to overwhelm her before she could use her Power. Cowley and Purvis let him go. They'd worked together enough times before that they knew Sullivan was a pro.

The elevator appeared, and Sullivan scanned the passengers through the gate as they descended. Four more people and another cart full of suitcases, and there she was. Delilah Jones was in the front of the car, borderline petite, delicate hands planted on lovely hips, tapping one high-heeled shoe impatiently. Jake had a moment to admire her legs before he was forced to lower his head. *The girl still has nice gams.*

They'd met in New Orleans not too long after the war, only a few years before he'd gone up the river. Back then she'd just been a petty crook at worst, using her Power like a can opener to rip open cheap safes, and Jake had been an idealistic idiot, thinking that people like them could make the world a better place. They'd been tight once, maybe even something special, but Jake Sullivan didn't have friends anymore. A stint in the Special Prisoners' Wing of Rockville State Penitentiary had seen to that. Now he just had jobs.

One of the male passengers lifted the gate and the others began to file out. Jake reached inside himself and felt the Power. Reality faded into its component bits. His surroundings now consisted of matter, density, and forces. The Power began to drain as he willed the pull of the Earth to multiply over the form that was Delilah Jones. Selectively increasing gravity was one of the more challenging things he could accomplish. It took a lot of effort and Power, but it was darn effective. It was a lot less draining to just Spike something hard, whereas this was more like delicate surgery. She wouldn't be able to move, no matter how strong she could make herself, and after a few seconds he'd manage to cut off the blood flow and knock her out. Go too soft and she'd Power out of it, go too hard and he'd kill her, but Sullivan was the best Spiker in the business. She would never know what hit her.

There was a shout and a gunshot. Sullivan's concentration wavered, just a bit, and the real world came suddenly flooding back. The Power he'd gathered slipped from his control and the elevator gate was sheared from its bolts and slammed flat into the floor under the added pressure of ten gravities. A passenger screamed as his foot was crushed flat and blood came squirting out the top of his shoe. "Sorry, bud." Sullivan turned in time to see one of the G-men tumbling down the stairwell, a grey shape leaping behind, colliding with Cowley and Purvis and taking them all down, "Aw hell," he muttered, then spun back in time to see Delilah's lovely green eyes locked on his.

"You were trying to *smoosh* me, Heavy!" she exclaimed, eyes twinkling as she ignited her own Power. She grabbed the big man by the tie and hoisted him effortlessly off the floor, even though he was almost a foot taller. The tie tightened, choking him as he dangled, and she finally got a good look at her assailant. "*You!* Well, if it isn't Jake Sullivan. Been a long time."

Then she hurled him. Suddenly airborne, he flew across the waiting area. Instinctively, his Power flared, and he bounced softly off the far wall with the force of a pillow. Jake returned to his normal weight as his boots hit the floor. He loosened his cheap tie so he could breathe again. "Hey, Delilah."

"You lousy bastard." She stepped out of the elevator and cracked her knuckles in a very unladylike manner. The other passengers had no idea what was going on, but they knew that this was not where they wanted to be. They took off at a run except for the one with the crushed foot, who hobbled as fast as he could. Every Normal had the sense to stay out of this kind of fight. "I'd heard you'd gone all Johnny Law now," Delilah said.

"Something like that," he replied slowly. "Bounty hunter."

"Hypocrite."

There was the sound of several quick blows. Off to the side, the grey shape rose and took on the form of a man in a long coat with a nightstick in hand. The G-Men were down. Purvis moaned. The man in grey stepped off the fallen agents and took a wary step away from Sullivan. He was short and tanned, with a pointy blond goatee and nearly shaved head. He picked his hat up and carefully returned it to his head. "Delilah Jones?" he asked quickly. Cowley started to rise and the stranger kicked him in the ribs, sending the agent back down.

"Who's asking?"

"I'm here to rescue you," he stated with a German accent, "from him." He nodded in Sullivan's direction. "No offense, *Mein Herr*."

"None taken, but I'm gonna give you an ass whoopin', you realize that, right, Fritz?" Jake stated calmly. He checked. The majority of his Power was still in reserve and he began to gather it.

"I can take care of myself, buddy," Delilah told the stranger. "Were you planning on arresting me, Jake?"

"If I don't want to go back to prison, yeah," Sullivan answered, glancing back and forth between Delilah and the new threat. Delilah was a known quantity, the other guy, not so much. "That's kinda the plan."

"Too bad," she answered as she grabbed the heavy metal luggage cart, picked it up as if it weighed nothing and threw it at him.

Sullivan reached out and increased the pull on the cart. It slammed into the floor, digging a divot through the tiles and coming to rest at his feet. At the same time the stranger hooked his shoe under Purvis's shotgun and kicked it into the air, smoothly caught it, and turned it toward Jake's head. Sullivan barely had time to Spike, gravity's pull changed direction, and the stranger was jerked off balance to the left. A round of buckshot harmlessly shattered a window. The Power twisted him again, pulling the German in the opposite direction, as if he were in sideways freefall.

But rather than collide with the wall, the stranger turned blurry and passed through the concrete as if it were water and was gone. "Damn, Fades," Sullivan muttered, turning his attention back to Delilah, just in time to see that she had crossed the room and her fist was flying at his face. He ducked and the concrete wall exploded into dust overhead.

Delilah had gotten faster over the years. Sullivan leapt back as she just kept swinging. He'd boxed in the service, but nothing like this. He went between her fists and slugged her in the face with a brutal hook. Pain crackled through his knuckles, down his bones, and through his torso as he drove all his considerable weight forward. The blow was hard enough to topple a gorilla.

She blinked. "I think you smeared my makeup."

He barely had time to Spike himself dense before she hit him in the chest. Mass increased, his boots cracked into the floor, and she still managed to shove him back ten feet in a cloud of broken tiles. His back hit the wall and shattered a mirror, leaving a cracked indentation of his shoulders in the concrete. He stepped out, shrugging off the broken glass.

It was not something that a normal Heavy could do, but apparently Delilah didn't have the time to think through the philosophical implications. "I've punched trains that were softer." The Brute paused and shook her aching hand. "You've learned some new tricks!"

"You too," he answered, breathing hard. "Too bad you took to murdering innocent people."

"Innocent?" she sputtered, reaching down and grasping a wrought-iron bench and ripping its bolts out of the floor. "You've got a weird take on *innocent*." She swung the bench like a baseball bat and Sullivan barely had time to throw himself to the ground as it whistled past.

Sullivan rolled aside, finding himself staring up Delilah's dress as she brought one foot down to stamp him through the floor. Distracting as that was, he managed to focus, Spike, and Delilah suddenly fell *up*. "Son of a b—" she shouted before crashing into the glass ceiling, twenty feet above. Sullivan held the pull for a moment, but he'd burned through too much of his reserve, too fast, and lost control. Gravity returned to normal, and Delilah fell in a cloud of broken glass, screaming, to the ground.

She must have used her own Power, as she slammed into the floor hard enough to shatter the tiles in a six-foot circle, but immediately rose, unharmed but angry, dusting off her dress. She'd lost the fur stole and the fancy hat was stuck in the ceiling. Delilah picked at the shredded red dress in disgust. "You know how much I paid for this thing? It's *French*!"

Sullivan was still on the floor. "I hate France," he said as he drew his Colt .45 from his belt.

"That's because last time you were there you were running

alongside a tank," Delilah said, slowly raising her hands. "It isn't polite to shoot a lady."

He snorted. "You're no lady, and you're mostly bulletproof, but this place is surrounded by thirty bulls with choppers, and you ain't *that* bulletproof." He swiped the thumb safety off and aimed at Delilah's chest. He could feel his Power scattered. It was going to take a moment to gather enough to use it again. Good thing he always packed a heater. "So I guess you're coming with me."

She tried to look innocent, and failed miserably. "Come on, Jake, let me go, for old time's sake. I'll make it worth your trouble."

"Tempting, but I've got the law outside. It's over." *For both of us.*

"Yes, it is over," the German stranger said, materializing as he placed the muzzle of a pistol against the back of Sullivan's head. "The policemen will not be a problem. My crew made sure of that. Don't try anything stupid, Heavy. Magic is always slower than a bullet."

The Spiker calmly raised his big .45, put the safety back on, and let it dangle from his trigger finger. "I never did like you guys that could walk through walls. That don't hardly seem fair."

"Life isn't fair, friend," the stranger said. A wooden nightstick slammed brutally into Jake's skull, hard enough to knock any normal man senseless, and he flopped to the floor.

"Hit him again. He's got a real thick head," Delilah suggested. The stranger complied. The last thing Sullivan saw was a torn red dress towering over him and a finger shaking disapprovingly.

Delilah

Chapter 2

The learned gentlemen from the university have asked me if I relied on Einstein's General Theory of Relativity or if I used the simpler rules of Newton's Law of Universal Gravitation on the evening in question when I accidentally took Sheriff Johnson's life . Shit. I don't know. I just got angry and squished the fucker. But I've gotten better at running things and I promise not to do it no more.

—Jake Sullivan,
Parole Hearing, Rockville State Penitentiary, 1928

El Nido, California

THE OLD PORTUGUESE FARMER sighed in frustration, ankle-deep in cow shit, as a panicked Holstein ran past, flinging shit in every direction, with his adopted girl on top trying to ride the animal like a horse.

"Off the cow!" he bellowed, but it didn't matter anyway, because people rode horses instead of cows for a reason, and a thousand pounds of beef slipped and landed on its side in a great grunting heap. The girl Traveled at the last second to avoid getting hurt. She appeared next to him, still in forward motion, and her rubber boots slid through the muck until she stopped.

She was taller than he was now, so he had to stand on his tiptoes. He smacked her hard on the back of the head as he shouted in English. "Mean to cows? You don't be mean to cows!"

"Sorry," Faye said sheepishly. "I wanted to see what would happen . . ."

The farmer just shook his head. He'd tried that himself once a long time ago, with similar results, but she didn't need to know that. "You upset the cows. Upset cows don't give so much milk. No milk, no eat." Times were hard, and they were paid by the hundred weight. There was a 1,000 gallon tank in the barn, and if it wasn't full when the milk truck came, then that meant less money from the creamery, and they would be eating cows to stay alive instead of milking them.

The cow got up and trotted away, shaking her head and snorting. Its ear tag told him it was Number 155, and she was a pain in the ass anyway. In the barn, she was a kicker, so it served her right. His hand still hurt from the evening milking when that cow had kicked him again.

"Sorry, Grandpa," Faye said again. "I was done putting grain out for the night and she was just looking at me like she was *daring* me to mess with her." Everybody who worked in the barn had gotten a hoof to the hand by that particular boss cow at some point. 155 was particularly good at pissing on her own tail and then hitting you in the face with it when you were just squatting down to put the milking machine on her. She was an *angry* cow. "155's a bitch."

He thumped her on the back of the head again. "Ladies don't cuss." He wanted to smile, but had to stay stern. "So you Traveled and landed on her back?"

The girl shrugged. She had really grown the last few years. She didn't really fit in with the rest of the family, being so much taller, paler, skinnier, with hair that was always long, tangled, and the color of damp straw. Her Portuguese had gotten better than his English, she got dragged to a proper Catholic mass most Sundays, and she worked hard for a girl. So it was almost like she wasn't a damn Okie anymore, but she would certainly never pass for an Azorean *Festa* princess.

"Never told you not to. Told you to be careful," he chided her. He had taught her everything he knew about magic. He'd taught her to Travel only to things that were in her line of sight, and how to use her instincts to avoid getting hurt by stray objects. He hated to admit it, but she was already better at it than he had ever been. She could go further, had a better feel for it, and could store more Power than any other grey eye he'd met, but she was still young, and therefore dumb.

"What if the cow moved and you got your foot stuck in it? I'd have a kid with one leg. You can't milk with one leg!"

"Sure I could. I'd get a stool with wheels."

"But who'd want a cow with a foot growing out it?"

Faye thought about that problem for a second. "The circus!"

He groaned. The girl's head just didn't work in the same direction as most folks. "People like us got to be careful. One mistake . . ." he made a gagging noise and crossed his eyes. She giggled. She still giggled a lot.

She hadn't really talked much for the first few months. Faye had always been a strange one, reacting to things only she could see, with lots of strange looks and scowls, and when she talked she didn't make much sense, usually the first thing that popped into her head. The farmer never found out much about her life before, and frankly he didn't care to, but he knew it must have been lousy, even by miserable Okie standards.

His wife, Maria, may God rest her soul, had taken to the little Okie girl, and doted on her. When Maria had passed on that winter, Faye had watched the family mourn, and he thought that it was probably then that she had figured out she was one of them now. Once Faye decided she finally fit in, she'd been nothing but smiles and mischief ever since. She really brightened the farm up, and though the old farmer missed his wife every single day, the skinny little Okie girl had given him something to live for.

Faye was the best ten bucks he'd ever spent.

"Come on, girl. Let's feed the calves, then we can turn in," he said, and the two of them climbed over the corral pipes and dropped down to the hard dirt of the yard. His knees were killing him but there was always more work to do on a dairy farm. She hopped down with the effortless grace of a young woman instead of a clumsy kid. He hated to admit that she was growing up. Even some of the local Portuguese boys from the other families had started sniffing around, but so far he'd kept them at bay with a stern glance and his reputation.

"Grandpa, can I tell you something?" After the first year she had started calling him Grandpa instead of Mr. Vierra. He'd never minded.

"What, girl? You gonna fess up to scaring more cows?"

She didn't giggle for once. That got his attention, because she was hardly ever serious. There were always random thoughts spinning in that girl's head, but it was rare when she shared. "It's about my magic. Something don't make sense to me." He waited for it. None of it really made sense to him. He'd just learned to control it by instinct. Most of the others like them weren't so lucky. "You taught me to *feel* ahead before I Travel . . ."

"And you always do, right?"

"Of course," she said defensively. "But lately, it's been more than feeling. If I try real hard, it's like, I don't know, like I can *see* the space before I get there. I don't know. I don't have the words to explain it good. It only happens if I try real hard."

The old farmer nodded thoughtfully. According to everything he had learned over decades of practice, that was impossible. You didn't see until your eyes actually got there. A Traveler could get a sense of *wrongness* if he was about to jump into a bad place, and that could save your life, but you couldn't actually see anything until you arrived. "I don't know how magic works, just that it does. I teach you what I know, don't mean you can't learn more than me."

Faye seemed perplexed by that. "Why is it that some of us can do some kinds of magic, but only some of us, and we can only do one kind? If we got one magic, why can't we get more?"

He knew that she was wrong. There was at least one person out there with more than one Power, but she was too young to have to know about *him*. "That's how God wants it, I guess."

"What if magic was something that could be learned, and we're not just born with? What if regular people could learn it, like from books or a school or something?"

This train of thought made him uncomfortable. Faye assumed what most people did, that there was only one kind of magic, but he knew that there was the other kind. The *old* kind, the *bad* kind. He grunted. "Less talk, more work. Come on. Calves are hungry."

Faye sighed. "They're always hungry."

Springfield, Illinois

"SULLIVAN! ARE YOU OKAY?"

He blinked against the brilliant light. His head was throbbing, pulsing like somebody was running a blacksmith's forge inside his brain. "Ohhh . . . that Fade cooled me good," he muttered, pulling himself up. Cowley was kneeling at his side, blood leaking from his nose. Sullivan wasn't the only one the Fade had worked over.

The Spiker mashed one big hand against the side of his head, and it came away stained red. He'd really gotten belted. Sullivan knew that he should have been out for a lot longer, but he'd spent a lot of time using his Powers to toughen his body. It wasn't like there was much else to do inside an eight-by-ten windowless cell all day. "Which way did they go?" He picked his fedora up and tugged it down tight on his head.

Cowley pointed up.

The blimp. Sullivan got to his feet. "How's Purvis?"

"I'll live," the senior agent grumbled from off to the side, his left arm hanging at a very unnatural angle. "Everybody's alive, but they're hurt bad. I don't know where the locals are. They should have come running when they heard shooting. They've got a gang of Actives, Sullivan. There are more of them that went up there. A Mover bounced the boys I left on the door. There was another girl, who knows what she does?"

Sullivan stood. His head hurt, but everything seemed to be attached. No bones were sticking out, and he wasn't *squirting* blood, so he'd been worse. He checked his Power. It had automatically returned and he could feel the weight in his chest. He had about half of what he'd started the night with. There was a sudden clank as the docking clamps were retracted from the dirigible. "Take care of your men, Melvin. I'm going after them."

"There are at least three Actives," Purvis warned.

"That's suicide," Cowley said, grimacing as he picked up his tommy gun. "I'm coming with you."

That kind of bravery would probably get the agent killed someday, but Sullivan could respect it. "Fine, let's go." His .45 was on the ground and he returned it to the leather holster on his belt.

"The car won't come down from the top. They probably wrecked the controls," Cowley said. "And the door to the next stairwell landing is steel, and it's been sorta . . . twisted. It's stuck. I already tried— Wait, Jake, what are you doing?"

Sullivan stepped into the elevator shaft. There was no ladder and the interior of the shaft was made up of a grating that would be extremely difficult to climb. The Spiker paused long enough to pull a pair of leather gloves from his coat and put them on before grabbing the swaying cable in the center. It was extremely greasy and he looked with distaste at the mess it was making to his best shirt. Money was tight. "*Don't* try to keep up."

He reached inside and used some Power. It always took less energy to affect his own body than others. Perhaps it was just a question of range, but either way, it didn't take much Power to make gravity shrink away to nothingness around his person. Sullivan reached high and pulled, launching himself up the cable, hand over hand, almost flying up the whipping strand. Within seconds he had left the first floor behind.

"Wow . . . and I get a lighter," Cowley muttered from below.

Why am I doing this? Sullivan wondered, but he already knew his answer. He had a few certain principles, and one of those was that when he started something, he finished it.

The bottom of the elevator car was black with grime and collected petroleum sludge. Sullivan almost collided into the soft mass, so great was the speed of his ascent. He held onto the cable with one hand and dangled, looking for the trapdoor. He found it, but had magically deprived himself of the weight to push it open. He concentrated on the trap's iron hinges. It took a great deal of effort to channel his Power in two separate directions at once, to make himself lighter, but to make the door heavier than its hinges could bear.

Good thing he'd done nothing but practice for six years . . .

"Sam! Get out of the way!" he shouted. He had no idea if the Bureau of Investigation agent was actually crazy enough, or physically fit enough to follow him this way, but it was worth the effort to yell. "Incoming!"

The trapdoor, now drawn toward the Earth as if it weighed five hundred pounds, tore free and toppled down the shaft. Sullivan reached out with his Power, just in case, and lessened the pull on the trapdoor so it fluttered down with the energy of a broken kite. The length of the reach overcame his concentration, and for a brief moment, Sullivan slipped. He barely held onto the greasy cable as he returned instantly to his natural weight. Sliding, almost losing it, he managed to shove one hand through the open trap. Grasping the edge, he pulled himself through onto the elevator's carpeted floor with a grunt.

The shaft terminated inside a glass enclosure. UBF signs encouraged mothers to secure their children while on the platform. Sullivan crawled forward, glancing around the darkened enclosure. Rain was streaking the glass and lightning crashed. Three UBF employees and the last of the passengers were standing there, gawking at the dirigible beginning to rise just outside the windows. Delilah was getting away.

"Hey!" he shouted. "Can you clamp it down from here?"

"Are you crazy? You want them to *stay*?" an older man in a blue UBF captain's uniform shouted. "That's my bird they're glauming out there, and even I don't want to mess with those freaks! He bent the door with his *brain*, son!"

Sullivan swore as he tried the door to the platform. The metal frame had been twisted and distorted somehow. It was like what Cowley had said had happened in the stairs. He didn't even know what kind of Power that was, and if it was the Mover, then it was from an Active far stronger than anybody he'd met before.

That gave him an idea. The dirigible companies were employing lightning directors now, and their safety records had gone way up as a result, but he'd also seen what an offensive weapon they could be during the war. "Who's the Crackler?" Sullivan asked. "Come on!"

One of the younger UBF employees stepped forward. Sullivan kicked himself. It should have been obvious. His coverall had a big yellow lightning bolt sewn on it. "We prefer being called Edisons," the young man said stiffly.

"Whatever floats your boat, pal. Can you blast them out of the sky?"

"It doesn't work like that," he said quickly. The others looked at him suspiciously. Even if he could, he wasn't going to admit it in front of people who could get him fired. "Of course I can't."

"It was worth a try." The dirigible was rising, loose cables whipping about it in the wind. "Cover your ears," Sullivan ordered as he drew his 1911 Colt. There was no way he could heed his own advice and his ears stung from the concussion in the enclosed space. A hole puckered through the thick glass. He stepped back and kicked the window out, careful not to slice himself open on the jagged edges, and stepped onto the platform. The rain was pounding around him in giant sheets.

The dirigible's cabin was thirty feet up and rising quick. He could have shot at it, but he might as well try to poke holes in the moon. He could empty an entire magazine into that gas bag and they'd still have enough helium to make it to California. A few .45 caliber holes weren't going to make a lick of difference. They were far enough away from the tower now to safely fire up the propellers, which coughed and began to turn. The stubby wedge wings started getting lift and the rate of climb increased dramatically. There was no time for hesitation. Sullivan took three quick steps and vaulted over the railing into space, drawing deep on his Power the whole time.

The safety cable snapped past, slamming into his chest, flinging him about as if he weighed nothing, which in fact was almost true. He wrapped his arms around the cable and his fedora disappeared into the darkness. Sullivan grimaced as the sharp corner of the platform's metal roof caught his leg and slashed through his trousers and into the muscle of his calf.

It hurt unbelievably bad. He didn't know how deep it was. He could let go and float to the ground now, or he could wait, pass out from blood loss and drop like a stone. But Sullivan ignored the pain, despite every rational part of his brain telling him that he was cuckoo, and began to climb, throwing himself up the cable with maniacal force. The wind was increasing as the dirigible picked up speed and the incandescent lights of Springfield were winking by under his kicking legs.

Thrashing through the rain, he could see that the cable terminated on a spool at the aft end of the cabin. There was a catwalk under it, and Sullivan concentrated on reaching it. He blinked away rain and tears long enough to notice the form of a man walking down the catwalk, right toward the spool. Sullivan knew he was a sitting duck. There was no more time.

Altering gravity took Power. The further he reached the more it took, and changing the direction of pull entirely burned up Power like coal in a blast furnace, but he had no choice. Sullivan Spiked as hard as he could as he let go of the rope and returned to his normal weight. There was a rip in space as one bit of it was temporarily *wronged* and inverted. Up became down and he fell through the sky, upward toward the climbing dirigible.

It was the Fade, moving down the catwalk, reeling the cables back in to avoid lightning strikes. He paused, noticing that something was wrong as the raindrops in front of his face slowed, hesitated in midair, and then began climbing. The German turned just in time to catch Sullivan's massive fist with his jaw.

"Lights out, Hans," Sullivan said as he crawled over the railing and dropped into a crouch on the steel catwalk. The German was out cold, flat on his back, one leg dangling off the edge. Sullivan knelt next to the unconscious man and patted him down. No papers, no wallet, the only thing distinctive was a gold ring with a black stone on his right hand. Sullivan found a diminutive little .32 in the man's coat, and frowned as he examined the baby Browning. "Europeans . . ." he muttered, stuffing the tiny pistol in his own pocket.

The German moaned, so Sullivan grabbed a handful of shirt with his left, and gave him another big right, before dropping him back to the deck. He wouldn't be going anywhere for a while. "Now we're even."

The big man moved quickly down the catwalk. Through the portholes he could see that the lights were on inside the cabin, which meant that he could see in, but they'd have a darn hard time seeing out. But he didn't see anybody as he passed. The dirigible was going even faster now, and the wind was screaming past, whipping his tie and coat behind him. Sullivan leaned into it and plodded on until he found an entrance door and ducked in.

The door opened into a wood-paneled hallway that bisected the cabin. It was a lot quieter inside. Sullivan paused, catching his breath, dripping rainwater, and made sure his Power was ready. The cut on his calf burned, but didn't appear to be as deep as he'd originally feared. The blood was leaking, rather than pumping, and he removed his tie and wrapped it around the cut as a makeshift bandage. Once he caught Delilah, the feds were definitely going to have to spring for a new set of duds. He drew his Colt and proceeded slowly down the hall, boots squeaking slightly.

The next door was marked GALLEY. Sullivan moved inside. The rectangular space was filled with two long bars and bolted-down swivel stools, but empty of people. There was a door at the far end, and Sullivan started toward it. Somebody was driving this blimp, and he had to be in that direction. Delilah was probably with him, and if he could capture her, then he was finally a *free* man.

There was a tinkle of glass and a crash from the other side of the door and Sullivan automatically raised the Colt. A head moved on the other side of the circular glass window, and then the door swung open.

It was a young man, tall and thin, with disheveled brown hair and a skinny mustache, wearing a wool overcoat, but no hat, and his tie was undone. He had a bottle of wine in one hand and a corkscrew in the other. He was grinning and all of his attention was on getting that bottle open. Of course alcohol was illegal, but everybody knew that the passenger blimps always had something good stashed for the rich passengers.

"Hey," Sullivan said calmly. The 1911 made an audible click as the safety was moved into the off position.

The young man looked up in surprise. "Hey, yourself," he replied slowly. "Who are you supposed to be?"

"The one with the gun, so get your hands up."

He paused. "But if I do that, I would have to drop this . . ."

Sullivan nodded slowly. "Beats getting shot in the face."

"This is an 1899 vintage Merida-Claribout. I can't *drop* it."

"Well, I could drop you instead."

He sighed in resignation. "Fine . . ." He let go of the bottle and the corkscrew and quickly raised his hands.

But there was no crash. No breaking of glass. Sullivan jerked his eyes down and saw the bottle hovering an inch off the floor. The young man smiled.

The bottle streaked across the galley at insane speeds, faster than Sullivan could Spike, and hit him in the arm as he jerked the trigger. Rather than break, the bottle impacted like a club. Sullivan tried to reacquire his target, but the bottle came flipping around out of nowhere and hit him over the top of the head and this time it shattered.

"Shit," he growled as he landed against the bar, alcohol burning his eyes. The Colt came up, but pain flared through Sullivan's hand, and he looked down in disbelief at the corkscrew embedded just behind the knuckles of his gun hand. His fingers twitched uncontrollably and the .45 hit the bar. He grasped for it with his left, but the gun flew down the bar and disappeared. "Damned Movers."

"Yeah, we get that a lot," the kid said. There was a sudden noise as several of the drawers on the service side of the counter slid open. There was a flash of silver and a cloud of knives, forks, and spoons rose over the bar. All of the items turned in the air so that they were pointed at Sullivan. "So who are you supposed to be?"

"I'm here to help arrest Delilah Jones for murder," Sullivan said with more calm than he felt as he stared at a particularly large steak knife. He grasped the corkscrew and slowly withdrew it, turning it so as to not pull out a plug of meat, grimacing against the pain. From his understanding of Movers, it took a lot of effort to even direct the smallest of objects with any control. Let alone whole bunches of them. This kid was *good*.

"You a G-man?" the Mover asked. He was frowning slightly, so it was taking some effort to hold up all those things, but Sullivan had to admit that it was mighty intimidating.

"Hardly . . . I suppose I'm a bounty hunter." Sullivan took his time responding. It had to be using up a lot of the kid's Power to show off like that. Being flashy was a waste of energy, and everybody had limits. "Maybe I'll get a reward for you too. What's blimp-napping worth nowadays?"

"Actually this is a dirigible. Blimps don't have internal frames."

"Everybody knows that."

"You must be the Heavy that's working for the feds."

"Yeah," Sullivan answered, Spiking hard. "Guess so." Each piece of silverware suddenly gained fifty pounds. The kid gasped as he lost control and the objects crashed down.

The kid was at the far end of the bar, which was a little too far for an accurate Spike, so Sullivan reached across his body with his uninjured left hand and rummaged through his right coat pocket.

"You're going to regret that!" the Mover shouted. "You Heavies can only concentrate on one space at a time. Watch this!" Then he theatrically spread his arms, and every loose object in the room shook. Plates, cups, bottles, trash, silverware, even the stools spun and the light fixtures pulled against their cords. "It's like a thousand invisible hands, bucko. Let's see how you do in the middle of a tornado."

Sullivan came out with the German's .32. "You talk a lot." And then he shot the kid in the knee.

"Oww!" the Mover screamed as he fell to the floor. "Oh damn!"

he grasped his leg and blood came pouring out between his fingers. All of the telekinetic Power was lost and the various objects fell with a clatter. "You, you bastard! That *hurts*!"

"You have to learn to focus through the pain to use your Power, kid," Sullivan said patiently. He'd crossed the room quickly and was standing over the Mover. "You're lucky. I was aiming for your head, but I'm right handed." He held up his bleeding hand, indicating the corkscrew hole. The fingers didn't want to close. "I don't aim so good with my left."

The kid gritted his teeth, gathering his Power, and a meat cleaver rose from the bar. Sullivan just shrugged, Spiked, and the injured man lofted to the ceiling and rebounded off a steel beam in the roof, then Sullivan let gravity return to normal and the kid fell, crashing in a moaning, broken heap at his feet.

Sullivan returned the .32 to his pocket. He removed his handkerchief and wrapped it around his hand to stop the bleeding. The white quickly turned red. It hurt like a son of a bitch. He spotted his Colt near the kid and picked it up, limping onward.

Two down, but how many others were there? Sullivan was feeling woozy. He was losing blood. Had the others heard the gunshot? Would they be waiting for him?

He crossed another empty hallway. The control deck was up a short flight of metal steps at the end. The coast appeared to be clear. Sullivan checked his Power. There wasn't a whole lot left. He should have just shot the talky Mover again and saved the juice.

There was only one way in, so Sullivan moved up as quietly as possible for a man of his stature. If he hadn't been so worried about running low on Power, he would have given himself the weight of a dainty ballerina and made no noise at all. He set his boot down carefully, so the steps wouldn't creak. The space around him was a mass of darkened pipes and shadows. This section wasn't meant to be seen by the passengers, so UBF had saved the money on making it pretty. This end of the dirigible was noisy and vibrating from the front propellers and the wind. It was possible that the pilot of the stolen blimp hadn't even heard the guns.

Creeping forward, Sullivan could see a man sitting in the driver's seat. He could just see the back of a balding head. The captain's chair was empty. He went a little further around the corner, until he saw a second person, a woman with long blonde hair, at the radio operator's station. She had her back to him and seemed intent on whatever she was listening to.

"All-points bulletin. The state police are just waiting for the storm to pass so they can get some biplanes up," the woman said. She had a touch of an accent like some of the eastern European immigrants Sullivan had served with in the First. "They think we're heading for Canada."

"Good thing we had Heinrich kill the spotlights," the driver said. "Canada? Please. That's like they took Vermont and made a whole country out of it, only more boring, and without the good maple syrup." His voice was deep and smooth, almost like a radio news man.

Sullivan couldn't see Delilah, and she was the one he was worried about running into at close range. He stepped into the room and aimed his gun at the back of the pilot's head.

The girl at the radio turned and spotted Sullivan. "Uh, Danny, we've got company." Sullivan realized she was rather attractive, probably thirty, with her hair bounced up like they were doing in the new color picture movies. "There's a large man pointing a Colt at you . . . and he looks *mad*."

The pilot chuckled, but didn't bother to turn. "No need to be rude, Jane. Hello there. My name is Daniel Garrett. You can call me Dan. Pardon me for not standing and greeting you properly, but we're at two thousand feet and climbing and these winds are getting worse. I'm trying to keep from plowing this unwieldy beast into the ground and being the death of us all."

"Is that a threat?" Sullivan asked. "Because I can get out and walk."

Dan laughed. "Oh no, friend, nothing of the sort." His voice was calming. Sullivan felt like this man was a likable sort, a real reasonable guy. "Please, lower that gun and relax. I'm trying to drive this pig here, and I could sure use a hand. I'm sure we can work out this misunderstanding."

The Colt bobbed down. Yes, this was just a misunderstanding. *No big deal.* They could always sit down and talk it out over a drink. Dan seemed a decent sort. He reminded Sullivan of an old friend, not that he could think of who specifically.

The entire front of the cabin was glass, and Sullivan could see nothing but blackness. Then lightning struck and he could see again.

Sullivan frowned. He'd felt this kind of intrusion before, though this one was a lot more subtle, a lot more cunning. "You're in my head." The Colt came back up. "Get out of my head, Mouth."

"You're sharp . . ." Dan said. "I thought you Heavies were supposed to be dimwits."

"Not all of us." He kept the gun on the driver, but kept one eye glued to the blonde. In this crew, he wouldn't have been surprised if she'd started tossing undead flaming grizzly bears at him or *something.* "I don't have time for your games—"

"No kidding," said the girl. "You've got a three-inch laceration on one leg, a puncture in your hand, a minor concussion, two injured vertebrae in your lower back, and you've just picked up a nasty cold, though you won't know about that until tomorrow morning. And you *really* need to quit smoking."

Sullivan sighed. "I'm gonna ask this one time, then I'm gonna beat you until I'm bored. Where's Delilah?"

A painted fingernail tapped his shoulder. "Right behind you, Jake."

She'd been hiding between the pipes, Sullivan realized as he Spiked, but Delilah had already been channeling her Power, increasing her strength tenfold as she grabbed Sullivan by the shoulders and slammed him through the duralumin bulkhead and out the side of the airship.

Didn't see that coming, Jake thought before blacking out, hurtling through the dark night.

It was the cold that finally brought him back to consciousness. Jake Sullivan gradually awoke, coughing at the bottom of a hole. He was on his back, soaked to the bone, encased in freezing mud. Water was falling down the hole, splashing him in the face, and every inch of his body ached. He was dizzy and wanted to puke, but he knew that was just the blood loss talking.

Not sure where he was, or how he'd gotten there, Sullivan pulled himself out of the mud. Roots and bits of rock were stuck in what was left of his clothing. His right hand still didn't want to close, and he was surprised to find that he still clutched the Colt in his left, though when he looked at it, found that he only had the badly crushed frame. The slide was just gone. It looked like the magazine had exploded under the pressure and the magazine spring was dangling out the bottom like a half-gutted fish. Jake tossed the ruined Colt in the mud with a splash, saddened by the loss of such a good piece.

He checked, and found that he was totally out of Power, utterly drained, and feeling unbelievably weak. It took him nearly ten minutes to crawl to the top of the hole, finding purchase on severed roots and bits of leaking pipe. Finally he crossed the top, where he discovered five splintered railroad ties and one side of a railroad track that had bent into a U before shearing. On top of that was the broken floor of an empty freight car, and above that was a perfect Sullivan-shaped hole through the freight train's metal roof.

That's a first, he thought as he crawled out from under the railcar and rolled onto his back into a puddle. He was in the middle of a train yard. The North American logo was right over his head. He'd fallen two thousand feet, blasted through a train car, dug an impact crater, and still nothing felt broken. Somehow he'd used up the last of his Power unconsciously before impact. He must have gone *real* dense. He hadn't known he could do that, but then again, he didn't routinely fall off blimps.

A shape appeared. "Looks like we got us another filthy hobo."

There was a second voice. "I'll fetch my beatin' stick."

Sullivan grunted. *It was gonna be a long night . . .*

Chapter 3

As soon as the idea was introduced that all men were equal before God, that world was bound to collapse. Behold the failed America, a culture steeped in rot, their magics used publicly in the streets, without control, even allowed to the despicable Jew.

—Adolph Hitler,
Final Munich speech before his arrest and execution by firing squad, 1929

Chicago, Illinois

THE PAPER DIDN'T HAVE MUCH MORE about the theft of the UBF dirigible. There had been a small article about how it was found abandoned in a field in Missouri the day before yesterday, but nothing new today. The headlines were mostly about the upcoming election, and FDR was talking about some New Deal, which just smelled a little too much like what the Marxists in Europe were shoveling for Sullivan's tastes. A group of his fellow veterans had gathered in Washington as what they were now calling the Bonus Army. Some anarchists were going on trial for something or other, but those assholes were always causing trouble. Besides that, the rest of the front page was about how the Bolsheviks had signed a new pact with the Imperium and the Siberian Cossacks to divide up Manchuria. The embargo was forcing the Japs to use hydrogen in their airships, but other than the inconvenience, they were busy as could be taking over everything in the Eastern hemisphere. The sports page was still going on about the baseball scandal, after the Yankees had been caught illegally using magic to hit more home runs, and the boxer he'd put $5 on to win last night had gotten knocked out in the second round. *Figures . . .*

The door opened. "We're ready for you."

Sullivan carefully folded the paper, put it back on the table, adjusted his tie, and entered the conference room.

"So, how are you feeling, Mr. Sullivan?"

He didn't answer for a long moment. Mostly he was feeling angry. Lied to, cheated, used . . . and that wasn't even counting the physical injuries he was still recuperating from. His back hurt, headaches were making it hard to sleep, his right hand still wouldn't close all the way, he had itchy stitches in his leg . . . and he was fighting a miserable cold. So overall, Jake Sullivan was in a lousy state, but when the man asking the question was also the man that had the power to put you back in prison, it did bring out a certain level of politeness.

"Fine, Mr. Hoover, sir. I'm doing fine," he lied. The bandage around his hand gave him an excuse not to shake J. Edgar Hoover's hand.

"Excellent," the Director of the Bureau of Investigation said as his assistant pulled a chair away from the table for Sullivan. It was at the far end of the conference room. "Have a seat. We were just discussing your actions in the Jones' case."

Hoover was a stocky man. His eyes were quick and a little too crafty, and he spoke too well. Sullivan had never liked him, and had developed an instinctive distrust from the first time they'd met in Rockville.

Purvis looked uncomfortable. His arm was in a thick cast. The Fade had broken it in two places with that club. Cowley and the other four agents from that night were also present, as well as a couple members of Hoover's entourage and a grey-haired secretary who was poised to scribble some furious shorthand.

He was too much of a professional and a gentleman to speak badly about his superior to somebody like Sullivan, but it was obvious that Purvis didn't like Hoover much. It was understandable. Purvis worked his ass off and had busted some of the most dangerous Active criminals there were, but Hoover was always the big hero in all the papers. And now the special agent in charge of Chicago looked real uncomfortable since his boss had felt the need to hop a dirigible and fly all the way here from Washington to get a personal debriefing.

Sullivan had sat out in the hall for that part. He wasn't one of them. In fact, he was a convict, a low-class criminal dirtbag. He'd heard how some of these men spoke about him. They thought he was just a dim-bulb Heavy that they could bring in once in a while to smack around some Active hooligan they couldn't handle. Sure, there were a few Gs who treated him with respect, like Purvis and Cowley, or the Treasury guy Ness, but most of the others were openly hostile.

From the beaten feel of the Chicago agents, it looked like Hoover had given them a good ass chewing. "We were just telling the Director about your bravery—" Purvis started to speak, but Hoover scowled hard and Purvis shut his trap.

Hoover coughed politely before continuing. "These men were impressed by your actions, Mr. Sullivan, but I, on the other hand, am a bit let down."

Sullivan raised a single eyebrow. *Oh, this ought to be rich.*

"When you were released from Rockville *early*, you made an agreement that you would assist the government in capturing people like you . . . And my understanding is that you now wish to *stop* helping? Do I have that correct, son?"

Sullivan was pretty sure he was about the same age as Hoover, and he didn't cotton to being called son. "Yes, sir. That is correct, sir."

Hoover didn't like that answer, so he stopped and picked up a piece of paper and began to tap a golden pen on the table in front of him as he pretended to study it. His frown made the other agents shrink a bit. "You've been a valuable asset, one which I'm not prepared to lose."

"With all respect, sir, my agreement with you and the warden was that I would help arrest five Active murderers." Sullivan held up his bandaged hand and began to count. "Tommy Gun Smith in Philly, Jim McKinley in Kansas City, the Crusher in Hot Springs, the Maplethorpe brothers in Detroit, which *should* count as two, and Delilah Jones was the last, and I did everything I could to catch her."

Hoover nodded. "So a Heavy *can* count. I see we've got us a jailhouse lawyer here, gentlemen . . ." The members of Hoover's entourage laughed. The Chicago agents knew better. "You want math, Sullivan? I'll give you math. Jones got away. So that makes four." Now Hoover held up his hand, thumb curled in. "And you did not manage to arrest the Maplethorpe brothers." Hoover lowered a chunky finger. "You gunned them down, in the streets, in broad daylight. Maybe you're right. They should count as *two*." He lowered another finger.

"They didn't leave us much choice, sir," Agent Cowley stated. "I was there. They came out shooting and—"

Hoover glared at the agent. Purvis shook his head angrily. Hoover had ended men's careers for far less than interrupting him. Cowley wisely backed down. Hoover turned back to Sullivan. "So by my calculations, that means you owe me *three* more arrests."

The big man's nostrils flared, but he kept his outward cool. "That wasn't the agreement."

Hoover leaned back in his chair. "Tolson." He opened his hand, held it out, and one of the functionaries immediately stepped forward and placed an open folder in it. "Thank you. This is your agreement, Mr. Sullivan. Let me educate you for a moment. An agreement is a contract between two men that is legally binding. Except that's the rub. You're not a man, you're a *convict*. So . . ." Hoover pulled out a sheet of white paper, crumpled it into a ball, and tossed it at Sullivan. It fell short and rolled to a stop right in front of him. "The agreement says whatever I say it says. You *will* help arrest Delilah Jones, and you *will* do whatever else I tell you to do. Lincoln freed the slaves, but he never said anything about the convicts."

Sullivan just sat there, staring at that crumpled piece of typing paper. His anger fed the Power in his chest, and he thought about just reaching across the table and Spiking Hoover through the floor; then he could pull the pile of smashed guts and pulverized bones up out of there, launch it through the ceiling and spray it as a red rain over downtown Chicago . . .

But he didn't, because despite what the jury had said, Jake Sullivan was not a murderer. Sure, he was a killer, he'd lost count of how many lives he'd ended in the war and in fights in Rockville, but he wasn't a murderer. There was a *difference*.

He spoke very slowly. "You lied to me . . ."

"I work for the government, son. Deal with it." Hoover pushed away from the table and stood. He addressed the entire room. "Carry on, agents, and this time, when you let a felon escape, do *not* let it get in the papers. That will be all." One of his men opened the door, and Hoover turned to leave.

But Sullivan wasn't done. "Hoover." His deep voice reverberated through the room, and there was no Mister attached. The crumpled paper floated off the table, and hovered, spinning, in front of his face. Hoover visibly paled, hesitating in the doorway. It was a well-known fact that the man was terrified of magic. Sullivan slowly enclosed the paper in one big fist and took it away. "You lied about Delilah too. I was suspicious that a bunch of Actives just happened to know we were going to be there to catch her. I did some checking yesterday. I've got some cop friends in that area, and they say she didn't kill anybody during any bank robberies."

That seemed to take Purvis by surprise. Apparently the Chicago agents had been in the dark too. "So who were those dead men in the photographs?" Purvis asked.

Hoover exchanged glances with the agent named Tolson. The taller man seemed baffled. Apparently they hadn't prepared an answer. Finally Hoover spoke. "That's not important. Just know that she murdered them. And the highest levels of government want her caught. Do I make myself clear?"

"Yes, sir," all of the agents answered simultaneously.

Sullivan didn't say a word, but inside he was seething. He just squeezed the crumpled contract in his hand, pummeling it with his Power as Hoover walked out. When Sullivan finally let go, a hard ball of compressed wood pulp the size of a marble hit the floor and rolled away.

San Francisco, California

THE ROOM WAS KEPT DARK, thick curtains closed. The lights hurt the boss's eyes, and Garrett also knew that despite what his employer said, the boss was ashamed to let anyone see him closely. He had been a proud man once, an unbelievably strong man, and it hurt Garrett to see him in this state.

"So let me make sure I got this straight," his employer said from the bed. "A single Heavy fought a Brute to a standstill, caught a dirigible that was already in the *air*, knocked out Heinrich, beat the ever living hell out of Francis, and resisted your Influence?

"That about covers it," Daniel Garrett replied. It was rather embarrassing to have his entire crew defeated by somebody with one of the most mundane of all Powers. "Every other Heavy I've known was employed as manual labor or on a construction job. I thought all they could do was make heavy things light enough to temporarily pick up. This one was different. It was like he had more than one type of Power."

The General shook his scabrous head in disagreement. Even that small motion seemed to pain him. "No," he rasped. "There's only *one* man in the whole world who possesses more than one type of Power. This man, everything he did came from the same Power, the magical alteration of gravitational pulls. He's just . . ."

"Different," Garrett said.

"Resourceful." His employer had to stop for a moment to cough into his towel.

Garrett wasn't so sure about that. He did not have a head for science, but the tools the Heavy used seemed to go beyond just altering gravity's strength and direction. His gut told him that something was different about this one.

The General's coughing fit continued. The sound was painful as his lungs ground and struggled for purchase. The hacking continued for another thirty seconds and Garrett started to rise to get Jane, but his employer waved for him to stay seated. Finally the white cloth came away stained with blood, and the man continued as if the spasm had never happened. "Recruit him," he gasped.

"Excuse me?"

"Hire him, Garrett. Find this Heavy and make him a job offer."

"No offense, General, but the new girl threw him through the dirigible. I'm relatively certain he's dead."

"No," he said, gesturing with one skeletal hand at the telegram on the desk next to the bed. "After you reported in I did some checking. Apparently he doesn't die easily."

He took the telegram and read it. Finally he whistled. "Impressive."

"Apparently that power-mad imbecile, J. Edgar Hoover, agrees with you. That's why he was sprung from jail. Hoover doesn't understand Powers. He just tries to wield them like clubs. Treats Actives like mushrooms. But *we* could use a man like this."

After looking over the telegram, Garrett didn't feel quite as bad about losing to the Heavy. Very few Actives had survived the battle of Second Somme.

"Time is growing short, Daniel," the General warned.

Garrett didn't know if he was talking about his declining health or the impending threat of the Imperium. Either was terrible in its own way. "I'll be on the next flight."

The General must have fallen back asleep immediately after Garrett had left. It was getting harder to remain conscious for any period of time. He returned slowly, aching, eyes burning at even the tiniest bit of light. His body was dying, rotting from the inside out, and he had been in such terrible pain for so long that he knew all he had to do was wish for death and it would blissfully come. He was only alive because of Jane's Healing magic and sheer stubbornness.

He still had too much work to do.

There was another reason he'd dispatched Garrett to recruit the Heavy. His sources had confirmed what he'd first suspected when he'd heard the man's name. It had been too much of a coincidence for there to be another Sullivan out there that was that talented a Heavy.

It seemed appropriate to use this man to balance the scales, he thought, but then a new pain appeared in his stomach that distracted him. It was hard to concentrate when your body was falling apart. Whenever the suffering grew too much to bear, all he had to do was recall the memories of Tokugawa, and he found renewed determination. That man would never rest. If he even was, or ever had been, a man . . . the General had his doubts.

His memory was still sharp. The spreading tumors in his brain had left that at least. It had been back in '05 when a handful of western military observers had been sent to document the war between the Russians and the Japanese, and he could still recall it like it was yesterday. The Tsar's forces had been utterly destroyed, fleets sunk in oily flames, and a hundred thousand men had been butchered in the first engagement.

The Imperium was born.

And that had been the day that Black Jack Pershing had met the devil himself.

El Nido, California

THE DAY WAS LIKE any other summer day in El Nido—work, work, work. Try to get the hard stuff done before it got too hot so you could take a nap when it was really miserable, and then back to work for the evening chores. Always up way before dawn to milk and feed. Only to dairy farmers did waking up to the cock's crow at sunrise feel like sleeping in. It had been a long time since the old farmer had slept in. He figured he could sleep when he was dead.

The morning's work was done. Gilbert and most of the family had gone into town. That just left him and Faye to finish moving hay, but he didn't mind. The girl worked harder than most boys her age. Better company too.

Usually.

"So I been thinking some more . . ." Faye said as she threw a pile of alfalfa into the feeder. She paused to lean on her pitchfork, wiping the sweat from her face.

"Uh-oh," he replied, rolling his eyes.

"Is magic *alive*?"

He kept forking the hay over. He thought about it for a long time. "Is electricity alive? Is fire alive?"

"Hmm . . ." Faye frowned. "That's what I thought. That's bad then."

"Why's that bad?" The girl's brain was always spinning around about something.

"Because if magic ain't alive, and it's just stuck to some people, then why couldn't it be stuck to some *thing*?"

He froze, pitchfork stuck in the hay. She didn't seem to notice.

"Why couldn't somebody figure out how to take someone else's magic and put it in like another person? Or an animal? Or a machine even?"

"Stop it," the old farmer ordered sternly.

Faye was confused. "Stop what?"

"Just . . ." How could he explain? He didn't want to expose this poor girl to what was out there, waiting. But she was just too damn smart for her own good. "Just never mind. Don't think about stuff too hard. Keep working."

She sniffed. "Are you mad at me, Grandpa?"

"I could never be mad at you, girl." He kept working, letting the rhythm of the movement calm his thoughts. After a few seconds Faye went back to her fork. Someday he would explain everything he knew to her, but he wasn't a man who liked to talk, especially about things like that.

A few minutes later the girl looked up. "Somebody's coming," Faye said, pointing at the road. Sure enough he could see the dust of approaching automobiles. "Probably more thieving Okies passing through. I'll lock the tool shed."

He nodded. He had taught her well. But these autos weren't coming from the main road. They were coming from the direction of Potter Field, the little airfield a few miles away.

They'd seen a metal single-wing cargo plane fly that way earlier. The whole family had stopped whatever they were doing to watch. It was quite the sight. There were just a few fabric biplanes at Potter. It wasn't like they got any fancy planes out in the San Joaquin Valley.

The old farmer suddenly had a bad feeling. "Throw the cows over the fence some hay," he told her, watching the approaching dust suspiciously. "Do the dry cows first. Go." Faye hesitated, then did as she was told. He wanted her away. The rest of the family had taken the Dodge into Merced, and wouldn't be back until it was time to start the 4:00 P.M. milking.

There was nothing else along this road except for his dairy. The cars pulled up the lane and stopped in front of the house in a cloud of white dust. He went out to meet them. He didn't bother to hose off his boots.

There were four men in each car, and all eight of them stepped out at the same time. Their clothes were fancy-boy city clothes, black or pinstriped suits and nice hats. The farmer didn't even dress that nice to go to church. He could tell these men might have been from the city, but they weren't fancies. They looked hard and dangerous.

The old farmer knew right away why these men were here. His wide straw hat covered his grey eyes, and he risked a glance back toward the barn. Faye had done as she'd been told and was out of sight.

The tallest one seemed to be the boss. He was square and thick, one of the biggest men the farmer had ever seen, with a jagged scar crossing half his face that had left one eye a blinded white orb. "Are you Joe?" that one asked. That didn't mean much. Half the Portuguese men in the world were named Joe. "Travelin' Joe?"

They had been bound to catch up with him eventually. The old farmer tipped his hat.

Faye was sweating, using a pitchfork to toss alfalfa over the barbwire fence to the dry cows. The hay was dusty, collected in her hair and inside her too-large, hand-me-down work shirt, and it made her nose itch. She stopped to sneeze a couple of times, then went back to work.

It was hot. The valley was always extra muggy in the summer, probably from the irrigation, and the sun was always beating down on her head. Her rubber boots were heavy with dried poop, too big, and made her feet sweat.

And she was as happy as she could be.

The Vierras were good people. They were always loud, frantic, and yelling about something, but that's just how they were. At least here she didn't get beaten daily for having the devil in her. Grandpa was actually proud that she was different. And unlike her life before, there was always food. Faye liked to work. She didn't even mind the Holsteins much.

Life was simple, and it was hard, but she was content, because it wasn't *mean*.

A cow stuck its head through the fence, curious, smelling her. It chuffed and blew green snot all over her pants. She wiped it off with a handful of hay and patted the cow on the nose. She licked Faye with a giant rough tongue and the girl giggled.

A gun fired. The line of Holsteins jerked, ears all cocked suspiciously in the same direction. It had come from the other side of the milk barn. A flock of black birds leapt into the air and flew over the roof. Grandpa was probably shooting at crows, but Faye frowned, since that sure hadn't sounded like Grandpa's shotgun. One of the dogs started barking like crazy.

Then there was a whole *bunch* of guns. A giant mad bumblebee passed overhead and it took Faye a second to realize that it was actually a bullet. Something was terribly wrong. She clutched the pitchfork tight and the dry cows bolted from the fence and ran for the far side of the corral.

The Okies are robbing Grandpa! It was like the bank robbers they talked about on the radio. Still holding the pitchfork, she ran for the barn, big boots clomping, but that was too slow, so she focused on a spot fifty feet ahead, which was as far as she'd ever Traveled before, touched the magic, sent her senses ahead, *clear*, and was just there.

She'd done just like Grandpa had taught, appearing an inch or so off the dirt so she wouldn't melt her soles to the ground, and hit the ground still clomping forward. Now she could see around the block edge of the barn and there were two black automobiles, and a bunch of men in suits running toward the house and shouting. There was another boom and one of the men fell off the porch and into Grandma's rosebushes.

A hand landed on her shoulder, and Faye nearly jumped out of her skin. "Girl!" Grandpa whispered in her ear. He had Traveled right behind her. He dragged her back around the corner as he broke open his shotgun, pulled the spent shell out, and fished another one out of his coveralls. He didn't seem any more upset than when he was dealing with a particularly nasty cow. "Go hide." He snapped the shotgun closed and pointed with it toward the haystacks, but then he scowled. "Shit. Forgot."

"Where are you going?"

"Something in the barn I need. Go hide." He closed his grey eyes and disappeared.

Faye focused on the haystacks. A man's voice came from behind her. "There's somebody el—" And then her boots landed in a pile of straw and she didn't hear the rest. Scared, she scrambled behind some broken bales, just her eyes sticking over the top, and she searched for the men. The nearest one was rounding the barn, silver gun in his hand, and he was jerking his head back and forth, wondering where she'd gone. She squeezed the pitchfork even harder, though she didn't know what she planned on doing with it.

Then she saw something strange. Another man, a giant, seemed to fly over the edge of the barn and landed easily on the tin roof. It was like he'd jumped right out of the yard, but Faye knew there was nothing to stand on over there, so he would have had to have leapt twenty-five feet straight into the air. The man crouched, scanning slowly, perched effortlessly next to the lightning rod. He reached into his suit and pulled out a huge gun. Faye ducked lower so he couldn't see her. This man was special too. Like her, but different. *Scary.*

Grandpa Traveled and appeared right behind the first man, stabbing the shotgun barrel into him. The man never knew what happened as the Sears & Roebuck shotgun blew him near in half, but Grandpa didn't see the big man on the roof.

"Grandpa!" Faye screamed.

The old farmer looked up, seeing her, surely focusing on the safety of the haystack and—

BOOM!

Grandpa lurched forward as the man on the roof shot him. He Traveled, and was instantly before Faye. Grandpa took two steps and fell to his knees. "Oh . . ."

Faye dropped the pitchfork, grabbed him by the straps of his coveralls, and dragged the little man behind the broken bales. "Grandpa!" she screamed. Blood was welling out from between the top buttons of his shirt, way too much blood. "Hold on, Grandpa!"

He grabbed her wrist, his fingers hard as rocks, and he shoved an old leather bag into her hand and squeezed it shut. Blood came out his mouth when he tried to talk and she had to put her ear down next to his mouth to hear him. "Don't let them get it. Find Black—" and then she couldn't hear the rest because it turned into a gurgle as he breathed out. He didn't inhale. Faye pulled away, and Grandpa Vierra's grey eyes were staring at nothing.

"Grandpa?"

A man in a suit came running around the edge of the hay. Faye saw him coming and she was filled with an emotion she'd never felt before. The wood of the pitchfork was hard in her calloused hands as she rose, straw-colored hair covering her face. Fifteen feet away the man raised his gun.

He shouted to the others. "I got th—" but then Faye Traveled, screaming, and drove the three narrow tines of the pitchfork through his ribs. Still screaming she pushed the man, driving him back, until his knees buckled and she drove the fork all the way through him and into the ground. The man grabbed onto the handle, but Faye put all her weight on the shaft and held him there while he kicked and cussed. After a few seconds he quit moving.

"Hey, girl," a very deep voice said. She turned, and the giant man from the roof, the man that had killed the first person who'd ever loved her, the man who'd murdered *her* Grandpa, was standing there, calm as could be, with the biggest revolver she'd ever seen pointed at her head. He cocked the hammer. One of his eyes was white. "No reason for any more killing today," he lied. "I'm looking for something. That's all."

Faye wrenched the pitchfork out of the fallen man and pointed it at the big man. Blood dripped from the tines. "You . . . you killed . . . killed my Grandpa," she gasped.

He nodded. "I guess that's how it's got to be then." He pulled the trigger.

The bullet passed through the space where Faye had just been as she materialized off to the man's side. She gasped in pain. She'd gone too fast, hadn't used her instincts, and done something *wrong*, but there was no time, and she stabbed the pitchfork deep.

The man looked down at the iron embedded in his body. The top was in his ribs, the middle had to be through his guts, and the bottom went in just under his belt. Faye drove her weight forward, trying to stick it in deeper, but the man calmly grasped the shaft and wouldn't let her. It was like pushing on a wall. The man hauled the fork out of his body, several inches of bloody metal from each spot, and in the process knocked Faye on her butt.

Grandpa's leather bag hit the ground, spilling something metallic into the hay.

Blood leaked out the three holes in the one-eyed man's side, but he didn't seem to care. His attention focused in on the bag. Faye scrambled for it, fingers hitting the drawstrings just as he pointed the big revolver at her, and desperate, she Traveled further than she ever had before.

The .50 Russian Long dug a divot in the dirt, but the girl was already gone.

"Gawdamned Travelers," he spat. It was a good thing most of them died young, because he hated them especially hard. He checked his side. The little whore had got him good, but not good enough. It took more than getting stabbed to hurt him, but it sure made him mad.

Carefully scanning back and forth, waiting for the girl to reappear, he picked the small piece of machinery off the ground. He'd been briefed enough to know that this was a part of what he was after, maybe the most important piece even, but it wasn't all of it, and his orders had said to bring it all back. He carefully stuffed the piece into one bloodied pocket.

Next he checked the old man's body, but he didn't have it on him. He must have given it to the girl . . . His remaining men caught up a moment later. "Have you found it?" he shouted. The men shook their heads. "Find it or I'll kill you all!" he bellowed. "There's a girl. She's a Traveler too. Find her and put a bullet in her. What are you waiting for? Move!"

Terrified, the goons went back to searching. *Better be afraid, fucking pussies.*

One man hesitated. "You're bleeding, Mr. Madi."

The big man just growled at him. "Naw? Really?"

"Uh . . . what do you want me to do with the bodies?"

Madi scowled. He'd lost two men to that damn Portagee and one to his brat. "Drag 'em inside. We'll burn everything 'fore we go. That's what they get for being weak. Now quit jawin' and find that girl."

Frustrated, he stomped over to the dead Portagee, lifted his LeMat-Schofield and pumped the rest of the hot loaded slugs into the body. Then he thumb cocked the second hammer and gave the old man the 12-gauge barrel just to be sure. He rapidly broke open his empty gun. The spent moon-clip kicked out automatically under spring pressure, and he stuffed another moon-clip of cartridges into the cylinder and a single shotgun shell into the overbarrel, then snapped it shut and shoved the Beast back into his shoulder holster. The bloody mess he'd caused made him smile.

He sat on a bale of hay and waited for the bleeding to gradually stop. Travelin' Joe was dead, but without all the goods, the Chairman wasn't going to be happy.

Faye watched the one-eyed man from under the overturned trough halfway across the pasture. He yelled at his men, shot

Grandpa a bunch more times, and then took a seat. Cows had sensed her, and, always curious, were gathering around the trough. The metal was old and had rusted through in places, and she kept her eye against one of those holes, spying, until she could no longer see through all the Holsteins.

She couldn't stop crying.

Her foot hurt. She'd Traveled without checking first. Grandpa had been gone for all of ten seconds before she had violated his first commandment. She knew that there was something stuck in her heel. Maybe a piece of straw, maybe a rock, and the pain was almost unbearable. Every pulse of her heart felt like somebody was driving a nail through her bones with a carpenter's hammer.

But that wasn't why she was crying.

Faye kept Grandpa's leather bag clutched to her chest. It was splattered with his blood. The pain made her want to just close her eyes and curl up into a ball, but she didn't know what time it was, and didn't know how soon it would be until the rest of the family came back from town. If these men were still here, then she knew that she would have to try to stop them before they could hurt her family, but she didn't know what to do, and she was so very afraid.

Finally, the pain had grown too much to bear. She kicked her filthy boot off, and drew her bare foot into a shaft of sunlight. Faye grimaced when she saw what it was. One of those big black crunchy beetles, the kind that was so tough that you could stomp on them and if the dirt was soft they would just pop back up alive. Its back half was fused into the flesh of her heel, its front legs and mandibles still thrashing.

There was no hesitation. She just wanted it out. Biting her lip, she unfolded her pocketknife, and started cutting. It hurt too bad, so she pulled off her bandanna, rolled it tight and stuck it in her mouth to bite down on so the one-eyed man wouldn't hear her scream, and went back to digging. Tears poured from her eyes, but she forced herself to keep going. The beetle ruptured, squirting a thick white juice that quickly mixed with her own blood. She knew she had to be thorough. After a few seconds of carving, the beetle was gone, she had a hole that hurt so bad she could barely think, but she felt immensely better. She stuffed her bandanna into the wound and held it there.

The cows had moved enough for her to see again. The big man had stood, lit a cigar, and then used his lighter to casually set the haystacks on fire before wandering off. A minute later the barn was burning too, and she could see black smoke rising from where the house should be.

She waited until she saw the dust from the cars as they drove back up the road. Then she waited longer, just to make sure it wasn't a trick. Finally Faye crawled out from under the trough and limped across the pasture to the burning ruins of the only *real* home she'd ever known.

The grey-eyed girl vowed never to cry again.

Chapter 4

I do not know why almighty God saw fit to give to man, within this very decade, magics of the elements and a quickening of the mind, Powers beyond reason and comprehension, and spells of energy and the spirit, when we were already so poised to destroy ourselves on our own. We enter tumultuous times. Left to our own devices I believe that I could stay this nation's course, to hold this Union firm, but now I fear. Only five years have passed since the magicians began to appear seemingly at random from our people and I know not where this path will lead.

Oh why, Lord, did you see fit to give that accursed Stonewall Jackson the strength of ten?

—Abraham Lincoln,
Document discovered in the
Smithsonian Archives, date unknown

Merced, California

FAYE'S FOOT HURT WITH EVERY STEP, but she was a girl on a mission, and she had a train to catch.

Gilbert Vierra, Grandpa's son, who was really more like an older brother to her than anything, had found Faye passed out in the yard. He'd gotten her foot washed out with iodine and stitched shut before she had even come to.

The law had gotten there soon after, but the sheriff had been useless. Merced County was a sleepy place, and a murder investigation was over their head. Nobody knew the three dead men and it didn't help that they'd all been burned along with the Vierras' home. A few people at Potter Field had seen the one-eyed man arrive, but no one knew who he was, only that he had chartered a flight from back east and the others had been waiting for him to arrive. The law was on the lookout, but somehow she knew he would evade them easily.

She was bitter, angry, and alone.

The family was gone. With the farm ruined, there was nothing left for them in California. The land, cows, and equipment would be sold and they would go to work on relatives' farms. Gilbert had asked Faye to come with them, but she knew that the one-eyed man was still out there, and she couldn't bear to put the others in danger.

So now she found herself at the train station, limping along the platform, ticket in hand, her worldly possessions in a satchel tied behind her back, and Grandpa's little pouch under her shirt. It was no longer that odd for a young woman to travel on her own, and even if it had been, she wouldn't have let that stop her. She was going to take care of Grandpa's dying wish.

Gilbert had wanted to help, but he had a young wife and four small children, now homeless, counting on him. He had not known about the pouch, nor had he ever heard his father talk about anything from his past that would suddenly cause a gang of killers to show up on their doorstep. Gilbert had given her the huge sum of $240, which was all of the family savings he dared spare. It represented a fortune to Faye, and was nearly half the cost of an automobile.

The first few dollars went to purchase the train ticket to San Francisco, and then another ten was spent at the hardware store for a used Iver Johnson revolver and a box of fifty .32 S & W cartridges. The owner had sold tools to Grandpa for twenty years, and promised her that it worked fine, but she went behind the shop and shot two cylinders' worth of ammunition into an old stump to make sure. Grandpa had taught her how to use a shotgun, but the revolver was a lot harder to aim. It was loud and kind of scary, but she hit wood most of the time.

The stubby little gun fit snuggly in the pocket hidden in the pleats of her traveling skirt. She just knew she would see the one-eyed man again, and when she did, she was going to pretend he was that stump behind the hardware store.

Grandpa's bag had a strange mechanical implement inside. It was a bunch of metal cylinders twisted together inside a wire frame.

It looked like it was part of something bigger, like an engine. The mystery object fit in the palm of her hand, and she couldn't understand what could possibly make it worth killing people over. There was a hole in the top where the other part she had lost had probably gone, and a slot in the bottom where it had to connect to something bigger. A few words had been stamped on the back: N. TESLA. 1908 WARDENCLYFFE GEO-TEL. MK. 1.

Faye listened to the radio. She knew that Tesla was the brilliant Cog inventor who had designed many incredible things, including the amazing Peace Ray that had ended the Great War, and that kept all nations at peace today. The news said that the rays had made it so that there could never be a big war again. Maybe Grandpa's device was part of a Peace Ray? The radio had always talked about those things in hushed tones. She had never seen one, but knew there were mighty fortress towers on the coasts, guarded by hundreds of soldiers and fleets of balloons. But how had Grandpa got a piece of one? All he had ever done was milk cows.

There had been one other thing in that bag, a scrap of old paper with a few words, a rough map and an address in San Francisco. She did not know who J. Pershing, B. Jones, R. Southunder, or S. Christiansen were supposed to be, but Gilbert had told her that the Presidio was some sort of army base right on the ocean.

The train pulled into the Merced station nearly twenty minutes late and Faye boarded, alone but determined.

Faye did not know exactly what she was going to do when she got to the spot on the map, but she would figure it out when she got there. She was Portuguese now, and Grandpa had always told her what brave explorers their people had been.

Chicago, Illinois

JAKE SULLIVAN HAD SLEPT most of the last couple of days, trying to shake his miserable cold. He still felt like death warmed over when he walked out that evening. He didn't know his way around the city, so he hailed a cab outside his hotel.

Staying in hotels had gotten to be second nature. He did not really have a home, other than a $10 a month rented room on top of a diner in Detroit. It was a place to sleep, stash some guns, his library, and served as his office, not that he'd had many regular clients lately. The money was tight for everyone, even for wives who would normally want their husbands tailed to check for mistresses. His only real work recently had been standing around intimidating the striking labor lines at the UBF factory, and J. Edgar's *assignments*.

Sure, there was always honest work to be had for a Heavy. Somebody like him was worth five Normals on a construction crew, but that seemed too much like breaking rocks, and Sullivan had already had his fill of breaking rocks.

The cab smelled like Burma Shave. "Where to, buddy?"

When Sullivan had a question that he couldn't answer, it tended to just stick in his craw, bugging him, gnawing away until he figured it out. Hoover had lied to him and his own agents about Delilah, and he wanted to know why. Purvis had mentioned that she had been coming into town to do a job for the mob, so that was where he would start.

"Lenny Torrio's place."

The speakeasy was in a warehouse near the new super-dirigible station. For something that was supposed to be a secret, it sure was busy, especially on a Saturday evening. There were two dozen automobiles parked inside the fence, including some Packards and even an expensive Duesenberg, plus there were three cabs waiting to drop off at the curb ahead of his and more coming up behind. The Chicago cops knew about this place, but the upper crust needed a place to kick back.

Sullivan had traveled the country extensively since his parole. Prohibition was brutally enforced in some states, especially in the South and Midwest, and in others . . . not so much. It hadn't been that long ago that one Eastern governor had promised to keep his state as wet as the Atlantic Ocean. The 18th Amendment was a joke from the start, and most everyone outside Kansas knew it. It was just American nature that when some authority told you that you couldn't do something, that just made you want to do it all the more.

Sullivan was not much of a drinker by nature. Mostly because he was too cheap, and the only thing Prohibition had truly succeeded in doing was raising the price of booze. On the other hand, if somebody else was buying he was in favor of violating the Volstead Act as much as the next guy.

He followed a group of well-dressed men and women down the stairs to a large metal door. The others were far more presentable than he, the men in crisp seventy-five dollar jackets and the dames in silk dresses with their hair in tight curls. Sullivan looked a little ragged, since his good black suit had fallen through a train car, so all he had left was his old brown suit, and it had already been unfashionable when he'd bought it used for $3 the day he'd gotten out of jail. He waited his turn while they gave the password, some of the rich kids giving him the crusty eyeball.

The door opened and music spilled out. The sheiks went through the metal door and it clanged shut behind them. Sullivan waited a moment, then knocked.

A slot opened and two beady eyes scoped him. "Password?"

"I need to talk to Mr. Torrio."

The eyes looked him over suspiciously. "You the law?"

"Do I look like the law?"

Apparently. "We got a dress code." The bar slid back into place.

Sullivan just shook his head. He waited a moment, and then knocked again, harder this time. The slot opened. "Password?"

Sullivan stuck a gold eagle through the hole. "Tell Mr. Torrio that Sullivan from the First Volunteer needs a minute of his time."

The goon grumbled as he closed the peep. Sullivan pulled out his pack of smokes and settled down to wait. He had one on his lips when he remembered what the blonde, most likely a Mender, had said on the stolen dirigible. She'd certainly got the part about picking up a cold right. These things were supposed to be good for you, but Healers could see your insides . . . He frowned and put the cigarette back.

Maybe that was why he was so spun up about this case. There were enough Magicals around nowadays that you were bound to have some in gangs. With the times being so tough, there were four times as many people making a living from crime as there were from carpentry, so you were bound to have Actives in there too. They had to make a buck, just like everybody else.

But this crew that picked up Delilah had been different. They weren't just magical. They had all been hardcore Actives. The

German had shadow-walked while being tossed around when every other Fade he knew could barely pull it off taking their time without getting stuck in the wall. The Mouth and the Mover had been better at their Powers than any other he'd met. And the way the blonde had diagnosed him, she had to have been some sort of Healer, and those were so rare they were worth their weight in gold. Even a weak Passive Healer could write their own ticket, so it didn't make any sense to have one slumming around in a gang.

Sullivan's thoughts were interrupted when the door flew open. There were two burly toughs there. One leveled a Remington Model 8 rifle at his chest. The other had a Winchester pump and stuck it against his nose. Jake slowly raised his hands. "Bad time? 'Cause I can come back later."

"Mr. Torrio says he knew *three* Sullivans in the Volunteers," the one with the shotgun said. "Which one is you?"

"Well, I ain't the dead one. So I guess I'm the pretty one," Sullivan answered. The goon pumped a round into the shotgun's chamber for emphasis. "Jake . . . Sergeant Jake Sullivan. The one that saved Lenny's sorry ass at Second Somme."

The goombas exchanged glances, and finally the weapons were lowered. "You's good. That's what he said you'd say. Mr. Torrio will see you now." He put one arm over Jake's shoulder and steered him into a long brick hallway. The door slammed behind.

"Welcome to the Grid Iron."

The club was about the ritziest thing Sullivan had seen. The exterior was a crumbling warehouse, but the inside was a palace. The brick walls had been covered in blue and white curtains, and an actual chandelier had been hung from the rafters. There had to be fifty folks on the dance floor, and double that sitting along the bar, drinking themselves stupid on quality Canadian booze. The front of the space was filled with round tables and diners. The smell of fine cooking made Sullivan's stomach rumble. The waiters were even wearing tuxes.

The back of the warehouse had a stage, and the music was both loud and good. A sparkling bridge spanned the stage over the band, darn near big enough to be an orchestra, and a long-legged dame was crooning a tune. She had great pipes.

One goon had remained at the door, and the other led Sullivan along the wall and up a flight of metal stairs. A balcony circled the room, and once at the top, they entered the private lounge, consisting of some leather couches overlooking Lenny Torrio's kingdom. There were tables in darkness along the back, and Sullivan could make out a few shapes behind the glow of cigarettes. He had entered the inner sanctum.

There were two more muscle types camped at the top of the stairs. Jake saved them the trouble of the pat-down and handed over his spare gun. It was a beater Smith & Wesson Military & Police .38, but he couldn't afford to replace his precious .45. "I'm gonna want that back," Jake stated as the guard carried the revolver away.

Lenny Torrio was sprawled between two chippies in slinky gowns. He was wearing a red silk robe over his clothes. "Sarge! How you been?" he shouted in greeting. He snapped his fingers and the girls jumped up to leave. "Get outta here. Can't you see I've got business to conduct?" He smacked one on the rump as they hurried away. "Have a seat. Have a seat!"

Sullivan settled his mass onto the couch across from Lenny. Physically, Lenny Torrio hadn't changed much. He was still a skinny, bug-eyed, hyperactive type. The con was going bald now, but he'd slicked what was left over to one side in a failing attempt to hide it. "Hey, Lenny. Been a long time."

"Sure has. You want a drink?" He didn't wait for an answer, but clapped his hands. "Yo. Amish, get my boy a drink! What're you waiting for?" Lenny turned back to Sullivan and frantically rubbed his nose. "Help these days . . . What can you do?"

Sullivan just nodded. "Nice robe . . . you supposed to be Rudolph Valentino?"

Lenny cackled, way too hard, slapping his knee. "You were always a crack-up, Sarge. Mr. Truth, Justice, and the American Way. Funny, huh? That I'm on top of the world, and last I heard you were a slave to the feds." A pair of glasses and a bottle were placed on the table between them by a cross-eyed man, who quickly hurried away. "How's that treating you?"

"Pays the bills."

"Good thing I'm a legitimate businessman." Lenny poured them both a drink. "And Rockville? Is it as tough as everybody says?"

"Worse." Sullivan took the whiskey, pounded it down in one gulp, and set the glass back on the table. It burned going down. He'd never liked Torrio. The man was slime, always had been, always would be, and the only reason he'd been in the First was because a Brooklyn judge had given him the choice between serving his country or serving hard time, and for somebody like Torrio, that meant Rockville Special Prisoners' Wing.

"So . . . you talk to Matthew lately?"

So that was why his door goons had asked him which Sullivan he had been. Torrio had always been scared of Jake's big brother, and for good reason. He had been the meanest bastard in the First, after all. Sullivan shook his head. "You don't want to go there. I ain't my brother's keeper." He changed the subject. "Thanks for talking to me."

"What? Just because you'd sell your own kind out to the government, I'm not supposed to entertain an old friend?"

Sullivan let the dig flow off him like water off a duck's back. He didn't rile easy. "My own kind? You mean crooks or Actives?"

Torrio shrugged. "Both. I heard why you went upriver, so in your case it's the same thing. Guys like us are better than everybody else, so you got made an example. You should know that better than anybody, Sarge. We should be running this show, not them. Normals just keep us down. Times are gonna change though, I tell you that."

Sullivan nodded like Lenny was just *full* of wisdom. He was full of something, but it sure as hell wasn't wisdom. He scanned the room. The men at the tables weren't clearly visible, but they were far enough not to eavesdrop over the music. The one named Amish was standing with arms folded about ten feet away. "I need some information . . ." Sullivan paused, frowning, as he sensed the intrusion. "And tell your boy to get out of my head before I open his."

Lenny was surprised that his man had been caught, but he played it like he was offended. He turned toward the cross-eyed man. "Amish! Are you trying to Read my guest?"

"Sorry, boss," the man replied sheepishly.

"Beat it, retard!" Torrio threw his glass at the goon, missed, and it shattered on the far wall. The goon scurried away. "Sorry about that. You know how it is."

"Yeah. I know how it is." He decided to get right to the point. "I heard Delilah was coming to do a job for you."

"Who's asking? You? Or J. Edgar Hoover?"

"Just me."

Torrio shook his head. "I got no idea what you're talking about."

Sullivan leaned back on the couch. *Let the games begin.* "I can't afford to pay for information, Lenny. I don't give a damn about the government, and they don't know I'm here. I got lied to about Delilah, and I want to know why."

"I make my living by knowing what's going on, Sarge. That'd be like me asking you to . . . I don't know . . . lift something heavy for free."

"I saved your life."

Torrio snorted. "Are you kidding? You didn't go out of your way for just little old me. You saved everybody you could. I just happened to be one of them."

"You did happen to be one of them," Sullivan said. "Remember that, and every time you look around your fancy club, and your fancy whores, and your fancy booze, you should remember that you should be too busy being dead to enjoy any of it."

"I worked hard for what I got."

"And you'd be fertilizing a field in France if I hadn't carried you, on my back, through a quarter mile of hell."

The mobster seemed to think about that. "You know, Sarge, the Chicago family could use a tough man like you . . ."

"I just want to know about Delilah."

"You were sweet on her back before Rockville, weren't you? She sure was a babe." Lenny's teeth seemed too big when he smiled. "Gotta be nice for a guy like you to have a girl he can't break by accident."

Sullivan was tiring of this. Maybe it was just the cold giving him a headache, but he was about done with the mobster's nonsense. "My business is none of your business."

Torrio sighed. "All right . . . for old times' sake. But then we're even, and I don't ever want to see you again. *Capisce*? Talking to somebody like you hurts my reputation. I show weakness and that asshole Capone will run me out in a box." He paused to pour himself another shot, got confused as to where his glass had gone, so took

Sullivan's instead. "The Grimnoir was looking for her, but she was on the run. They paid me to find her. I got her to come out of hiding so they could pick her up. Looks like they did, though from what I heard, you gave them one hell of a fight."

The name meant nothing to him. "What's a Grim Nor?"

The mobster downed his drink. "Not *Nor. Nwarr.* You'd think you'd spent enough time in France to not butcher everything. But they ain't French as far as I can tell. That's just what they call themselves. I don't know who they are, real secret bunch, but they seem to know everybody, and their money is green and there's lots of it. I think they're some sort of crew, but they're connected, big time."

"What did they want with Delilah?"

"Beats me. The one I talked to said they were on the same side and wanted to protect her. Delilah was hiding out up north. The law's been hunting her since she killed those lugs that went after her."

The Chicago agents had been told the five mutilated corpses had belonged to innocent victims of her rampage. That had never sounded like Delilah's style. "Who were they?"

Torrio looked at Sullivan like he was thick. He licked his teeth. "You got no idea what you're getting into, do you?"

"You know us Heavies are dumb, Lenny. Humor me."

"They were men you don't want to cross, Sullivan. When they missed her, they stuck the law on her. Nobody messes with *them.* Not the feds, not the mob, not the *army.* They're bad news. That's all I'm saying." He thumped his glass back down and stood. "You need to get out of here, and stay out of this if you know what's good for you."

Sullivan stayed seated. The couch was comfy. "So . . . you told this Grimnoir bunch which blimp Delilah would be on. Was that before or after you told the Bureau of Investigation?" Lenny's face slipped for a second as he said that, and that second told Sullivan he had called it right.

Torrio composed himself, playing offended. "You calling me a snitch?"

"The BI prefers the term *informant,*" Sullivan smiled. "How much was the reward on that? Here you are, giving me lip about working for the Man . . . At least I'm honest about it. I like to pick one side and stick to it. But you . . . you were always good at playing all the sides."

"Get out of my club." Torrio's robe whipped dramatically as he pointed at the stairs.

Sullivan stood. "See you 'round, Lenny."

Lenny Torrio waited until Sullivan had picked up his piece and was escorted out before summoning his imp. The spindly little creature crawled out of the shadows under the couch and clambered onto the table. Half monkey, half reptile, its bat face opened in a hideous grin of jagged black teeth as it waited for the evening's orders.

"Follow him," Lenny ordered. "I want to know where he sleeps."

The imp shrieked, leapt from the table and scurried up the bricks and out the nearest barely-open window. Spreading leathery wings, it disappeared into the night. Lenny poured himself another shot as his guest inevitably joined him. The Oriental had been waiting patiently in the darkened recesses of the balcony. The man made Lenny uncomfortable because he just stood there, like he was at attention or something. "What?"

"Will this man be an issue?" His English was perfect.

Jake Sullivan was probably the stubbornest, most single-minded, unwavering, bravest, and therefore dumbest son of a bitch Lenny had ever met. "Probably. He was asking about your outfit, about those men the Brute girl killed."

"What does he know?"

"Not much. He hadn't even heard of the Grimnoir."

The man nodded. "So . . . You *told* him then?" There was a thinly veiled threat in the words.

"Not about you people, of course," Lenny sputtered. "I'm not stupid. Look, if I had known you wanted Delilah, I would have turned her over to you, and not them. That wasn't my fault. I've got my sources looking for these Grimnoir people and the other two men you want, and as soon as I hear anything, you'll be the first to know. Your boss can take that to the bank."

The Japanese man raised a single eyebrow. "The Chairman will be pleased to hear that, and you will be exceedingly well paid for your services. By the way . . ." He reached into his suit and removed a heavy pouch. It clinked as it hit the table and a few octagonal gold coins spilled out. "Your source in California was correct. We found Traveling Joe, but we still desire something that was in his possession. Part of a device. It was missing."

Lenny nodded as he took the piece of paper, examining it briefly. It was part of a mechanical drawing way beyond his understanding. He stuck it in his robe with one trembling hand. "I'll see what I can do." Lenny Torrio could find anyone or anything, because that's what he did, that's what had made him a powerful man. He was the best Finder in the business.

"Is there any chance that this man would be willing to be in the Chairman's service?"

"Hardly." Torrio laughed, then stifled it quickly. "No offense intended of course. But old Jake has always been set in his ways. He sees things real simple in black and white, and once he sets his course, you can't sway him."

"An admirable quality. Alert me when your demon returns. Your *friend* is too curious and will need to be dealt with. I will require the services of your staff." He bowed slightly before returning to his table.

Lenny tried to pour himself another drink, but his hands were shaking too bad, and he spilled a bunch of the expensive hooch on the table. His old pal, Sullivan, had been right. He had a knack for playing more than one side. Unfortunately he'd just been drafted by the worst side of all, and there wouldn't be any turning back now. "Sorry, Sarge." He finally gave up and took a long drink from the bottle. "This is just business."

Chapter 5

Gentlemen, we have now reached the last point. If anyone of you doesn't mean business let him say so now. An hour from now will be too late to back out. Once in, you've got to see it through. You've got to perform without flinching whatever duty is assigned you, regardless of the difficulty or the danger attending it. If it is steering the clouds and calling down lightning, if it is hurling fire or steel, if it is breaking the Germans' will, or dragging their Battle Zeppelins from the sky, if it is the closest kind of fighting—be anxious for it. You must know your Power, how to shoot, and how to stay alive. No matter what comes, you mustn't squeal. Think it over—all of you. If any man wishes to withdraw, he will be gladly excused, for others are ready to take his place.

—General Theodore Roosevelt,
from speech given to First Volunteer Brigade (Active) before second battle of the Somme, 1918

Chicago, Illinois

SULLIVAN TOSSED AND TURNED, fevered dreams eating at his peace.

Finally he gave up, and lay there, shirtless and sweating, miserable and sick, partially awake, his mind still running through the remnants of a muddled dream. Fields of mud and broken trees sticking out of the ground like splintered bones and so many Zeppelins in the air that they seemed to blot out the sky the Germans they just kept killing over and over and over while the Kaiser's sorcerers would just wake them up and send them back into the fray until their bodies had been so pulverized that they could no longer hold a rifle and his brother getting half his face torn off by artillery and General Roosevelt dying in a spray of blood and fire under the claws of a Summoned and . . .

Then he was awake. Sullivan sighed, staring at the dark ceiling. His internal clock told him that it wasn't even close to morning, but he wouldn't be falling back asleep any time soon. He decided that the dream must have been from talking to Lenny. It had reminded him of the bad old days.

He heard flapping at the window, and at first he dismissed it as just a pigeon. But it sounded too . . . *leathery*. Sullivan just kept breathing deep. Listening.

Amish McCleary didn't like being called a retard, but he was too scared of Mr. Torrio to complain about it. He would prove to the boss that he could pull his weight around here, and that he wasn't just good for eavesdropping on meetings with bootleggers and hustlers.

He was going to pop the Heavy himself. The big lug had a reputation. He was supposed to be a real tough guy, a hard case, but Amish knew nobody was that tough when they were asleep in bed and you kicked in the door and sprayed them down with a Tommy gun. Who cared if he was asleep? The word on the street would still be that Amish McCleary had been the man who'd had the balls to take down Heavy Jake Sullivan.

That would show Mr. Torrio. Even Al Capone would have to respect him after that, and maybe then nobody would make fun of his cross-eyes anymore.

The Jap sat next to him in the front of the Packard. Amish was scared of Mr. Torrio, but he was terrified of the Jap. One time Amish had gotten curious to see if the Japs thought the same as white men, so he'd used his Power to try to Read him, even though Mr. Torrio had warned him not to. It was like his Power had hit a brick wall. Amish wasn't a very strong Reader. His Power barely worked once in a while, and he could only really get into the heads of the really dumb. When he tried to read smart people he just kind of bounced off. The Jap hadn't just bounced him, he'd booted him out of his head and across the street. Amish's head had ached for the last three days straight.

The Jap didn't bother to look at him, like he was too good to give Amish the time. "The demon returns," he said simply.

The Jap must have had really good hearing, because Amish didn't hear the wings flapping until ten whole seconds later. Mr. Torrio's imp settled on the side mirror and squawked at him. Amish listened for a second. He didn't speak Demon good like Mr. Torrio, but he could get the gist of it. "The Heavy's asleep. Let's go."

The Jap held up a hand. "Send one man in first to make sure the lobby is clear."

Amish hesitated. Mr. Torrio had put him in charge, not the Jap. He didn't know who the Jap was supposed to be or who he worked for, but all of a sudden he thought he could give the orders? But Amish hesitated, because first off the Jap scared him to death, and second, it was a good idea.

Daniel Garrett checked his pocket watch for the fifth time. It was almost three o'clock in the morning.

"It is exactly two minutes from the last time you checked," Heinrich stated, not looking away from the window. The German seemed nonchalant as he watched the nearly empty street and the front of the Rasmussen Hotel, but Heinrich was always composed. The entire world could be exploding around them in flames and Heinrich would still play it cool.

"Well, sorry. I don't have your Teutonic nerves of steel," Daniel muttered. "Are they moving?"

"*Nein.* Only the one went inside, probably to check the registry. The others are still waiting. We should take them now."

"There's at least six of them."

"All the reason to go now. Element of surprise, my friend."

The two of them had arrived on the last dirigible of the evening. A contact at the Chicago police had told them where Jake Sullivan was staying. The Grimnoir Society prided itself on having contacts everywhere.

Daniel leaned forward so he could see out the stolen Chrysler's passenger side window. He did not like stealing automobiles or blimps, but they were in a hurry, and besides, they always left the things they'd *borrowed* where they could be found when they were done. He had to shove his glasses back up his nose. His natural vision was terrible. "You don't even know who they are . . ."

"We're staking out this particular hotel because of our mysterious

Heavy, and a group of suspicious men arrive and are also watching the same hotel . . . Coincidence?"

Daniel thumped his head dramatically on the steering wheel. "Figures. I wonder what Sullivan did to tick them off?"

"I do not know, but he seems to have that effect on people." Heinrich rubbed his jaw. Jane had Mended it good as new, but Daniel knew from personal experience that a magically fixed bone would still ache for days afterward. It was obvious the Society's best Fade felt guilty for letting a Heavy knock him out. You don't sneak up on Fades, they sneak up on you. "I've already said it once, but I do not have a good feeling about this Heavy."

"Don't feel bad. You should have seen the information the General gathered on this one. You're lucky he didn't *eat* you. Wouldn't be the first German he's done in, I figure," Daniel said, trying to make his young friend feel better, and failing. "They quit pinning medals on his chest when they ran out of room, and you saw how big he was."

"I don't trust him. Maybe the Imperium is here for the same reason as we are?" Heinrich mused. "What do we do then?"

Daniel didn't answer at first. He didn't think he had to. It was open season on anybody who worked for the Imperium, and if they hired the Heavy, then he was fair game too. "You don't even know they're Imperium."

"I can smell s—" Heinrich shifted. "He's coming back."

Daniel leaned forward again so he could see a man walking quickly from the hotel entrance to the parked autos. They conferred through the windows for a moment. After some discussion, doors opened, and men began to pile out. Long guns were removed from the vehicles and quickly covered in loose coats. The man who stepped from the passenger seat of the lead vehicle was familiar, Japanese, dignified, and Daniel swore under his breath as recognition came. He looked just like the photographs smuggled out of Manchuria. "That's Rokusaburo."

"Told you so," Heinrich said. "Imperium *Scheisse*."

The Japanese killer pulled a thin, three-foot, black object and held it under his long coat as he walked casually toward the hotel entrance.

"An Iron Guard, here in the U.S.? I can't believe this! Damn it. I wish we had the rest of the crew." Dan moved to start the car. They would need to alert the General that one of the Chairman's best men was in the States. There was no way just the two of them could take on an Iron Guard. There were other Grimnoir in the Midwest, and if he could raise enough of a force in time, they might be able to—"Heinrich, what're you doing?" he hissed as the young German opened his door.

"I'm going to go and talk to this Heavy, like *Herr* General ordered," he smiled as he got out. "Coming?"

"Are you crazy?" Daniel said. "Rokusaburo will cut us to bits. He can't be killed!"

Heinrich shrugged. "He is magic. He is not immortal."

Daniel banged his head on the steering wheel again.

Amish and two Torrio men, Brick and Hoss, stepped out of the elevator on the tenth floor. The Jap trailed them silently a few feet behind, his long black coat almost hitting the carpet. Amish had left the two others covering the lobby. He wasn't expecting this to be too hard.

The imp couldn't tell them a room number. It wasn't like it could hop down the brightly lit hallways like a miniature kangaroo checking room numbers. It peeked through windows. That's about all the stupid thing was good for, but the logbook at the desk had Sullivan's blocky signature under Room 109, so that's what Amish was looking for.

He'd draped his overcoat on top of his Tommy gun, not that he needed to bother. The desk clerk had been passed out drunk. He tossed the coat over his shoulder as he rounded the corner and spotted the gold numbers for 109.

Daniel Garret went straight for the front door while Heinrich went for the side. Fades worked better in the dark. Mouths always preferred the public.

There were two gangsters in the low-class lobby. One was sitting in a chair next to the desk, pretending to read the newspaper. The other was acting like he worked there, behind the counter, except he hadn't even bothered to remove his hat. Both of them looked good and stupid. Dan kicked his Power up a notch.

"Good evening!" he said, friendly as could be. "I'm in need of a room."

"We're all full. Go away," grunted the man at the front desk. His posture told Daniel that he was holding a gun under the table.

Dan always did enjoy a challenge. He reached out, his magic telling him the emotional state of the two. They were small-minded and brutal men. The beauty of being a Mouth was that the dumber your audience, the easier they were to steer. Strong minds were much harder to sway, and they could usually sense the intrusion. "Hey, don't I know you guys? You look really familiar." So far, so good, so Dan pushed harder.

The two men glanced at each other, feeling a sudden deep sense of camaraderie. "Uh, yeah . . . I think I know you," said the one with the paper.

"We're friends, don't you remember . . . that one time? We all got together?" Dan asked, pushing as hard as he could. There was no time for subtlety. He was their buddy, their old pal. His magic was based on lies and coercion, but any moral qualms he'd had about using it had been put to rest once he'd seen the Imperium schools in action.

"Oh yeah!" said the one behind the counter.

"I need a favor."

Both of them were smiling now. "Anything, bub."

"What room is Jake Sullivan staying in?"

The goon flipped open the book and scanned down the page. "Tenth floor. Ninth room. Our buddies are up there now to whack him."

"Good. Good. Thanks a lot. That really helps me. You know what else would help a ton?" Both were smiling and nodding.

"What?"

"Anything for a pal!"

Dan hesitated. He wasn't as heartless as he'd thought. First he had to know. "Are you *bad* men?"

"I've killed three people for Lenny Torrio!" said the first one proudly.

The second one snorted. "Big deal, I once broke an old lady's hip because she owed Mr. Capone protection money; then I beat her head in 'cause she got lippy."

That would do. "Great, guys, just great. Do me a favor, would ya?"

"No problem." They both were grinning stupidly.

"Give me a second to get out of the way, then I want you to kill each other."

A Mouth couldn't force someone to do something that they normally wouldn't consider. It didn't work like that. Even someone as strong as Dan could only sway someone down his natural path. All he could do was push what was already there. If he'd asked a decent person to murder a friend, it would simply break the spell. Only a real piece of work would take such a small amount of Influence to do something so heinous. Dan wasn't even in the elevator before they started shooting.

Heinrich caught the door right before it closed and slipped inside. "That didn't take long."

"Not much loyalty amongst gangsters, I suppose. Tenth floor, please."

Amish checked the safety on his Thompson. He wasn't going to screw this up. Brick was the biggest, so he moved up to kick the door. Hoss reached up and unscrewed the hall light, plunging them into shadow. The boys had done this kind of thing before. The Jap just hung back, looking bored.

There was a big glass window at each end of the hall, and enough street light was coming in that Amish could still see his buddies. This was going to be great. He squeezed the Thompson tight. "Do it. Do it!"

Brick reared back and kicked hard. His considerable weight tore the lock right through the jamb, and the door flew open with a bang. Amish leapt through, screaming, turned toward the bed, spotted the lump in the middle of the blankets and mashed the trigger. He fired from the hip, stitching hot slugs through the bed, the headboard, and the wall. He jerked the foregrip back down and kept ripping the bed, flinging feathers and bits into the air, until he'd hammered through the entire 50-round drum in one continuous smoking burst.

"Take that, stupid Heavy! Yeah!" Amish shouted. "That'll learn you up real good."

Hoss rushed past him, double-barrel shotgun in hand, grabbed the blankets and yanked them off the bed, revealing nothing but a pile of bullet-riddled pillows and clothing. Hoss started to shout, "Where is—" but then his chest and head erupted in a shower of red as a swarm of giant bullets stitched him. Hoss tumbled dead to the floor.

The Heavy stepped out of the bathroom, shirtless, holding an enormous black cannon to his shoulder. The smoking muzzle swiveled toward the doorway where Brick had appeared and there was a terrible thunder. Brick disappeared back into the hall and Amish blinked as something hot and wet splattered him in the face. It took him a second to realize that he had just been hit with part of Brick's skull.

The cannon settled on Amish last and the Heavy paused, with a little smile that seemed almost sad. "Lenny couldn't even bother to come himself?" Amish pushed the release and yanked the drum out of the Thompson, then fumbled at his pocket for a stick mag. The Heavy just shook his head, disappointed.

Then everything was wrong, down was now behind him, and Amish screamed as he fell through the door and into the hallway. *How—* He felt his collar bone snap as he hit the wall. Gravity came back suddenly and Amish spilled onto the hall carpet. Pain washed through him in waves. The Heavy appeared in the doorway, glanced quickly both ways, and saw the Jap.

"Who are you supposed to be?" the Heavy asked.

The Jap didn't answer. He just opened his big coat and showed his sword. Amish looked back and forth between the two terrifying men and knew that he was about to see one *hell* of a fight.

But the Heavy just did his trick with gravity again, and now down seemed to be the end of the hallway. The Jap began to fall, but whipped his sword out and jabbed it into the floor, and he was hanging there as Amish tumbled down the carpet past him. The window barely slowed him.

Amish opened his eyes inside the shower of glass to see that he was gliding over the street ten stories below. *I'm flying!* It was the most wonderful thing he'd ever experienced, until he reached the end of Sullivan's range, then gravity returned to its normal direction and the street rushed up to meet him.

⁂

"Who are you supposed to be?" Sullivan asked.

The man at the end of the dim hall threw open his coat, revealing the blue-wrapped hilt of a sword. His hand hovered over the handle of the blade, waiting.

Jake's curiosity did not run as deep as his apprehension at facing a crazy guy with a giant razor. He Spiked, bending gravity's pull to a different angle. The dead body and the cross-eyed Reader slid down the floor, but the other drew his sword in a flash as the Power hit, took it in two hands, and drove the silver blade deep into flooring. The Reader zipped past, hit the window, and took the whole assembly with him into the city.

The swordsman hung from the end of the blade, parallel with the carpet, dangling, patiently waiting for the Spike to subside, watching Sullivan curiously the whole time.

The Power needed to distort gravity for so long was too much, and Sullivan let go, letting himself fall against the doorway. The swordsman landed on his hands and knees, then took his time getting up. He pulled his blade from the wood, then spun it once quickly through the air, before letting it dangle loose in his hand. His fedora had gone out the window with the Reader, but other than that, he seemed fine.

"I did not realize the Americans had developed their Heavies to this extent."

"I'm big on self-improvement." The man was an Oriental. Sullivan had worked in a few Chinatowns before, and the truck drivers that had driven the First Volunteer around France had been Vietnamese, so he had more cultural exposure than a lot of his countrymen, but this man spoke English better than Sullivan did, and had a much nicer suit. Probably almost fifty, but strong and fit, he was remarkably tall compared to the other Asians Sullivan had known, probably just under six feet, and appeared a little too confident. "You ain't from around here, are you?"

"I am impressed with your level of mastery, Mr. Sullivan," he gave a very formal bow. "It is a great honor to battle one such as you."

Sullivan raised the Lewis gun to his shoulder. "There's nothing honorable about battle," he replied, pulling the trigger.

A short burst of 30 caliber bullets hit the swordsman square in the chest. Sullivan lowered the machine gun, but the swordsman was still standing. "Impossible." A string of .30-06 should have put even the toughest Brute on their ass.

The swordsman started forward slowly, raising his weapon, both hands on the hilt, blade held rigid next to his head.

Sullivan leaned into it this time. When the first Heavies started drifting into the First Volunteer, they had been put to work as machine gunners. Even the least powerful Heavy could carry five times as much weight as a Normal. An Active Heavy could lower the tug of gravity on his weapon, so even a pig like the Lewis Mk3 was handy to run around with. But the less a gun weighs, the more it recoils, and the harder it is to control, so a clever Spiker actually *increases* the pull on his weapon when it's time to put the hammer down.

The giant barrel barely moved as Sullivan pounded the remainder of the drum magazine into the swordsman. Each .30-06 bullet hit with an impact sufficient to quarter an elk, but instead of tumbling through flesh, the bullets exploded into fragments against his body. The hallway was pummeled with noise, the air was thick with unburned powder, and shining brass cases bounced along the floor.

When the Lewis bolt finally fell on an empty chamber, the swordsman was still there, clothes tattered, but flesh unharmed, and his slow walk turned into a charge. The sword descended as Sullivan desperately used his Power, hurling his attacker back. The swordsman fell a few feet but instantly adjusted, and drove himself back toward Sullivan in a leap. The big man shouted as the end of the blade flickered through his skin.

Sullivan stumbled back, blood pouring down his bare chest. He Spiked again, totally reversing gravity, and the swordsman fell toward the ceiling. Again, his foe adjusted, twisted, and took the impact with his hands, rolling across the roof, getting closer. Sullivan cut the Power and the swordsman dropped, hitting the ground in a perfect crouch, coat billowing around him, sword extended behind. He looked up and smiled.

"What are you?" Sullivan gasped, reaching deep, gathering Power. He had one last trick.

"I am Rokusaburo of the Iron Guard, Herald of the Imperium, warrior of the Emperor of Nippon. Know that before you die." he said with pride. He rose and extended his sword, aimed directly at Sullivan's heart. "I represent the *future*."

"Not if we can help it."

A grey shape appeared through the wall, colliding with the swordsman, locking up on his extended arm. Both of them crashed into the wall, cracking through the boards. The swordsman roared, the grey shape was instantly flung off, and the German from the stolen dirigible landed at Sullivan's feet.

"Need a hand?" the Fade asked.

Sullivan shrugged. "I suppose."

The swordsman came out of the wall swinging. The blade was insanely fast, and Sullivan was barely able to raise the Lewis to block. The German started pumping rounds from a pistol into the attacker and Sullivan was rewarded with bits of bullet jacket hitting him for the effort as they ricocheted off the Jap's skin.

Rokusaburo spun into the hall, and they had to leap back to avoid being eviscerated. The sword lanced forward, and Sullivan barely blocked it, the Lewis flying from his hands under the impact. The blade instantly returned, humming through the air, and the tip pierced his bicep. The steel came out in a splash of red that painted the wallpaper, and Rokusaburo stepped back, triumphant, as Sullivan crashed, bellowing, into the wall.

The sword flicked back to finish him, but the swordsman's head rocked as he was struck from behind, and the blade passed within a hair's width of Sullivan's throat. He jerked his eyes up to see a bespectacled man walking down the hallway, firing a handgun repeatedly into Rokusaburo's back. It was just as ineffective as before, but at least it was distracting. The swordsman turned toward the new threat.

The Fade came off the floor, leaping past Sullivan, and kicked the Imperial in the back of the legs. The Japanese went to his knees, but simultaneously reversed his sword and drove it up, right through the German's guts. The Fade was too quick with his Power, and the silver blade erupted through nebulous grey smoke. The mass sidestepped, re-formed into solid flesh and bone, and kicked Rokusaburo square in the skull.

The swordsman's head snapped back hard, but then came right back wearing a vicious snarl, and the German had to dive away to avoid the sword.

Apparently hitting him did about as much good as shooting him.

Sullivan pushed himself off the wall and stumbled forward, splattering blood in great pulsing gushes from his arm, but still he was calm, analytical, trying to find a way around Rokusaburo's Power. Even while bleeding out, Sullivan was able to note that the Jap's clothes were shredded, but it was like his skin turned to hardened steel on impact. He had never heard of the Power of indestructibility before, but like any other Power it had to have limits. It had to run out eventually, or break when pushed too far.

Sullivan cleared his head, using his Power to see the world as it really was—mass, density, and force. He could feel the Power of his opponent, and he understood then what was happening. The Jap was like a reverse Fade. Instead of making himself hazy until his body could pass through solid things, this one was increasing it until nothing could pass through. It was taking a staggering amount of energy.

It was time for Sullivan to play his final hand.

He needed to get real close for this to work. He was too big and slow to get past that three-foot razor blade without losing a limb. He needed a distraction. The man in glasses had reloaded his pistol and started shooting again, diverting Rokusaburo's attention long enough for Sullivan to hiss, "Fritz. Take the sword again. Then get back." The German nodded quickly and moved in.

The Fade charged in one way, going grey, just as Rokusaburo swung through him, and Sullivan dove straight at the swordsman. Superbly trained, the sword was already coming back around in a killing arc.

They collided. Sullivan took every bit of Power he had and let it all go at once, channeling it through his body, increasing gravity's strength, bellowing at the world to pull them down under the strength of fifty Earths. The swordsman gasped as the magnificent force crushed down on him. He fired his own Power, and Sullivan could feel his own hammering like bombs against a bunker as the two magical forces slammed together. The floor beneath splintered and exploded, and the two dropped through, hitting the next floor down without even slowing, blowing through landing after landing, ten stories in an ever quickening cascade, until they crashed through a series of pipes and into the concrete of the foundation.

Still Rokusaburo's Power held, invulnerable, struggling, taking the impossible force. The foundations cracked and turned to powder under the pressure, but Sullivan kept pushing. The walls bent. The lights crackled and died. Sullivan could feel something burning beneath the swordsman's clothing, some other alien source of Power that he was drawing upon to sustain his invulnerability. Then finally, inexorably, he felt his enemy weaken. Rokusaburo screamed in frustration. His Power flickered like a flame deprived of oxygen, and then it was extinguished.

The full impact of Sullivan's Power hit him then, and Rokusaburo was just *gone*, replaced by a sudden pressurized red mist that instantly coated the entire basement.

Sullivan lay there for a moment as the world returned to normal. It took a few seconds before he could breathe again. He slowly pulled himself out of the dripping crater, and spit a mouthful of blood that he was relatively certain was his own. His Power was gone. He'd never felt so tired. Gradually realizing that he was bleeding, he mashed one big hand against his torn arm, but the blood just leaked between his fingers.

The Japanese sword was twisted like a pretzel and embedded in the floor. The damaged boiler was hissing and screaming. It hurt to turn his head, and he was certainly no boiler mechanic, but all those gauges breaking and steam shooting out like that had to be a *bad* thing.

A grey shape fell through the broken ceiling and the Fade landed softly next to the indentation. He took in the majestic mess in awe, then looked down at his shoes in disgust and kicked away something that had probably been one of Rokusaburo's more elastic organs. He paused long enough to pick up a piece of the broken sword. "Souvenir," he explained with a smile, then noticed the hissing boiler. "Come, my large friend. I believe this building is going to fall down on our heads very soon."

Sullivan didn't know if he could trust the German, but he was too tired to argue.

Rokusaburo

Chapter 6

I swing as hard as I can, and I try to swing right through the ball. The harder you grip the bat, the more magic power you use all at once, the more you can swing through the ball, and the farther the ball will go. I swing big, with everything I've got, muscle and magic. So now they're talking about banning us Actives from baseball because we're not fair, not sporting? Hell, I hit big or I miss big. I am what I am and I live as big as I can.

—George "Babe" Ruth,
interview after hitting his
200th season home run, 1930

New York City, New York

BILLIONAIRE INDUSTRIALIST Cornelius Gould Stuyvesant had many offices, but the one that had the best view was at the top of the relatively new Chrysler Building. Not only did he like this particular office because it enabled him to look out over the city, which he considered his personal fiefdom, but he also found the building aesthetically pleasing. It was pointy.

His favorite pointy building had briefly been the tallest building in the world, before the Empire State Building had been completed. He had a suite there as well, but preferred this location because from this position he could watch his fleet of trans-Atlantic passenger dirigibles docking at the Empire State, or his cargo airships landing at the industrial pads closer to the ocean. It made him feel like a child with a model train set.

Cornelius stepped away from the window as a servant brought him the morning paper. He took his place in a comfortable recliner and opened first to the obituaries, as was his daily custom, to see if anyone he disliked had died, but sadly the announcements held no joy.

On the bright side, that meant that his most hated enemy was still suffering and wasting away under the curse of the Pale Horse. His spies had confirmed that he had taken gravely ill, and he had not been seen in public in almost two years. The thought made Cornelius smile as he turned the pages. He still owed that foul Harkeness a favor, but whatever it was would be worth it.

The *Times* spoke of more war in Asia as the Imperium annexed another bunch of islands he'd never heard of, Herbert Hoover looked like he was going to be trounced by Governor Roosevelt (not that Cornelius minded, since he had donated plenty of money to both sides), and more general lawlessness and moral decay around the country. Most of the news was old hat for a man who had informants everywhere, but one item caught his attention.

"Well, I'll be . . ." he muttered around his morning cigar as he studied the photograph. It was a grainy shot of one of the Imperium's new tri-hulled super-dirigibles, taken over some Dutch colony. It would look like a big blurry blob to most viewers, but he recognized the design because it had originated amongst the Cogs employed in his engineering department at UBF.

He disliked Cogs, just as he disliked all magical people, himself and immediate family excluded, but he had grown fabulously wealthy from their genius. Every Cog was already a genius in their own way, absolutely fanatically brilliant at something, but then they could occasionally use their Power to push them over the top, to achieve the most amazing of all creative achievements. The Imperium's new Kaga-class flying battleship was a perfect example.

Nine hundred feet long, with three separate hydrogen-filled hulls, each hull cordoned off into ten separate armored chambers, the Kagas were the biggest thing to ever take to the sky. Hydrogen was far more dangerous than helium, but provided more lift. The Imperials had asked for hydrogen in the specifications probably became the main source for helium in the world was unavailable to them in Texas. With the redundant mechanical and magical provisions, the Kagas would be virtually indestructible, with armaments that outclassed the best dreadnoughts of the Great War, but with four times the speed, its own parasite air force, and a virtually unlimited range.

The picture was a bit different than the blueprints he had seen, more bulbous. The Imperials had added a few things that he did not recognize, but that did not concern him. UBF had been paid to provide the hull and engine design. His eldest son had arranged the deal while serving as the ambassador to Japan, may God rest his soul.

The government had forbidden the sale of superscience to the Imperium as part of the embargo, but Cornelius Gould Stuyvesant knew that laws were to keep the lower classes in line. Whereas, he did what he wanted, but did so in secret to avoid the hassle of know-nothings' petty harassments. The embargo forbid UBF from the construction of any warships for a foreign power. Cornelius was currently overseeing the construction of the Emperor's personal flagship at the UBF plant, but since it was officially a diplomatic and scientific vessel, it was perfectly legal. The warships, like the Kagas, on the other hand, were quite illegal, but with the economic slump, the Imperium were the only people with money to burn.

He'd sold them the Kaga design a few years ago. He was just surprised to see that the Imperium had gotten the bugs worked out so quickly. Once they started using their new super-dirigibles to further their domination of the East, the U.S. Navy would be forced to come to UBF for their own next-generation airships.

Cornelius loved a good arms race as much as the next robber baron.

Chicago, Illinois

THE GRID IRON CLUB was usually quiet on Sunday mornings, but today was the exception. Lenny Torrio was pacing up and down the bar, throwing bottles and whatever furniture he could pick up in a fit of rage.

His remaining seven men were standing around, waiting for the bout to pass like they always did. These spells had earned Mr. Torrio the nickname of Crazy Lenny, but they always eventually subsided.

They'd lost five boys last night, shot to death, and poor Amish tossed out a window. The old Rasmussen Hotel had been evacuated right before the boiler had exploded, and they'd just got word that the city inspectors were saying the building was unsafe and was going to fall down. They all knew that it was a mess and the public outcry would bring the law down on them hard.

Mr. Torrio was going on about how Al Capone was sure to move in on them, when some new faces arrived. The first was another Japanese, this one younger than the last one. It made the men uneasy when they saw how unnerved the new arrival made their boss.

"I'm sorry about your friend," Torrio sputtered. "Really I am. Please, give your Chairman my full respects." The Japanese did not speak or move.

Another man entered behind the Asian. This one was white, tall, muscular, with a badly scarred face and one milky white eye. Apparently, seeing him really shook Mr. Torrio. "Whoa, hey old buddy, been a real long time. I'd heard—"

"Heard wrong," he grunted. "Call me Mr. Madi now, Lenny."

"Is this about last night? About Jake? Look, I'm sorry, 'cause I just did what I was told . . ." Torrio looked back and forth between the two newcomers, apparently confused. "I didn't know you were working for the Chairman now."

The big man with the bad eye shrugged. "I don't care about Jake. I go where the action is, Lenny . . . Your sources find anything on these other guys the Chairman's lookin' for?"

Torrio raised his hands defensively. "You know how it is with demons, man. You got to sort out what's true and what's not . . . but that device you were looking for, that your—" he nodded respectfully toward the Jap before continuing—"*dear* deceased associate showed me the drawing . . . it's in California. I saw a skinny girl on a train, not far from where I found that old Portagee for you. She was easy, 'cause she don't know about Finders."

"Turns out that bit ain't so important. What about the others?"

"They've hidden themselves too good, but I know Christiansen was last in the mountains and Southunder was on the ocean somewhere. I'll track them down for you, I promise."

"Well, that narrows it down a bunch." Madi turned to the other man and spoke real slow in a language that none of the men understood. The Japanese gave a quick reply. Madi asked a question. The Oriental nodded once, and the big white man went back to Torrio. "My associate doesn't think we need your services anymore and that you brought too much attention."

"Aww, come on, Madi," Lenny begged. "It ain't like that. Where else are you going to get another Finder as good as me?"

"Oh, somebody else told us where to find them already, and if we need to summon any critters . . . I figure we'll get by," Madi answered as something strange moved in the shadows of the warehouse rafters. Everyone looked up as the Summoned fell from the ceiling, spread its eight-foot wingspan, and settled gently to the floor. It hissed at the men with both heads and they instinctively stepped back. Claws clicked on the hardwood as it scuttled around the end of the bar and out of sight. Something squealed, and the dragon came back with Mr. Torrio's imp clenched in one set of jaws. The other head came around and snapped onto the creature's legs.

"Mildred!" Lenny shouted as his imp was ripped in two. "No!"

The dragon kept chewing as the imp's body dissolved into smoke. The whole crew was so distracted by the sight that they didn't see the man called Madi reaching for his shoulder holster.

Ten seconds later Crazy Lenny Torrio and his entire gang were history.

San Francisco, California

IT WAS ALL a little overwhelming, and all Faye could do for her first few minutes in the big city was gawk like the country girl that she was. There was an astounding number of people packed everywhere, scurrying along in every direction. The train station was easily ten times the size of the station in Merced, and there were more human beings milling around the platforms in those first few minutes than she had seen cumulatively in her entire life.

The air smelled like diesel, and humanity, and all sorts of unfamiliar perfumes. She tried to shrink down, uncomfortable, not used to moving through a crowd. The people were so packed that they moved in waves, almost like a herd of Holsteins, only far more colorful.

Many of the men were in suits, some were in work clothing, and Faye saw military uniforms for the first time. One handsome young man in white (Gilbert had said that meant Navy) winked at her as he went past, and Faye looked down, blushing. The young man was elbowed in the side by one of his friends and they all had a laugh.

The women were astounding, their dresses so pretty and flashy that Faye instinctively felt drab and boring in comparison. Their hair was all done up in ways that she had never even imagined, while hers was just flat. Many of them had jewelry and more wore furs, and almost everyone had a hat far nicer than her simple straw one.

Feeling underdressed compared to the other women, Faye paused long enough to put on the only piece of jewelry she possessed, the gold and black ring from Grandpa's bag. It wasn't nearly as fancy as the big things with all of the sparkles like the others had, but Faye figured it would do. The ring was too big and flopped around on her finger, but at least it was something.

She made her way through the masses, walking in the direction that most of the other disembarking travelers were heading. Somehow she ended up inside a building with really tall ceilings and big stained-glass windows and then she was swept out onto a sidewalk along a street where more fancy cars than she had ever imagined were speeding back and forth.

She had seen Mexicans before. They came through the San Joaquin valley and picked the crops every year, but the Mexicans here were different. They didn't seem to be passing through, they looked like they lived here. Faye saw other colors of people for the first time too. They were just part of the crowd, working just like everybody else, and nobody here seemed to pay them any extra mind. She tried not to stare, because that just didn't seem polite.

When she looked up, the sheer massive *tallness* of the surrounding buildings took her breath away. A great black shadow was moving down the street, and she nearly broke her neck craning her head back to watch the super-dirigible passing overhead. She watched the giant bag until she could no longer track it behind the big buildings and it was the most magical thing she had ever seen.

San Francisco was supposedly one of the least harmed cities by the depression, being such a mighty cosmopolitan hub of commerce. Having all of those military folks stationed at the nearby Peace Ray

Station spending all their money here had to help things. Faye could only begin to imagine how this place could have possibly been any fancier four years before. Compared to the Vierra farm, or especially the shack she had lived in before that, San Francisco was astounding.

Gilbert had told her about how taxicabs could drive her right to the address on Grandpa's note for a fee. At first she thought that sounded absurd. Paying somebody good money to ride when you could just walk? But her foot still hurt from the stupid beetle and the city was so overwhelming that the idea of walking across it was terrifying, so she got in line behind the other travelers waving at the curb, and studied them, so that when it got to be her turn she wouldn't look too much like a stupid hick.

Faye was so distracted by her new surroundings that she didn't see the man watching her from the steps of the train station. He paused long enough to crumple and toss a telegram sheet before following.

Unknown Location

SULLIVAN'S HEAD HURT, and the inside of his mouth was dry and tasted like he'd been chewing on rotten mouse-flavored cotton balls. The first thing he saw as he came to was a cup of water sitting by the side of the bed. Forcing himself up with a groan, he reached for it, but the fresh stitches in his arm and chest pulled and burned. His head swam, so he had to give up and lay back down.

The water just sat there, taunting him.

At first Sullivan thought that he was really dizzy, because the tiny room seemed to be swaying, but then he saw the vibrating ripples in the water cup, and realized that it was the room that was moving, and not him. There was a rhythmic noise coming from under the floor, and after a moment his fogged brain put together that it was steel wheels on a train track. The thick curtains had been drawn, but enough light leaked around the corners to indicate it was afternoon.

He was on a train, in a private luxury car, apparently.

He vaguely remembered stumbling up a ramp under his own power, being led by the German on one arm, and the fellow with glasses on the other, and at some point he had wound up in a wheelchair. The trip from the Rasmussen was a blur, and Sullivan knew that he'd lost a lot of blood on the way. That swordsman had stabbed him good. It was only through luck and the timely intervention of the two strangers that he hadn't got his head chopped off.

Sullivan frowned at the water, contemplating his next move.

There was something fishy about the swordsman. The goons he'd popped had been Lenny Torrio's boys, but the Japanese was way out of Lenny's league. He'd never met someone with a Power like that, or with the ability to adapt so quickly. Sullivan had been challenged by all sorts in Rockville, and he'd always won because he was meaner, tougher, and faster than the other guy. This one had been different. But he'd still managed to squish him like a bug, nonetheless. He hadn't used his Power like that since he had last lost his temper. That time had got him sent to prison, but strangely enough he felt equally justified in both uses.

It hurt to move his head, but he tried to rise a bit. There was a wheelchair shoved in one corner, blocked in by a regular wooden chair so it wouldn't be able to roll about. Several bloody towels were piled on it. Beside the water cup was a leather surgeon's bag, still open, and a few implements were sitting on a white cloth. He couldn't remember a thing, but apparently he'd had one hell of a night.

One wood-paneled wall slid open, revealing itself as a door. The man that entered was in his forties, short and chubby. "Good afternoon, Mr. Sullivan. Glad to see you're awake," he said, walking over to the bedside, humming absently. He spared no time manhandling Sullivan's arm so he could inspect the stitches. Sullivan cringed in pain, but the man didn't seem to notice. "Hmm . . . Not my best work, but you're not dead, so I'll call it a win."

Sullivan nodded his head at the water. "What? Oh yes? The side effects of opiate-based pain relievers can include cotton mouth, which can be rather unpleasant," the man stated matter-of-factly. It took him a second to realize that Sullivan didn't want a medical lesson, he just wanted a drink. "Oh, yes, sorry. Here you go."

He managed to spill half of it, but Sullivan cherished the victory over his enemy, the cup. "Who are you?" he finally croaked. "Where am I?"

"Dr. Ira Rosenstein. I was harassed by Mr. Garrett into coming on this trek. Mr. Koenig is in the next room getting some sleep. They had a late flight. I believe Mr. Garrett is in the dining car. I tried to tell him that I would prefer for you not to move for several days, but he was adamant that you must return to California immediately. The General must be briefed on the presence of an Iron Guard. Can you imagine? An actual Iron Guard acting with impunity within the United States? But of course you can, obviously. You did kill him after all, and in a particularly spectacular manner, if Heinrich is to be believed, though he does tend to embellish."

Sullivan just nodded, as if he had any clue what the doctor was talking about.

"You will need to take it easy for a while. Your physical condition indicates to me a rather intense life-style. In addition to what I attempted to fix last night, without my regular staff or equipment, in a moving train car rather than a proper operating room, but I digress . . . As I was saying, you are suffering from several other very recent punctures, contusions, and lacerations. I would strongly suggest that you tone down your activities, Mr. Sullivan."

"You a Healer?"

Rosenstein snorted. "As *if* . . . No. I am a doctor. I *work* for a living. Yes, I do happen to be a Cog, so I am a particularly gifted surgeon when the opportunity arises, the finest in Chicago. But I went to medical school and have continually educated myself at every opportunity to further my knowledge of anatomy and the most cutting edge surgical techniques, if you will excuse the pun." He smiled.

Sullivan didn't get it, but he'd had a really hard week. "Sure . . ."

The doctor continued. "Most people do not realize that Cogs are not just limited to machines or theoretical equations capped with bursts of magical brilliance. Some of us prefer to toil in fields of a medical nature. Whereas Healers"—he waved his hand dismissively—"know absolutely nothing of anatomy or biology, but work their magic from base intuition, and oh how everybody just *loves* Healers. They just put their hands on you and poof, you are all better. And then everyone showers them in money. Do you know how many years I went to school, Mr. Sullivan?"

"Uh . . . a lot?" He could tell it was a sore spot.

"Yes. A *lot.*" Rosenstein raised his voice. "Have you ever met an Active Healer that wasn't an insufferable bore? Full of themselves with a God complex and an ego bigger than Lake Superior?"

Sullivan had never actually had a conversation with a Healer. They were, after all, the rarest of the rare of Actives, or so he had thought, until he met a Jap who could shrug off dozens of rounds of .30-06. He shrugged.

"Well, trust me, sir. They're all pompous, the lot of them. The only thing they're good for is publicity."

Sullivan nodded. The miraculous ability of the Healer and the wondrous ingenuity of the Cog were the single biggest reasons Actives had been so accepted, even celebrated in American society. Some types of Powers did not fare so well. Heavies were generally valuable as dumb lugs, useful in industry, so he was in the middle of the pack. Other types were actually discriminated against, even despised.

Rosenstein checked the chest wound next, clucking approvingly at his work. "I am rather surprised that you survived this wound. It struck bone, but managed not to shear through. It is almost as if your bones are extremely dense . . . hmmm . . . You should be dead."

Sullivan didn't say anything, but he knew that it was probably because of all of his experimentation at Rockville. When breaking rocks had become too easy, he'd broken rocks in increased gravity. Sullivan had made his body as hard as his attitude. Even when he wasn't altering his weight through magic, he tipped the scales at eighty pounds heavier than he looked. Toward the end, when he was using all his Power, he'd broken rock with his *bones.*

"Good thing Garrett thought to call me. Helping out is the least I can do." He held up his right hand and used his thumb to wiggle a black and gold ring. "Considering I owe the Society my life." Then he went back to work.

"Who's the Society?"

The doctor paused, fingers on the bandage. "Excuse me?"

"The Society. What is it?"

"The Grimnoir, of course." A look crossed Rosenstein's face, partway between confusion and embarrassment. "I thought you were . . ." He grew even more troubled. "Oh my. Excuse me a moment." And the chubby man leapt up and hurried from the room like he had just discovered his patient was inflicted with a highly contagious plague.

Sullivan sighed and watched the ceiling. He was a patient man.

Three minutes later the German entered the room, rubbing sleep from his eyes. Rosenstein stayed in the doorway, fidgeting nervously. The German pulled up the chair, knocked the bloody towels on the floor, and sat on it backwards, arms resting on the back, studying Sullivan. "I will handle this, Doctor," he said finally. The doctor gladly fled, closing the door behind him.

The new visitor was young, with extremely short hair and a neatly trimmed goatee, the guy he punched out on the blimp. He waited a minute before grinning. "Ira is worried he said too much about us. Very good surgeon, but he's always fretting about something."

The smile seemed genuine, but Sullivan knew better than to trust anyone. "Who are you?"

"Heinrich Koenig, at your service," he said. "Fade extraordinaire and all-around problem solver."

Sullivan nodded. The German was probably in his early twenties, so at least a decade younger than Sullivan, but behind that easy smile was something dangerous. Sullivan could recognize a fellow traveler of the hard life, a survivor. Underneath the friendly veneer lurked the soul of a killer. "Thanks for stepping in there."

"We did the world a favor by ending that man, perhaps more than you will ever know," Heinrich replied. "No thanks necessary. That is what we do."

"We?"

"I cannot say that yet."

"What are the Grimnoir?"

"That isn't my place to explain. My associate will be back soon, and he is supposed to give you the pitch. Believe it or not, the reason we were at your hotel room was to make you a job offer. Daniel's the one that's good with words. Me, I'm more a man of action."

"I got a couple of G-men who'd agree with that."

Heinrich shrugged modestly. "I have my talents."

So did Sullivan. "How's the jaw?"

The smile left. "You broke it in two places. Luckily we have a Mender on staff. She put it back together, fixed Francis's knee too. Having a Healer around is nice."

"The blonde on the blimp?"

"Yes." Heinrich reached up and rubbed his jaw. "A very good one. It still hurts though."

"Yep. Imagine it would." Sullivan grunted. He wasn't the apologizing type, and he was still waiting on some answers. "So you going to tell me what the straight deal is, or are you just here to waste my time?"

The German chuckled coldly. "The *straight deal* is beyond your comprehension. You have no idea what you have just walked into. We are in a war, the likes of which even you have not seen."

"Don't get lippy," Sullivan replied. "I managed to stack a few of your relatives back in the biggest war ever, so don't tell me what I haven't seen, kid."

The German frowned. He was too young to have fought in the Great War, but Sullivan knew the country had fallen apart after the armistice. There were some tough feelings there, he could tell, but Heinrich kept his cool. "I just ask that you be patient, and your questions will be answered."

"I'm about done with this nonsense." Sullivan gasped as he tried to sit up, all of the stitches pulling in his chest and arm like strands of fire. "I'm walking out that door, and don't you try to stop me."

Heinrich uncurled his arms from the chairback, paused as if in thought, then reached into his grey suit coat and pulled a revolver from the inside pocket. Sullivan tensed, ready to Spike, but Heinrich just smiled again as he flipped the revolver around and handed it over butt first. "I believe you left this at the hotel. Your big gun was unfortunately smashed to bits."

Sullivan warily took his Smith & Wesson. He swung out the cylinder. It was still loaded.

"You wish to go? Your clothes, or should I say, the bloody remains of your pants and your shoes are under the bed. Unfortunately, neither I, nor my associates have anything that will fit you, my large friend. Feel free to leave at any time. I believe we are in Kansas by now. You should have no problem wandering around the Midwest, especially missing half your blood. Oh, and the police are looking for you. Apparently *Herr* Hoover is a little upset about you destroying a downtown hotel in a rather newsworthy manner and wants you brought in.

I am sure he will understand why the mob and an Imperium assassin were trying to murder you."

He would also want to know why exactly Sullivan had gone to meet with Torrio. Hoover would more than likely send him back to Rockville just for being a pain in the ass.

The German continued. "*Or* . . . you could continue to rest until my associate returns, and then everything will be explained in full."

It hurt to move. It hurt to think. Just rising this far had made him dizzy. Sullivan glowered and slowly lowered himself to the bed. He kept the .38 in one big hand.

Heinrich stood. "Very good. Daniel should be back in a moment." He turned to leave.

"Answer me one thing," Sullivan said just as Heinrich reached the door. "You say we're in a war . . . what side are you?"

Heinrich paused. "This war is in the shadows beyond nations. I am on the side of righteousness, of all that is free, or holy, or good, *Herr* Sullivan . . . Rest. You look like death." He closed the door.

Of course, the Grimnoir thought they were the good guys. Everybody thought they were in the right. The evilest bastards he had ever met had still thought of themselves as the good guys. It was just his dumb luck to blunder into a bunch of true believers. Sullivan closed his eyes and went back to sleep.

Chapter 7

MAGIC LEADS TO TERROR - City Firemen were unable to contain the FIRE that ripped through a Mar Pacifica estate on Sunday evening until there were only charred remains of the home, belonging to famous big game hunter L.S. Talon. A TERRIBLE DISCOVERY was made once the DEADLY flames were extinguished. So far, SEVEN human bodies have been recovered from the scene. Local residents say that there was a great commotion and much GUNFIRE before the conflagration spread. RUMOR is that Mr. Talon was a supporter of MAGIC and was himself an ACTIVE. He has been missing since Sunday and is believed to be amongst the DEAD.

—Article,
San Francisco Examiner, 1929.

San Francisco, California

THE ADDRESS on Grandpa's note was on the far west side of the city. The neighborhood was called Richmond, and a lot of things must have changed from when Grandpa had drawn his little map. The area was filled with new houses, stores, and churches. Every now and then they would pass an area that was nothing but sand dunes, but then quickly enough there would be more homes. Some of the larger places had been started, but then abandoned when the developers' money had run out along with everyone else's.

"Lots of Jews and Irishmen in this part of town," the driver told Faye helpfully. "The Russians built a great big church up over that way." Faye just kept watching out the window. As Grandpa had always said, her brain would just get to spinning sometimes, and the real world would fade away. She lost track of time as the town turned into suburbs, and then into an area of gentle green hills as they went south.

She snapped back to reality as the cab stopped. "We're here. This is the address you gave me."

"This? This is it?" she asked, staring out the window. "Are you sure?"

"Yeah," said the driver. "Not what you were expecting, I guess."

There had been a house here once, that much was obvious, a really large one from the remains of the foundation that was poking out of the ground. Weeds had grown up over the crumbling brick and what had once been a big chimney stood like a monolith.

"Looks like it burned down a long time ago," the cabbie said. "You want me to take you back?"

There was a strange smell in the air when Faye stepped out of the cab. It was kind of fishy but not too offensive. It took her a moment to realize that she was actually smelling the ocean for the first time. This couldn't be it. This had been her only clue from Grandpa. She started to wander toward the ruins.

"Lady?"

There had once been a fence of iron bars around the property, but whatever had engulfed the house had been so hot that the metal had softened and bent, and now the fence just looked lopsided. She ran her fingers across the bars and they came away orange with rust.

"Hey, lady! Pay me," the cabbie growled.

"Oh, sorry," Faye mumbled as she returned to the cab and carefully counted the money out exactly. The cabby looked at it in disgust before driving off, and it was only a moment later that she remembered Gilbert warning her that people in the city also expected tips.

The gate was lying in the weeds. The grass was hip deep on what had once been a lawn. Faye thought that she could just barely smell the ash as she gingerly put her weight onto the charred boards of what had been the porch, and it reminded her of another, more recent, fire. She noticed that somebody had etched strange symbols into the crumbling floor, and she stepped over them carefully.

There was nothing else there.

Somehow she knew that something bad had happened here,

something worse than the fire. Lives had been lost in this place. Death was in the air.

"I'm sorry, Grandpa. I didn't expect this," she said as she slowly turned around. "I thought maybe somebody around here would help me." She had been so certain that the address would hold the answers that she had not thought about what she would do next if there were no answers to be found. She was on the outskirts of a strange city, had no friends, and no idea what to do. She picked out a pile of bricks and sat down.

Why am I here?

Faye wasn't sure. Grandpa hadn't even really given her any last words, he'd just choked out half a sentence before dying, given her some weird metal thing, which she'd managed to already lose half of, and now she was just alone. She wanted to cry, but she felt like she'd already cried all her tears, and now she was just all dry and hollow inside.

A fat brown squirrel crawled up onto a nearby board. It cocked its head at her curiously, as if wondering what this strange human girl was doing sitting on some ashy bricks in the middle of its forest.

"Hello," said the squirrel.

Oh, great, now I've gone crazy.

"Hi," Faye responded.

The squirrel just kept looking at her, twitching nervously like squirrels do, and for a minute Faye thought that maybe it had just sounded like the little animal had spoken. Grandpa had always said that she got her brain spinning too fast sometimes and that if she spun it too hard it might break. The squirrel examined her for what seemed like an abnormally long time, and Faye started to doubt that she'd heard anything at all, and felt stupid for talking to it.

"Nice ring," the squirrel said. Its voice didn't seem to match, like the sound wasn't coming from the animal, but *through* it. It had a deep, scratchy, male voice. "It set the ward spells off. Where'd you get it?"

"My Grandpa gave it to me," she answered, holding up her hand to show off the black and gold band. She could have sworn the squirrel nodded thoughtfully. "He gave me a list with some names on it. I'm looking for somebody named Pershing. Could you help me, little squirrel?"

"We've got a live one at the old place," the squirrel said, like it was talking back over its shoulder. Faye looked into the grass for other squirrels but didn't see anything else hiding in the grass.

"Are you okay, Mr. Squirrel?"

"You ain't from around these parts, are you, kid?" asked the squirrel.

"Is it that obvious?"

"Well, yeah, actually . . ." The squirrel twitched and swiveled its head back toward the road as it sensed something. A large black automobile was coasting to a stop on the road. Its whiskers twitched violently as the doors opened. "Shit! If it ain't some Imperium motherfuckers!" exclaimed the squirrel, then it swiveled back to her. "Damn it! Hide, girl! Hide! Go!" Then it leapt off the board into the grass.

Faye watched the profane little animal disappear, then switched back to the car. Three men had gotten out and were heading straight for the fallen gates. They reached into their coats and came out with guns. She scrambled behind the pile of bricks and ducked down low. It was just like what had happened to Grandpa, and she realized that she was shaking uncontrollably.

She could hear the crunching of the grass as the men moved. They were obviously city folk, not hunters, loud and clumsy. She risked a peek around the side of the bricks, and the closest was going to be on the porch in seconds. And there, right in the soft ashen wood, clear as day, were her footprints, leading right to where she was hiding.

"*Psstt.* Over here." The squirrel's head poked up out of the weeds. "Stay low."

It was either follow the squirrel, or Travel before they found her, but she didn't know where to Travel to, and if she appeared in front of one of the other men, they'd shoot her dead just like they had done to Grandpa. Faye crouched down, bunched up her dress so she could crawl, and hustled after the squirrel. The animal was gone by the time she got there, but there seemed to be an indentation in the grass. When she pressed on it her hand went right through into an empty space.

There was a footfall a few feet away. With no time to think, Faye shoved her head through the grass and found herself staring down an ivy-coated chute. There was only a foot of light before everything was masked in shadow. She kept going, scooting down a gentle slope. Spiderwebs hit her in the face and insects skittered across her body. A second later her hands landed in soft dust, and she pulled herself into a tight black space. A few spikes of sunlight pierced the darkness from holes in the floorboards above. Every time one of the men took a step, ash cascaded through the light. Something furry and warm pushed past her lips and she almost screamed.

"Easy . . ." the squirrel said softly.

"Where are we?" Faye whispered.

"Coal cellar . . . Hurry up, Francis. Imperium assholes right on top of us."

"I'm not Francis. Who's Francis?"

"Shut up, kid. I ain't talking to you," the squirrel hissed. "Move your ass, boy." There was a thud directly overhead and one of the men shouted something. They'd found Faye's tracks. "Shit . . . They're gonna find us. Never a grizzly bear or a moose or a Doberman around when I need one . . . Hey, girl, you got any Powers?"

"Yeah," Faye whispered. "I'm a Traveler."

The squirrel sighed. "What? Son of a bitch. I was hoping you had super strength or shot lightning bolts out your eyes or something because these Imperium goons are gonna find us any second."

"My name's Faye."

"Did I ask for a life story? We're about to get killed here . . ." The squirrel let out a long sigh. "Aw hell . . . My name's Lance. You just scoot for the woods. I'll hold them off."

She wasn't sure what exactly the squirrel, Lance, was going to do to fight off three men with guns, so she reached into her pocket, and pulled out her little revolver. She cocked the hammer as slowly and quietly as possible. The squirrel rubbed up against her face again. "Are you daft? The only thing you're gonna do with that little thing is piss them off. What is that? A .32? Jesus, you ain't hunting squirrels. Gonna use that to put us out of our misery?"

There was a sudden crash. A pile of ash broke loose from the ceiling, obscuring the tiny shafts of light. Then another crash, and a much larger shaft of light appeared as one of the men smashed a hole in the floor with his boot. "Go!" Lance shouted. The furry shape left her face, bounded up into the light, and launched itself into the air.

One of the men screamed. "It's crawling up my pants! Kill it! Kill it!"

"Quit being a punk, and step on it, Al. We've got business."

There was a commotion, shouting, and then one of the men started to laugh at his companion's problem. They didn't know they were dealing with a *magic* squirrel. Faye thought about the area near the front gate, concentrated, feeling her magic. She hadn't Traveled since getting the bug stuck in her foot, and for the first time in her life, she was scared to use her Power and hesitated.

I can do this.

Her thoughts went ahead of her. The air was clear of objects, the grass was tall, waving, not a concern for a Normal, but for her, every piece represented potential death, a single blade of grass potentially as deadly as a steel knife. No leaves in the air. No big pieces of sand or grit, no bugs, only particulate so small that her passage would brush it aside. Nothing was about to enter that space. She saw *everything.* And it all happened within a tenth of a second and she was gone.

Faye appeared an inch over the tall grass, still in the same prone position she'd been in the cellar, and dropped like a stone. Her landing was cushioned by the weeds and she popped right back up.

The three men were standing in a circle over something. One of them was pointing his pistol at the floor, and she knew that the magic squirrel was just as dead as Grandpa had been. "Lance!"

The men looked up simultaneously, guns rising toward her, and Faye prepared to Travel again, but their eyes collectively jerked upward as something passed through the air over her head with a rustle of cloth in the wind. A petite shape landed in a crouch between the men, knocking one of them sprawling.

It was a woman in a red dress. She rose quickly, slammed her palm into another's chest with a terrible crack, throwing him back and completely through the brick chimney, collapsing the entire structure in a cloud of red dust. She spun back toward the last man, just as his gun stabbed out toward her, and Faye screamed. There was a gunshot.

The man's head snapped back. The pistol dropped from lifeless fingers before he collapsed into the ash.

"Good shot, Francis," the woman shouted, then she turned back to the first one she'd knocked down. She kicked a giant beam casually out of the way, bent down and grabbed a handful of hair, dragging the struggling man from the ashes.

There was the sound of an action being worked, and Faye turned to see a man standing back at the gate with a bolt-action rifle. Faye almost Traveled, but he didn't point the rifle at her, instead he gave her an easy smile. "It's going to be all right. We're here to help you."

The man was young, probably not much older than her. "Are you Lance the magic squirrel's friend?"

"Huh?" At first he seemed bewildered by that, then he started to laugh, like she'd said something hilarious.

Faye was confused by his reaction. "Come on! I think they squished him!" she cried, then Traveled back to the house. Her shoes hit the ashen floor, just as the lady in the red dress was smacking the last man senseless. The scary woman glanced up, surprised. She was holding the much larger man effortlessly by the neck, one arm cocked back to hit him again, her delicate knuckles covered with his blood. Faye paid her no mind. These new people seemed to be on Lance's side, and he had saved her life.

"Oh no!" Faye cried, falling to her knees next to the hole in the floor. The squirrel was inside. It moved weakly. "You're alive!" She picked up the tiny body and hugged it close. The magic squirrel blinked stupidly. It must have gotten hit in the head.

The young man joined her a moment later, putting one hand gently on her shoulder. "Come on, we've got to get out of here. There might be more coming."

"I wish they would," said the woman. She appeared with a limp form thrown over one shoulder. The man was much bigger than she was, but she didn't seem to notice the weight. "I hit that other guy through the chimney a little hard, but this one's alive. I can remedy that real quick if you want . . ."

"Naw, the General will want to question him," said a gruff male voice. "Francis, bring the car up and stick him in the back. Looks like some tough guys working for hire. They probably won't know anything about the Imperium, but it's worth a shot." He sounded strangely familiar and Faye looked up. A burly, dark-bearded man was standing at the base of the porch with his thick arms folded. He was wearing rough work clothes and a wide-brimmed hat. He was shorter than Faye, but nearly two men wide in the chest. Faye stood, still cradling the squirrel.

"Lance?"

The man's eyes twinkled as he grinned. "That's me . . . Hell, kid. What're you doing with that squirrel? I'm too proud and not near hungry enough to eat that flea-bitten thing for dinner."

Faye looked down at the squirrel just as it regained its senses and bit the hell out her thumb. "Ow!" She flung her hands wide and the little animal scurried into the grass.

Lance turned and started to walk away with a pronounced limp, realizing a moment later that she wasn't following. "You coming or what?"

Somewhere in Colorado

WHEN JAKE SULLIVAN WOKE UP again it was later in the day and there were brown mountains outside blocking the sunlight, but a pair of electric lamps lit the train compartment fairly well. They were still moving and the air felt thinner when he inhaled. Someone was sitting in the chair next to the bed, reading a newspaper. The banner proclaimed that it was the Denver something or other, and the headline was about some anarchists causing trouble, but Sullivan didn't feel like trying to move his head far enough to read it. He must have groaned, because the paper dipped down, revealing a thick pair of glasses and a friendly smile. "Evening, Jake. How're you feeling?"

"Not dead. So could be worse."

The man chuckled as he folded the newspaper. "Understandable. We haven't had the pleasure of being formally introduced, though we've met twice now, I'm Daniel Garrett. I've been sent by my employer to make you an offer—"

"Not to be rude, Dan, but which way's the toilet?"

That caught him off guard, and he pointed to the rear of the compartment. "Well, you *have* been asleep for a really long time . . . But Ira said you shouldn't try to move—" Sullivan sat up abruptly, feeling the stitches pull and ache. "Never mind, I suppose." Sullivan swung his legs off the bed, heaved himself up, and stumbled for the back. Walking would have been difficult under normal circumstances, but the rocking of the train made it worse.

"Never been in a train car that had a private toilet. Now that's high-class," Sullivan stated on his return. This time there was a whole pitcher of water at the bedside instead of just a cup. He picked it up and started drinking

"Yes, I bribed our way onto the very best . . ." Garrett said as Sullivan pounded down the entire pitcher. "It was the first thing out of Chicago, well, this or a freight car, and the doctor said he needed something decent to work on you, so I made sure I passed around enough dough to keep the crew from talking about the big, busted-up fella in the wheelchair."

Sullivan slammed the pitcher down. "That's better." He leaned against the rocking wall, feeling every ache, stitch, and bruise, and he *still* had a cold. "I'm starved. Any chance I could get you to spring for a couple of steaks?"

"Of course . . ." Garrett replied. "I-I thought you wanted to know what was going on first?"

Sullivan grimaced as his stomach growled. Burning that much Power always made him hungry, and that wasn't counting the blood loss. "You talk. I eat."

Chapter 8

Why did I join the First Volunteers? That's a tough one. My older brother, Matt, he just liked to fight, and figured Germans would serve as good as any. My other brother, Jimmy, he was simple. He went wherever we went. Me . . . I was the one that liked to ponder on stuff. Roosevelt did like he did before with the Rough Riders. My daddy was a Rough Rider in Cuba. President Wilson didn't want him to go, but General Roosevelt wanted to prove that Actives were good for the country. Got himself killed in the process. Never did like his politics, too progressive for me, but I'd follow that man into battle anytime. Lousy politician, great leader . . . Sorry. The question . . . Why'd I go? I guess I felt a duty to show that Actives could be useful . . . that we could be the good guys . . . I was a fool.

—Jake Sullivan,
Parole Hearing,
Rockville State Penitentiary, 1928

Mar Pacifica, California

THE THREE STRANGERS drove Faye south along a road overlooking the ocean. The young man, who introduced himself as Francis, was driving. Lance was sitting up front, and the woman, Delilah, was in back with her. The man that had tried to hurt her was on the floor, with his ankles and wrists bound and a burlap sack over his head. Every time he started to move Delilah would kick him again as a reminder.

Lance had taken a piece of charcoal from the ruined house and drawn a complicated mark on the unconscious man's forehead before pulling the sack over his head. She didn't know what that was supposed to do, but it seemed to satisfy Lance.

Faye had started to ask questions in the car, but Delilah had shushed her, explaining that if the General, whoever that was, decided to let this man go, then the less he knew the better. Faye had a suspicion that Delilah had just said that out loud so the man on the floor would have some hope, and maybe that would make him more cooperative. Or maybe she just didn't want to talk. After all, Faye thought, why would a beautiful, sophisticated woman, that could jump across a vacant lot and throw men through brick walls want to waste her time talking to a hayseed bumpkin from El Nido by way of Ada, Oklahoma?

The only other conversation was when Lance apologized for his swearing and called her *little lady.* He said that he tended to cuss more when his mind was in more than one body at a time.

So Faye went back to spinning in her head, examining the car, the finest thing that she'd ever ridden in, all shiny chrome and bright blue paint and soft leather, intricate mirrors on top of the spare tires, and a little golden angel on the end of the hood. She watched the ocean, amazed at how far it seemed to go until you could see the curve of the world at the edges, and even the people she was riding with, at least two of them just as special, if not more so, than she was. It was all very intimidating.

They turned off the main road onto a windy gravel path. They drove under a stone arch with elaborate writing on it. Faye could read, but these letters didn't look right. They looked more like what had been scratched in the ashes of the burned house than normal words. There was a blocky shack behind the gate, and someone watched them through a dark window as they passed. Or maybe *something,* Faye thought, as the shape swiveled to follow them, and it looked entirely too triangular to be a person, unless they were wearing a very strange hat.

The house at the end of the lane was spectacular. It was three times the size of the Vierra's milk barn, only instead of holding cows, it was made for rich people, and it was on top of a giant finger of land that stuck out into the ocean. Three sides around the house turned into cliffs that ended in waves crashing on black rocks far below. The front of the house had tall white pillars and more windows than she could quickly count.

They parked inside a garage, which seemed strange that there would be a space actually *inside* the house to leave your car, but this was big enough that they could probably park four tractors inside and have room to spare. She was having a hard time wrapping her brain around the kind of wealth it would take to build something like this, and suddenly the little wad of money hidden in her traveling skirt seemed pathetic.

"Delilah, would you kindly drag this piece of trash downstairs and lock him in the basement?" Lance asked. "We'll get to him in a bit."

"My pleasure." Delilah grabbed the man by one ankle and yanked him out onto the cement like he was a piece of bad luggage.

"She seems kind of scary," Faye said to the two men once Delilah was gone, the man bumping painfully down the stairs behind her. "Is she going to kill him?"

Francis shook his head. "That gunsel? The people he works for shot Delilah's father down in cold blood. For all we know, he might be one of the ones that did it. Serves him right."

Faye studied him. Francis seemed like a nice young man. Polite, friendly, well spoken, she even had to admit that he was rather handsome. He talked like he came from the big city, but not from the poor big city, but a place with schools, and houses like this. He turned and caught her staring and she looked away quickly. Then again, he had blown a man's head off earlier without hesitation. She reminded herself that she needed to be on guard. It wasn't like she knew these people.

Lance gestured for the door. "Let's go get that thumb looked at. Never been bit by a squirrel before, though I *have* bit people *as* a squirrel. It looks like it hurts. You're probably hungry too. We'll get you a room where you can clean up before supper."

Faye looked down at her shabby dress. It was covered in dirt, coal dust, and speckled with dull red drops of dried blood. She had even gotten the seat dirty in the car. "Sorry for the mess," she said sheepishly.

"What?" Lance said gruffly. "This?" He snorted loudly. "Girl, you don't know much about what goes on around here, but let's say that I've seen a whole lot worse. Come on. You've probably got a bunch of questions, and I've got a few myself, like who your grandpa was, why he gave you a Grimnoir knight's ring, and why those goons were following you."

That reminded her. "I need to speak with someone from that note. Is Pershing here? Or Christiansen? Jones? Southunder? It's really important. My Grandpa's last words were that I needed to talk to somebody named Black something."

Francis and Lance glanced at each other. The muscular Lance only came up to Francis' shoulder, so he actually had to look up. "Your call," Francis said. The younger one was dressed in a fancy suit, and Lance was wearing worker's clothes and a dusty hat, but it was obvious which one was in charge.

"Nothing personal, but I want some of our people to talk to you first. I'm in charge of security around here, and *nobody* gets to see General Pershing until I say so."

She had not come all this way to be turned back now. "You listen here. I need to talk to Black somebody, my Grandpa said so." Faye reached into her voluminous skirt and pulled out the little Tesla device. "I think this has something to do with it." She held it out, and Lance took it, scowling as he read the plate. "My Grandpa was murdered by men looking for this, and I'm not going anywhere until I find out why."

"Aww . . . this ain't good. Not good at all." Lance hesitated, like he was going to keep the device, but then he shook his head and passed it back. He looked at Francis. "I hope this ain't what I think it is. Keep an eye on her. Don't let her snoop in anything." Then he limped away, grumbling.

"He's grouchy," Faye said when Lance was gone.

"You'd probably like to freshen up," Francis suggested.

When she returned from the washroom, Francis was waiting with a sandwich on a plate. "I had the cook make this for you," he said.

"You have *servants*?"

"Well, of course, this was one of my father's estates," he answered proudly. "The Society has been using it since the old headquarters was destroyed."

She took the sandwich. "It must be nice to be rich. Servants *and* indoor plumbing."

"I . . . well . . ." he stammered. "I wasn't meaning to brag. But yes, I suppose it is rather nice. Please, sit down." He gestured toward a nearby table.

The interior of the home was amazing. Electric lights were on every wall. "This is the nicest dining room I've ever seen," Faye said, settling into a padded chair.

"Well . . . actually, this is where the help eats. The dining room is back there . . ." he drifted off, uncomfortable. "Sorry, bragging again."

For some reason his embarrassment made Faye smile. She liked this Francis. She ate her sandwich. It was good.

Lance returned a minute later. "Here's the deal, you seem like an all right kid, Faye, but we deal with some . . . strange types, and there's more than a few folks who'd want nothing more than to see him dead. In fact, the predicament we're in now is because I didn't do my job a few years ago, and somehow somebody got through and put a curse on him. It ain't nothing personal, but I'll be needing to hold onto your little gun, and if you try to use any magic on the General, I *will* kill you. Do you understand?"

"No need to be impolite," Francis said.

"I once saw a six-year-old slash a man's throat with spikes that came shooting out his fingers," Lance pointed out.

"Fine," Faye said, removing the Iver Johnson from her pocket and passing it over to Francis. "I want that back. It cost ten whole dollars."

They left the kitchen area, through some sort of service room, past a workshop full of machines, out into a giant foyer, then up a flight of stairs. Lance's limp was more pronounced going up the stairs, almost like one leg was shorter than the other.

"What happened to your leg?" Faye asked.

"I left part of it in a demon's stomach," he responded without turning around.

Francis leaned forward and whispered in her ear. "You can't get a Healing if too much time's passed. If it's healed on its own wrong, it'll stay that way. A surgeon tried to fix it later by cutting out all the poisoned bone. He's *sensitive* about it."

He heard. "Shut up, Francis."

"You can control animals?"

"Sorta . . ."

Faye smiled. "That would be the best Power *ever* back on the farm. No cow would ever kick me in the hands again! What was that mark you put on that man's head? What's with the funny writing on the gate and in the house?"

"Magic spells. Do you ever get tired of asking questions?"

Faye thought about that for a second. "No. Where are we?"

Lance sighed as they reached the top of the stairs. He knocked politely before entering the first room. A beautiful blonde woman, wearing a white sundress, was sitting in a chair, reading a thick book. "Hey, Jane."

She looked Faye over as she stood. "Oh, honey, what happened? You've got a hole in your foot! And something bit your hand! You should have called me and I would have come down . . . Imagine, making the poor thing walk up here with a hole in her heel."

"How'd you know?" Faye asked, but was ignored.

"She didn't tell me nothing about foot problems," Lance said defensively. "Damn, woman. How was I supposed to know?"

"Is she *okay*?" Jane asked, looking to Francis for confirmation. "She must be since you brought her up here."

"She didn't burst into flames when we crossed the barrier, did she?" Francis said, pointing back at the doorway. There were more of the curious letters carved into the wood.

"Hold still," Jane ordered as she set her hands on Faye's shoulders. Jane's hands were extremely warm, so warm that Faye could feel the heat through the coarse fabric of her traveling dress. Then her hands were ice cold, and now Faye was hot, like she was burning with fever. She wobbled for a moment, dizzy, as the flash of warmth passed.

"What just happened?"

"The hole in your foot will be closed by supper," Jane answered. "I just gave you a little help is all."

Faye's thumb felt puffy. She held it up and the punctures from the squirrel bite were now just purple indentations. *An actual Healer!* Only millionaires had Healers. Faye felt lightheaded. "I can't afford to pay you . . ."

"Oh, honey, you've been listening to too many radio programs," Jane clucked reprovingly, picked up her book, and returned to her chair. "Don't keep the General up too long. He's having a bad day."

"It's about to get worse," Lance muttered.

Western Colorado

THE DINING CAR was nearly empty. Sullivan grunted politely as the waiter dropped off his third thick steak, then he went to town, carving the beef into huge triangles and hungrily gulping them down. "Oh . . . yeah . . . that's better," he mumbled. To him, magic was almost like physical exercise, and running his Power dry always left him exhausted and famished.

Heinrich Koenig and Daniel Garrett watched how much he consumed in amazement. The bookish Garrett pulled out a pack of smokes and offered them to his companions. The German turned him down, but Sullivan never turned down anything free, took one, and stuck it behind his ear for later.

They had procured clothing for Sullivan at the last stop. He would have to get it tailored later, as no one made clothing sufficient to fit his shoulders and arms, but Sullivan was forced to admit that this was now the nicest suit that he owned. The bandages were thick and itchy under his new white shirt. Once Dr. Rosenstein had decided that Sullivan wasn't going to die on him, he had gotten off in Denver to catch a flight back to his practice.

"So, about this job . . . I'm listening."

Garrett lit up his smoke and leaned back in the booth. "So, Sullivan, where do you think magic comes from?"

"Well, that's an odd question," Sullivan answered, still chewing. "The best scientists in the world don't know that. How should I? I'm just a po' dumb ol' Heavy, Mr. Garrett." His voice dripped sarcasm like the rare steak dripped juice.

"Call me Dan, and we both know you know more than you let on."

Sullivan wiped his mouth on a napkin. "The first documented case of Powers occurred in 1849, a Chinaman in California who could bend steel rails with his hands. Newspaper attention brought in some scientists, and the rest is history. Dr. Spengler's research indicates that there may have been isolated individuals in rural communities as early as the late 1830s, but those were usually hushed up or run off by the superstitious. Dr. Kelser from the

University of Berlin claimed to have proof of one in 1818, but I think his methodology was flawed . . . and he was a quack."

"You know your history," Heinrich said.

"I read a book once." In reality, his tiny apartment was filled with them, and he'd visited every university library he could. He could devour a thick book faster than most educated men could get through the daily paper, and he never forgot any of it. People tended to equate well-spoken with well-read, but that was a mistake with Jake Sullivan. "It didn't even have pictures."

Garrett smiled. "You evaded my question rather nicely. Do you know where magic comes from?"

"I can only guess," Sullivan answered. "Some folks say it's hereditary, but you can have two parents with Powers, and there's no guarantee their kids get anything. You have lots of cases where the same Power seems to run in a family. Those eugenicist assholes have been tinkering with that for generations, trying to breed Powers, and they've still got nothing. Rumor is that the Japs are heavy into this, even doing some scary medical procedures to the people they conquer to try and make more Actives."

"I can tell you that the Soviets are doing it as well," Heinrich said. "I've seen things with my own eyes that you would not believe. Cog science creating terrors beyond your wildest imaginings."

"Disgusting," Sullivan agreed.

"So you don't like eugenics?" Garrett was curious.

"We're people. Not horses."

"Agreed," Heinrich said, taking a drink from his coffee. "There was a movement back home that espoused that sort of thing. Luckily, their crazy leader, some washed-up painter, got the firing squad. Good riddance."

"So if it isn't from . . ." Garrett paused, trying to think of the proper word.

"Mendelian genetics," Sullivan said, pointing his fork at Heinrich. "Your people produced some clever monks."

"Actually, he was Austrian," Heinrich replied.

"Close enough."

"So if it isn't *genetics*, you're saying that it must come from God?"

Sullivan shrugged. "Beats me. I don't get real religious in my line of work. Sure, I believe in God, but I don't think magic is his gift to man to make the world a better place, or any of that Father Coughlin radio show nonsense. If it was a gift from God, I think he'd be a little more picky in who he gave it to. I doubt God gave the Kaiser the ability to trap the spirits of men inside bodies that should have died ten times over, until they went crazy with a taste for human flesh, damned Teutonic zombies." Sullivan looked over at Heinrich. "No offense."

"None taken." Heinrich gave a long sigh. His tone indicated that he had some familiarity with the Kaiser's necromancy. "Please, do not discuss *them*."

"Magic has revealed Hell is a place, so perhaps magic can come from both God and the Devil . . ."

Sullivan frowned. Garrett was fishing now, testing him. He concentrated, but couldn't sense any intrusion into his mind. The Mouth was just getting a feel for his beliefs, not trying to influence him, so Sullivan answered truthfully. "Finders and Summoners have the Power to bring in beings from other worlds to do their bidding, and just because the easiest one to get to happens to look a lot like what we think of as Hell, doesn't mean that it is. I've dealt with demons. Both sides were using them in the war, but they were basically really smart monkeys. The Summoned aren't bright enough to be the fallen angels from the Bible."

"Very good," Garrett said, letting out a puff of smoke. "The personal beliefs of the Summoner tend to influence the form that the Summoned appear in, and they're not bright enough to tell us about their home. Since ones conjured by westerners tend to look like devils or angels, people tend to make assumptions. So, do you at least have a theory as to where Power comes from?"

Sullivan chewed his last bite of steak, thinking. "Oh, I do. Don't mean I'm right, or that I can prove it. I think magic is a force. I don't know from where. I don't know if it is alive, or if it's intelligent, but it picks people here and attaches itself to them. I can't make heads or tails out of why it picks who it does, but some of us can touch a little piece of it, some more than others, and we can use that little bit to do something to influence the physical world. What we can do depends entirely on what little bit of the Power we can personally reach."

The other two shared a surprised look. "Not bad . . ." Heinrich said. "You come up with this on your own?"

"Yep." Sullivan didn't add that he'd figured out a whole lot more than that. As far as he knew, he was the only person who'd put together how a few different Powers were related, and how he'd been able to stretch his into the adjoining areas a tiny bit. But that was his secret. It was time for the Grimnoir men to share some of theirs. "Funny, I've been doing all the eating *and* the talking, and I still ain't got no more answers."

"What if I told you that *we* know the real history of magic?"

"I wasn't born in Missouri, but I'd say show me, Dan."

Mar Pacifica, California

FRANCIS STAYED in the back of the room. He'd known General Pershing for most of his life. He was almost like a second father, especially since he'd done a much better job being an example of manhood than Francis's real father, and it pained him deeply to see the General in his current state. His body seemed to deteriorate a little more every day since he'd been cursed by the mysterious Pale Horse. Jane exhausted her Powers on a daily basis fixing all of the new health problems, and even she had to admit that at this point, Black Jack was living off of sheer determination alone.

If they could just figure out who it was that had cursed their leader, then the Grimnoir would kill the wretched Pale Horse and break the spell. They all suspected that it must have happened during the Imperium's attack against their old headquarters. The General had fallen ill shortly after. A Pale Horse had to touch his victim to bind the curse, so it must have been during the chaos of the battle. They'd done everything they could over the last few years to track down the Imperium's agents, but even after assassinating every one they could lay their hands on, they still hadn't found their Pale Horse.

The General's hands were so paper-thin that sunlight could be seen through his skin. It was hard to believe that those were the same hands that had taught him how to throw a ball, how to ride a horse, how to shoot a gun. *It won't be much longer now*, Francis thought, then hated himself for thinking it.

The girl, Faye, was showing the General her Grandpa's treasure.

Whatever it was had certainly gotten the attention of Lance Talon, and he wasn't a man who riled easily. Lance had told Mr. Browning what had been printed on the device, and the second-in-command had immediately said that they needed to take it directly to the General.

The old gentleman, John Browning, had joined them. He stood on the other side of the bed, tall, regally thin, and extremely bald. Nearly eighty, his mind was still the sharpest amongst them. He studied the device with intelligent eyes, obviously worried by what he saw. So that meant that two of the most experienced American Grimnoir were distressed by whatever the presence of the device suggested. The General gestured with one palsied hand, and Mr. Browning lifted the small piece of metal, carefully reading the nameplate again. He let out his breath in a long, low whistle. "I would be forced to say that this is the real thing, General."

"I was afraid of this . . ." the General rasped. "I told them that we should have destroyed the pieces when we had the chance . . . The fools thought we might need the weapon someday . . . Who else knows where the other pieces are hidden?" The weakness of his voice made Francis cringe.

"Only the senior members of the Society," Browning replied. "The elders of course, it was their order. Here? Only you, I, Mr. Talon—" he nodded at Lance—"and Mr. Garrett. We were all sworn to secrecy. The others that knew were lost in the last attack. Even the knights entrusted with a piece did not know the others' whereabouts. None of the junior members should know."

"The Chairman has found out somehow . . . I feared this day would come."

"We thought them finding Jones was a coincidence, that the Imperium ran into him on accident. He had the blueprints for the Geo-Tel, but we thought they'd been burned." Lance was speaking. "We've got to assume that the Chairman has got the plans. I tried Christiansen, but no response on his ring, and he don't have a phone."

"What's going on?" Faye asked. "What are y'all talking about?" But the seniors were too involved in their discussion of mysterious devices and conspiracies to pay the young lady any mind.

Francis caught himself staring at Faye, even though she wasn't his type. He was no stranger to the ladies. That's what happened when you grew up in a family with money to burn and a line of eligible women who wanted to marry into that kind of money. Then when he'd gone off to school his father and grandfather had encouraged him to sow his wild oats and get such foolishness out of the way. He'd bedded half the lovelies in Boston, all of the reputable prostitutes, and still had plenty of time left over for drinking and gambling, but that was before he'd turned his attentions to the more serious business of saving the world and pissing off his family.

In comparison to other girls, Faye seemed rather drab, with her simple clothes that only hid too skinny a figure, plain features, and a complete lack of refinement. At best he'd consider her *cute*. She obviously came from poverty and a total lack of education, but something about her kept snagging his attention, and he couldn't put his finger on it. Maybe it was those strange grey eyes.

Or perhaps it was her refreshing directness. "Excuse me, you old mummy." Faye raised her voice. "That's my gizmo you're pawin' over. My Grandpa died for it, and I came a long way to find out why." Browning and Pershing ceased speaking immediately. "That's more like it."

"My apologies," the General whispered. "Your grandfather was a very good man, and you have my condolences. We are members of the Grimnoir Society, an organization that stands against the darkest magics."

"He was once a member and helped in one of our gravest missions," Browning said. "This item you brought here is a part of the most destructive weapon ever created by the hand of man, and in the summer of 1908, we stopped it from being fired on the United States. Thousands, perhaps hundreds of thousands, would have perished."

"And now if you'll let the grownups finish talking, we've got to figure out how to keep the evilest bastard in the world from putting it back together and killing us all," Lance finished. "So shush."

Western Colorado

"So, you're a secret organization that protects Actives . . ." Sullivan took a long drag from the second cigarette he'd bummed off of

Garrett. The train was rolling into the sunset, and the dining car only had a few other people in it, including a young couple, a businessman, an old woman, and the bored waiter loafing at the far side of the cabin. Nobody was close enough to listen in. "And fights evil magic?"

"Basically, yes."

"Define evil."

"It's pretty self-explanatory," Garrett exclaimed.

"Dan, one man's evil is another man's politics." Sullivan had once gone to prison for doing what he knew to be the *right* thing, and that wasn't too long after fighting in a war where both sides thought of themselves as the good guys, but that didn't stop them from slaughtering each other by the thousands with every tool at hand.

"I can't define evil, but I sure as hell know when I see it," Heinrich said.

Sullivan grunted in affirmation. "And I thought you said Dan was the one that was good with words."

"We do whatever it takes to stop those who would use magic to enslave others. On the other hand, we also fight those who would punish all Magicals for the actions of a few. There are powerful Actives who would like to put the entire world under their boot. They see themselves as the logical end of the eugenicist's argument, the answer to Darwin's theory. On the other side are the Normals who are so scared of magic that they would love nothing more than to just stamp us out of existence."

Sullivan had smoked the fag down to nothing, and stubbed it out in the ashtray. *If it sounds too good to be true, it probably is.* "So if it's so good, why's it secret?"

"Those of us that join the Society must fight in the shadows. There are forces at work, whole nations, and things even bigger than nations that would have us fail. They'd hunt us down, and if they couldn't destroy us, they'd kill everyone we love."

Sullivan pondered Dan's last few words. He seemed to be telling the truth, or at least he believed he was. "Does the U.S. government know about you?"

"Parts of it . . ." Garrett said hesitantly, glancing around the room. "It's complicated."

"I'm an American first, Active second," Sullivan growled. Despite it being run by a bunch of idiots, Sullivan loved his country, and his loyalty ran deep. His older brother, Matt, had often made fun of him for it, but Sullivan was at heart a patriotic man.

"There are Grimnoir in every country. We'd never ask any of them to do anything that goes against conscience. Listen, I can't tell you too much. I've been asked to make you an offer. Your talents would be invaluable. But if you turn us down, the less you know, the better off you are. You join us and *then* I can answer all your questions."

"What's in it for me?" Sullivan asked, expecting the usual answers for when someone was trying to hire out some muscle. *Cash, booze, dames . . .*

Daniel cleared his throat and leaned forward, looking him square in the eye. "You get to learn more about magic than you ever thought possible *and* you get to make a difference."

That wasn't the answer he was expecting. That answer felt good, but it also made him suspicious. He checked his head again, but unless Garrett was the best Mouth ever, he could sense no intrusion. But life had bit him too many times to not be apprehensive. "Who runs the show?"

"What?" Heinrich gave a sardonic laugh. "So maybe when you take that bit of intelligence back to J. Edgar Hoover, all will be forgiven?"

That was a sore spot. "Screw you, Fade."

"So, you're ashamed that you hunted down your own kind? Aren't you?"

Sullivan raised his voice slightly. "I agreed to help the BI, but I only went after murderers. That was the deal."

"Like Delilah Jones?" Heinrich spat.

It was being lied to about Delilah that had sent Sullivan down this path to begin with. "They told me she was a cold-blooded killer. I bought it. How is she?"

"Alive. Which is more than I could say than if you'd succeeded. All she had done was defend herself from the men who had already shot her father to bits. Good work there. If we had not come to save her, she'd be dead by now, picked out of the jail cell you put her in for the convenience of the Imperium." Heinrich's face was getting red. "And you question *our* honor? *Our* judgment? I think not, Heavy."

Something he'd said had set the young German off. Maybe

Sullivan had finally met somebody as distrusting as he was. "Easy, Heinrich," Garrett cautioned. "I can't answer that yet, Jake. You must understand."

Damn it. He was tired of being lied to, sick of being kept in the dark by everyone around him. His patience was done.

Sullivan lurched out of the booth, hands on the table to hold himself steady. His body ached beyond comprehension and he was in a foul mood. "I'm not taking a job if I can't even know who I'm working for. So I'll just be getting off at the next town. Thanks for the dinner and the duds, but I consider them payback for the ones I wrecked falling off that blimp."

Garrett shook his head sadly. "Sorry to hear that, pal. I'd say that this was a wasted trip, but we did kill an Iron Guard, don't get to do that every day . . . What are you going to do about the BI?"

"We'll work something out . . ." Sullivan muttered, dreading the thought of Rockville. He'd need to come up with a story that would satisfy Hoover as to why he'd gone to visit Torrio and then managed to destroy an entire hotel. *Easy as pie.* "So long, boys. Thanks for helping me ice that Jap . . . And tell Delilah I'm real sorry."

"So long, Heavy," Heinrich said. "I knew this was a mistake from the—" He froze, looking down at his fingers. Garrett suddenly flinched and curled his hand into a fist.

Sullivan paused, noticing that both men were looking at their rings. Heinrich suddenly rose and swept all of the dishes and cups onto the floor, spilling coffee across the linoleum. The other patrons startled, and the old lady glared at them disapprovingly.

Daniel jumped into the aisle and shouted. "Attention passengers, everyone needs to go back to their cabins, right now. This is not a big deal, and you will remember being asked to move by the conductor." The other passengers got up and headed vacantly for the exits. Sullivan felt the words slamming around inside his skull. Garrett's Power was staggering, and he felt a strong urge to walk right out, but he focused on a spot on the wall until the feeling subsided.

"Thank you, everyone. Have a pleasant evening." Garrett made eye contact with Sullivan as he passed, as if surprised to see him sticking around. "Hey, waiter! Lock the doors and get out. You need a ten-minute smoke break."

"Right away, sir!" The waiter complied without question. There had been no finesse there, just the Power of suggestion wielded like a club. Garrett may have looked like a balding, nebbishy librarian, but he was one of the strongest Actives Sullivan had yet encountered.

Heinrich grabbed the saltshaker, unscrewed the lid, and poured it onto their hastily cleared table. He stuck his finger into the pile and stirred, until he'd made a circle four inches across. "Don't just stand there, Heavy. Fetch me a glass of water."

Curious, Sullivan complied, picked up a cup from the next table and handed it over. Heinrich stuck two fingers in the water and swirled it about, then took them out and drew two symbols in the center of the circle of salt. Garrett returned from checking the doors a moment later. "You better get out of here. We just got the kind of signal that means one of those things that you don't want to know about is going down."

"Well . . . *now* I'm curious."

Heinrich said a few words under his breath as he stared into the circle. At first Sullivan thought it was German, but it was something different and unfamiliar. There was a drumming noise, at first indistinguishable from the wheels on the track, but it grew in pitch, until it was just a ringing in the ears. The room seemed to flex, almost like when Sullivan was testing his own Power, and then a white glow appeared as the salt seemed to ignite. It burned brightly, as if it were being fused into a solid object. It floated up from the table, and rotated, until it was facing them at eye level.

It was like looking at a tiny motion picture, like one of those new television devices. There were people moving in the circle, but they were slightly hazy, and he could see the train's window through them. "Daniel, Heinrich, this is Lance. Can you hear me?" A face appeared in the floating circle, a blunt-nosed man with a lumberjack's beard.

"Got you, Lance," Garrett replied.

Injuries forgotten, Sullivan moved around to the side. No matter where he stood, the porthole seemed to turn to face him so he could see the same picture. He couldn't believe it. This wasn't a Power that resided inside someone. This was magic on its own, like something from an old fairytale. Heinrich had just cast an actual *spell!* Which, according to everything he'd ever read, was totally impossible.

"Do you remember the stories about the Geo-Tel?" the man in the circle asked.

"Of course," Daniel replied. "Oh no . . . did he find part of it?"

"It looks like he got part of the Portagees' and probably the blueprints from Jones."

The Mouth swore under his breath. "This is bad, very bad. Will he be able to build one?"

"The Geo-Tel? What's that?" Heinrich asked.

"No time to explain," Lance said. "We don't know if the Chairman's got enough to figure one out yet or not. Where are you?"

"We're on the Pullman, Denver to Ogden, we're almost in Utah now," Garrett responded.

"You're the closest to Christiansen. Make sure he's all right. Hold on, the General needs to speak with you." The view of the circle shifted, careening wildly about, and Sullivan saw several other people, including an old bald man who looked strangely familiar, and a young girl in a rough dress. Then the view seemed to lift, and settle downward, so that it was looking into the face of a man lying flat on his back in bed.

The man had to be over a hundred years old. His face was like a skull, crossed with purple veins, milky cataract-filled eyes, with grey skin stretched tight over it, mottled with blotches and bruises. Tubes had been run into his nostrils. "Garrett . . ." His voice was almost a whisper and Sullivan was impressed that he could do that much. "Get to Sven as quickly as you can. Recover the device that was in his protection."

"Yes, General."

Apparently those eyes could still see. "Is this the Heavy?"

He stepped forward. "I'm Jake Sullivan. Who are you?"

"We've met before, Sergeant Sullivan. Turns out I pinned a Citation Star on you myself after the armistice. It was too bad you served under General Roosevelt, because from your reputation, I certainly could have used a man like you."

Sullivan scowled, studying the diseased face. *It couldn't be.* The man who had done that honor had been a strong man, and it hadn't been *that* long ago. "General Pershing?"

"In the flesh, or what's left of it."

Sullivan was speechless. John J. Pershing, supreme commander of the American Expeditionary Force in the Great War, had disappeared from public life three years before. This was the greatest military commander alive, the highest ranking general in U.S. history, and they'd even talked about running him for president a little while back. "Sir, what happened?"

"I've been assassinated. I just haven't given the bastards the satisfaction of dying just yet. Welcome to the Grimnoir, Sullivan."

"I haven't exactly enlisted yet."

"Then consider yourself drafted, son. All hell's about to break loose."

Sullivan hesitated, unsure what to say. "Sir . . . I don't—"

"I'm asking you, one soldier to another, for your help. This is not a small thing I ask, and it will be dangerous, and it will be a sacrifice, but it is the right thing to do. It is the right thing for your country, and your people, and your God, and for all that you hold sacred. You have my word."

It ain't like you've got anything better going on.

"I'll need to get J. Edgar Hoover off my back. I won't be much good to you as a fugitive."

"Important men owe me favors. It's done . . . Garrett, bring this man up to speed. Go get Christiansen. Protect that device at all costs. Burn any Imperium that get in your way. Burn them *down*. Then get back here. Any questions?"

Heinrich and Daniel simultaneously said, "No, sir." Sullivan had a thousand questions, but he just nodded.

"Do not fail." The picture disappeared, leaving a circle of fused salt hanging in the air. The glow dissipated. The circle fell to the table and shattered into bits.

"I suppose that answers my question about who calls the shots," Sullivan said.

Chapter 9

My cavalry unit was camped eighty-two kilometers south of the Podkamennaya Basin that morning. Despite driving the Green Cossack army back for nearly three months, the Nipponese troops had withdrawn earlier in the week. Their retreat was unexpected, but a welcome chance for us to regroup, tend to our wounds, and fatten our fighting bears on the local reindeer herds. We discovered the reason for the Imperials' retreat around breakfast. A blue light appeared in the northern sky, rising from the horizon as a pillar, until it disappeared into the clouds. Scouts estimated the disturbance was near the position of our main infantry encampments. Kapitan Kurgan had a pocket watch. He said the disturbance started at exactly 7:00. Flocks of birds and large numbers of forest animals retreated past our camp in the direction opposite the light. At 7:05 the light had grown so bright that it was as if there was a second sun. Then the noise came, like the sound of artillery. The earth shook. All of us were knocked to the ground. The sky split in two and the light turned to fire. The fire grew until the entire north was fire and it came toward us. The hot wind came after the thunder, snapping down all the trees of the forest and flinging our tents. The temperature increased until it was unbearable. Our clothing caught fire and our bears went mad from the pain, turning on their Controllers and rending them. I was thrown approximately two hundred meters into the river. The water boiled. That is all that I recall.

—Leytenant D. Vasiliev's animated corpse.
Testimony to the Tsar's Investigative Council on the Tunguska Event, 1908

Ogden, Utah

He'd gotten hurt pretty bad back at the cabin, though he was a lot better off than the hired thugs they'd brought with them. Thanks to the Chairman's gifts, his body would be back up and running in no time. The goons would still be dead. Madi shook his head and went back to stuffing his guts back in. The old Grimnoir had turned out to be one hell of a fighter, but Madi had gotten of what he'd been after. He always did.

"Hold still," his companion ordered in Japanese. Yutaka was the only other survivor of their morning's work, and the Iron Guard was up to his elbows in Madi's blood. He ran the needle back and forth expertly, holding the muscle together with thick cord. The healing kanji etched in scar tissue on Madi's back had kept him alive despite being disemboweled for over an hour now, and the overtaxed Words of Power were burning as hot as the day he'd first been branded. "This is slippery."

"It don't have to be pretty," Madi grunted. The stitches just needed to hold everything in the right place until he could heal up in a few hours. He should have been incoherent with pain, but the more kanji he'd had burned onto him, the stronger he became. Since he was also the first white man to have the honor of being an Iron Guard, the fact that he was the only one of them strong enough to bear over a dozen kanji pissed the other slant-eyed bastards off to no end. "Hurry up. I don't want to look all busted up when we report in."

The heat from the kanji was making him sweat. He had them carved into his back, chest, legs, and arms. The downside of so many brands was that he couldn't really feel *anything* anymore. Madi had taken to hurting himself just for fun. He'd actually enjoyed getting shot on this mission. The brief pain had reminded him that he could still feel anything at all. It had taken forever to drive back to the hotel from the Grimmy's podunk town, and he'd relished the suffering every mile of the way.

Once Yutaka had him closed up, the Summoner prepared a circle, so they could confirm the success of their mission. This was no normal circle either, and Yutaka was having to draw the most intricate of magical kanji in special ink made from human blood and demon smoke on the floor. Telegrams and radio could be monitored, even the best codes could be broken, but nobody could eavesdrop on this communication, plus it did have another added benefit. Madi washed up and put on some clean clothes so he could be presentable.

Twenty minutes later he stood in front of a glowing blob floating in the center of the hotel room. The surface rippled like water, finally solidifying into a view that Madi recognized as the Imperial Council Chambers. Madi marveled at the clarity of the link; it was almost like looking through a door into another room of a house. He had to admit that Yutaka was an artist. Madi's personal gifts tended to be more direct.

Madi was taken by surprise by who appeared in the rift. It was the Emperor's chief advisor, Lord Tokugawa himself, Chairman of the Imperial Council, and de-facto leader of the Imperium. Madi and Yutaka bowed with the utmost respect. Madi had not expected the big boss, and felt a little giddy from the excitement. It was late in the evening in Tokyo, but everyone knew that the Chairman never slept.

The Chairman appeared to be a man in the physical prime of his life, but the word around the Council was that he looked exactly the same when he first arrived at the Japanese Court forty years ago. It was rumored that he did not eat or drink either, but that he was sustained on Power alone. He was regal, handsome, distinguished, with jet black hair, wearing a western suit tonight, but with the red sash badge of his office around his waist. Madi had personally seen the Chairman's displeasure cause his enemies to weep blood. He'd seen the Chairman heal the incurable, kill the unkillable, break the laws of physics, and warp the fabric of reality with his mind.

Madi only respected one thing, and that was strength. You were either weak or strong. Whoever was the strongest was therefore the best, and no one could be stronger than the Chairman. He'd never believed in his father's god, only in the Power. The strongest wouldn't preach about mercy, peace, forgiveness, or any of that bullshit. That was all sissy talk for the weak to pretend that they still mattered. The Chairman was *force*. He was going to inherit the world, crush the meek, and Madi planned on being at his side when he did.

The Chairman was all business. "It is done?"

"Yes, Chairman," Madi answered enthusiastically. Yutaka stepped forward, deferentially, and passed the parcel containing the device through the rift. It flickered, but Yutaka's spell was perfect, and the package landed softly at the Chairman's feet. No living thing could pass through a fold in space except for the wretched Travelers, but a master magician could send through small bits of matter, and Yutaka was certainly a master.

"Very good, Iron Guard," he said, and Madi felt his chest swell with pride. He bowed again.

Another figure scurried into the bottom of the rift, retrieving the package. Madi recognized one of the Cogs from Unit 731, the Chairman's special science group. Even after all of the things that Madi had done, those weirdoes still gave him the creeps. They'd been the ones to modify his body into the perfect killing machine he was today, and that had been years ago. Their work had come a long way since. He'd seen the camps in Manchuria, the experiments they were doing to the people they'd enslaved, and the *things* they were turning Actives into.

The Chairman must despise weakness as much as Madi did.

"Our spies should be giving us the position of the final piece shortly. You will return to California immediately. Await further instructions." Madi didn't know who was feeding them information from the Grimnoir, but he didn't need to know. Madi was a weapon that just needed to be pointed in the right direction.

Sullivan stepped gingerly from the train platform. He was running his Power just a bit, easing gravity's pull, and that made walking much more comfortable. His injuries weren't life threatening at this point, but the last thing he needed to do was push it, rip something open, and start bleeding all over the place.

Heinrich was procuring them transport to the little town that Sven Christiansen lived in. Garrett was helping to make sure Sullivan didn't tumble down the ramp. He paused to catch his breath and to admire the scenery. The mountains were huge and brown.

He felt a strange sensation a moment later, something odd, but familiar. Sullivan paused, scanning the crowd, but couldn't see anything out of place. The whistle blew and the North American Pullman began to chug away.

"Sullivan? You all right?" Garrett asked.

It was like . . . he wasn't sure, just instincts kicking in, as if he were walking the deep woods, and everything had gotten too quiet, like there was a dangerous predator hidden somewhere in the trees. The sensation faded.

He shook his head. "Naw . . . . I'm fine. Let's go."

❖❖❖

Madi watched the station out the private train car window, scowling. The hair on his arms had just stood up.

"What is it?" Yutaka asked, suspicious.

"I don't know . . ." Then he saw the broad-shouldered fella standing at the end of the ramp next to a short, dumpy man in glasses. "It can't be . . ." he muttered, placing one hand on the warm glass. "Well, I'll be damned."

Jake.

Yutaka stood up and moved to the window, trying to figure out what was going on. "Trouble?"

"You have no idea . . ." Madi muttered. There was no way it was a coincidence, damn Lenny Torrio for ever talking to him to begin with. If he hadn't already killed Torrio, he'd kill him again, and make it hurt more this time. Madi despised weakness and worshipped strength, but Jake was something different, one of the strong who felt the need to protect the weak, and that made him dangerous. "Summon a demon. Have it follow the big man."

Mar Pacifica, California

THEY ATE BREAKFAST in what Francis called the *nice* dining room. Faye thought that it was a little ridiculous to have a chandelier that obviously cost more than her Grandpa's farm, but she did have to admit that it was very sparkly. The food consisted of a bunch of items that she'd never seen before with names that sounded vaguely European.

General Pershing was in his room. Apparently he no longer ever left his bed, not that it mattered, since the Healer, Jane, said that his stomach couldn't handle solid food anyway. Other than that, everyone else that she'd met so far was gathered around one end of the enormous table, and there were enough seats remaining for another twenty people.

"My father liked to entertain," Francis explained, when he saw her looking down the empty expanse. "We used to have some grand parties here when I was a child. More marmalade?"

She didn't know what that was, nor did she know what to do with all of the extra forks and spoons on each side of her plate, and it was really odd that servants kept bringing more plates, when she could just as easily served herself. Breakfast at the Vierras' had consisted of one big pot of something dropped in the middle of the table, and all the milk they could drink of course, and then everybody helped themselves until they were stuffed. Breakfast in her old life had happened sporadically. Actually, all the other meals had been kind of like that, too. She'd spent a lot of time hungry.

Most of the others had the same gold and black ring. Francis had asked her not to wear hers yet. Apparently there was some sort of oath you were supposed to take before you could wear one. She noticed that Delilah didn't have one either.

"Any word yet from Garrett?" Lance asked.

"His train should be arriving in Ogden now," Browning said. "My home town actually. I do miss it. I'd love to see it again before I die."

"Why can't you visit?" Faye asked.

The old man paused, muffin halfway to his mouth. "Well, my dear, as far as the world is concerned, I died of a heart attack a few years ago while in Belgium. If our enemies knew that I was Grimnoir, they would go after my family. That is how they operate. That is a sad byproduct of our mission. Now I use my knowledge to help protect those in need of our aid."

Faye scowled. His name sounded familiar from the radio. "You're famous, aren't you?"

Lance grunted a laugh. "Half the world's guns have his name on the patent. Except mine, because John Moses never bothered to make a revolver."

"I'm a simple inventor," Browning answered modestly. "I designed a few firearms. Nothing important."

"Semiautos jam . . ." Lance muttered, obviously trying to get a rise out of him.

"Mine don't," the older man responded with a gentle smile.

Faye decided she liked Mr. Browning. He seemed like a very nice man.

"I'll drink to that, my deceased friend." Lance raised his glass. It seemed a little early to Faye to be drinking that much whiskey, but the others seemed used to Lance. "According to the papers, I died in a sudden fire. But I suppose by definition, fire is *sudden* if it kills you."

"What were you before?"

"Big game hunter, adventurer, automobile racing driver, explorer . . ." Lance paused to think. "Cow puncher, spent a year as a coal miner, let's see . . . come from a long line of cowboys, great-great grandpa was a pirate." That sounded farfetched to Faye, but then again, when they'd first met, Lance had been a talking squirrel. She was willing to go with it.

Faye turned to the remaining three. Jane was reading a book again and apparently wasn't even listening to the conversation. She always seemed to be reading something. Delilah hadn't spoken yet either, she was sullenly stabbing at her food with a fork. Francis looked up.

"Well, if we're telling our stories, I'm still alive. Everybody knows I've got magic, but they don't realize how much, but most folks think I'm a sort of fop that gets by on his family name and attends lots of parties. I play it dumb."

"Really?" Lance raised one bushy eyebrow. "How ever do you pull that off?"

"I . . ." Francis frowned. "Never mind."

Faye glanced at Delilah. The dark-haired lady was about the prettiest woman she'd ever seen. "I bet you were a movie star."

Delilah started to laugh. "Oh, come on . . . Wait . . . you're serious?"

"Yes," Faye said. "You're very beautiful."

Delilah just stared, surprised, green eyes blinking rapidly. "Why yes. Yes, I am. And yeah, that's paid a few bills for me, but probably not in the way you're thinking, little girl."

Mr. Browning coughed politely.

"Oh, don't get all huffy, *Moses*," Delilah said coldly. "I won't talk about it in *polite* company." She stood up and tossed the napkin on her plate. "I'm not hungry." She walked from the room without another word.

"What did I say?" Faye asked.

"Ms. Jones has had a difficult life," Browning said. "Her father was one of us . . . *once*. I'm afraid that sometimes the Society does what it thinks is best in the big picture, but it misses the suffering of the individual . . . never mind. I apologize."

"Oh, don't worry," Lance said. "John here is our moral compass, but he can be a little disapproving of certain vices." He downed the rest of his whiskey in one gulp. "Ahhh . . . That's good stuff. I'll grab

Delilah and we'll have a little talk with the prisoner. Socking him in the head will cheer her up." Lance left as well.

Jane spoke without looking up from her book. "I've been Grimnoir my whole life, and my parents, and my grandparents before that. They were some of the first founders. I was born into this. I don't have to pretend to be dead, because I've never gotten to really be alive." She turned the page. "You have to actually exist first, you know."

"That's . . . that's kind of sad," Faye said.

"Eh . . ." Jane shrugged. "You get used to it. This is all I've ever done, so I can't complain. I'm a Mender after all, that's my God-given gift, and I've got no shortage of injured people this way. My friends have left things behind to do this. I never had to, and even if I did, I'd still do it anyway. I'm just glad that I never had to make that choice."

Faye understood. "I don't really have anything either. I guess if my Grandpa was still alive, I'd still be there, with him, happy. Now? I think it's awful nice of you folks to let me stay here for a spell." Faye didn't know what she was going to do next. She was still figuring out what had happened, as secret societies and Tesla superweapons were a bit over her head, but General Pershing had said that she was welcome to stay with them as long as she wanted.

"Leaving things behind is tough." Jane placed a bookmark to hold her page then finally set her book down. "You haven't met my boyfriend yet. That's how it was for him. He was a radio star. Had his own show on the American Broadcasting Network and everything, best voice in the world, people used to say. He read the news, he was half the voices on the detective shows. Everyone loved him, and then one day they didn't anymore. They hated him."

"What happened?"

"People found out he had Power, that he could influence people with his words, get inside their heads. They pretty much ran him out on a rail. It ruined his life." Jane sniffed and reopened her book. "Poor Dan."

"Don't be hasty. Young Mr. Garrett turned out to be one of our finest operatives," Browning suggested as he rose. "He would never have met you either, my dear, if he'd continued in the radio business, and I don't believe he would have it any other way." Jane blushed. "Now, if you will excuse me, I do have some business to conduct."

⁂

His eyes fluttered, open enough so that he could see who was at his bedside. He made out the scarecrow form and shiny baldness, decided that it was John Moses Browning, and closed his eyes again because any light was particularly painful today.

"Yes, John?" Pershing whispered. "Did Garrett recover the device?"

"We've not heard anything yet," Browning replied.

"I see . . ." That meant that there was another reason for the visit, and Pershing already knew what it was. Browning was his second-in-command, one of his oldest surviving friends, a deeply honorable man, and keeping the truth from him was more painful than the cancers eating his bones.

Browning sighed. "I'm concerned, Jack."

"The Chairman's trying to reassemble a weapon that blew a thousand-mile hole in Siberia," he laughed, but it came out as a painful wheezing noise. "I'm a touch concerned, myself."

"That Cog, Einstein, figured that it was such a release of Power that it would have been felt in other realities. Concern is an understatement, but we both already know that . . ." Browning paused. "That's not why I'm here. I'm a little worried about your recent recruiting."

Pershing would have nodded if he could have. "Please, continue."

"In the past we have always thoroughly checked people out before we revealed ourselves to them. That's always been the Grimnoir way. That's the only reason we've stayed alive as long as we have. The Chairman's spies are everywhere, and if we brought one of them into our ranks, it would destroy us."

Pershing knew that Browning was utterly correct. It was the single biggest reason he could no longer even trust his own government or even the Army that he'd helped build. The Imperium's tendrils were deep into everything. "Our numbers are too few. We've lost so many good men. If we do not increase our numbers, we will fail."

"I agree, but first it was Delilah Jones. We barely knew anything about her, except that her father was a bitter, miserable crank of a man, who would surely have drunk himself to death if the Imperium hadn't found him first . . . and she herself is of questionable character, a criminal even."

"We've recruited criminals before, John. They can go places that others can't. You're just offended because she was a New Orleans whore."

Browning sighed. "No need to be vulgar, but yes."

"She did what she had to do to survive. When she discovered her Power, she turned to more lucrative crime."

"You say that like it's a good thing. And this Heavy you have running around with Garrett and Heinrich. He's a murderer."

Pershing couldn't deny that. "And a war hero." He knew that if Browning found out the other reason he'd recruited Sullivan, he'd surely think that the Pale Horse's curse had finally driven him mad. "It balances."

"Well, we should just take a trip up to Rockville and clean the place out then . . . Either one of them could have been co-opted by the Imperium. We've not investigated either as we normally would."

"We can't spare the manpower to investigate anyone." The American Grimnoir had borne the brunt of the secret war against the Imperium. The international leadership had their own fights, as the Imperium was active in virtually ever corner of the globe, but it seemed to him that all the tough jobs had been assigned to his people, and the Americans had paid for it in blood. *As usual.*

"And now you're letting this young lady, Ms. Sally Faye Vierra, stay here. Do you plan on giving her the oath as well?"

"Oh, please don't tell me you think that little thing is an Imperium spy?"

He snorted. "Unless the Imperium has found a magic kanji for channeling the Power of irresistible cuteness, no, of course not. She's a wonderful child, but she's only a child. Consorting with us has put her in danger."

"I've led men into battle that were younger," Pershing responded.

"Those were men." Most of the knights of the Grimnoir were male, most of their female members served in a support or intelligence fashion. Brutes, like Delilah, were historically an exception for reasons so obvious that even the harshest misogynist had to agree. "You want to start sending women into this meat grinder? Are we that desperate?"

"Look around. We've taken seventy percent casualties over the last decade. We can't protect the honor of the fairer sex if our entire nation is in slavery under the Chairman's heel."

"It's not right."

Pershing gave a noncommittal grunt. "She's a girl, but she's also a Traveler. We both know how rare those are. Think of the possibilities. Look what the Imperium has accomplished with their Travelers."

Pershing couldn't see, but he knew Browning well enough to know that he would be shaking his head sadly. "You would turn that little girl into our own personal Shadow Guard?"

The Imperium had a few pure-Active units that they knew of, the warrior Iron Guard, the experimental Unit 731, and the Shadow Guard assassins. They were often referred to by their common name, ninja, and the Grimnoir had lost many to their poisoned blades over the years. "We're better than them, but we'll do whatever must be done to win. Our way of life, our freedom, depends on it."

"That's the same thing you said to Traveling Joe twenty years ago, if you recall. And he walked away and never looked back. He'd rather be a farmer than another murderer in the night. At least there's honor in milking cows." There was a rustle of cloth as Browning got up from the chair.

Pershing had caused quite the stir when he'd been the first Grimnoir leader to invite coloreds into the Society. He doubted anyone would be surprised should he start drafting children. "Fine. We'll give the young lady a home and a proper education, Lord knows she needs one, and I won't ask her to do anything, but mark my words, her nature is such that she'll want to give some payback to those Imperial bastards."

"And to think that I'd come up here worried that you were losing your judgment. Rather, it turns out you're as ruthless a man as ever."

"I have a history of winning wars, John. That's why I was given this job."

The door closed and he was alone in the dark. Browning was right to question his wisdom. It did seem foolhardy on its face, but he had his own reasons for bringing in these new people. It was time for some fresh blood.

He no longer knew whom he could trust.

In 1908 he'd led a small team on a suicide mission. The Tunguska Event had been a mere test-firing of Tesla's Geo-Tel. If the Peace Ray was a scalpel, the Geo-Tel was a battle-ax. Only by the grace of God had they succeeded just as the blue pillar was starting to form over the East Coast and the Power itself was rising from the bowels of the Earth. The knights of New York had succeeded only by the narrowest of margins.

He'd been so enraged that if they'd had the ability, Pershing would have turned it around and fired it at Tokyo. With that being an impossibility, he'd wanted the thing destroyed, but the international Grimnoir leadership had vetoed that, in the hope that someday they might be able to utilize it themselves. He'd broken up the device and given it to the surviving members of his team to keep safe. Only the inner circle of the Society knew who had the pieces.

But now those men were dying one by one, which meant that someone had betrayed them. He alone knew where the final piece was, but did not dare tell any of his people. He needed outsiders.

The bedroom door flew open with a bang. "It's Garrett!" Lance shouted. There was a bustle of movement and the nervous voices of at least three people as the focal circle was activated. Of course, Pershing hadn't felt the contact. His fingers had become so arthritic that his Grimnoir ring couldn't be worn anymore.

The flash of white light could be seen through his eyelids, but he didn't complain. He was as anxious for the news as everyone else.

Garrett's voice came through a moment later.

"Christiansen is dead. The device is gone."

Chapter 10

It was nearly eleven o'clock at night—an immensely late hour for those latitudes—but the whole town was still gathered in the Gatlinburg courthouse yard, listening to the disputes of theologians. The Scopes trial had brought them in from all directions. There was a friar wearing a sandwich sign announcing that he was the Bible champion of the world. There was a Seventh-Day Adventist arguing that Clarence Darrow was the beast with seven heads and ten horns described in Revelation XIII, and that the end of the world was at hand. A charlatan magician was escorted from the premises for pulling a rabbit from a hat, while nearby a fundamentalist of the Merlin-Baptists pontificated on the epistles of St. Paul while shooting lightning from his eyes and none dared interrupt that sermon. There was the eloquent Dr. T.T. Martin, of Blue Mountain, Mississippi, who had come to town with a truckload of torches (the wooden, not the human kind) and hymn books to put Darwin in his place. There was a singing brother bellowing apocalyptic hymns. There was William Jennings Bryan, followed everywhere by a gaping crowd. It was better than the circus.

—H.L. Mencken,
Editorial in the Baltimore Mercurium
about the Tennessee Magic-Monkey Trial, 1926

New York City, New York

CORNELIUS GOULD STUYVESANT was enjoying the view from the top of the Empire State Building's super-dirigible dock. A mighty six-hundred-foot hybrid lifter was in the final moments of docking. Cables were coming out of the sky in great unfurling masses and his

UBF employees were scurrying about securing the great beast. Two smaller dirigibles had been serviced in the last hour, and each one had been moved along with shocking efficiency.

The wind over the city was potent today, but with two full-time Weathermen dedicated to calming the skies, dirigibles would be able to dock safely on even the gustiest of days. There were two more Cracklers on staff to deal with the static electricity and lightning issues, and even a single underpaid Torch just in case there was a fire. This might not have been the largest United Blimp & Freight station, but it was certainly the crown jewel of innovation.

One of his retainers arrived, moving familiarly past his security man, and passed over the latest daily business summaries. There were two new orders from the British for small patrol craft and two complete air trains for Belgium, and they'd received the third installment payment for the Imperium's diplomatic flagship vessel. Construction was complete and it was being taken for its test runs at the Michigan facility. If everything shook out to spec it could be shipped to Japan in a matter of days. He looked forward to the last payment, since the Japs always paid in gold bars, and he couldn't care less if some of it had surely been melted down from Chinamen's teeth.

A further note indicated that one of the admirals he was paying under the table at the Navy Department had confirmed that the general staff were very frightened of the new Japanese Kaga-class super-dirigibles, and would be ordering their own fleet upgrades in the next fiscal year. *Perfect.* "It's a good day to be me," he said aloud, then chuckled. Every day was a good day when you were the richest man in the world.

"Yes, Mr. Stuyvesant," his bodyguard agreed. Cornelius couldn't remember this one's name, but he was a big Brute, and had come highly recommended.

"I wasn't talking to you, idiot," Cornelius snapped. The Brute nodded politely. It was best to keep such men in their proper place. Fighting dogs should always be kept on a leash. He made a few notes on the file and passed it back to his retainer, who then retreated from the balcony with ratlike swiftness.

Cornelius leaned on the balcony and savored his cigar. The dirigible was almost locked down. Who said that it was an economic depression? He was doing just fine.

"Hello, Mr. Stuyvesant."

The voice had come from behind. Nobody was supposed to be out here except for him and his immediate entourage. Somebody was getting fired for this. He turned around, ready to bellow his fury, and stopped, surprised.

"Harkeness . . ."

The Pale Horse had returned. He was standing there, calm as death, in a pitch-black suit, a craggy shadow of a man. One bony hand was resting on his bodyguard's shoulder, and the giant Brute collapsed to the deck, grey-faced and gasping for air. Harkeness removed his hand and stepped forward.

"Good evening, sir. I have come for that favor."

Cornelius took an involuntary step back and crashed violently into the railing. "Don't come any closer."

Harkeness smiled with his yellowed teeth. "I'm a businessman, Mr. Stuyvesant. Why would I hurt you now? I'm just here to collect on our deal . . . You weren't thinking of backing out now, were you?" His accent seemed to accentuate every wrong word. "That'd be rather upsetting."

The bodyguard turned on his side and vomited blood in a great gushing mass. He convulsed violently, then was still. Cornelius screamed.

"Oh, sorry about that. I get carried away sometimes. You're going to want to have a Torch clean that up. Perhaps throw down some peroxide as well. Now as I was saying—"

Cornelius thought fast. "He's still alive! I don't owe you anything until he's dead. That was the deal."

"Come now. We both know General Pershing is as good as dead. I've given him three years of terrible suffering, and I stand in awe of the man's will. Anyone else would have eaten a bullet by now. I know that you know I speak the truth."

"It hasn't accomplished what I wanted," Cornelius shouted. "I wanted results."

"No. You wanted to fill the hole your son's death left in your soul. You wanted to fill it with revenge, and you wanted the once-favored heir that had forsaken you to come crawling back to your fold, his pride broken. That did not occur, but that's not my concern. You came to me for one thing, and one thing only: Death.

Painful, lingering death." Harkeness stepped forward, crowding Cornelius, until he could smell the tobacco on his breath. "Black Jack Pershing will be dead soon, but I need my favor *now*."

Cornelius briefly contemplated throwing himself off the ledge, but he was too scared. His fear seemed to cause his own Power to flare, and he reached inside, gathered all his energy and threw it at Harkeness.

The Pale Horse was hit by the telekinetic wave, and his polished dress shoes slid across the marble and into the puddle of blood. Harkeness looked up in disbelief. "That's it? That's all you have?"

Cornelius tried again, but his Power was exhausted.

Harkness stepped forward, glaring down at his shoes in disgust. When he looked up again, his face was flushed with anger. "You think that Power is something you can mistreat your whole life and never respect, and then when in your time of need it will somehow rise to the occasion?" He covered the distance the feeble push had moved him in two steps and grabbed Cornelius by the lapels. "You have to earn Power, fool!"

Cornelius screamed when he saw the hands curled into claws next to his body. He could almost see the flesh crawling with disease. One narrow finger came up and stroked his lips with a yellow nail. His bladder let go. "Fine! Fine! Name it. Name your price, fiend! Please, just don't hurt me. I beg you! I'll give you anything."

"I do not want anything more than our agreed-upon price." Harkeness released him. "You will make a change to one of your client's specifications and you will not inform them." He removed an envelope from his jacket and shoved it between the buttons of Cornelius's shirt. "You will follow the instructions on these blueprints exactly, down to the most precise measurement. These changes will be made under your direct supervision. It will be done in utmost secrecy."

Cornelius slid down the balcony, curled his knees up to his chest, and whimpered in a puddle of his own urine.

"You've been touched by the Pale Horse. You've heard what's happened to Pershing despite the constant ministrations of Healers. Failure to follow these plans exactly will result in you sharing his fate. I will know if you try to betray me. I am inside your skin now, Mr. Stuyvesant. Goodbye."

When Cornelius finally looked up with tear-filled eyes, a set of bloody footprints were all that remained of the Pale Horse.

Tremonton, Utah

SULLIVAN SAT UNDER THE SHADE of a scraggly tree. The narrow box canyon was covered in the little trees, hardly more than sagebrush, and the grass was tall and yellow. The gentle hills were broken with occasional gashes of ancient stone. It was a beautiful spot in its own rugged way. He could see why the old Grimnoir had chosen this as his hiding spot.

The Box Elder County Sheriff's Deputies were still combing through the wreckage of the cabin, but Sullivan pieced together what had happened after a few minutes of wandering around.

Two cars full of men had come up the dirt road. Sven Christiansen was no fool. He'd abandoned the structure, which was the obvious target, and headed up one of the hills. Despite Garrett saying that the old Dane was in his late sixties, he'd managed to lug a Browning 1919 and its tripod up there, and when the men in the cars had proven to be who he'd expected, he'd hosed them down.

Christiansen had picked his targets and fired short, controlled bursts, just like Sullivan had been taught as a machine gunner in the First. There were six bodies between the cars and the front of the cabin, all in various states of destruction. A large blood trail through the soft dust showed Sullivan where another man had been plugged bad, but had somehow kept moving.

One car was abandoned, hole through the radiator, puddle underneath. Tracks showed where the other had turned around and left.

The walk had left Sullivan winded and his wounds aching, but he'd found the ambush spot. There were over a hundred shell casings, and since the Browning ejected straight down, they tended to collect in a pile. Deep pockmarks in the rock showed where the goons had returned fire.

It was the other set of tracks that appeared suddenly behind Christiansen's position that showed what happened next. The cloven hooves were massive, but the spacing told Sullivan that they came from a bipedal creature. He put his own considerable weight down in the dirt, and saw that in comparison the creature had been far heavier. Then the signs became confusing as the Summoned had descended on Christiansen. There was a claw mark scored into the rock where it had swung and missed. The three talons covered almost twice the space as Sullivan's big hand. The dried blood splatter told how it had ended.

So now Sullivan sat under a tree, pondering what it all meant, while Heinrich and Garrett were having their turn being questioned. They had arrived twenty minutes after the law. Someone had seen the smoke rising from the valley and called it in. As strangers in the tiny community they were automatic suspects. A few radio calls and a bit of investigation had confirmed that they'd arrived in Ogden too late to be the killers, but that didn't make them any less suspicious.

Garrett was doing the talking, which was for the best, since with a little gentle magic, Garrett could probably talk his way out of near anything. Sullivan figured that Dan would have been smooth even if he didn't have magic. The man sure didn't look like much, but he'd probably make one hell of a door-to-door salesman. Sullivan had taken a liking to him, despite having to constantly check his head to make sure that it wasn't the Mouth's magic talking. Heinrich was polite, but it was obvious that he personally didn't like Sullivan much. Jake was fine with that. He didn't really have any friends, and wasn't looking to start collecting them, either.

The two Grimnoir joined him under the tree a bit later. "Sheriff says we're free to go," Garrett said. "I guess that ol' Sven had a reputation in the local Danish community of having a lot of secrets in his past. They didn't seem too surprised to see him end up like this. What do you think happened?"

"One big-ass demon got him," Sullivan said. "Probably eight hundred pounds. Which means we're dealing with a Summoner like I ain't seen since the war."

"You can read sign?" Heinrich asked, surprised. "You struck me as a city boy."

"I come from a place not much different than here. If we didn't kill it our own self, then we didn't get to eat. I moved to the city because that's where the work was."

Garrett squatted down next to him and pulled out a smoke. "Anything else?"

"Another one of them got shot real bad, lost most of his blood, but his tracks say that he walked around under his own power for a long time. Looks like a big old boy. Probably three hundred pounds and I bet he has to get his boots made special, like me. Plus he was shooting this." Sullivan reached into his pocket and pulled out the moon-clip. It consisted of six fired, brass cases snapped into a sheet-metal circle. He tossed it toward Heinrich, who caught it easily and held it up to read the head stamp.

".50 RL? These are huge. This come out of a cannon?"

"Russian Long," Sullivan said. "Cossack cavalry had a limited run of them made for their war against the Japanese. Smith & Wesson filled the contract. Cossacks wanted something portable and short, but could still punch a Jap helmet at three hundred yards. The shells were clipped together so they could load easier from the back of a moving bear. Damn thing even has a shotgun barrel for when they were up close in the trees. Most powerful handgun in the world, made specifically for Brutes, because it was loaded so hot it could sprain the wrist of a normal man."

"Don't see those around very often," Garrett said.

"So this big boy with the big gun got hit a bunch of times, but kept moving. At first I thought he'd been killed from all the blood, then brought back as a damn filthy zombie."

Heinrich scowled. "You've got a real problem with zombies, don't you?"

"I only want to have to kill somebody once. Killing them twice seems like work. But the tracks aren't from a zombie. They shuffle, stumble, like their balance is all gone, and they don't take cover like this one did. So he got opened up, dumped most of his blood, and didn't worry about it. Either of you know what Power that could be?"

"There are other things besides natural Powers . . ." Heinrich suggested. "We've not had a chance to tell you about those yet. The Imperium has special soldiers. The Chairman picks them himself."

"They're called the Iron Guard," Garrett added. "They're all strong Actives to start with, but then he changes them."

"What do you mean *changes*?"

"There are two kinds of magic, Sullivan." Garrett explained.

"Natural occurring Powers. One Power, one person. Everybody knows how that works."

He didn't correct him, though he personally knew Garrett was wrong. Sullivan figured he was good for at least one and a half himself.

"Then there are spells, where with different tricks you can capture some of the Power and use it."

"The Power can be chained to certain signs and words," Heinrich said. "All Grimnoir learn a few, but we don't delve too deep. It's too dangerous. You screw up a chaining the Power to a word and *bad* things happen. Some of us are more talented than others."

"We stick with the easy ones, and we practice the hell out of them before we're allowed to do them on our own," Garrett said. "The Imperium, though, they push the limits. They mark their servants, even ones that have no magic of their own. They'll mark multiple words permanently on their Guards. It makes them into something else, something not human."

The swordsman. He'd been different. Not only was his Power something Sullivan had never seen before, it had been too strong. As they'd grappled, he'd felt the unnatural heat coming from under his shirt, like there had been something on fire against his skin. "Rokusaburo?"

"Normally we don't try to take an Iron Guard unless we've got at least five-to-one odds, preferably more. We got lucky . . ." Daniel grunted as he stood up. "Come on, boys, we've got a long ride ahead of us."

Mar Pacifica, California

THE IMPERIUM GOON was tied to a chair in the center of the empty storage room. As nicely equipped as the family estate was, it had not come with a proper dungeon, so they had to make do. A single naked light bulb hung directly over their prisoner's head. Francis and Delilah were standing back in the shadows, watching. Lance was the most experienced at . . . well, everything, and was going to do the actual questioning.

Francis found himself praying that the man would roll over and talk quickly, because he didn't have the stomach for violence. Sure, he'd killed his fair share of evil men. He'd even shot one of this particular fellow's associates in the face with a P17 Enfield, but pulling the trigger or using his Power to bash someone's head in during a battle was different than hurting someone who was completely at your mercy.

Remember the Imperium schools, Francis . . . He curled his hands into fists and steadied himself for whatever would come next. He and his family and other important delegates had been given a guided tour of one of the premier facilities in Tokyo. As many bored young men tended to do, Francis had wandered off the approved path and gotten lost. He'd seen the parts of the school that weren't shown to the outside world, and it had changed him for the rest of his life. *Never forget what they did to the children.* Anyone who supported the schools deserved whatever they got.

Lance limped up to the chair and pulled the burlap sack from their guest's head. He glared at his captors with angry eyes, and surely would have started shouting if it wasn't for the fact Delilah had taped his mouth shut. The spell of weakness was drawn on his forehead with ash from the old place, which seemed somehow appropriate.

"I'm sure you know who we are," Lance said with his rough drawl. He produced a hunting knife from behind his back and quickly shoved it through the man's shirt. He twitched and jerked away in sudden fear. The blade was so razor sharp that it sheared through the cloth like it was nothing, and Lance laid the man's chest bare. A series of red scratches had been cut into the prisoner's chest. Francis couldn't read the Japanese version of spells, but he'd seen this one before, and knew that it granted increased vitality. It made the Imperium thugs harder to put down unless you got them right in the heart or the brain.

"And I sure as hell know who you work for . . ." Lance made a show of studying the marks. "I'm gonna ask you some questions. You're gonna answer or you're gonna regret it."

Lance roughly pulled the pressure tape from the prisoner's mouth. He screamed as the tape removed most of his moustache. "Grimmy bastards!"

"So you do know who I am. What's your name?"

"Albert," he spat. "Albert Rizzo."

"Where you from, Albert Rizzo?"

"Montauk, New York."

It never ceased to amaze Francis that Americans would join the Imperium cause, but from what he understood from the international society, it was the same in every nation. The Imperium recruited mostly from the poor classes. They usually picked Normals, gave them a taste of having their own magic, and put them to work. The smartest and most brutal were able to rise in the ranks, and the rest turned into cannon fodder in their never-ending war against the Grimnoir.

"Who do you answer to, Al?"

"I answer to the Chairman!"

Lance sighed and stabbed the knife into Albert's arm. the man screamed. "You know what I mean." The knife came out, the last inch dripping blood. "Unfortunately for you, your recruiter marked you with the kanji for health, which means that I can cut on you for *twice* as long as a regular man 'fore you croak. Plus I know all the places that hurt, but don't have any arterial bleeding. See where I'm going with this?"

Albert growled at him. "Madi. He said his name was Mr. Madi."

Francis twitched. He'd heard that name before. The man was a legend, even by Iron Guard standards.

"Big fella. Got one bad eye?" Lance asked.

"Yeah, that's him."

"Wait!"

Francis jerked toward the female cry. *Faye? What's she doing in here?* She must have followed them down, but he hadn't heard her. *She can teleport, idiot.* The girl walked into the circle of light and right up to the chair. Lance raised his hand that wasn't holding a giant knife.

"You don't want to see this, kid," he said gently. "This ain't for you."

"Where's the one-eyed man!" Faye shouted.

"Go to hell."

Lance turned around and stabbed him in the thigh. Albert squealed. "See? Look what you made me do. My daddy fought Apaches, and he taught me every damn thing he learned from them when I was little. So don't make me take a trip down memory lane, and answer the damned question."

"I don't know," Albert said. "We work in little groups. They call us cells. They send telegrams when they need us for jobs. We don't know how to reach nobody else. Especially the bosses. I swear. That crazy brunette done killed everybody else in my cell."

Lance wiped his knife on Albert's shirt before returning it to the sheath on his belt. "See, that wasn't so hard now, was it? I didn't even have to skin you or nothing."

Albert started to cry. "You don't get it, Grimmy. It don't matter what you do to me. My brothers are gonna win in the end. The Chairman's way is the only way. We need his leadership. Freedom is a lie. People are starving. There ain't no jobs. The rich keep getting richer while we're dying. The Chairman can fix everything. He's just like Jesus!"

Lance rolled his eyes. "Damn useful idiots."

"No! He's not just magic. He works miracles. He's the real second coming. He's the new messiah, only this time he's making the weak into the strong. His plan is to make man better, the perfection of humanity. People like you say that he's taking away freedom, but he's really just protecting us from our own bad choices. The Chairman will save us all. When he's done, everyone will have Power. This isn't just a movement, this is true religion. I see that look on your face, you think we're crazy. Oh, you think you can stop us, but you're wrong. I've seen Madi kill your stupid kind like it was nothing. You think you're so powerful? You ain't got nothing!"

Faye began to shake, but Francis didn't think that it was because of what Lance had done. "Were you with the one-eyed man in El Nido?"

"Is that where that old Mexican lived with his stupid brat and his stupid cows? Yeah. His magic was supposed to be so rare and special and shit, but it was nothing compared to—" Albert's eyes widened and he looked down in shock at the knife planted squarely in the center of his chest.

Francis jerked in surprise. Faye had Traveled directly behind Lance. She slowly took her hand away from the quivering knife. "He was Portuguese. And cows aren't *stupid*!" she shouted. Albert tried to say something, but then his read rolled forward, limp. When Francis blinked again, Faye was gone.

"Aw hell . . ." Lance said, reaching around and realizing that Faye had relieved him of his hunting knife. "That ain't good. A single kanji won't save you from getting knifed in the heart."

"Faye!" Francis shouted, realizing what had just happened. He ran for the stairs.

Delilah stepped into the light, grabbed the Imperium man by the hair and lifted his head. He was obviously dead. "You know, I like her. She's a firecracker."

Faye's boots landed in the soft grass of the front lawn. Taking a few steps, she folded her arms around her chest and sunk down to her knees, sobbing.

That's another promise broken. I said no more crying.

She was supposed to be tough now. She'd just killed one of the men who'd killed Grandpa. He deserved it. He deserved to die just as much as the one she'd gotten with the pitchfork. She'd taken Lance's knife and she'd driven it right between his ribs and into his heart and killed him dead as meat. It served him right.

Then why am I so sad?

Her whole life had been hard. It never let up. She tried not to think about her first family. She had been routinely beaten for her weird grey eyes, just for being different, and her father had beaten her mother occasionally for spawning a demon. They'd kept her around though, because somebody who could steal food so good was okay, even if she'd been sired by the devil.

And even then she'd been happy. If everything was miserable, then as a little girl she'd decided that she'd be happy, just to spite them. Once she'd made that decision, nothing else mattered. She made up her own world in her head, one that wasn't filled with hunger and terror, and she lived there instead. And then one day she found out that there was a place in the real world that was every bit as good as the fake one . . . and then she wasn't alone anymore.

The one-eyed man had taken that away from her. That's why she was crying, she decided. It wasn't about the fact she'd just put a knife into a man's chest, it was because he wasn't the *right* man.

"Faye!"

She turned to see Francis running from the house. *Oh no.* She didn't want him to see her like this. She sent her thoughts ahead. "Are you—?"

She landed on her knees at the top of a rock cliff, looking down into the crashing waves far below.

Grandpa had told her about crossing an ocean like this crammed into a tiny room on a steamship. He told her all sorts of stories about working hard, fishing, cutting up whales, about his first few cows, but he'd never bothered to teach her about any of this Grimnoir stuff. "Oh, Grandpa. You were probably scared to tell me. You knew about people like the one-eyed man, but I could have handled it. I'll sure handle it now. You taught me a lot, and one of those things was to always finish any chore I start," she told the ocean. "I promise."

A seagull landed on the rocks next to her.

"Who you talking to?" Lance asked. His deep voice seemed strange coming from the goofy white bird.

"None of your business," she snapped.

"Sounded like you were talking to the dead." The seagull waddled up to the edge and looked over. "You gonna jump?"

Faye snorted. "That's stupid . . ."

"Damn right it is . . . You know, nobody blames you for doing that, though next time ask me before you swipe my knife. I'm particular like that."

She wiped her eyes. "Sorry."

"If we had to apologize to everybody every time we screwed up around here, we sure wouldn't get much done . . . How old are you anyway?"

"I don't know," she answered truthfully. "My first family said I didn't deserve no birthdays, because I was the devil's child."

Squawk! "What? That's a bunch of bunk!"

"I figure I'm maybe sixteen or seventeen, give or take."

The gull clucked. "Damn, that makes me feel old . . . Well, for what you've been through, you're doing just fine for your age. You ain't the first person 'round this place that's got a need for revenge."

"Do you need any revenge?"

"Well . . ." he seemed hesitant. "The Chairman destroyed everyone I loved and took my whole life away and part of my leg. What do you think?"

"I think I liked you better as a squirrel."

Lance flapped his wings indignantly. "That's not what I meant. You're a strange kid, but I do agree. I've got a belly full of garbage and

I smell like shit. You want to come back to the house? Francis is running around like a chicken with his head cut off looking for you. I think he's worried."

"Oh . . . he seems really nice."

"He's a good enough kid, but he's had a sheltered life compared to people like us, so don't hold that against him . . . He means well."

"He's nice looking."

"Oh my hell." Lance shook his narrow beak back and forth. "That boy's been around the block . . . more than a few blocks I might add, and he's at least four years older than you. Plus, I don't want to have to snap his little twig neck for dishonoring you, okay? Let's keep our minds on business for right now. Remember, evil empire trying to get a superweapon?"

"I want to help stop them, and I'm gonna kill the one-eyed man myself. I swear it."

Lance was quiet for a long time, his head automatically cocking from side to side as he stared out to sea. "He's in the big leagues, kid. You might as well say you're gonna kill the Chairman while you're at it."

"He's the one-eyed man's boss? Fine. I swear I'll kill him too then."

Lance sighed.

"You're really good at the *other* magic, aren't you?" Faye asked. "You've got your animal Power, but you can write spells too. If you taught me what you know, then I could be more help."

"It ain't easy," he said. "And it's more than spells. Being Grimnoir means that you hold the line. It's learning how to fight, how to tail somebody and be a good spy, how to shoot, all the tricks of the trade. It takes a lot of practice and hard work."

"Well, if this Chairman is as tough as everybody says he is, we better get started if I'm gonna kill him anytime soon."

The seagull laughed. "Delilah's right. You are a firecracker. All right, I'll teach you how to be a Grimnoir knight, but on one condition: no more murdering unless I say so, or you got a real good reason!"

Hakeness

Chapter 11

People ask me how I do it. It is hard to explain. There is just this thing inside, like a battery. It charges up on its own, and I can turn it on when I really need it. The battery runs down fast, too fast, and it takes time to charge back up, but when it is on . . . I can feel the individual pistons thumping, the air over the wings, I can see the propeller turning . . . everything. It is like time slows down. Well, mister, let's just say that when I'm on, I own that sky.

—Lieutenant James H. "Jimmy" Doolittle,
Interview after breaking the world airspeed record in a Curtiss R4C Parasite, 1927

Mar Pacifica, California

"YOU'VE ONLY GOT A FINITE AMOUNT of Power available at any one time." Lance was limping back and forth on the estate's back yard near the swimming pool. The sound of crashing waves could be heard in the distance. "If you get stupid and burn it when you don't need to, then you'll be weak when you *really* need it . . . Right, Francis? How's the knee feeling?"

Francis's head snapped up from where he was loafing on a nearby bench. He'd obviously not been paying attention. "Uhm . . . better?"

"Wake up, Francis. I need your help. Yeah, like I was saying. Don't waste Power on flash. Flash is for chumps. Get in, kick their ass, and get out. If you run through too much Power, too fast, you're on your own until it replenishes itself. Got it?"

"Sure," Faye said happily. The last two days had been rather exciting for her. She'd already mastered a couple of the simplest spells, which had impressed everyone. She was playing with magic in ways that Grandpa never would have allowed. It was even more challenging than attempting to ride a cow. "Don't mess around. Go fast. Get out."

He grabbed the rope that was tied to the cloth dummy that was hanging from a big wooden frame. A pair of boards supposedly representing swords hung from it. A red rising sun had been painted on its chest. "Show me!"

She Traveled directly behind the dummy and stabbed the wooden practice knife Lance had given her into its back. By the time Lance had jerked the rope to spin it, she was already gone, standing in front of it, and jabbed it again. Lance pulled it straight up so a board would hit her, but she was too quick and leapt back, disappearing and reappearing on the other side, still in motion. She planted the knife square into the rising sun.

"Now, Francis," Lance ordered as he let go of the rope.

This time the board moved way too fast, and a different angle, and it clipped her right in the shin. Faye screamed as she Traveled, coming at it from another angle, only to catch another board in the arm. The knife fell from limp fingers. She Traveled back, just as she hit the ground at Lance's feet.

"Ow ow ow!" Faye's fingers weren't responding and a big purple bruise was spreading on her leg. "Thanks a lot, Francis."

"Hey, you said you wanted to go faster," he said, as he released his Power and the dummy collapsed in a pile of fabric and wood. "Sorry."

"Just imagine if that was an Iron Guard's katana instead of a chunk of hickory." Lance sighed. He did that a lot when teaching her. "Jane, would you kindly put our young Traveler back together, please?"

The Healer frowned as she looked up from her book. She was wearing a white bathing suit, enormous black sunglasses, and reclining on a pool chair, enjoying the sun. Healers had the advantage of sunbathing without worrying about getting burned. "This is the last one for today, Lance. I used up most of my Power fixing up the General this morning."

"Fine, fine, we'll do something a little less physical next."

Water was rolling involuntarily from Faye's eyes but she didn't think that fell under her self-prohibition on crying when she'd just got her arm broken. "Less physical? Can I drive the car again? Can we go fast?"

"It ain't a tractor. Of course we'll go fast."

"I'd be happy to shoot more of Mr. Browning's machineguns too!" Shooting those off the cliffs had certainly made the little .32 Iver Johnson she'd bought seem inadequate.

Jane padded over daintily. The soles of her feet were soft and there were plenty of hard spots in the ground. It made Faye want to laugh. She hadn't owned her own pair of shoes until she'd arrived in El Nido. Jane's gentle hands rested on her arm, and a moment later, the now familiar hot feeling moved through her body. The swelling began to go down immediately. "Be more careful next time, hon. I won't always be around to fix you up," Jane admonished her.

Delilah had wandered up to see what was going on. She was the most standoffish of everyone at the estate, and Faye still hadn't really had a conversation with her. She didn't think that Delilah was a snob at all, just that she had a hard time talking to people. She seemed like she was kind of broken inside. Faye could understand. She'd probably be bitter herself if she hadn't been able to explore the world inside her own head.

"What're you doing?" Delilah asked.

"We're teaching Faye how to use her Power to fight," Francis said proudly. "She's improved immensely."

"That's what you call it . . ." Delilah scowled at the dummy. "Can I try?"

"I suppose," Lance said, taking the slack out of the rope. "Get ready, Francis."

She cracked her knuckles and walked over to the dummy, pausing to look at Faye still sitting on the ground. "Let me show you how it's done, little girl."

The dummy started to spin. Delilah closed her eyes for just a moment. There was no physical change, but suddenly she just seemed different, her posture shifted, and she hunched low, the visible muscles in her forearms, neck, and ankles seeming to harden. She covered the remaining distance faster than Faye could comprehend. She put her fist right through the rising sun.

Francis's brow furrowed in concentration as he swung the

boards at her. Delilah blocked one with her forearm. She caught the other one in her bare hand, wrenched it free, and used it to cleave both the dummy's legs off in one swipe. Next she grabbed it by the face, tore it clean off, snapping the rope in two, spun once and pitched the head clear into the ocean before the body had even hit the ground.

It had taken about two seconds. She stepped back and straightened her dress. Her body seemed to soften and her posture returned to normal. "There you go."

Francis and Jane stood there with their mouths agape. Lance just grunted. "Great. Now we need a new dummy."

Delilah came over and sat on the grass next to Faye. "Listen, you're not gonna learn to fight by hitting a canvas sack. How about you work with me? I don't think you could hurt me if you tried, anyway, and it would be a lot more realistic."

Jane spoke up. "I can't Mend her if you rip her head off."

"Shove it, sister," Delilah called back. "What do you say?"

It couldn't hurt. Well, actually, it could hurt a whole lot. But this was probably Delilah's idea of being nice. "Sure. Tearing someone's legs off with their arm could be useful."

"You'll probably have to work up to that. Come on, stand up." Delilah arched her back, kicked her legs, and was instantly on her feet. "Hit me as hard as you can. I'll just give you a little love tap when you screw up."

"Delilah . . ." Lance muttered.

"Relax, squirrel boy. I won't hurt her . . . much." Her smile was kind of scary.

"You don't have to do this, Faye," Lance suggested. "Brutes are the reason I carry a .44 Special stoked with hot wadcutters." Delilah growled at him. "I'm just sayin' is all."

Faye stood up. Her arm and leg were feeling much better already. Delilah was waiting for her in the center of the lawn. Francis and Lance stepped back. Jane picked up her book, but apparently she'd found something more interesting for once, and didn't open it. Lance had shown her how to hit something without breaking her hand, explaining that you always used your hard bits to hit their soft bits, but she wasn't good at it. Surely Delilah would help her get better.

"Okay, what do I do?"

"Hit me, stupid," Delilah said.

Faye didn't like being called names. She Traveled, landing right behind Delilah, and punched her hard in the back. Faye screamed on impact as the bones in her fist crashed into something that felt like a concrete slab. Momentarily distracted, she didn't see the backhand that rattled her brain and sent her rolling across the lawn.

"See, just a little tap for when you screw up. That's how you learn."

It was like being run over by a mad cow. Jane started forward, but Faye managed to spit out something that sounded like "I've got it." She struggled to her feet.

Delilah seemed impressed that Faye had gotten back up. "Lesson one. Never hit a Brute with your bare hands. Our Power makes our tissues tougher than normal. When I'm burning full Power, pistol bullets bounce off."

"You've got skin like a rhinoceros," Jane suggested. "I can see that from here."

"Don't go there, porcelain doll, or I'll show you a rhino." Delilah snapped. "Lesson two, only suckers fight fair. Come on, Faye. I heard how you swore you'd kill Madi. That goomba could snap me in half. If you can't hurt me, how do you expect to put a dent in the big man? Let's see what you've got."

Faye Traveled, appearing just off to Delilah's left side, and this time she used her heavy boot to kick her in the leg. By the time the arm came flying around, she was gone, back on the other side, and kicked her in the back of the other leg. She Traveled back to where she'd started, smiling, proud that she'd tagged the Brute twice and gotten away.

Delilah was wearing a sort of work dress. It actually cut off above the knees, which Mr. Browning surely found scandalous, but it made more sense when she covered half the yard in two steps and kicked Faye in the teeth.

When the fuzzy lights quit spinning around her head, Faye realized that she wasn't dead, this wasn't heaven, and that the white angel looking down at her was Jane. "—way to go, you big bully." The heat of Jane's Power radiated through her face, but her skull still felt like it had been broken in half.

"She said she wanted to learn. Poor little white-trash Okie wants to run with the big dogs, life is hard. She better get used to it. I even turned my Power off before I hit her that time," Delilah said. "My dad was one of the toughest Brutes the Grimnoir had ever seen, and Madi beat him like a rented mule. He'll *eat* her."

"Your father was probably drunk at the time too," Lance spat. "Back off, Delilah."

"Look who's talking."

The Healing was done. The heat died down, and Faye used Jane's shoulder to pull herself up. "I'm ready."

Delilah was stunned. "You don't give up, do you?"

"Nope. What was the lesson that time?"

Delilah shrugged. "Don't mess with a Brute."

"Okay," Faye answered as she Traveled. Delilah tensed but Faye didn't land anywhere near her. Instead she landed next to the practice dummy and grabbed one of the heavy hickory boards. She reappeared directly in Delilah's face and clubbed her like she was swinging at a baseball. Delilah rocked back, and Faye appeared behind her, and hit her in the back of the head so hard that the wood stung her palms.

Faye reappeared twenty feet away, still holding the board and panting. "Grandpa liked baseball. Said it was the best American sport. He taught me how to bat," she shouted.

"You little snot!" Delilah said, striding forward, rubbing the back of her head. She charged, leaping across the space, and landed in the empty spot Faye had just left. "Where—"

Faye clocked her with the club again, this time in the back of the leg. She was gone by the time Delilah kicked through the air. She spun, searching, and didn't see the fist-size rock launched from the other end of the pool. Faye shouted with glee as the rock hit her straight in the nose. "He taught me to pitch overhand too!"

Delilah cursed and raised her hands, serious now. Faye ran up onto the diving board, screaming, as she leapt into the pool, except there was no splash. Delilah spun expecting her to appear from behind, but instead Faye came out of the air over her head. The impact was so loud that everyone in the yard cringed. Faye Traveled before she hit the ground and was gone.

Delilah went to her knees, cringing at the indentation in her shoulder. "Oh, I'm turning it up now."

Faye came around from behind Francis. He jumped in surprise. "Remember, don't tear my head off, 'cause that would be cheating," Faye taunted. She could tell that Delilah was angry and burning her Power hard now. Her body seemed different, hard and dangerous. Just like Lance had said, she was using it up too fast. Faye was only using hers in tiny pops, and she'd never actually run out of Power before in her life, but she figured she would know when she got close. She just had to outlast her opponent. "You're right, Delilah, this is fun!" Then she Traveled.

Delilah spun, lashing out randomly as Faye disappeared. She hesitated, but the Traveler didn't arrive anywhere near her. "Where are you?"

"Up here!" Faye waved from the roof of the estate. "Come and get me!"

Delilah was mad. She ran across the yard, took two big strides, and landed in a crouch on the roof of the porch, two more bounds and she was on top of the shingles with Faye. Brutes could climb *fast.* "Oh, you're dead meat, you hick."

Faye waited until Delilah was almost on top of her before Traveling. She landed in the yard back where it all started. "What're you doing up there, silly?" she called, waited for Delilah's frustrated scream, then focused hard, appeared in the air directly behind the Brute, and swung the hickory stick with all of her strength. Faye was a skinny girl, but she'd been doing manual labor and bucking hay for three years, and had busted more than a few bulls in the snout with a shovel handle, and she laid into Delilah like she was a particularly nasty Holstein. The stick broke in half, but Delilah rocked forward, off balance, and tumbled from the tall roof.

She landed flat on her back on the tiles next to the pool with a terrible thump.

Faye appeared next to her a second later and squatted down. Delilah grunted as she tried to sit up, her Power momentarily exhausted from hardening her body for the impact. "What was the lesson that time?" Faye asked innocently.

Delilah closed her eyes and sank back to the tiles. She held out her hand in truce, and Faye slowly took it. "The lesson that time is that you aren't as stupid a hick as you pretend to be." She actually smiled. Faye could tell that it was a real one this time. She'd made a new friend.

***

Sullivan was impressed, and he didn't impress easily. The mansion was epic, probably the single biggest house he'd ever seen excluding pictures of palaces and castles from books. He actually recognized the European architectural styles, but since he'd only read the words and had never heard them pronounced, he didn't even bother trying to say them out loud. He whistled. "Nice digs you boys got here."

"It belongs to one of our operatives. His family burns money during the winter to keep warm. You might remember him. You shot him in the knee," Heinrich said.

"Well, I broke your jaw, and we're best buddies now," Sullivan responded. "How many of you Grimnoir are there anyway?"

"Not near enough," Garrett said. "That's not my place to say. You've not taken the oath, so there's only so much I can tell you. That's between you and the General." Sullivan could respect keeping mum for security's sake. He had no doubt that anyone who showed up on the Chairman's doorstep with a roster of Grimnoir would be rolling in the green.

Garrett sounded the Ford's squeaky air horn as they pulled up to the front porch. From the funny markings he'd seen on the way in, he figured that the people inside already knew they were coming.

He unfolded himself from the car. A fountain bubbled nearby. It was a giant gold fish spitting water straight into the air at a golden UBF-style passenger blimp. The illusion created was that the water spout was holding up the dirigible, but Sullivan found the whole thing gaudy. Heinrich began to unload the luggage from the trunk. Sullivan had no bags at all, just the clothes on his back. He didn't need much, though he did miss his Lewis gun. It had sentimental value.

A group of people came out onto the front porch. An absolutely gorgeous blonde in a white bathing suit came running off the porch. He recognized her as the Healer from the stolen blimp. Dan Garrett broke into a huge grin, opened his arms, and the blonde jumped on him, showering the pudgy little man with kisses. He looked over at Heinrich. The German just shrugged. *Go Dan,* Sullivan thought.

"I'm so glad you're home!" she said, squeezing Dan tight.

"It's good to be back," Dan answered as she broke free. He had to adjust his glasses. "Jake Sullivan, this is my fiancée."

The blonde turned to him. Sullivan tried not to stare impolitely, but he hadn't seen a woman that attractive in a bathing suit, even a very modest one, for a long time, as in *ever*. "Jane," she said, holding out one hand. Her nails were painted bright red. "What have you done to yourself this time? Every time I've seen you, you have more holes in you! Hang on."

Sullivan's hand suddenly felt very warm. The heat rolled across his body, and seemed to collect in his injuries. His lungs filled with fire, and he jerked his hand away. "What're you doing?"

Jane looked offended. "Well, I was trying to help you, but I suppose I should save what Power I've got left for today in case the General has any more attacks. I'll fix you right up tomorrow." She studied his chest. "And stop smoking, or you'll develop miserable emphysema in three years, and be dead in six."

The heat seemed to dissipate except in the spots where he'd recently been hurt. Those bits were so hot that he started sweating profusely. "Well, thanks . . ." He'd never actually met a real live Healer before. "But if I schedule a regular checkup with you, can I keep smoking?" Jane just sniffed indignantly.

Two men came off the porch, shaking hands with Dan and Heinrich. The first was a squat, but powerfully built man. Sullivan recognized the beard from the salt circle on the train. The second was tall, extremely thin, and completely bald. He would have made a convincing undertaker. He looked familiar, and Sullivan could almost swear that he'd seen his picture in a book.

"John Moses Browning?" he asked.

"Indeed. Hello, Mr. Sullivan." The tall man came over and shook his hand. His grip was firm and callused.

"But you're dead."

"Greatly exaggerated," he said with a smile.

Sullivan was not an emotional man, but he couldn't help himself. "Sir . . . I just have to tell you that the M1911 is the finest fighting handgun in the history of the world. It's an honor. I killed a mess of Germans with one of those. It was very dear to me."

"Thank you, sir." Browning looked a little embarrassed. "Hmm . . . I'll have to show you my workshop then. I have some new prototypes that I think you would like."

The short man came over with a pronounced limp. When they

shook hands, it was obvious that he was trying to put some extra squeeze in there. "Lance Talon. Good to meet you, Sullivan." Sullivan squeezed back. Both of them were too strong to hurt the other. Finally Lance grinned at him and let go. "Welcome to the Grimnoir. The General's looking forward to seeing you."

"Wait . . . Talon? The famous hunter? I read your book about Africa." Sullivan didn't admit it, but he'd thought the whole thing had been fabricated. Lance Talon just sounded like too much of a radio serial hero's name to actually be a real person.

"Glad somebody read it." Lance turned back toward the porch as the doors opened. "And here are the others that are staying with us. I believe you know Delilah?"

She was standing there in the doorway, watching him carefully, wearing a short grey dress with her hands resting on her hips. She was just as beautiful as the day they'd met. As pretty as the night he'd tried to arrest her . . . he lowered his eyes, uncomfortable. When he looked up, she was still smirking at him, and he had no idea what to say.

Faye was walking through the house with Delilah. The others had been alerted to something by their rings, and had gathered at the front. Apparently somebody Faye didn't know was arriving. She was excited to meet these new Grimnoir, as everyone else she had met had been very nice.

Delilah had been talking about fighting, and Faye had only been half paying attention. She knew that she should be trying to learn more, because Delilah was like an encyclopedia of ways to hurt people, but she'd learned so much over the last few days that she felt like her brain was full. She was exhausted, and just wanted to take a nap. It was true what they said: a Healer could fix you, but you still felt the pain for a while after, and every single part of her body hurt from the training.

So she was distracted when Delilah opened the front door. She was saying something about how she was nervous, because one of these new arrivals and her used to be real close, but Faye was too tired to care.

When she looked past Delilah's shoulder, the world came to a screeching halt. *He* was there, the thing from her nightmares. Faye froze, suddenly choking on her own terror.

His face was down, covered by a black fedora, but she recognized him anyway, the way he stood, the way he moved. He was huge, his chest wide as two men, arms like tree trunks, and when he looked up toward Delilah, she saw the square profile of the left side of his face.

It was him!

The right side of his face would be a hideous scar and one gleaming white eyeball and Mr. Browning and Lance were standing right next to him, unaware of the evil they'd invited into their house, and she just knew that when that bad eye came around he was going to kill all her new friends just like he'd killed her Grandpa.

Madi!

She began to shake uncontrollably.

Delilah said something to him, and he actually smiled, friendly as could be. His voice was exactly the same, deep and dark as a well, and he even used the exact same slow words as when she'd first met him, when she'd been staring down the barrel of the gun that had killed Grandpa. "Hey, girl."

"No reason for any more killin' today. I'm looking for something. That's all," he'd said. Faye screamed and the paralysis was gone.

I have to save them. She forced herself to move, reaching into her pocket and grasping the little .32 as she focused, sending her thoughts ahead, discovering that the space right behind Madi was empty, and she Traveled.

Sullivan had tried to think about what he would say to Delilah on the ride here, but he couldn't think of anything. Words had always failed him when he needed them most. He knew that he needed to apologize, to try to explain, to hope that maybe it could be like it was once before . . .

Delilah finally spoke first. "Hey, big boy." It was exactly how she had woken him every morning in New Orleans.

"Hey, girl . . ." He smiled. *Maybe the two of us will be all rig—* Then a terrible pain pierced his back. He stumbled. Confused. The others looked past him in shock. He reached up, trying to feel what had struck him, and something felt like it was stuck, burning, between his shoulder blades. His hand came back covered in blood. A terrible buzzing filled his ears. Delilah leapt off the steps screaming something that he couldn't understand as he fell toward the soft grass.

Faye jabbed her little gun forward, jerking the heavy trigger. She aimed right for where his heart should be. There was a pop and a puff of smoke. She kept shooting, pulling the trigger as Madi lurched, not even hearing the noise anymore.

The others were shouting. Delilah charged off the porch, obviously burning at full Power. She'd recognize Madi too. She'd help. But instead of tearing Madi's head off, Delilah caught him as he fell, lowering the giant to the ground.

His head rolled around. His other eye was brown . . . Not white. His hat fell off. There was no scar.

And she looked up, confused, to see a young man with a blond goatee raise a skinny black pistol toward her. She started to speak, to explain that something was horribly wrong, but the gun barked and he shot her squarely in the chest.

Faye

Chapter 12

Man found that he was faced with the acceptance of "magical" forces, that is to say such forces as cannot be comprehended by the sciences, and yet having undoubted, even extremely strong, effects. The false idea of some comprehensive, unexplainable "power" was thus born in the collective unconscious . . . Now that the realm of magic had opened for man, our greatest neuroses are laid bare, so we explain them away with imaginary things.

—Sigmund Freud,
Letter composed just prior to his death by cocaine overdose, 1925

San Francisco, California

Madi had not wanted to contact the Chairman again so soon. He liked being the one who took care of business on his own and came back with results. Having to cry to the boss all the time struck him as a habit for weaklings, but this opportunity was too good to pass up, and as he stood before Yutaka's shimmering portal, he could barely contain his excitement. The Edo Court came into focus, clear as day, despite being an ocean away, and there stood the Chairman.

He bowed deeply.

"What is it, my son?"

Madi liked that. *Son.* The Chairman didn't say that to any of the other Iron Guards as far as he knew. A smile split his scar. "Chairman Tokugawa. We spotted Grimnoir in Utah."

"I assume you eliminated them?"

"No, my lord. Better." He finally looked up from his bow. "I had Yutaka dispatch a demon to follow them. We found one of their hideouts. The Summoned couldn't enter the property because of the warding spells, but we know about where they are . . . It is only a few miles from where we burned out their last nest in California."

"Pershing . . ." the Chairman muttered to himself. "Excellent. He may have the last piece of the Tesla device. If it is present, retrieve it. If it is not, try to discover its location." Eradicating every last Grimmy went without saying, obviously.

Excitement was building in the pit of his stomach. It felt good to feel *something*. "I would like permission to call up all our reserves."

The Chairman's expression didn't change, but his words indicated his displeasure. "The fiercest warrior strikes and holds nothing back, assuring an enemy's demise with a single blow, yet wastes all his strength for the rest of the battle. The wise warrior strikes with skill, retaining his strength to fight again."

Madi bowed in submission. He'd gone out of his lane. It wasn't his place to jeopardize the Imperium's many secret operations inside the United States. Madi had only the slightest idea of the number of agents they had in the military, government, media, and industry. America was riddled with corruption, and when the time came, it would fall. "My apologies, Chairman Tokugawa."

The Chairman appeared deep in thought. "But for Pershing . . . I'll make an exception. Activate as many cells as wisdom dictates. Make an example of him that will strike fear into the hearts of the few Grimnoir that remain. Yet we must have complete deniability. The time for open war with the Americans has not yet come."

He did have a plan. Something that had been simmering in the back of his mind, and this seemed like the best opportunity he'd ever have to put it into effect. "I have an idea for something *spectacular* . . ." Madi said. "It'll accomplish multiple goals." Madi outlined what he had in mind. He was rather proud of it. Normally he was a straightforward type, but this struck him as particularly devious. He'd put a lot of thought into it.

"I am impressed . . . Your mind is as fearsome a weapon as your body," the Chairman said. Madi felt like he could explode.

"I'll need Shadow Guard."

"You will have them . . . and my complete faith. Kill them all, my son." The leader of the Imperium cocked his head to one side, as if listening to something very far away. "I am needed elsewhere."

The shimmering ball of light flickered into nothingness. Madi turned to Yutaka. "Send a telegram to every cell in five hundred miles. We strike as soon as the Shadow Guard arrive." He could almost taste the blood.

Mar Pacifica, California

FRANCIS HAD ARRIVED at the reunion a little late, just in time to see Faye shoot the big man in the back for no apparent reason. Heinrich reacted instantly like the soldier he was and drilled Faye. He was too surprised to act, but then Heinrich stepped forward and aimed his Luger between Faye's eyes, ready to finish her off.

"No!" Francis shouted, surging his Power. Heinrich was knocked aside as he pulled the trigger, blasting a hole in the dirt next to her head. Francis ran toward them. "Wait!"

"Heinrich, stand down," Browning ordered. Obviously confused, Heinrich stepped back, lowering his pistol to his side. The entire group was shocked.

"What the hell!" Lance bellowed, dropping down beside the girl. "Faye! Damn it! Stay with me, girl."

Francis arrived in time to hear Faye whisper something. "Madi. Thought he was . . . Madi . . ." She coughed and blood came shooting from her mouth. Francis dropped down at her side and did the only thing he'd been taught to do in this situation, and put direct pressure on the hole.

"What was she doing?" Delilah screamed, rocking the big man back and forth in her lap. His eyes were open, flickering. They rolled back in his head and he was out. "Come on, Jake, come on."

"Save them," Browning said to Jane.

"I . . . I can't." The Healer stood between the two, hesitating. She closed her eyes and held her hands out. "Too much internal damage. I can't save them both. They're dead in minutes. I've only got enough Power to do one or the other." She looked to Browning imploringly.

Browning, unsure, stated to speak, but bit his tongue, looking between them.

"Are you insane?" Garrett shouted. "She must be a Shadow Guard. Help Sullivan."

"No, she's not," Francis spat. There was no way that Faye was some sort of Imperium assassin. There had to be an explanation.

"She's a damned teleporter! She's a ninja, Francis!" Dan grabbed Jane by the arm and pointed. "Save Sullivan."

"Don't you *dare* use your magic on me, Dan." Jane ripped her arm away.

Heinrich had holstered his gun, and was walking in a slow circle, rubbing his hands on his face. "*Scheisse*," he said, snapping back and moving to Delilah. "Roll him over." She did, and Heinrich pulled the big man's coat down, revealing a white shirt soaked red. Blood was pouring from multiple entrance wounds.

Browning spoke. "Which one has less time?"

She stopped at Faye and closed her eyes. "Damage to the aorta." Then back to Sullivan. "Lung, superior vena cava, spine . . ." She opened her eyes. "Sullivan's tougher. Faye's dead first."

"Save her," Browning ordered.

Jane shrugged off Dan's hand and ran to Faye.

"What!" Delilah shrieked.

Browning ignored her. "Do we have time to get him to the hospital, or could you walk us through an operation in time?"

Jane was concentrating on Faye, but she shook her head in a vigorous *No*.

"Very well. Lance, help me." The old man removed his coat and tossed it on the ground. "Place him on his back. Heinrich, open his shirt. Garrett, go to the library and fetch the third volume of *Rune Arcanium*. Hurry!" Dan ran up the steps and disappeared into the house.

"Are you crazy?" Lance hissed. "That never works."

Browning pulled a small pocketknife and opened it. "The Imperium makes it work."

"If we screw up even the slightest, it could warp him into who knows what. Almost every Grimnoir who's tried has died, or *worse*, and most of them weren't bleeding to death at the time."

"He's a very strong man," Heinrich said.

Lance cursed under his breath. "Blood or Smoke, John?"

"You've the steadier hand with a blade. Here, this is finer than yours," Browning said passing his pocketknife over handle first. Lance took it hesitantly. "Just pretend you're cleaning an elk."

"What are you doing?" Francis asked.

"Something stupid," Lance said as he took a vial out of his pocket and handed it to Browning. "Delilah, don't let him move. If we get one line even sorta wrong he's done." Delilah put her weight down on Sullivan's shoulders and awoke her Power. Lance kept talking as he put the blade against Sullivan's flesh. "This is like what the Imperium does to their Iron Guards . . ." Talking seemed to steady his nerves.

Browning unscrewed the vial. Smoke hissed out. "I will attempt to make a pattern in Summoned's ink while Lance interlocks one into his skin. If we succeed, we will connect a direct link to the Power. This is the old spell for health."

"Like what the Imperium goons have?" Francis sputtered.

"Something like that, only stronger," Lance said slowly, cutting an intricate curve deep into Sullivan's muscle. Dark red blood came welling out from behind the blade. "Except that pathetic scribble wouldn't survive a bullet in the spine . . . *Come on* . . ."

"Francis, get a mark of weakness on that girl before she wakes up," Browning said. "I don't want her Traveling out of here if she is a Shadow Guard." He raised the vial, but hesitated, and bowed his head first. Francis realized he was saying a prayer. A second later Browning opened his eyes, and started carefully dripping the smoking liquid. Delilah had to turn her head away as it sizzled on the impacted skin like bacon.

Francis looked for something to write with, couldn't find anything, realized his hands were covered in Faye's blood, and quickly drew the simple little mark of weakness on her forehead. All it should do was screw up her access to her magic. He didn't feel right doing it, but he didn't know what to think right then. This strange little girl had just murdered *another* person in front of him.

Jane's hands glowed pink around the bones, almost like she'd placed them on top of a brilliant spotlight. This was the most Power he'd ever seen her expend at once. A deformed 9mm bullet rose through the hole in Faye's chest as the tissue closed up behind it. Francis could feel the heat from a foot away. Jane removed her hands from Faye's head, and fell into the grass. "I got it beating," Jane gasped. She struggled back to her knees, blonde hair covering her face, exhausted. "She'll live."

"Jane, do you have anything left at all?" Browning asked.

"Give me a sec," she panted, crawling over. "It won't be enough."

Browning frowned as he got to a difficult part. Sullivan's blood was obscuring Lance's cuts. "Wait until I tell you, then channel whatever you've got left into the dead center of this design. Understand?"

"Yes, sir . . . You'd best hurry. Blood pressure is dropping. His heart will stop in ninety seconds."

Garrett returned with a thick leather book. "Page one hundred and twenty-three," Browning said, and Garrett started flipping. Lance stared at the intricate picture, swore, and started cutting faster. Browning took one look, scowled, and said. "If any of you have faith, I'd suggest prayers for a steady hand."

"Miracle would be good too . . ." Lance said, "Ask for one of those."

Jake Sullivan was back in his cell at Rockville, wearing his issued black and whites, sitting on the end of his tiny bunk. The fifty-pound iron ball chained to his ankle was a familiar old friend. It had been a joke to a man with his magic, but rules were rules, and he'd worn it for six straight years.

It was exactly the same. Every day was exactly the same. *You sleep. You work. You get put back in your cage . . .* but somehow Sullivan knew that today was different. Today he'd been a free man, but someone had shot him full of holes and murdered him.

So, this is what hell looks like . . . Figures.

There was a rattle as the eye slit on the steel door slid open. A pair of black eyes appeared. "Greetings."

"You the devil?" Sullivan asked.

"Yes," the voice answered. "You could say that."

Sullivan scowled as he got a better look through the slit. He hadn't expected the devil to be Japanese. Those black eyes were set in a handsome, strong face, but they belonged to someone far older. They were the eyes of an ancient. "You're the Chairman, aren't you?"

"I have many names. That one will do for this place . . . The land where the dead come to dream."

"What do you want?"

The cell in Rockville was gone, and he was standing knee deep in mud made from ground dirt and blood, his Lewis gun smoking hot in his hands in the dead center of no-man's-land. Coiled barbwire entangled thousands of mutilated corpses and the yellow cloud in front of the sunrise told him that the poison gas was coming again.

"I've come to witness your failure," the Chairman answered. Sullivan turned to see the Chairman walking on top of the liquid mud. He was average height, wearing a fine black suit with a red sash festooned with medals and ribbons draped over one shoulder. He paused to pet a rising zombie's scabrous head as if it were a faithful pet. "I want to see you burn."

"Why?"

"It brings me pleasure. Few things do these days. I always come to see when someone tries to touch the Power directly. The Grimnoir are trying to save your life as we speak."

The sensation of them mutilating and burning a spot on his chest seemed distant, somehow absent. "How do you know?"

"I am closer to the Power than they are," he said simply. "I know when someone tries to steal my birthright. Their smallest spells are beneath my notice, but now they try the most complicated of links in desperation, but they are as children, toying with the things of adults. They will fail, as they always do." The Chairman paused, studying Sullivan. "Too bad . . . I can see that you are a man of character."

The Somme was gone, and they were in a familiar bar in New Orleans, another place where he'd tried to build a life, and failed. Sullivan stood over the splattered mess that had been Sheriff Johnson. The other patrons were fleeing or hiding. The negro serving boy that he'd saved from the Sheriff's wrath was huddled in the corner, afraid of what he'd just seen Sullivan do. "He was gonna hurt you 'cause you're an Active . . . Like me . . ." Sullivan tried to explain, but the little boy was too terrified of him to move. "It's gonna be okay. I won't hurt you . . ."

"Here you have dispensed the same justice as I would have. Pathetic Normals, afraid of magic, afraid to bow to their betters." The Chairman strolled around the bar and kicked what was left of the Sheriff's skull across the plank floor with one polished shoe. "They chained you for this? This was a work of righteous fury. They should not have imprisoned you for destroying this vermin. They should have rewarded you. What do you owe such a world, such a failed system? Especially after all you had sacrificed for them."

He was back in France, in the final hours of Second Somme, the fiercest battle of the war. There were more Actives collected here on this day than any other point in history. Dirigibles and biplanes were exploding and dropping from the sky like a meteor shower. Lightning, fire, and ice danced back and forth, destroying like a reaper's scythe. Men leapt impossibly high through the air, screaming down into their enemy as demons erupted from the ground in geysers of bone.

"A great and terrible thing to behold. You thought that you could show the Normals the goodness of the Active race. That you could be their champions, their protectors, but instead you gave them this." He waved his hand at the carnage. "You gave them *fear*. They did not see heroes, they saw savagery beyond comprehension, and understood that it was only a matter of time until their betters turned their glorious fury upon them. You are not men to the lesser Normals. You are but tools. Dangerous beasts of burden to be kept locked away until needed, nothing more."

Jake Sullivan held his little brother Jimmy as the blood pumped from the stumps where his legs had been and a dozen other lethal wounds. His other brother was trying to reach them. "Matty!" Sullivan shouted, unheard through the artillery shells exploding all around them. "Matty!" His older brother leapt through the shrapnel, heading for them, but a chunk of steel sheared cleanly through the right half of his face and he went down.

Jimmy stretched out his hand as Matt Sullivan crawled the last few feet toward them. Matt's right eye was nothing but a globe of blood. He grabbed his dying brother's hand. "I'm here, Jimmy," Matt gasped. "I got you."

Jimmy had been the simple one, the good one. "We're gonna be okay . . . okay . . . Brothers are here. Nothing hurts us when we stick together. Right, Jakey? Right, Madi? *Sullivans stick together* . . . ." Then he was dead.

"Your brother, Matthew, serves me now," the Chairman said, walking between the deadly shrapnel to kneel beside Sullivan's only surviving blood. "He relived this same moment with me as well, and he came to understand how our race has been mistreated. I showed him the way of the strong. Under my tutelage, he has been born again, stronger than you can imagine, a champion of righteousness.

Never again will he allow the weak to soil *our* world. He has become one of my finest Iron Guard. He has taken the name Madi in honor of the fallen."

Sullivan began to cry.

"Serve me and I will help the Grimnoir's feeble magic successfully link to the Power. You will soon join one brother or the other. Your decision."

The battlefield was frozen in time. In real life he'd gotten up from this trench, thrown Matty over his shoulder and carried him back to the lines. Then he'd gone back out and ended so many lives that he lost track. Fueled by rage, he'd reached parts of the Power that other Actives only dreamed of. He'd broken the wall between Powers, and had gone beyond being just a Heavy. In a fever driven by blood and hate, he'd killed and killed until he began to not just feel the Power, but to actually *see* it, until he could reach out and take it for himself.

Sullivan looked up through the land of the dead ones' dreams, and saw the Power itself, a great glowing world that filled the center of the real world. It was divided into sections, each one a geometric shape, all of them linked together into a seamless whole. He could tell that the spell markings he'd seen were just representations of those geometric shapes.

"You can see it . . ." the Chairman said, following Sullivan's gaze upward from the battlefield. "Fascinating. It has been so very long . . . I thought that I alone could behold its beauty."

There was a faint line leading from the center of his chest where his own Power connected to the great mass above. It linked directly to one point of a shape that Sullivan understood was where the Power interacted with the laws of gravitation. He followed the shape to other sections—mass, density, velocity—until they formed one tip of a triangle. He rose from the mud, coated in his brother's blood, and *knew*.

Thousands of other glowing connections linked the Somme to the magic above, each line attaching a different Active to a different geometric area of the Power, until the thing draped down over the real world like a cloud of Spanish moss made of pure crackling energy. Sullivan could see the triangle he'd been born linked to. His line led to the gravity point. The next point pertained to the realms of electromagnetism, while the final point represented nuclear forces far beyond his comprehension.

There were other shapes inside the triangles, hundreds of them, each tied inexorably to the fabric of reality, all of them working together in a tight seamless mass. An artist's interpretation of all the laws of the universe, only this art wasn't imitating life, it was influencing it.

"Magnificent, isn't it?" the Chairman asked softly, standing at his side.

Sullivan's link was stronger, brighter, than almost all of the others at the Somme, and it was then that he realized that it wasn't a one-way street. Energy wasn't just coming down from the Power. It was also rising up in great clouds from the Actives that died. As they lived, exercising its energy, the energy grew, and when they died, a greater sum returned to its source. More links descended to the world, touching others, creating more Actives, increasing the cycle.

It's eating. That's how it grows . . .

"It's alive, ain't it?"

The Chairman nodded. "Yes. It came here from somewhere *else*." He saw that the Chairman's link was the brightest of all, and it played about, choosing between several of the geometric patterns as he saw fit. "I was the very first it chose," he said wistfully. "It learned about humanity through me."

"Why's it here?"

The Chairman smiled and held out his hand. "Follow me and I will show you, my child. It wants us to cleanse the world and make it pure."

Sullivan returned to the Power and knew that the Chairman lied. The Power wasn't good or evil. It wasn't God or Satan. It was a symbiotic parasite. It lived through them, and in return, they got magic. "You don't get it," he said. "You actually believe what you're shovelin'." Sullivan laughed in the face of the most powerful wizard in the world. "It doesn't want anything, you idiot. You *moron*. You've killed millions . . . for this?"

Then pain beyond anything he'd ever experienced tore through his ribs. He crashed into the mud next to his dead brother. A circle of fire ignited on his chest. This link was different, wrong, somehow misdirected, not to the Power, but to something else entirely, beyond what he could see. The Grimnoir trying to save his life had just failed.

"I am afraid you have died," the Chairman said sadly.

"Heart's stopped," Jane said. She put her gentle hand on the big man's brow. Her white bathing suit was stained with blood. Lance had blood up to his elbows. He and Browning were doing something to the big man's chest.

"It ain't working!" Lance shouted. "The healing ain't taking."

Faye was lying on her back, too weak to move. "I'm sorry . . . I thought he was—"

"Shut up, Imperium bitch!" the man with glasses shouted, pointing a gun at her face. "We'll deal with you in a second."

Her first instinct was to Travel, but something was burning on her forehead, and the magic inside her was all strange and fuzzy. Francis was looking down at her. "I'm sorry . . ." she whispered. "I was trying to help."

"Hush," he said. His eyes were sad.

She wished she could help. This was all her fault. It wasn't Madi at all, though the big man looked *exactly* like him. Faye closed her eyes. If only she had a useful Power, like Jane, she could do something, or if she were smart like Lance or Mr. Browning. Instead all she could do was Travel. She'd never thought of it as a stupid thing before, but it was.

She hadn't prayed since Grandpa had died. *Please, God. Don't let this man die because of me. I'm so sorry. It was a mistake. I was only trying to save my friends.* She concentrated as hard as she could, just like she was about to Travel and she needed to check to make sure the space was clear so she didn't get killed by a bug lodged in her brain or something. Her mind spun, went ahead, and she saw the dead man and all her friends from above, but it wasn't clear. Something was wrong. Something angry and red was stuck to the man's chest, a bad piece of magic.

Faye knew that she had to knock that bad magic out of the way so the good magic could work. She couldn't Travel with her whole body, but she could use her brain.

Sure, God. I figure I can do that. Thanks! Amen.

❖❖❖

Sullivan was fading away, turning into smoke on the wind exactly how the Summoned died on Earth. The red link was tearing him apart. It came from behind the Power . . . from whatever mysterious place the Power had fled from.

"You should have come with me," the Chairman said as he leaned on the side of the trench. The mud didn't get on his suit. "Think of what we could have learned together—" He stopped, puzzled, as a brilliant light erupted through the mud at Sullivan's side. "Remarkable."

It was the purest link to the Power that he'd seen yet. While the Chairman's was bigger and broader, this one was just simple, and shot in a beam as straight as a Tesla cannon. It actually had an audible hum like a high voltage wire.

Excuse me, mister. Sorry about shooting you and stuff. Then the failed design on Sullivan's chest quit burning. The red link was severed. He gasped as his senses returned. *I hope that helps.*

The Chairman was nodding in appreciation at the display of raw strength. "This has been a most interesting day. Unfortunately your body is already dead."

Come back with me, mister, please. Everybody is gonna be real mad if I murder you too. Follow me home, please.

Sullivan scanned the Power. Time was short. There was his area of expertise, his triangle of gravitation. If he could follow that link, he could follow others. He reached out with his mind, searching the dreaming dead of the battlefield. The Menders he'd carried Matty back to had been . . . *there.* Finding that clump of lines, he followed it up to a second shape. Their odd triangle connected primarily to laws concerning biology and two other unknown sides, and the Healers landed near the middle. The two triangles superimposed into a sort of hexagram and he memorized the shape.

He found that purest line of Power and grabbed hold.

"See you 'round, Chairman," Sullivan said.

"Farewell, Mr. Sullivan. I have enjoyed our most enlightening conversation. When we meet again, I will destroy you."

"He's gone," Jane pronounced.

Browning slowly sank to the ground. The old man was totally spent from the effort. "We did our best . . ."

Lance stood up with a pained grunt. He was covered in blood. "Wasn't good enough. How! How can those Imperium bastards do this and not us!"

Faye closed her eyes. She knew that she'd been able to touch the big man with her brain, but she didn't know if he'd been able to follow her home. She hoped he had, because being a ghost here was sure to be a lot nicer than in that scary place with the mud and bodies and barbed wire, and the big glowing jellyfish thing in the sky. She knew what jellyfish looked like because Grandpa had once shown her a picture of one because it was called the Portuguese man-of-war, and he'd thought that any animal named after the Portuguese had to be pretty neat. That scary place was probably hell, and that's where she was going because she had just murdered somebody, so she had probably better get used to that big jellyfish because she was going to spend the rest of eternity there.

Delilah was crying her eyes out. This had to be the man she'd said she'd been close to. That made Faye feel extra sad, because she didn't think Delilah had ever had very many people who loved her.

The man who'd shot her came over, grabbed her roughly by the arm, and jerked her violently to her feet. He stuck his pistol hard into her face. "Start talking, Shadow Guard." He was hurting her arm bad, but she knew she deserved it. Francis rose and grabbed the man with the goatee, but he just turned around and punched Francis right in the nose. Francis fell down, holding his face.

"It was an accident," Faye pleaded.

"What were you thinking, John?" the man with glasses was shouting. "Why'd you save her instead of him? Jane . . . How . . . How could you?"

"I did what I had to . . ." the blonde stammered, then looked down at the big man's body, puzzled. "Wait."

"No, you wait, damn it—" the bespectacled man stopped and took a few steps back. The big man sat up and looked around, confused. Delilah shrieked. "Great, you turned him into a zombie!"

"Hang on . . ." the big man grunted, looking down at the bloody mess on his chest. He held out his hand. "Knife." Lance hesitated. "Please."

Lance hurried over and gave him the knife. The big man studied the mangled gashes for a second then cut a new line. He thought about it for a second, then made one more adjustment, grimacing in pain the entire time as he cut. He studied his work and nodded. "There . . . that's better." Then his eyes rolled back in his head and he hit the ground like a sack of wet grain.

Chapter 13

I am by heritage a Jew, by citizenship a Swiss, by magical gift a Cog, and by makeup a human being, and only a human being, without any special attachment to any state or national entity whatsoever.

—Albert Einstein,
Letter to Alfred Knesser, 1919

Detroit, Michigan

THE UNITED BLIMP & Freight Michigan facility was the size of a small town, and it did actually have a company town in it. UBF provided housing to its workers, and despite that, communist agitators had still managed to get them to strike the previous summer. Cornelius Gould Stuyvesant could not understand the sheer ingratitude, but then again, he wasn't in debt up to his eyeballs to the UBF company store. That was his workers' fault for being greedy. Debt was a tax on the stupid.

His arrival had surprised the management, but they had learned over the years that he liked to drop in on his properties unannounced. He could tell from his manager's reactions that this visit was slightly off-putting. It was probably because he couldn't stop *itching.*

Ever since the Pale Horse had touched him, he'd felt an unbearable creeping sensation. Spending a fortune in the process, he'd exhausted five Healers, and still he was certain that he was ill. He'd banished his mistresses, afraid that he might catch something terrible from them, since his immune system was in such a weakened state. He had taken to wearing an antiseptic scarf, and had made all twelve of his new security men do the same. The only reason he'd ventured out from the safety of his private floors atop the Chrysler Building was to fulfill the damnable Pale Horse's mission.

The Cog engineer in charge of this project was the only other person in the drafting room when Cornelius unfolded the new blueprints. He'd made the Cog wear a face mask as well. "You can see the necessary changes here," he said, stabbing his fat finger into the diagram. "This is your number one priority. You will do this with the fewest possible employees, in the utmost secrecy. Make sure they are hand-picked men. Hand-picked!"

It took him a minute to decipher the complicated design. "Uh . . . sir, I'm afraid that I don't understand. This change serves no mechanical purpose. It's merely some geometric designs stuck together. It does not even have an artistic purpose, since that's an interior wall in the bowels of the ship . . . behind a hydrogen piping system, in fact. No one will ever see it."

"You have," he pulled out his pocket watch, "twenty-four hours. Then we will be shipping the Imperium their new diplomatic flagship."

The Cog's eyeballs bulged over his mask. "That's impossible. She's out on trial right now. There's no way we'll get the piping system moved in time and still get everything—"

There was no time for this. He could feel the bugs crawling under his skin. Cornelius grabbed him by the protruding Adam's apple and squeezed. The Cog choked. "Listen, here, boyo, you will get this done, in secret, right now, by God, or I'll have you fired—no, wait, I'll have you tossed out of one of your own dirigibles from five thousand feet. Can your fancy magic brain handle that?"

The Cog stumbled away, coughing and red. After he composed himself, he replied. "I'll get right on it."

"Damn right you will," Cornelius sputtered, indignant, and then he fled to wash his hands.

Mar Pacifica, California

JOHN MOSES BROWNING knocked politely before entering Black Jack Pershing's room. He wasted no time and did not bother to sit. The General already knew why he was there.

"How long have you known that the Heavy was an Iron Guard's brother?"

Pershing coughed, but managed to contain it before it turned into a fit. "Soon after he single-handedly tore through half of our operatives. I requested his records. Roosevelt had three Sullivans under his command. One died, one lost half his face, and the last became a legend. The oldest one stayed in the service, but went AWOL from the expeditionary unit sent to support the Tsar during the revolution. Intelligence from the international leadership suggested that the missing Sullivan had been recruited by the Imperium, and the descriptions matched. I knew it was a possibility."

"It would have been nice of you to say something sooner, then perhaps our house guests wouldn't start shooting each other. Have you gone daft?"

"Didn't see that coming . . ." Pershing answered. "See? I told you the little girl would make a fine assassin. She's stabbed or shot half the estate by now. How is she?"

"Tied up in the basement until we decide how to proceed. Daniel and Heinrich are convinced she's a Shadow Guard infiltrator. Francis and Lance were ready to fight them over that conclusion."

"And you?"

"Oh, I do believe she's innocent. She's the only one of us who's actually seen Madi in the flesh. If I had been in her shoes, I probably would have done the same thing, only I would have used a weapon chambered in a proper caliber and he'd be dead."

"And his miraculous recovery?"

"As soon as Jane had regained enough Power, she gave him a proper Healing. However he should never have been around long enough for that to have happened . . ."

"So . . . he came back from the dead, and completed the most complicated of physical spells on *himself*?"

Browning shrugged. "I'm certainly not that good of a wizard."

Pershing had known that this one was special. "Send him in."

Sullivan paced back and forth in the guest bedroom, staring at the white wall. Occasionally he would pause, think about something, then make another mark with one of the charcoal pencils he'd found. He was interrupted by a knock on the door. "Come in."

Browning entered. "Mr. Sullivan, the General would like to . . . oh my . . ."

The furniture had been cleared from one side of the room. The white paint had been covered in marks, notations, and designs from floor to ceiling. Complex geometric shapes were interlocked, and lines led from the shapes to words. *Density light—Fade, Density thick—Rokusaburo? All related to Gravitation—Heavy. Electromagnetism—Crackler, Icebox, Torch? Biological positive—Healer; Biological negative—Pale Horse? The Brute seems to be a combination of Biological and perhaps a midpoint of the Density side (intersection of the hexagram?). Mental (didn't get good look but was it a dodecahedron?)—Mouth, Listener, Beastie? Where do Cogs fit in? Traveler—third corner of the Heavy triangle, unknown, folding space somehow. Is that related to Finders and Summoners? Do the Summoned come from the old world the Power left behind?* It went on like that for several feet, packed into tight block paragraphs.

Sullivan stepped back from his work and took it all in. Browning saw that the bullet holes from the day before were now just a series of white blemishes on his back. Jane had done her work well, but she had confirmed that the wounds had stabilized by themselves. "Yeah . . . Sorry about the mess. I needed something big. I've got to get this down while I remember it."

"I have a chalkboard downstairs . . ." Browning suggested. "I take it you did not sleep . . . much?"

Sullivan turned to face him. He was shirtless, corded with muscle, and the bandages had been ripped off and tossed aside. The terrible lacerations and chemical burns from the day before were now a complicated circle of raised, white, scar tissue. He covered it with one hand. "You did good work," then he pointed at another spot on the wall. "This is what it should have looked like."

Many of the designs were similar to the designs that the Grimnoir had collected through decades of experimentation into the *Rune Arcanium.* Browning had always excelled at the study of those, because he instinctively had an understanding of how things fit together, whether made of metal or magic. These designs were beyond even him. "How do you know all this?"

"Long story. I suppose I only want to explain it once. Any chance there's a shirt around here I can borrow? I've been running through those things like there ain't no tomorrow."

Sullivan thought about the mark on his chest while he waited for the skeletal man in the bed to address him. The other spots on his body that the Healer had sealed up still ached, but the geometric design over his heart just felt *different*. He could feel his own Power beneath it, where it had always lived since he was old enough to remember, but this was strange, like a warm weight had been sewn into his skin. Physically, it didn't hurt at all. It actually felt *good*.

The Power inherent in the design was nothing compared to what he'd developed over the years, and somehow he knew that this bit could never grow beyond what it was now. Yet he felt stronger, healthier, more alive than he ever had before. His own constitution had been augmented into something more. He could better understand why the Chairman's men would seek these things out, but at the same time, he now understood that the Power was using him as much as he was using it, and the idea of cutting more spells onto his body left him uncomfortable.

Either way, thinking about the mysteries of the Power kept his mind off of what had happened to his brother . . .

The old man had been propped up with pillows. The General spoke: "Give us a moment, John." He waited for Browning to leave, studying Sullivan with cataract-filled eyes. Once the door closed, he spoke. "At ease, Sergeant." Sullivan realized that he'd been standing perfectly straight. *Old habits die hard.* "In fact, sit. Staring all the way up there is wearing me out."

"Yes, sir." Sullivan pulled up a chair next to the bed. "Can I—"

"There's nothing you can do for me now, unless you happen to come across the bastard that cursed me, and if you do, rip his heart out. Other than that, just listen . . ." The General's voice was a whisper. Sullivan had to lean in close to hear. "There aren't many of us left. We've always worked in small units, in secret, but we've been hunted down like dogs. We're stuck in the middle of a war. One side's pure evil, the other side's too obstinate to realize it's even in a fight, and is more scared of its own best weapons than the enemy. Do you know who we are?"

"You're a bunch of mystics who fight evil."

"Mystic? Sullivan, I'm an Episcopalian."

"I only know what Dan Garrett told me, and he kept it close to the vest."

"But you came anyway?"

Sullivan shrugged. *Once again, getting involved in somebody else's fight.* "Yeah. I guess I did."

"That's because you're a man with a sense of duty. You do what you think you have to, no matter what. I can tell that about you," the General said. "Don't ask how I know. I just know the measure of a man, and I can see that duty in you. It's like a fire in your belly."

It was possible the old man's curse was affecting his mind. Sullivan didn't think he was anything special, just another guy trying to get by. A curious one though . . . "Why am I here, sir?"

"Jane would be quite cross if she knew I was about to do this, but we're approaching a time of reckoning. Let me show you *my* Power." One palsied hand drifted over and rested on Sullivan's own, and then he saw—

Macajambo, Philippines
1903

"YOU ARE THE ONE they call Nigger Jack?" the weathered old Filipino asked in surprisingly perfect English.

He'd been given that nickname after commanding the 10th Cavalry, made up of Buffalo Soldiers. He held open the flap to his tent. "I am Captain Pershing." He glanced about the darkened camp and saw that the guards were still at their stations. *How had this man come this far into the camp?* He placed one hand on his flap holster. "Who are you?"

The old Filipino was dressed rather nicely, with a red silk vest, probably one of the local leadership they'd been protecting from the Moros. "I am the one who has come to teach you about magic."

"I do not know what you are talking about," Pershing said firmly. He looked around. No one was close enough to overhear them. Even rumors of being Actively Magical could ruin his career.

The visitor raised his hand. A gold and black ring glimmered in the torchlight. "You have seen this before, yes?"

He had, several times in fact. As a boy, that ring had been on the hand of the man who had stopped a Missouri mob from lynching a child who could make fire with his thoughts. That ring had been on the finger of the man who'd thwarted his assignment to capture a Magical Lakota girl. Then in Montana, a Cree medicine man had brought down real medicine and caused a plague to erupt, but they'd been cured by a woman wearing that same ring. In Cuba, a Spaniard who'd frozen them with his breath and shot ice crystals from his hands had been killed by an unknown soldier with a gold and black ring.

All of them had come, whether as enemy or ally, done something to protect a Magical, and then disappeared as mysteriously as they had come.

"We defend those who would be ruined because of their birthright, but we police our own, and will not allow magic to be used for ill. We keep the balance."

Pershing only had to think about it for a moment. He held the flap open wider. "Come inside."

Vladivostok, Primorsky Krai
1905

THE INTERNATIONAL OBSERVERS had been invited aboard the new airship *Kurosawa*, to watch the bombardment of the Russian fort. Officers from France, Britain, Germany, and the United States were on the command deck, gaping in awe at the destruction. The ocean was covered with burning oil slicks. A giant steel hulk exploded far below them and rolled on its side, breaking ponderously in two and heading for the bottom. The Russian fleet had been totally annihilated.

The United States military attaché removed his pocket watch and checked it. "Fifteen minutes," Captain John J. Pershing stated.

The Brit, Nicholson, looked like he was going to fall over the railing in shock. The Kaiser's man was scribbling furious notes. The French major was still airsick. Pershing had to admit that he himself was a little nauseous, though not from the altitude. The Japanese airship creaked and shifted as it turned into the wind and headed for the port city. Already other dirigibles had gathered over the heavily fortified walls and the Emperor's magical shock troops were leaping down, causing chaos among the defenders. Transport ships were steaming in for an amphibious assault, while the regular army attacked overland. It was absolutely seamless.

"As you can see, gentlemen, the Emperor's forces are as well trained as I have promised," their guide said. Today had been the first time Pershing had met the guide. He had been introduced as Baron Okubo Tokugawa, and had recently been appointed as the Chairman of the Ruling Council and chief advisor to Emperor Meiji. He was wearing a European style military uniform, with a chest full of medals, but with the Asiatic touch of a red silk sash and a traditional sword. Pershing's gut told him that this was the man running the show. "Perhaps now, our nations can come to an understanding as to the Imperium's natural supremacy in this area."

The Chairman's sure enjoying the view. Pershing grunted a noncommittal response. He was no diplomat. What he cared about was how the Japs had integrated magic into their war machine. Incoming shells had been deflected by coordinated Movers on the naval vessels. Heavies and Brutes were storming those walls. Damage control had been conducted by Torches who could put out the most terrible fire just by thinking about it. Hell, they were even riding on an airship designed by Cogs.

This was the beginning of the end. Either magic would be used to conquer the world, or the backlash would cause Normals to become so terrified of his kind that they would be exterminated.

"How did you get so many wizards?" Nicholson asked.

"Excuse me?" the Chairman asked, raising a single eyebrow.

"You're utilizing magic on a scale we've never seen before . . . How?"

The Chairman nodded respectfully. "Unlike in the West, here in Nippon, we respect those with such gifts. We take them in as they are discovered and give them the finest education possible. In exchange, they serve a term of six years in the Emperor's military or bureaucratic corps."

"Brilliant . . ." said the German.

Pershing gave a bitter laugh.

"Yes, Captain Pershing?" the Chairman asked politely.

"My understanding is that you steal children away from their families as soon as you see a sparkle of magic, and then you put them in a prison where you can turn them into machines. Those who don't make the cut get experimented on until they're either useful or dead. The really strong get additional magic branded right to their souls."

"I can assure you that the Imperial schools are a strictly voluntary affair. It is considered a great honor for a family to send their children to such prestigious institutions." The Chairman was not easily riled. "May I inquire who told you such lies?"

Pershing turned away from the destruction at the rail and looked the Chairman in the eye. "Maybe I was told by a Manchurian, driven gibbering mad with pain, who escaped from one of your schools with failed kanji branded all over his back?"

The Chairman looked down at Pershing's ring and scowled. "I see . . . Would you walk with me for a moment, Captain?"

He hesitated. The Chairman struck him as a very dangerous man, but he was on a diplomatic mission. If any harm were to befall him, the repercussions would be severe. Japan was strong, but not strong enough to risk a war with the West . . . *yet.* They were still modernizing, though at a shocking pace. It would come though, he could feel it. Pershing nodded and followed the Chairman toward the end of the observation deck. Guards with bayonets mounted on their rifles bowed and moved out of their way.

The wind was louder now that they were steaming toward Vladivostok. Pershing could smell smoke and gunpowder on the wind. "You are a knight of the Grimnoir?" the Chairman asked.

"Yes."

"So the Society plans on standing against me then?"

God, I hope so. "That's not my place to say. I'm here representing the United States Army. But as one Active to another, what you're doing here is wrong, Baron Tokugawa. I've heard about you. I know you're like me."

The Chairman folded his arms. "I am far beyond you."

Pershing tested his Power. Baron Tokugawa's thoughts were far too well guarded for him to get even the briefest Reading. "No good can come of this. I'm begging you. If you follow this path, it will change everything."

"Splendid." He smiled for the first time. Pershing knew it was the smile of a predator. "The time for change has come. Tell your Society if they want a war, they will surely have one."

New York City, New York
1908

THE LAST IRON GUARD stood at the end of the brick tunnel. Fetid water dripped down the walls and had flooded the bottom foot of the narrow space. The Imperium man balled his hands into fists and they burst into blue flames. The water striking him turned instantly into steam and began to boil around his legs.

"You will not pass!" the Iron Guard shouted in Japanese. "Glory to the Emperor! Glory to the Chairman!"

Ten yards. Pershing leaned back against the damp wall and peered around the corner as he shoved more shells into his Winchester '94. He worked the lever and chambered another round. Time was running out. The same Geo-Tel that had destroyed a thousand-mile swath of Siberia in one stroke was now targeted here and was due to fire any second. They had to get past that Iron Guard. They'd already killed three of the bastards but lost half a dozen Grimnoir in the process.

"Sven, Bob, on my signal, hit him from the left." Southunder and Christiansen moved quickly through the muck. Browning was still reloading his pump shotgun. "John and I will throw down some covering fire. Bill, you rush him." The Brute, Jones, just nodded his head vigorously, his courage surely fortified with alcohol.

"What 'bout me?" Traveling Joe asked as the little man squatted behind him.

"Once he's distracted, you get that device and break it. No matter what."

He muttered something in Portuguese and disappeared.

The famous Cog, Nikola Tesla, had given them the information about his invention. The Imperium had tricked him into building it, and had kidnapped his pigeon to keep him quiet. It drew the Power itself up from the core of the Earth and spiked it on the surface, drawn to a complicated targeting spell. They did not know where the design was drawn, but they'd been able to intercept the Iron

Guards before they could flee with the device from Wardenclyffe laboratories, but rather than give it up, they'd decided to destroy themselves along with it in suicidal fire.

The single test firing of the Geo-Tel had managed to wipe out the entire Cossack army, and now it would slag the East Coast of the United States of America.

Not if I can help it . . .

"NOW!" Pershing and Browning leapt into the tunnel and opened fire. The gunshots were devastatingly loud in the enclosed space. The bullets and buckshot struck, sending the Iron Guard staggering back, but his body was laced with kanji of durability and vitality. He raised one hand and blue fire erupted down the tunnel. Pershing dove into the foul water to avoid certain death.

He was hugging the bottom when the telepathic message from the surface arrived. *Blue light growing in the sky. We've only got seconds left. Hurry!*

Working on it, Isaiah.

When he broke the surface, Browning was at his side shrugging out of his burning coat and holding a shotgun with a wood stock scorched from the heat. The Iron Guard was distracted by Southunder's rapid gunfire as the other Grimnoir flanked him. The Iron Guard moved toward them, hurling fire, but jerked as the water around his legs was frozen into a solid block by Christiansen.

The Iron Guard lowered his hands, blasting fire into the ice to free himself. Pershing had once been the best shot in the Army and showed it as he snapped the Winchester to his shoulder, lined up the front sight, and drilled the distracted Iron Guard in one eye.

Jones crashed down the tunnel in a wave of water, his muscles driven with superhuman strength as he burned his Power. The Iron Guard was snapping around, blood spraying from one socket, kept alive only by kanji spells and fanaticism, liquid flame shooting from his fingers as Jones tackled him with a roar.

Pershing was up and sloshing forward as he worked the lever. The Power was rising up through the ground with a crackling rage. Soon it would supercharge the atmosphere and the resulting explosion would reach from Canada to Washington D.C.

It's firing!

Jones was on top of the Iron Guard, fists hammering up and

down like pistons as he slammed the man's head into a misshapen pulp. He rose, still bellowing, meat and hair dripping from his hands. "Nobody messes with Wild Bill! NOBODY!" He kicked the body down the tunnel.

We're all going to die.

"Vierra!" Pershing shouted. "Break it!"

Traveling Joe appeared with a splash next to him, holding a strange mechanical device. It was humming and crackling with Power. "You mean this?" He raised it overhead and slammed it down into the bricks, cracking it into several pieces.

The electric tingling in the air died. The Power was returning to the core.

It's . . . it's dissipating. You did it!

"Yes . . . yes, we did . . ."

Paris, France
1909

THE INTERNATIONAL LEADERSHIP of the Grimnoir Society had come together for the first time in a decade. The meeting room was plain, the building drab, and little would a passerby know that some of the most important people in the world had gathered there in secret.

"General Pershing, we are honored to have you as the newest member of the international leadership. Your bravery has saved the lives of thousands."

He hadn't come all this way just to get his ego stroked. "What about my proposal?"

"As commander of the American members of the Grimnoir Society, you are aware of the mighty challenges that face us. I'm afraid that we cannot honor your request at this time."

Pershing pushed away from the table and stood. "Respectfully, I think you're wrong. We need to recruit more people. Not just Actives, but anyone who has the courage to stand against the Imperium. The Chairman is our greatest threat. The time to strike is now. The longer we wait, the stronger he becomes. We need to build an army and take the fight to him. We need more knights. There's strength in numbers."

"There is more strength in secrecy," one of the younger Europeans said, his English rough, his pronunciation stilted. "War is brewing here, and I fear that our kind will be drawn into both sides. The Kaiser is already building Active units. I, for one, fear our own governments more than I fear the Japanese."

"Then you're a fool," Pershing snapped. There was a collective gasp. "The Kaiser is a Barnum clown compared to the Chairman. He's no mere politician. He's a force. The Geo-Tel events have been blamed on meteorites, but we all know what they really were." *No one in the American government believed him, but these people should understand. They had to.* "What if it had been your country that was about to be evaporated?"

"Then I would still listen to the knowledge of my elders," the European looked to the three men at the head of the table for confirmation.

The elders deliberated quietly amongst themselves for a moment, before the one in the middle finally spoke. "Our strategy remains the same for now. We will contain the Imperium, but we will not risk an open battle. Secrecy is paramount. General Pershing, you will protect the Geo-Tel device in the event that we ever, God help us, grow desperate enough to use it, but I do not ever foresee the need to use a weapon so terrible that its firing would be felt through the very fabric of all worlds. You will report the location only to the Grimnoir elders, in the case that something should befall you."

"You're all making a terrible mistake." Pershing stormed from the room in disgust.

Mar Pacifica, California
1932

SULLIVAN PULLED HIS HAND away as dozens of memories flooded into his mind all at once. He remembered frustration riding in pursuit of Pancho Villa, confusion at the aftermath of Wounded Knee, the bitter soul-crushing sadness of losing his wife and three young daughters in a terrible fire, everything, the thrill of victory and the agony of defeat, and finally three years of unbearable suffering, but those were blurry, and had probably come over by accident.

Others had been very specifically stamped into him, as harsh as the light of day. "What are you?"

Pershing appeared even weaker than before, if that were possible. "I'm a very weak Reader. I barely qualify as an Active, but I've been saving up a lot of Power . . . I thought it would only be fair to try and answer your questions while I answered my own . . . Thank you. I finally got to see the Power . . . It all makes sense now."

"You read my mind?" Sullivan asked.

"Yes . . ." he closed his eyes. "I *was* right about you. And now I must rest . . ."

"Why'd you show me all those things?"

Pershing's breathing had grown shallow and erratic. "Because . . . someone must know the truth . . . Only a handful of us knew . . . about the Geo-Tel . . . I need you to destroy the final piece . . . Don't let *him* get it . . . Because we have a . . . traitor in our midst . . . I can't even trust people who are like my . . . children . . . Whoever it is . . . they're too strong for me to Read . . . Because . . ."

Pershing moved slowly, pushing something toward Sullivan. He took it, and found that it was one of the Grimnoir rings.

Because you are the man for the job. Carry on.

Pershing sent that last thought with his Power, then let out his final breath.

"General?"

His chest had quit moving. It was as if he'd found someone to pass the torch to, and had finally moved on. Sullivan sat there for a moment, stunned. Jane arrived a moment later, studied General Pershing's still form and began to cry.

Chapter 14

You can go a long way with a smile. You can go a lot further with a smile and a gun. A smile, a gun, and a Brute get you the key to the city.

—Al "Scarface" Capone,
Interview, 1930

Detroit, Michigan

THE PALE HORSE AWOKE feeling more refreshed than he had in three years. It was as if a great burden had been lifted from his soul.

It is done.

Harkeness had followed Cornelius Stuyvesant to Michigan. His sources had confirmed that the billionaire had completed his assignment, and the proper modifications were being made to the Chairman's personal airship. He could not have asked for better timing. Pershing finally succumbing to his curse on the very same day as the completion of his favor would be seen as a sign of his Power. It was a coincidence, but Stuyvesant would be terrified. Having a man such as that under his thumb could prove valuable in the future.

Pershing had been a strong one. When Harkeness had first touched him, he had expected him to last a few months, perhaps a year at most. He had underestimated the willpower of such a man, not to mention the remarkable and surprising skill of his Healer. That thought made Harkeness swell with pride.

This assignment had been draining, but it would be worth it. He dressed in his finest suit and took the elevator to the lobby. He would send a telegram to Isaiah. The powerful Reader would not know of Pershing's demise until it hit the papers, but he needed to get to work. It was almost time to provide the Chairman with the location of the last piece of the Tesla device.

Their plan was almost complete.

Mar Pacifica, California

ARRANGEMENTS HAD BEEN MADE to take the General's body into the city for transport to Arlington for burial. By the next day, word would spread over the wires, and the entire nation would mourn the loss of one of their greatest heroes.

And they only knew the half of it, Sullivan thought bitterly. He wasn't sure if it was the recent shock of Pershing's memories that caused him to be so angry at the powers that be and their isolationist blindness, or if it was his own memories. Either way, he had a job to do, and with a rock breaker's dedication, he knew it was going to get done.

The American Grimnoir were taking their leader's loss hard. Command fell to John Moses Browning until the Society's elders appointed someone else. Sullivan could tell that Browning didn't want the responsibility. He was very old, but he'd fulfill his duty. Sullivan could respect that.

They had called a meeting, and the group had gathered around a long rectangular table. Browning stood at the head, exhausted and drained. At his right hand was the stocky Lance Talon, on his left was the bespectacled Dan Garrett. Of the others, he knew Heinrich well, but he only knew the kid, Francis, from when he'd kneecapped him. Delilah had come down and sat directly across from him, but she'd only greeted him with the slightest of nods. Jane was the most distraught by the previous day's events, but had still joined them. She sat next to Dan, who was discreetly holding her hand under the table. The last person to join them was the young girl who had shot him in the back then saved his life.

She was an odd one. Thin, gawky, with hair like wet straw, and the strangest grey eyes he'd ever seen. She held out one little hand to him in greeting. He took it, surprised that she had calluses that would make anyone running a pickax at Rockville proud. "You look just like your brother, only not evil. Sorry about murdering you."

"Attempted murder," he corrected her.

"Oh, no, you were totally dead when I found you under the magic jellyfish," she smiled. "Good thing you followed me back. I'm Sally Faye Vierra. You can call me Faye." She took her seat.

Browning got right down to business. "I have received a message from the Grimnoir elders. We are to take no action until we receive further orders."

"We've been sitting on our asses for too long," Lance complained.

Browning frowned, obviously not liking foul language, but used to working with Lance. "What would you have us do?"

"We need to get out there, find Bob Southunder, and get the last piece of the Tesla device."

Sullivan paid careful attention. The General had been certain that one of these people had betrayed them to the Chairman.

"Only nobody, not even the General, knows where Southunder went," Garrett pointed out. "We have no idea how to reach him, or even if he's alive or dead. How are we supposed to find him?"

I can . . . Sullivan thought, realizing that he knew exactly how to find the man. Pershing had kept that secret as his ace. He kept his mouth shut.

"If the Chairman already had the last piece, then we'd know as soon as he fired it," Browning said. "We have to assume Southunder is still alive."

Faye raised her hand. "What about my Grandpa's piece?"

Browning shook his head sadly. "Unfortunately, the part that was taken by Madi was the complex piece. What you have is not that important, and the Chairman's Cogs should have no problem replacing it."

"Oh . . ." Faye stared at the table. "Shoot."

"Who let her out?" Heinrich asked.

"I did," Browning said. "The General Read her. She's no Shadow Guard."

"I only shot Mr. Sullivan because he looks just like his big brother, Mr. Madi."

There was a rustle as most of the Grimnoir turned to Sullivan in surprise. He stared back at them coolly. "Yeah . . . Got a problem?"

"Jake, is this true?" Delilah asked.

Madi is the one that killed her dad. "He is, but I didn't know he'd fallen in with the Imperium till yesterday. He disappeared on AEF Siberia. I hoped he'd either died or settled down somewhere. Can't say I'm surprised though. It suits him." Delilah looked away, seemingly stunned by that revelation, and his stomach lurched.

"Your brother . . . is *the* Madi?" the kid, Francis, asked. "He's the most powerful of the Iron Guards!"

He shrugged his big shoulders. "You can't choose your relatives, kid."

Francis turned red with embarrassment. "Yes . . . of course . . . sorry."

Browning continued. "It's fine, Francis. Despite the General's issues with your family, we've been able to make good use of this estate. We needed a place where we could keep the General safe during his illness. Now, I imagine we'll need to be on the move again for our own safety. I have received word that the elders will be sending a new commander. I will step down as soon as he arrives."

"That ain't right," Lance said.

"Those are the orders. In the meantime, we are to do nothing, not even give the oath to any new members . . ." he dipped his bald head toward the end of the table that held Sullivan, Delilah, and Faye. "My apologies. If you wish to join the Society, you will need to be interviewed by the new commander. Otherwise, you will be asked to leave our protection. It is out of my hands."

Faye did not know what to make of this news. She had barely known Mr. Pershing, but he'd immediately accepted her like Grandpa had. He'd even taken the time to Read her mind and share some of his own memories with her. It had been especially fun to see Grandpa as a brave younger man. Some of the other memories had been strange, and she was still trying to figure out why he'd shared some of those with her.

Browning continued talking, answering the others' questions. They weren't happy. Faye could tell that they were like her. They wanted to take action, not wait around for someone else to tell them what to do.

She looked over at Mr. Sullivan. He seemed nice. He reminded her of a mature bull, big and strong, but not with a lot of snorting and kicking up dirt. Quiet, like he didn't need to show off. You could tell he was powerful just by looking at him. She still felt bad for shooting him. Delilah would watch him quietly every time Mr. Sullivan turned away, playing it shy, which didn't seem like Delilah at all, but Faye didn't pretend to understand such things.

She didn't like that part about not being allowed to be a Grimnoir, but that didn't matter to her. It was just a name. She had some promises to keep, and that included avenging her Grandpa, and killing Mr. Madi and his boss. The servants brought in food, and she dreamed absently about how she was going to shoot the correct Sullivan next time as she ate. She could get used to having servants.

When the meeting was over and everyone was dispersing and that scary German who had shot her in the heart was watching her suspiciously, she caught Lance by the arm and followed him outside. "Will you still keep teaching me how to fight?"

He stopped, thinking hard. "You didn't keep your promise."

"No murdering without good reasons . . ." Faye sighed. "I'll try harder this time."

Lance grinned through his bushy beard. "It'll be my pleasure."

Browning had sent a servant to have Sullivan meet him alone in his workshop. It had only taken a moment of looking into the butler's vacant expression to realize he was a Summoned, easily the most human-appearing one that he'd ever seen, but a Summoned nonetheless. It made perfect sense considering the Grimnoir's apparent fixation on secrecy.

The butler-creature led him to a room filled with machinery and left him at the entrance. Sullivan paused to admire the racks of beautiful weapons. He ran his finger down a perfectly engraved Auto-5, then a polished over-under, then he stopped to gawk at what must have been an early prototype of the deadly Browning Automatic Rifle. He whistled.

"So, you are an enthusiast?" Browning said, hunched over a workbench, a tiny part in one hand as he worked it over carefully with a round file.

"I grew up with one of your Winchester rifles, used it to put food on the table, an 1895 that my daddy brought back from Cuba. It even had the bayonet, but he never did let me use that on any deer," he chuckled. "You could say that I'm a fair hand with a gun. Got mighty handy with a Lewis during the war."

Browning did not look up from his work. "Colonel Lewis designed a fine weapon."

Sullivan wandered around the end of the rack to another filled with guns that he did not recognize. "May I?"

"Of course." Browning held up the part to the light and nodded in satisfaction.

Sullivan picked up a short weapon, and was surprised at its weight. At first he thought it was a BAR missing its stock, but rather the action was where the stock should be, enclosed in a housing so he could mount it to his shoulder like a proper stock. There was a pistol grip forward of the magazine. He realized that his face would rest on the leather pad on top of the receiver for a cheek-weld. "Interesting . . ." It made the overall weapon about a foot shorter, but still with a barrel length sufficient to generate good velocity. "No wasted space, but dang if you don't want to shoot that one left-handed . . . You'd eat brass."

"The English requested that. They called it a bullpup. Overall length is significantly shorter, plus it has improvements to the gas system and bolt. It is the BAR model of 1929, but it was never submitted since I suffered a *fatal* heart attack . . ."

He hefted the stubby weapon. Lighter, no bipod, it would have been much nicer in the close confines of a trench than his massive Lewis gun, though not nearly as good for laying down sustained fire. It even fired the same powerful cartridge. "It's weird, but I like it."

"This one has been personally worked over, including the addition of minor spells of durability and accuracy. Five hundred rounds a minute, feeding from twenty-or thirty-round box magazines. There is a case for it behind the counter. It has a Maxim silencer that can be attached to the muzzle, much quieter, though it does get rather hot . . . I would like for you to have it."

Sullivan paused. "Really?"

Browning nodded as he took the metal part and slid it into a pistol frame followed by a pin to lock it in place. "I know that you will be leaving us shortly. I've known Black Jack for many years, and he wasn't quite the cipher that he thought he was. I know that he had a special assignment for you, something so important that he did not dare tell any of his longtime associates . . . The least I can do is make sure you are as well equipped as possible."

"Thank you, sir."

He watched as Browning's hands flew about in a blur, quickly assembling a pistol. Browning may have been old, but he'd done this millions of times. He continued working as he spoke, "I hail from a persecuted people, Mr. Sullivan. My family was driven from place to place. We would build a home, only to be forced out by mobs and murderers. I've seen persecution firsthand. That is why I joined the Society. I became a knight of the Grimnoir because no one should have to bear such cruel treatment." He worked the slide several times and checked the trigger, nodding in satisfaction. "Excellent."

Sullivan did not recognize the pistol. It looked like the old favored 1911 that he'd broken, only fatter, and with a concealed hammer. Dozens of tiny designs had been hand carved into the metal grips.

"I have lived a very long time. The last few years have been on borrowed time thanks to magical Healing. Yet, even in my old age, I've yet to see the end of violence against the innocent . . . I provide the weapons to prevent such things. Whatever task Black Jack gave you, Mr. Sullivan, please do not let him down."

"Yes, sir," he answered as Browning passed the pistol over. He took it tenderly. It even felt like his old 1911, just thicker, which was more comfortable in his big hand. The sights were bigger and easier to see than he was used to. It felt like it had been made for him.

"The M1921, designed for Army Brutes, except the contract was cancelled. Based on my 1908, only with fourteen rounds of .45 automatic in a staggered column magazine. It is the only one of its kind, so please do not lose it. There are twenty magazines in the box on that top shelf. I will provide ammunition, as well as any supplies you need, including money. J. Edgar Hoover has been sent a telegram stating that the Army has requested your services at the American Battle Monuments Commission. Unfortunately, the Army will require you to be out of the country and unable to communicate for the foreseeable future. If anyone asks, you are detailed to the staff of one Colonel Eisenhower. Hoover will not like it, but the General had many friends. Do you still have his ring?"

He pulled it out of his shirt pocket. "I do."

"I believe he would want you to keep it. You will need it as a full member of the Grimnoir Society. Should you accept, I will administer the oath to you before you leave. It will provide a small measure of magical protection."

"I thought that your bosses said no new members?"

"Bureaucrats are the same in every endeavor, even Magical ones. I do not know what your assignment is, but I will not have Black Jack's dying wish denied because of me. When will you be departing?"

Sullivan thought about it for a moment as he inspected the pistol. He needed to get to Southunder as fast as possible, but he'd started on this quest for personal reasons, and he wasn't the type of man who left things unfinished. "I've got one last thing to do."

Lick Hill, California

MADI FOLDED HIS ARMS and rested them across the roof of the automobile. The summer sun beat down on him. Across the fields of waving yellow grass and small hills sat the power plant; beyond the smoking stacks was a ravine, and then the largest hill in the area. The narrow steel-strut tower that rose from the plant seemed somehow too tall. In a way, it was every bit as unnatural as he, an aberration in the laws of physics, created from wild Cog imaginings.

"What do you think?" he asked the advance scout from the Shadow Guard contingent.

The young woman removed her sunglasses and studied the tower's defenses. She did not need a telescope any more than he did, revealing that she surely wore the kanji granting the vision of a hawk. "They are complacent."

Her assessment matched his own. He'd studied this location carefully when the Chairman had commissioned the study of weak points in the American defenses. The fact that they were able to park so close was a testament to Americans' foolish pride. There were half a dozen other automobiles parked along the road here as well, mostly travelers stopping to gape at one of the legendary Peace Rays. *Pathetic.* "Can you take it?"

"Easily. Judging from the number of vehicles, traffic, and visible guards, I would say that they are understaffed. Even if they have any

Actives, we will take them by surprise," she stated. It was a well-known fact that the military had atrophied since the last war left the country in an isolationist stupor. After all, who could invade a country that had so many Peace Rays? "It will take at least twenty minutes for reinforcements to arrive. Their lack of fear has made them soft."

"We'll have to remedy that . . ." he muttered, glancing over at the Shadow Guard. The fact that she was female meant nothing. The Shadow Guard was made up of Fades and Travelers, perfect assassins. The Chairman would never waste one, even if they were of the weaker sex, but he'd been surprised to find that she was as white as he was.

She caught him looking, and turned her eerie grey eyes on him. Her hair was dark red. She obviously knew what he was thinking. "My parents were British missionaries in Burma when it fell. I was raised in an Imperium school. It was a great honor. As you are well aware, a Caucasian is able to do more among the Americans without arousing suspicion." She put the cheaters back on to hide her unnatural eyes.

She was beautiful, and she knew it. Madi was impressed with the way that her every unconscious move managed to display her perfect body just enough to keep his constant attention. The Shinobi Academy had taught her well. Seduction was a valuable tool of espionage. Even if she wasn't a Traveler, he had no doubt that she would be an effective tool. "What do they call you?"

"For the purposes of this mission, my identity is Gladys Mays of Toledo, Ohio. In the academy, I took the name Toshiko." She returned his gaze without fear. That was something else he would have to fix. Madi had masters and he had followers. He didn't have equals.

He'd taken so many kanji onto his body that all physical sensations had become dull. He had taken to cutting himself with a razor just so he could feel. It was a rare occasion to find a woman that got his attention. Madi decided he would take her for himself when this mission was complete. He'd see just what tricks the academy had taught her, and he'd consider it his reward. Being an Iron Guard had its privileges.

"Brief your men, Toshiko. We strike tonight . . ."

Mar Pacificia, California

FRANCIS HAD WATCHED Faye training for the last hour. She was learning at a frightening speed, and he found it nearly impossible to keep track of how fast she popped in and out of sight, appearing suddenly at totally unexpected directions and speeds. Lance was clearly befuddled trying to keep up. Though he knew it was impossible, the girl didn't seem to be capable of running out of Power.

He had needed to do something to get his mind off his grief, and his first inclination had been to raid the liquor cabinet and drink himself incoherent on his family's finest vintages, but he knew that the General would have disapproved. Pershing had been like a father to him, far better than the man who'd spawned him.

His father hadn't been a bad man per se, simply weak. He was a politician first, human being a distant second. He was the type who tested the wind before stating an opinion. There were no truths, only the path that had the least economic repercussions. When he'd been appointed ambassador, and had seen the Imperium's evil firsthand, even that hadn't been enough to goad him into taking a stand. Francis, on the other hand, had left Japan haunted with nightmares from the things he had seen.

He was a Mover from a long line of Movers, only he was far more talented than his forbearers. To them, it was just a parlor trick, something that could become an embarrassment should it ever become public knowledge, and he had constantly been admonished to keep his Power secret. General Pershing had seen his talent, recognized his potential, and had shown him how he could use it to make things right. Pershing had taught him how to be a man. He owed him his life, except now he was gone.

Francis jumped as Heinrich appeared on the bench beside him. The Fade always managed to move with unnerving silence. "Sorry," he said calmly. "I did not intend to startle you."

"Well, you didn't," Francis sputtered. "I heard you coming," he lied.

Heinrich was quiet as he watched Faye disappear just as Lance tried to hit her with a padded stick, only to reappear ten feet in the air over his head. "She's too talented to just be some poor country girl. I do not trust her."

"You're incapable of trust," Francis muttered, then regretted it.

"I've earned that right," Heinrich said softly. "Where I come from, trust is an honor given to very few . . ."

Francis was once heir to the world's greatest blimp magnate. Who was he to judge someone who'd grown up as a homeless urchin inside the walls of Dead City? Francis had never been inside the ruins of what had once been Berlin, but he'd heard the legends. The smoking blight left by the firing of the Peace Ray had ended the Great War, but had burned the land and poisoned the air. Then it was made hell on Earth as the Kaiser's undead soldiers had been rounded up and walled inside. He couldn't even begin to imagine what it had been like to be one of the humans trapped inside, especially as a child. "I'm sorry. That's not what I meant."

Heinrich continued as if he hadn't heard Francis's apology, which was probably for the best. All the Grimnoir knew that behind his friendly demeanor, Heinrich was a pained man. "This girl . . . She is not as dumb as she pretends to be." He couldn't disagree with that assessment. Faye was smart, just not in a *normal* way. "She shows up and immediately kills a prisoner just as he is starting to talk . . . That doesn't strike you as odd?" He didn't wait for a response. "Then soon after, we lose the General . . ."

"We all knew it was coming soon." Maybe that was why he didn't feel as sad as he thought he should have. Part of him was relieved that the suffering was done, and that made him feel even guiltier. "That big Heavy was in there when he died, not Faye." The very thought gnawed at Francis. He'd known the General since he'd been a little boy, had become a knight under his tutelage, had forsaken his family to serve under his command, and given him a home during his final years . . . and yet it had been a complete stranger who had been there at the end. "He's Madi's brother, but I don't see you getting all suspicious of him."

"I don't trust him either . . . I barely trust you and we've worked together for years." Heinrich's smile was apologetic. "I'm very sorry about your nose," he said. "I shouldn't have struck you."

Francis sniffed. Jane had fixed it, but it still hurt. "She's not a Shadow Guard. You know. Black Jack said so." It didn't seem right to invoke the General's name to win an argument, but he had, and Francis was going to be damned if his suspicious friend was going to cast doubts on anything that Black Jack had said from his death bed. "So lay off her."

Heinrich looked at him, raising his eyebrows. "Francis Stuyvesant . . . *mein Gott.* Have you taken a liking to that grey-eyed lunatic?"

"That's . . . that's absurd. Go to hell, Koenig," Francis said as he rose from the bench. He wasn't in the mood. "I'm going to go and get completely drunk."

"I'm sorry, Jane," Daniel Garrett said as his fiancée cried. "You did everything you could. Nobody blames you."

Jane blew her nose and wiped her bloodshot eyes. "It's my fault, Dan. I should have been able to save him." She pulled her knees up to her chest and rocked back and forth. "Why? Why couldn't I be strong enough?"

Her pain was killing him inside. Dan put his arm over her shoulder, pulled her close, cursing his own inadequacies. He knew that all he had to do was reach for his Power. Just a little push . . . the tiniest of pushes . . . He could tell the woman he loved that it wasn't her fault, that she'd done everything she could, that no Healer could stop a Pale Horse, and with his Power to influence minds, she would believe whatever words came out of his mouth.

Even if it was the truth, it would also be wrong, so he didn't do it.

"I love you, Jane," he said softly. He was careful not to even touch his Power as he spoke. He had no right. "It wasn't your fault. You did the best you could . . ."

"You're not trying to Influence me, are you?" she asked, almost, but not quite, laughing through the tears.

"Of course not," he answered as he brushed some stray hairs away from her eyes. "You already know how much crap I get for being a Mouth getting married to a babe like you. Everyone in the world thinks the only way somebody like you would end up with an ugly mug like me is because I've got you hypnotized . . ." he said it as a joke to cheer her up, but they both knew it was partially true, and it hurt him every single time. He smiled. "It sure isn't because I'm rich."

Jane hugged him close, her fingernails digging into the back of his neck. "When you can see everyone's insides all the time, we're all ugly . . . and squishy." They both had a laugh, then Jane began weeping again, and Dan did all that he thought an honorable husband-to-be should do, and gave her his shoulder to cry on.

Finally, she spoke. "I can't bear it. It's just too much hurt. I can fix physical hurt, but I can't do anything about this kind. I need to be strong. The others need me. Dan . . . I want you to *tell* me I did my best. I need to *believe* it."

He nodded, and pushed his Power hard. "It wasn't your fault." His words resonated like biblical truth.

"Thank you . . ."

Sullivan found Delilah standing at the edge of the ocean, staring out toward the setting sun. Her dress was whipping around her in the wind, and he could see her figure as the sun shone through the fabric.

"You're a tough one to find," he said.

"Who said I wanted to be found?" she said without turning around.

Sullivan paused, all the practiced words failing him once again. They always worked in his head, but turned to garbage when he tried to form them in his mouth. Instead he just said, "I came to say I'm sorry."

"For trying to arrest me? For bouncing me off a roof? For being ready to shoot me down for the coppers because you just took their word that I was a mad-dog killer? Or for before that? For when you ran away and left me alone in New Orleans? Maybe even for just being a lousy jerk . . ."

" . . . Yes . . ."

She finally turned around, placed her hands on her hips and gave him that same dangerous smirk. "You're leaving again, aren't you?"

She was so pretty that it struck his heart like a bullet. "There's something I got to do."

"Take me with you."

"It'll be too dangerous."

"I'm a Brute, remember?"

Sullivan didn't respond. He didn't know what to say. She had the

Power to pull a man's head off with her bare hands and anything short of a high-powered rifle would bounce off her skin. She was tough as nails and worth ten men in a fight . . . but she'd always be that same scared girl that he'd found abused and mistreated in Louisiana. He'd put her back together while she'd helped him heal from the nightmare of the war, a pair of survivors who'd started to cobble together a life. But then he'd gone away. Prison had changed him, leaving him hard and uncaring, and it had been easy to believe that she'd become just as jaded while they'd been apart. But he'd been wrong, and here she was, the same girl, only with a harder shell, and she deserved so much better than a lug like him who had already proven he couldn't protect her. There was no way he could live with her death on his hands. That was one thing that he wasn't strong enough for. He just wasn't eloquent enough to explain all that.

"You're doing this for Pershing? I know what it is, you know. It's the same reason he brought me here, only once he Read me, I think he decided I wasn't good enough . . . But by then, he was stuck with me . . ." She turned back to the Pacific. "Story of my life . . . Damaged goods. Nobody wants me."

Without hesitation, he moved forward and encircled her in his arms, crushing her tight against him, suddenly afraid to let her go. He whispered low in her ear. "I do."

They were two irreparably flawed people. Together they almost made a whole person, and he figured that might just be enough. She leaned her head back into his chest and he held her there for a long time.

Chapter 15

. . . And on this momentous day, let us remember the brave sacrifice of Junior Assistant Third Engineer Harold Ernest Crozier of Southampton, who was lost after an ice collision on our maiden voyage. His natural magical gifts, combined with his great moral fortitude, enabled him to control the incoming waters before there was any other loss of life. He was a credit to the Active race. We shall now have a moment of silence for Engineer Crozier.

—Captain Edward J. Smith
of the RMS *Titanic,*
on its fifth anniversary cruise, 1917

Lick Hill, California

THERE WERE FOUR GUARDS manning the main gatehouse. Three were playing a game of poker, while the last was watching the clock, knowing that they were due to be relieved at two o'clock in the morning, and he was dying to get out of the stinking concrete shed and back into his bed. He cursed the slow clock, lit another cigarette, and went back to being miserable.

It was a joke. The entire assignment was a big, stupid joke. Nothing ever happened at Lick Hill. After the Great War showed the absolute war-ending power of the Peace Ray, every nation that could afford it built at least one. America had three along its west coast alone. The Peace Ray was a marvel of superscience. It fired a near instantaneous beam of absolute death as far as three hundred miles in a perfectly straight line. No army could invade a country with a Peace Ray. Everyone knew that Tesla had made war obsolete.

The towers were absurdly tall, and usually put on top of the highest land available. They were a line-of-sight weapon. The higher it was, the further it could engage targets. When the war had first ended, strings of observation dirigibles had been stationed all along the coast, ready to call in a warning and firing coordinates to the huge crews of operators at a moment's notice. Hundreds of technicians were protected by thousands of soldiers. The sheer amount of electricity necessary to run the machine necessitated the building of huge power plants, but it was all necessary for national security.

The guards were well trained and issued the finest safety equipment. They had to be. A full-charge firing of the Peace Ray could actually turn the very air around the beam into poison. Only the bravest of soldiers were assigned to guard the most important weapon in the arsenal of freedom.

The Peace Ray was the key to assuring America's safety in the dangerous new world.

Or so they had said in 1920 when they'd built the damn things, but over time, thousands of soldiers had turned into hundreds, and then into two understaffed platoons. Hundreds of technicians had turned into a skeleton crew of thirty. Budget cuts had taken away all but ten of their blimps. Half of those were in the shop, and the rest were expected to watch the coast from Canada to Mexico.

Their gas masks hadn't been pulled out in years. The private wasn't even sure where his was. The Army budget had been so deeply cut over the last three years that he wasn't even sure if they had gas masks at all for the new guys. The power plants had mostly been diverted to feed the growing metropolis of San Francisco, and the last he'd heard from one of the techs, they were running at maybe fifteen percent of maximum power, but that wasn't supposed to matter, because nobody knew that, and as long as the Peace Ray rose over the coast like a deadly futuristic sentinel, it would do its job as a deterrent, or at least that's what the brass figured.

Guarding a Peace Ray was a crap job, but at least he had a job, the private thought ruefully, which was more than he could say for a lot of folks he knew. Times were tough, so three square meals and a bed in a barracks wasn't *that* bad of a deal if you thought about it, but one-thirty in the morning was a lousy time to be thinking about it.

There was a tinkle of breaking glass and a grunt. He turned, expecting to see that one of his buddies had dropped their coffee mug, ready to give them some grief about the mess, but he paused, realizing that the spreading stain on the floor was too red to be coffee. Somebody was moving around his friends, who had all put their heads down on the table. "Who are you?" Then the stranger dressed in funny black pajamas and a mask came across the guard shack with a flash of steel and separated the private's head cleanly from his neck.

Mar Pacifica, California

SOMETHING'S WRONG . . .

Faye woke up with a start. She was breathing hard, sweating, and had kicked her blankets onto the floor. The house creaked a bit, as the wind from the ocean was strong tonight, but other than that, it was quiet. Everything *looked* normal. The room was dark, but she'd never had a problem seeing better than most folks at night. She'd always figured it was because of her grey eyes.

Something ain't right. She knew to pay attention to her instincts. It was like when she Traveled. If she paid attention how she was supposed to, she just somehow knew when things were gonna be dangerous in the space she was about to fill. Faye got out of bed and pulled on a pair of pants under her baggy nightshirt. Some folks might think pants on a girl were scandalous, but frankly, she didn't care what people thought, and if you were going to go sneaking around because something bad was in the air, pants made more sense.

She didn't bother with shoes, as her soles were like saddle leather, but she did pick up the big .45 automatic that Mr. Browning had given her. He said that next time she needed to shoot somebody, this one would put a *proper* hole in them. Francis had told her that it was probably too powerful for a girl, but she'd been milking cows, and had a stronger grip than the city boy did, so what did he know?

The hallway was quiet. She padded down the thick carpet of the second floor balcony. There was nothing moving in the space below or on the stairs.

She used her Power to check her surroundings. Having had a lot of practice recently, she'd gotten even better at scouting before a jump, so good in fact, that it was like she could see everything in a big circle around her, not with her eyes, but inside her brain. The area around her had always been like a map in her head, and when she picked a spot to Travel into, she could focus more on that space, but she'd been Traveling so much lately, that she'd discovered that her head map had gotten bigger and clearer. It was almost like her thoughts could Travel on their own, and she didn't even need to send her body to see what was going on. A big book Mr. Browning had, written by a Dr. Fort, had called her Power by the name of Teleportation, but even it hadn't mentioned anything about being able to have a magic map in her head.

Faye checked her head map. It used to only stretch for about fifty feet in a circle wherever she was standing, but with practice, it now seemed to go about double that. It didn't have a lot of detail, so she didn't feel like she was invading anyone's privacy, and besides, something was fishy tonight besides the ocean. Mr. Sullivan's room was next to hers, but it was empty. Next was Delilah's room, and she was surprised to find that both of them were asleep in the same bed. That was a little shocking to her since they weren't married folk, so she kept going. She liked Delilah and just hoped Mr. Sullivan would make her happy.

Nobody was moving on the second floor, so she decided to Travel downstairs. Grandpa had always warned her not to Travel into a spot where she couldn't see with her own eyes, but she'd been breaking a bunch of his rules lately. She appeared in the fancy dining room. There was something in the shadows behind the piano, but it turned out to just be a curtain moving a little in the breeze from an open window.

The map in her head didn't show anything weird. Even the servants were perfectly still, sleeping standing up in their bare quarters. She didn't know what they were, they sure as heck weren't people, but darn if they couldn't fix a mighty fine sandwich. Then at the very edge of her map, something twitched. She checked the spot in the living room, *clear,* and Traveled.

Her bare feet appeared an inch off the carpet, and she landed with the lightest thump. In the dark ahead of her was a shape, dressed entirely in black, crouched low, doing something to the magic carvings on the wood around the big glass windows. There was a scratching noise as the visitor flicked a knife back and forth.

Her first inclination was to just take Mr. Browning's .45 and shoot the stranger in the back of the head, but she'd promised Lance that she'd try extra hard not to kill anybody else by accident, and she was afraid that this might just be another Grimnoir that she didn't know. Lance had said that there were hundreds of them. "Can I help you?" Faye asked politely.

The person's head whipped around. He was wearing a black mask under a hood. A pair of grey eyes seemed to glow in the dark, then they just disappeared.

Traveler!

Faye felt the air behind her move and she reacted on instinct, Traveling. She could almost feel the knife drive through the space she'd just occupied. She landed on the other side of the couch. The stranger's hand snapped through the air and Faye jerked to the side just as something metal passed her face. A four-sided metal razor embedded into the wall with a *thunk*. "Hey!" Faye shouted, then she disappeared just as the stranger threw another razor at her.

She landed on the second floor. She'd never been in Lance's room before and almost managed to impale herself on the antlers from a stuffed elk. "Lance! Lance! Wake up!"

"Huh?" Lance immediately sat up in bed, his hand flying to a holstered revolver hanging from the bed post. "Faye?"

"There's a Traveler and he's trying to kill—" Her instincts warned her that something was coming and she threw herself back just as the stranger appeared, swinging a knife for her throat.

There was a terrible bloom of fire and the man crashed back into the wall. "Damn ninjas!" Lance bellowed as he fired five more rounds in rapid succession. Faye covered her ears. The stranger was still sliding down, leaving a trail of blood on the wallpaper as Lance sprang out of bed and turned on the electric lamp.

"You hurt?" he shouted as he dropped the empty revolver and picked up a lever-action rifle from the bedside. "I hate damn ninjas." He worked the action. Faye realized that he was as hairy as the animals he controlled and buck naked to boot. She shrieked, pointing. Lance looked down, swore again, and covered himself with the rifle butt. "I sleep like this. Old camping habit . . . Never mind. Hell. Go get Browning," he ordered.

Faye Traveled to Browning's room and froze as the old man sat up in bed, aimed a shotgun right at her face, and pumped a round into the chamber. Faye screamed and Traveled off to the side. "It's me!"

"I near blasted you, young lady." Browning admonished as he lowered the shotgun. "Who's shooting? What's going on?"

The Grimnoir sure did wake up fast. At least he was wearing pajamas. "There was a Traveler, and he tried to stab me, but Lance shot him a bunch, and said he was a damn ninja!"

Browning just nodded, placed the shotgun on the bed beside him, did something with his Grimnoir ring, made a fist with his ring hand, and slammed it jarringly hard into his palm. "We are under attack," he said.

WE ARE UNDER ATTACK.

He was already waking up from the sudden banging, but Sullivan rolled out of bed even faster as someone bellowed the words directly into his ears. "What?" he shouted.

Delilah was already up and moving, throwing her clothes on. "Gunfire."

"Who was yelling?"

"What?"

Sullivan's sleep-filled head realized that it had been Browning's voice, but of course, Delilah didn't have a Grimnoir ring, so she wouldn't have heard. He had put Pershing's ring on his pinky, the only one of his massive digits it would fit. "Never mind." He grabbed the thick .45 from the nightstand.

There was enough light coming through the window that Sullivan could see her throwing her dress over her head in a terrible hurry. It reminded him of when he'd had to flee New Orleans just ahead of the law. Delilah looked at him, eyes wide. "Just like old times, huh?"

He drew back the slide of the automatic and let the oiled steel fly forward under spring pressure, chambering a round. "Yeah, just like old times." *Only I ain't running this time.*

⁂

Madi's improved hearing easily picked up the gunshots. Three hundred yards away lights started coming on inside the house. The scout he'd sent to disable their alarm spells had failed, but it was a worthwhile sacrifice. He'd been surprised that his men had made it this close to the property before alerting the Grimmys, and he was thankful for the fog coming off the ocean. The Imperium men around him tensed, ready for action.

He'd gathered nearly thirty men for this operation, most of them were new recruits from San Francisco or Los Angeles, desperate suckers willing to risk their lives in exchange for gold or a touch of magic. He'd given them a big pep talk, a gun, and promises of the Chairman's eternal gratitude. He figured they'd take terrible casualties, but they were expendable. He planned on letting the Grimnoir use up their Power on the chumps first so he wouldn't endanger any of his more valuable assets. If any lived, that would prove they were strong, and therefore worthy of further training.

"Get 'em, boys," he whispered.

To their credit, most of them didn't hesitate. They rose from the bushes, some screaming as they charged the house, in a terrible impersonation of a proper Imperium battle cry, naively believing that the single kanji of vitality he and Yutaka had carved on them would make them bulletproof. It would make them tougher, but that wasn't near the same thing. The smarter ones actually took the time to use cover and aim their guns at the lighted windows as they approached.

He turned to his second wave. He'd kept two Shadow Guards, both Travelers, for himself and sent the rest with Toshiko for the raid on the Peace Ray. He didn't like splitting his forces, but he'd promised the Chairman something epic, and he always kept his promises. Now it looked like he was down to just one. He glared at the little Jap Traveler.

"Get in there. Find Pershing. I want him alive. Then report back."

"*Hai!*" His black hood dipped in a quick bow and he disappeared.

Madi turned to Yutaka. "Send your scouts. I want that Tesla device." His companion was already working, channeling his Power to Summon creatures. If it wasn't for the possibility that Pershing had that device, he'd just use the Peace Ray to melt this whole peninsula into molten lava and save the men. If it wasn't there, he'd pull back and then blast them. If he killed all the Grimmys first, he'd burn the place down the old-fashioned way, then have Toshiko use the Peace Ray on the Presidio and San Francisco. She had both sets of coordinates, just in case.

Another pair of Iron Guards had arrived that morning. He'd kept Hiroyasu, figuring that his particular scary-ass Power might come in handy, but he'd decided to send his partner along with the larger group attacking the Peace Ray. He didn't trust that Shadow Guard dame to not fuck up *his* mission. Everyone knew the Iron Guard were the best of the best. Hell, he could probably take all of these Grimnoir by himself.

Except for Jake, he's strong, like me . . . he caught himself thinking, and then quickly dismissed that as a weak thought. He still hadn't decided what he was gonna do with him yet, but Madi found that he was kinda looking forward to the challenge. It had been awhile since he'd squared off against anyone he'd considered a challenge. They'd never been real tight. Jake had always been the know-it-all, always telling him that they weren't no better than regular folks. He'd put up with Jake always defending the Normals, and all he'd gotten for it was a mangled face.

Some little part in the back of his mind kept saying the idea of burning his brother with a Peace Ray should have been troubling, but the more he thought on it, he didn't find that the idea of killing Jake upset him at all. In fact, Jake was the last vestige of his old, weak life. Taking him out would be like cutting that last chain that was keeping him down.

He checked his pocket watch. He'd enchanted the glass surface with a direct link to Toshiko. From the view he could tell they were eliminating the soldiers in complete silence. Beneath the glass he saw the ticking hands, and knew that they were well ahead of schedule.

"Impys in the treeline to the south. I took an owl over them!" Lance bellowed as he limped down the second floor balcony, now thankfully fully clothed, with bandoleers of ammunition crossing his torso. "Kill the lights." Then he jerked back as the window across from him shattered. He calmly went to one knee to avoid any more stray rounds.

Someone turned the lights off as Faye crouched down next to Lance. The big man, Mr. Sullivan, came walking up behind her, surprisingly quiet, with an enormous funny looking rifle in his hands. He'd put on a brown canvas vest with lots of pockets, and had a huge backpack over one shoulder. It looked like it weighed a ton, but she had to remind herself that weight didn't matter to someone like him. Delilah was right behind him, holding a short gun with a drum magazine on it.

"How many?" Sullivan asked, squinting into the patchy fog. Faye had to remind herself that most folks couldn't see in the dark like she could.

"At least two dozen, maybe more," Lance answered. He closed his eyes and took back control of the owl. "They're charging."

Sullivan just grunted in response, moved up next to the broken window, leaned around, and started shooting. The rifle was loud as he cranked off two or three rounds at a time, shell casings flying out right under his cheek. Lance popped up, shouldered his Winchester and fired. There were more gunshots coming from downstairs as the other Grimnoir piled it on.

Holes appeared in the walls around them. Plaster flew past Faye's face as she crawled down the landing. Lance rolled away, swearing up a storm, as Sullivan calmly drew back, yanking a new magazine out of his vest. Delilah reached down, grabbed Faye by the back of her nightshirt and dragged her down the carpet like she was a naughty puppy. "Get behind something solid," Delilah ordered as she hurled Faye down the hallway. "Now!"

She scrambled behind a marble statue of a fat man holding a blimp, but it exploded into dust and she yelped as the fragments pelted her. Faye crawled further down the hall, and fell through a doorway. Everything was breaking or shattering, and she decided that the second floor was *definitely* not the place to be.

Faye thought ahead, realized that the hundreds of glaring bits of danger were bullets, picked an empty spot, and appeared in the entryway. Mr. Browning and Mr. Garrett were both at the front door, shooting into the night. She got behind the piano.

"Out of the way!" Heinrich bellowed as he charged past her, green metal can in each hand. He dropped the cans next to a piece of furniture covered in a lace cloth and potted plants. The plants crashed to the floor as he ripped the cloth away, revealing a huge metal object on three legs. It was so big that at first Faye wondered why that mean German would be messing with a piece of farm equipment at a time like this, and then she realized that the huge thing was a *gun*. Francis caught up a second later, his rifle bouncing around on a sling over his back. He opened a cover on top of the big gun as Heinrich opened one of the metal cans and pulled out a linked belt of the biggest gleaming brass cartridges she'd ever seen.

A second later Francis yanked a huge handle back and forth and grabbed onto the spade grips on the back end. He swiveled it toward the window. The barrel was as big around as the pipes that fed the Vierra's milk tank, and covered in a metal shroud with holes in it, and Faye instinctively knew to cover her ears. *This was gonna be loud.*

There was a brilliant strobe of fire coming from the front of the house and a sound like thunder. Madi cursed. His enhanced vision enabled him to see his men exploding into clouds of meat as the huge bullets passed right through the trees they were using for cover. The damned Grimnoir had a Ma Deuce. He'd thought about bringing a mortar, but he'd hesitated, worried that if the Tesla device was inside, he'd accidentally damage it. "Yutaka!" The other Iron Guard appeared instantly at his side. "Anything from your spirits?"

"No device yet," he answered, grimacing as he concentrated on the invisible creatures he'd brought up from a lower plane. "The spirits say there are nine Grimnoir and a number of weak Summoned. The house is so covered in spells that it obscures their senses."

"Shit . . ." Madi glanced at his watch. Toshiko was inside the Peace Ray control center, slaughtering everyone. No alarms yet . . . He still had time, but not enough to be dicking around. "Hiroyasu . . . get your ass up here." The other Iron Guard approached deferentially. Madi didn't like the reedy little man. He was physically weak. He'd only been able to sustain a few kanji brands, but the sheer menace of his Power made him a valuable weapon of the Imperium. "Do your thing."

"I will need a few minutes," he answered with that effeminate voice that just pissed Madi off even more.

"Make it quick." He needed Hiroyasu's Power *now*. He needed to throw something else at the Grimmys, and those damn Shadow Guards were nowhere to be seen, and he had to assume that the first one was probably dead. "Yutaka, call off your spirits. Bring out the Bull King."

Yutaka let go of the lesser demons and turned all of his considerable Power to pulling up the greatest beast he could possibly Summon. Madi leaned back against the tree and lit a cigar. If the stupid Grimnoir wanted to play rough, he'd show them rough.

Sullivan stepped back from cover, eyes searching the mist-shrouded treeline through the ragged remains of the window slats. There was a muzzle flash. He raised the bullpup BAR, aimed at the spot and cranked off a burst. He moved to the side before they could return fire, heading for the next window. The house-shaking thunder coming from below told him that one of Browning's M2 .50-caliber machine guns had been set up. From what he'd heard, they were awe-inspiring weapons, and the terrible mess it was making of the little forest was proof of that. Great plumes of dirt appeared wherever it hit, trees shattered into splinters, and men died.

The thunder stopped. The normal fire tapered off. He couldn't see anything else moving in the woods, so he took the chance to reload. Someone downstairs, probably one of the younger ones, let out with a whooping cheer. "I think we put a hurtin' on them." Delilah appeared from around the corner, smoking Thompson in hand. She was nervous.

Lance peered over the windowsill. At some point his hat had been removed from his head by a bullet and blood was trickling down his scalp. "Hang on . . ." he closed his eyes, concentrating. "We killed a mess of them, rest are hunkered down. There's a group hanging back behind cover . . . He's Summoning something . . ."

"Aw hell . . ." Sullivan stepped back, leaned over what was left of the railing and shouted downstairs. "Demons incoming!"

"Not demons, just one." Lance bolted up from the floor and started shoving more shells into his Winchester. "But it's the biggest damn thing I've ever seen!"

There was a roar from the woods., so deep and powerful that Sullivan could feel it vibrate his back teeth. He thought back to the hoofprints and mighty claw mark in Utah and knew that if this was the same Summoner, then this was about to get real bad. He turned to Delilah. "Whatever happens, stay behind me."

"Shut up, Jake," she answered with false bravado. "I've seen these things before."

He gripped the BAR harder and checked his Power. "Not like this you haven't."

A huge shadow moved in the shadowed woods, crashing through the trees. A few of the surviving attackers screamed as they struggled to get out of its way. A sliver of moonlight revealed something at least ten feet tall, blocky and misshapen, before it disappeared back into the fog. Delilah gasped in shock. It came out of the thicket then, driving itself forward with its hooves and too-long arms that ended in three eviscerating claws, snorting and shaking its bull-like head, tearing up chunks of turf, angry at being ripped from its home and knowing that it couldn't go back until it fulfilled its master's wishes. It stopped at the edge of the trees, pawing the ground and smelling the air, until its four red eyes, bright with licking fire, turned to stare right through them. The Greater Summoned opened its mouth and bellowed its fury, flaming spit spraying in a wide arc as it slammed its hooves down rhythmically and prepared to charge.

"I seen bigger," Sullivan said.

The demon came at them.

The .50 opened up a second before the rest of them, a line of glowing tracers zipping past, but the demon launched itself high into the air, giant wings unfurling from its back as it rose. It sailed upward as the .50 tracked up, after, and finally into it, huge bullets striking and tearing off chunks of toughened flesh until the machine gun finally ran out of elevation. The demon seemed suspended for a split second, hanging before the moon, but it descended directly at them, roaring, streaming tendrils of smoke from where it had been hit.

It was heading right for the balcony and it would tear the house down around them when it hit. Sullivan could hear the wings snapping like a tattered sail as it neared the end of its ballistic arc, and he had an idea. Throwing the BAR over his shoulder, he grabbed his Power. *Don't fail me now.* He ran toward the broken window, automatically doing the math.

"Jake!" Delilah screamed after him as he put his boot on the windowsill and launched himself into space.

Pull. Mass. Density. Velocity. His Power knew what to do. The demon's eyes narrowed as it dove, claws thrown wide, seeking to rend his head from his body. Sullivan extended his hands just before impact and Spiked with all his might. Gravity suddenly multiplied twentyfold and swatted the demon from the sky, snapping its wings and pulling it straight down as if it had been grabbed by a great invisible hand.

Sullivan sailed past in midair as the creature jerked violently downward. He barely had time to use his Power before hitting the sidewalk. The concrete cracked as he struck and rolled away, physically unharmed, but with his Power scattered. He came right back to his feet, unslinging the BAR as he turned.

The demon had hit the fountain, crushing the blimp statue to bits. Water was squirting from broken pipes and nothing moved in the wreckage. Sullivan didn't know if that sudden impact would have put a Greater Summoned down or not, so he approached cautiously.

But not cautiously enough. The demon exploded from the wreckage with lightning speed and backhanded him across the yard.

"Down!" Mr. Garrett shouted as several hundred pounds of gold-plated blimp statue were hurled through the front entrance of the Grimnoir house in a sparkling shower of glass and splinters. Mr. Browning went spinning across the tile on his back.

Francis cranked the huge machine gun around and mashed the butterfly trigger. It roared and spat a fireball from the muzzle the size of a fifty-gallon drum. Huge bullets tore into the fountain, raising a cloud of concrete dust.

The bull monster came out of the hole with water steaming from its burning hide. It jerked as the bullets hit, black smoke shooting from the wounds. It grabbed the pulverized statue of the fat man, raised it overhead and threw it too.

Time seemed to slow to nothing as Faye watched the broken statue spiral directly toward the machine gun. Francis was still shooting, silhouetted in the red flashes, as giant brass cases hit the floor and bounced away, and she knew that he was going to die there, smashed to pulp, trying to put the demon down to save the rest of them. She Traveled.

Landing dangerously close to Francis, she whacked her nose on his rifle's stock, threw her arms around his waist just as the statue hit, and they were gone, landing ten feet to the side, as half the wall and the machine gun flew back into the grand piano in a terrible crash of hot steel and wood.

Francis was on top, squishing her into the carpet. His eyes were squeezed tightly shut. They opened slowly, surprised to be alive. "How—"

She didn't know. She'd never Traveled with anything other than the clothes on her back before, let alone a whole 'nother person. She checked, but nothing seemed melted together like Grandpa had warned her could happen. "I didn't know I could do that!" Faye exclaimed as she shoved him off into a pile of broken glass. She would have giggled except for the killer bull monster coming to get them. She wasn't where she'd expected to land, and had only made it halfway, which made a kind of sense, since she was moving a lot more weight than normal.

A hoof came out of the crater and slammed deep into the pavement of the walkway. The demon, billowing smoke from a dozen wounds like a broken chimney, lowered its head and roared. It was coming for them. The Grimnoir kept shooting, but the smaller bullets didn't even seem to hurt it. She didn't know much about demons, but she figured when it ran out of smoke, it would be dead, but by the time that happened, it would probably have killed them all.

Something grey shimmered through the remains of the front porch, and Heinrich materialized right in front of the monster. He shouted something insulting in German. The demon turned its eyes toward him and growled. "Yes. Here I am. Come! Come and get me." He shot it with a skinny-barreled pistol. A three-clawed hand swung and Heinrich turned blurry right before impact and it zipped through him. He ducked under the next attack, and rolled across the grass, his long coat flapping behind.

"What's he doing?" Faye asked.

"Buying us time," Francis answered as he pulled himself up.

Heinrich turned grey as the demon lowered its head, snorting in rage, and threw horns through him. The mean, but very brave man appeared on the other side, grimacing from the strain. "What happens when he runs out of Power?"

"He dies." Francis looked her right in the eyes, desperate. "Can you find its Summoner? If you can stop him, it'll weaken that thing."

Some of the others were moaning. Jane was moving between them like a white battlefield angel. Bullets were landing around them again as the remaining bad men renewed their attack. She turned to the woods, and knew that it would take a few jumps to find the man controlling the demon, and she would have to find him out there in the dark, surrounded by the same kind of men who'd killed Grandpa.

I'm not losing another family. She gripped Mr. Browning's .45 tight in her callused palm, picked a spot as far away as she dared, and was gone.

His chest was burning.

Sullivan sat up with a grunt. His back was pressed into the end of a ditch, and it took him a second to realize that the trench had been dug by his body. He shook his head to clear it as he pushed loose from the dirt. His shirt had been ripped open, and the hexagram scar on his chest was hot to the touch. The new Power was streaming through his tissues, giving his already hardened body extra strength.

His Power was still recovering from the massive Spike, but he could feel it building along with his anger. He checked the BAR. The rugged weapon was unharmed, etchings of durability glowing slightly in the dark. He had landed close to the woods, and could hear voices around him in the night as the Imperium men cautiously approached the house. They were all around him, shapes in the fog. There was gunfire to his left as one of them opened up.

In the distance, the Greater Summoned was battling with Heinrich. Behind the spinning forms, the first floor of the Grimnoir house had been laid open like a disemboweled animal. Delilah leapt from the second floor, screaming, dark hair whipping in the moonlight, and landed next to the demon. She charged it, fists raised. It was going to rip her apart, and it was his fault. "Damn it," he muttered, rising. *Now I'm mad.*

He came out of the trench, covered the short distance to the man shooting the submachine gun, raised the heavy BAR overhead, and shattered his skull. Before the body hit the ground, Sullivan had picked up the subgun, some weird Jap thing with the magazine sticking out the side, and raised it in one hand, looking for his next target. There were two more men crouched ahead of him, so he pulled the trigger, working it across them, bullets tearing into their backs as they jerked and twitched. The bolt flew forward, empty, and he hurled it into the darkness.

Shapes turned toward him, aware now that something terrible was in their midst. Sullivan shouldered the BAR and went to town.

Faye hit the ground running. She figured she might as well be moving while she checked her head map, since the place was covered in bad men with guns. But she didn't need to worry, because off to one side, Mr. Sullivan was killing the ever-livin' hell out of the Imperium men. They were dropping like alfalfa in front of a scythe.

If I was a demon Summoner, where would I hide? She scowled at the trees. The fog was wispy and moving, and it made it hard for even her grey eyes to see good.

"Kid!" A deep voice came from above. She looked up to the noise of beating wings, and instinctively ducked as an owl swooped past. "Hundred and twenty yards, due east!" Lance shouted through the bird. "Careful. There's three of 'em!"

She could Travel that in a few hops. Back at the house, the demon roared its fury, and she knew she didn't have much time.

Madi stalked back and forth, enraged. Several Grimnoir were tangling with the severely damaged Bull King. His goons were dropping like flies. The stinking unreliable Shadow Guards were still missing. And his watch was telling him that Toshiko was in position, and needed to get a target in the next few minutes before the Army pulled their heads out of their asses, realized they'd been attacked, and sent reinforcements to the Peace Ray. And he still didn't know if the Tesla device was here or not. "Damn it, Hiroyasu, you better get your shit together or I swear on the Chairman's eyes I'll cut your balls off."

The thin man was concentrating on his Power, sweat beading his brow. "One moment . . ."

Yutaka was focused on his demon. Madi stomped over to him, scowling. They should have been done by now. "This is fucking unacceptable," he shouted as he drew the Beast from his shoulder holster. "I'll take care of these Grimmy bastards myself."

He flinched as Yutaka's brains hit him in his good eye. The right side of his partner's head had split open like a dropped melon. Yutaka opened his mouth, like he was trying to say something, but nothing came out except a trickle of blood as he fell to the ground.

Madi wiped his face with his coat sleeve. A skinny, grey-eyed girl was standing there, big .45 raised in one quivering hand. "You!" they said at the same time, and she cranked off several fast shots, and by the time he raised his gun, she was gone.

"Son of a bitch!" Madi bellowed, feeling the burn of the hot slugs embedded in his chest. It was that Portagee's brat. "You Travelin' whore!"

Hiroyasu was crouched low, afraid. Madi's improved senses couldn't pick her up. He knelt down and checked Yutaka, but half the contents of his head had already slid onto the damp grass. His partner had only been able to sustain a single kanji of vitality on his body, and that wasn't near enough to withstand getting your skull emptied.

He'd lost an Iron Guard. He'd lost a brother. The Chairman was gonna be pissed.

There was a flash of movement to his side, and he raised his .50, thinking it was that little Traveler bitch coming back for more, but instead it was one of the Shadow Guard. The little man in black bowed deeply, noticing the dead Iron Guard. "Sir, I have bad news."

"What now?" Madi spat.

"Our other Shadow Guard was lost to the Grimnoir. He was—"

"Frankly, I don't give a shit. Did you find the device or not?"

"Not yet, Iron Guard. I will return."

"Wait. You're taking me with you. You want something done right, you gotta do it yourself." He turned to where his remaining Iron Guard was cowering. The .45 bullet lodged in his lung was pissing him off. Madi grabbed Hiroyasu by the collar and hoisted the tiny Lazarus off the ground. "Listen up. Yutaka was twice the man you were. I'm going in there myself, and there damn well better be some gawdamned zombies doing some killin' out here or I'm gonna come back and hurt you in ways you can't even imagine. Got it?"

"*Hai!*"

Madi dropped him on his ass, put his hand on the Shadow Guard's shoulder, and said, "Move it. I got murdering to attend to." The two of them Traveled, disappearing into the darkness.

***

The Greater Summoned was confused, weakened. It stumbled as Delilah punched it in the chest with a crack that could be heard across the entire peninsula. It went to one knee, and Delilah immediately stepped up onto its leg, threw herself high, and crashed her elbow down between its four eyes. Fire billowed around her, scorching her dress.

The demon slashed at her stomach, but she was too quick, and only a thin trail of blood flew from her abdomen as she leapt back, landing on her hands and knees fifteen feet away. The demon rose, smoke billowing from wounds too numerous to count. It wobbled, disoriented, no longer being whipped on by its Summoner.

"Hey." Sullivan reached up and tapped it on the shoulder. The demon turned and opened its mouth to roar at the new challenge. Jake calmly drove the muzzle of the BAR in between the flaming jaws and pulled the trigger. Smoke exploded from its eye sockets, nostrils, and ear holes as the .30-06 bullets ricocheted around inside its armored skull. He wrenched the gun free, raised his left hand, and Spiked gravity sideways.

The demon tumbled down the lawn. It rose, shaking, onto its claws and knees. Wasting no time, Delilah ran up its back, crouched between the crumpled wings and grabbed it by the horns. She surged her Power, screaming as every vein became visible in her straining arms, and wrenched the head violently back. Its neck snapped, and smoke shot like a broken steam line from its throat as flesh ripped. Delilah kept pulling, her teeth grinding together, as her Power drove her strength to Herculean levels.

The demon's head tore free and she lurched back. The body seemed to deflate, smoke rising and oil dripping from the stump as it sank to the ground. Delilah raised the bull head over her like a trophy and shook it. "Take that, you magic cow son of a bitch!" She threw it over her shoulder as she appeared to shrink, her Power exhausted.

Sullivan stepped over the body. Heinrich was struggling to get up, splattered with blood and smoking oil, his grey coat in tatters, but he was grinning from ear to ear. "Damn fine work, my friends."

"You okay?" Sullivan shouted at Delilah, concerned. She was panting, exhausted, filthy, and injured, but still gave him a broad smile and a wink. They'd done it. They'd survived. And Sullivan felt a huge weight lift from his chest. Then a man in black appeared at Delilah's side and drove a sword deep into her guts.

"Jake?" Her eyes widened, one hand stretched imploringly toward Sullivan. She fell away in a flash of red as the ninja twisted and jerked the blade free. Sullivan screamed her name, bringing up the BAR, but the barrel was blocked by an open hand that hit like iron, and he was staring into the blank white eye of his older brother.

Bull King

Chapter 16

As an eminent pioneer in the realm of high frequency currents, I congratulate you on the great success of your life's work, but I am of the sad belief that your Peace Ray may have been inappropriately named.

—Albert Einstein,
Letter to Nikola Tesla
for Tesla's 75th Birthday, 1931

Mar Pacifica, California

"BEEN A LONG TIME, JAKE," his brother said, still blocking the rifle barrel.

Sullivan looked past the ruined face to where Delilah was lying on her back, hands pressed against her stomach, blood leaking between her fingers. "Go to hell, Matty," he snarled, reaching for his Power and Spiking it hard.

Magic crashed against magic. "It's *Madi* now." His teeth gnashed together behind ruined lips as he fired his own Power. Gravity collided and ruptured around them. "Matthew was my old name. My weak name. I had to take a new one as an Iron Guard. Remember where it came from?"

"Yeah . . . Jimmy had a hard time with t's." The destroyed body of the Summoned and the rubble around it fell into the sky. Delilah screamed as she was shoved across the lawn. Heinrich was heading their way when he suddenly tumbled backward, flailing, toward the house. *I forgot how strong he was.*

"I got baptized in the blood of the innocent. The only decent

Sullivan there's ever been." Madi's tie was whipping around his face, torn back and forth, as the pull of the Earth shifted. "Our brother deserved better."

"You think Jimmy would want this?" Sullivan hissed as the ground underfoot began to sink. Water from the broken pipes spun weightless around them. His Power had already been used hard on the demon and he could feel it weakening.

"He was too good and pure and dumb to know what he wanted." Madi didn't even seem to feel the strain. Heat was radiating from his body as dozens of kanji burned magic. "But he was *strong*. We all were, but we gave our lives to protect the pathetic. They used us. And how'd they thank us? You saved a thousand lives, and you come home to what? Going to prison because you tried to keep some Active kid from getting lynched?"

"Like you would have cared." His pulse was pounding inside his skull. It was almost like he could see the line of Power stretching from his soul to the center of the Earth, and it was flickering bad. He was almost done.

"They didn't even waste a Healer to fix my face."

"Whole unit only had a few Healers. They did just enough to keep you from dying. It's called triage, dummy," Jake said. Madi had too much Power. With the forces buffeting them, the first to slip would be crushed. "You were always the ugly one anyways."

Madi laughed. "And you were always supposed to be the smart one." Suddenly, Madi dropped his Power, but rather than being smashed by the sudden increase in pressure, his body flared in strength like a Brute as he took the hit. The dirt around them exploded outward in a shower. Sullivan staggered back, surprised. "Who's the smart one now?" Madi asked as he slugged Sullivan in the face.

Sullivan rocked back. The blow rattled his thickened bones. Madi kept coming, hitting him over and over and over again, moving faster than was humanly possible. It was like being worked over by a meat hammer. "See, Jake. I'm the strongest there is. I've got the magic of ten Actives now. What you got?" He knocked Sullivan's return punch aside with one casual forearm.

Sullivan ducked a hook, falling on his butt, then jerked up the BAR and fired. The magazine had mostly been expended on the Summoned, but at least five rounds struck Madi in the chest, exiting his back in gouts of meat and fabric. His brother fell, crashing hard into the ground.

Sullivan lay there, gasping, bleeding. His head was swimming from the beating. He had just killed his own blood.

Then Madi got up. "Ahhh . . . yeah. Felt that one." Blood was pouring from the holes in his chest. Sullivan scrambled back as Madi strode toward him. "Like I was sayin', I'm the strongest." He slammed a boot into Sullivan's chest, rolling him hard. "I can see that pissant little Healin' spell on your chest. You think that makes you a big man or something?" He booted him again. "Shit . . . I got *five* of those."

He managed to get to his hands and knees but Madi's next kick landed in his ribs and lifted him several feet off the ground.

"Madi is here!" Faye shouted as she appeared in what was left of the foyer.

"We know," Garrett said, pointing with one bloodied hand toward where a maelstrom of water, dirt, concrete, and fog was swirling across what had been the lawn. It was terrible to behold. Somewhere inside there were the two titans, slamming each other with Powers beyond comprehension.

Heinrich appeared, carrying Delilah's limp form in his arms. She seemed so very small and there was blood all over the German's coat. "Jane!" he shouted. "Help!" He set her down gently where the piano had been.

"One second!" Jane replied. She was crouched next to Mr. Browning, who was bleeding profusely from a bullet wound to his neck. "Keep pressure on her, Heinrich."

"Help the girl," Browning whispered, his teeth stained red. "I'm fine."

"No offense, John, but shut your yap and don't tell me how to do my job," Jane responded calmly, her hands glowing like molten gold.

Lance shrugged past Faye, working the action on his Winchester. "Undead are coming. All those assholes we killed once are back up and moving this way fast."

Heinrich closed his eyes and let out a long string of something that Faye could only assume was profanity. "Zombies. They've got a damn Necro . . . a Lazarus!"

Grandpa's Bible teachings hadn't been very good, but Faye didn't remember any of the dead people who came back to life in the New Testament going insane with a desire to kill like the radio shows said this kind did. On the other hand she'd slept through a lot of masses. "I got the one with the demon. If I shoot the man with the zombies, will that make the magic stop?" she asked.

"*Nein*. Undead are different," Heinrich said as he shoved what had once been the living room curtains against Delilah's wound. "Their spirits can't leave their bodies. They have been chained forever."

"How do we stop them?" Faye asked. The same show on the radio had made it sound like you could just shoot them in the head and they'd leave you alone, but she knew that those programs were just make-believe. This was real.

"You can't. You just damage them until they can no longer move, but that's difficult when they are still sane and have guns. How many, Lance?"

"Probably twenty undead. I don't know how many alive."

"More than we can handle," Heinrich stated with grim finality. "The Lazarus will whisper to them that the only way to end the pain is to destroy us. Poor bastards don't even realize they're dead yet." The way the others acted when he said that made Faye certain that the German was their expert on zombies.

The storm of flying debris finally stopped, and everything instantly fell as gravity returned to normal. All of them turned to see who had won, and sadly all they saw was Mr. Madi kicking Mr. Sullivan across the yard like a child's ball. Behind the two giants was a crowd of mangled bodies, running right for them.

The dead men were shrieking and crying, bones visible, flesh hanging off in strips where the slugs had hit, eyes bulging out of shattered skulls, bullet holes fresh and puckered in drained skin, white shards sticking out of broken limbs, and somehow she knew that they could still feel it all, every terrible unending ounce of hurt, and all those dead men held her and her friends responsible. The dead lifted their guns and Faye's insides turned to water.

Madi grabbed Sullivan by the throat and jerked him from the ground. "Hell, Jake," his brother said, punching him in the stomach, "I had this all built up in my head like you were gonna be a challenge.

This is just like when we were kids." Sullivan blinked through the blood and tears. He grabbed Madi by the tie, pulled him forward and rammed his elbow into the side of his head. Madi dropped him and stepped back, rubbing his face, grinning savagely. "That's more like it."

Sullivan stood shakily, spit a blob of blood, and raised his fists. "You always were a bully."

"You ain't seen nothing yet," Madi said. He paused as his watch spoke to him with a woman's voice. He lifted it and listened. "Hell . . . Fun as this has been, I'm about to fry this whole area with a Peace Ray. You're distracting me from my mission. You seen a piece of a Tesla device around here?"

Sullivan stepped forward, put his weight into it, and swung a big right at Madi's face. Madi dodged it so quickly that the air whistled around him. He responded by clubbing Sullivan effortlessly to the ground. "Guess not." Sullivan gasped as a heavy boot slammed onto his spine, pinning him down. There was a popping of snaps, a creak of a leather harness, and finally a loud metallic click as a hammer was cocked.

"So long, Jake. Any last words?"

"Mama always liked me best," Sullivan grunted, sputtering out a bloody laugh.

Madi aimed the Beast at the back of Jake's head. If he had more time, he'd let his brother know just how much this moment meant to him. He could actually *feel*. It was a bittersweet victory, and the old, weak, sickly part of him was screaming *no*, but he pushed that part back down into the deep well where he kept it chained in black poisoned waters. He pulled the trigger.

Then there was a snap of air and a pair of grey eyes shining in the dark as Jake vanished.

The bullet dug a .50-caliber hole in the ground. Madi looked up at the mansion, a snarl parting his ruined lips. "I'm getting *sooo* tired of her . . ."

Hiroyasu's zombies were passing him, charging blindly toward the house. The morons didn't even realize they were dead yet. Some of them were shooting, screaming, bones sticking out their faces, or dragging their intestines behind them in long steaming trails. *About damn time.*

A few of the living goons approached him cautiously, carrying their new Arisaka subguns, following the zombies. Those were the brave and stupid. The cowards in the ranks had probably bolted and run as soon as they'd realized he wasn't about to waste any perfectly good corpses. He glared at the remaining men. "What? We've almost got th—" A rifle bullet hit him in the shoulder, tore through his flesh until it struck his collarbone and shattered. He grimaced as the fragments tore a dozen separate wound channels through his flesh and a chunk of bone pierced his heart. "Damn it." Even he had his limits, and time was almost up. Toshiko was yelling at him that they needed to fire soon or risk discovery. No matter what, the Imperium couldn't afford to be implicated. It was time to finish this.

He followed the blood trail of the dead mob, murder in his wounded heart.

Francis worked the bolt of his Enfield. He'd plugged Madi square with an .30-06 soft-point, but the Iron Guard didn't seem to notice. He fired the remaining rounds at the closest zombie as fast as he could work the bolt. He was an excellent shot, since Black Jack had taught him well, and he pulverized the undead body, but it just kept coming. He used his Power to reach out and pick up chunks of concrete as heavy as he could lift, and started hurling them at the undead.

Garrett grabbed him on the shoulder, breaking his concentration right as he put a chunk of rebar through a zombie's face. "Fall back!" he shouted in his ear. Garrett hefted a BAR and laid down fire as he walked backwards. Francis took up his empty rifle and ran.

Faye and Sullivan popped into existence so close that he almost tripped over them. "Help me!" she cried. "He's too big."

He grabbed one of Sullivan's arms and pulled. *Jesus. He weighs a ton.* Garrett grabbed the other and they pulled his body further inside. The zombies would be on them in seconds.

The Heavy stirred, his bloody face scrunched up, and then he pushed Francis away. "We got to get out of here."

"No kidding. Zombies!" Francis jerked his head toward the front.

He shook his head. "Peace Ray . . . Browning! You got to get your people out of here. Madi's gonna fire the Peace Ray at us."

Jane had just left him and moved to help Delilah. Browning was holding himself up by leaning on the banister, looking pale and weak. "Are you certain?"

"Yeah. We ain't got much time."

Browning nodded. "Lance, get everyone to the tunnels."

Jane was starting to use her Power on Delilah. "No time, girl," Lance said as he leaned down and scooped the Brute into his arms. "We got to get deep underground. Now! Francis, send out your family's Summoned to slow them down. Everybody follow me."

Francis complied, twisting his ring. He knew that they wouldn't last more than seconds against maddened undead, but that might make all the difference. "I—" but then he was knocked aside as something fell from the balcony above and landed in their midst. He scrambled back as a hulking slab of a man turned toward him, half his face a ragged mass of scar tissue, soaked in blood, white eye gleaming. "Madi!"

His movements were a blur of fists and magic. Sullivan and Faye hit the far wall. Lance and Delilah went flying over a broken couch. Jane was knocked sprawling. Garrett had time to lift his automatic rifle and fire a single round before Madi swatted him down the hallway. Heinrich went grey as he charged, but Madi raised his hands and force exploded outward in a wave. Francis found himself falling down the floor until the wall rushed up to meet him. He bounced off the stone, screaming in pain as his shoulder popped.

"This the best you got, Grimmies?" Madi taunted, drawing a huge revolver from inside his ruined coat. He jerked suddenly as a chunk of meat exploded from his side, then again, as John Moses Browning pummeled him with an Auto-5 shotgun. Madi spun, firing his huge gun once, and Browning fell, crashing back through the banister and onto the stairs.

"John!" Lance's .44 flew out of the holster in a speed draw. He opened fire, slamming six rounds into Madi's chest, neck, and head in a continuous roar. Madi pointed and Lance fell upward, crashing through the chandelier and into the beams of the roof. Madi held him there for a moment, as he rolled something around inside his mouth and spit out a deformed bullet, then he jerked his hand back, and Lance fell, bellowing, until he hit the floor with a sickening thud.

Francis spotted a poker lying by the fireplace, concentrated, and launched it across the room like a spear. It impaled Madi through the bicep and deep into the chest, pinning his gun arm to his side. Francis started looking for something else to telekinetically grab when Madi unleashed another Spike, disrupting gravity again, and Francis found himself crammed upside down inside the fireplace when it subsided.

He crawled out of the ashes, coughing. Zombies were scrambling through the broken walls, screaming with pain that would never end. The servants, in tuxedos and maids' uniforms, collided against the undead, smoke and oil breaking against blood and bone.

A tiny man dressed entirely in black appeared next to Madi. "Iron Guard!" he shouted. "I've searched everywhere. The Tesla device is not present."

Madi was occupied dragging the poker out of his body. It made a sickening grating noise as it cleared his ribs. The tip came out with a chunk of tissue wrapped around it. He threw it on the floor with a clatter. "What a waste." He lifted his watch. "Toshiko, give me a minute to get out of here, then scrub it off the map." Madi rested his blood-soaked hand over the ninja's shoulders, started to speak, then paused. "Hang on . . ." his face crinkled as if he had a strange smell stuck in his nostrils. He walked over to where Jane was unconscious on the floor. "What do we have here? A Healer? You assholes actually have your own Healer?"

"Get away from her," Garrett gasped as he struggled to rise, blood streaming down his face.

Madi reached over and grabbed a fistful of blonde hair. He dragged Jane through the broken glass. "You know how *rare* these are?" He was talking to the Shadow Guard. "This should make up for losing an Iron Guard." He seemed to be having serious difficulty breathing. "Get us out of here."

Garrett had pulled himself up the wall with a trail of bloody handprints. "*Leave her alone!*" he shouted, and the voice that came out of him wasn't the voice of a man, but a roar of thunder. It was like a commandment from a burning bush and Francis cringed as the words struck him to the very fiber of his being.

Madi hesitated, his brow creased as he fought the Influence. "Damn . . . You're good." Then he raised his revolver and shot Garrett. The little man went down hard. The Shadow Guard laid his hands on Madi and Jane and the three of them Traveled right out of the mansion.

"Jane!" Garrett screamed. "Oh God no! No!"

Francis dragged himself across the floor. The zombies were still coming, and if they didn't kill the Grimnoir, the Peace Ray surely would. They only had one chance. "We've got to get to the tunnels," he cried.

Lick Hill, California

TOSHIKO'S SHADOW GUARD were efficient and that filled her with pride. Bodies were strewn from one end of the command center to the other. The vast majority had died unaware that they were even under attack. She stepped over a headless corpse and took a seat in the observation area. The coordinates had already been dialed in. Unfortunately, all indications were that there was only enough energy for one brief firing, which would be more than sufficient to burn the entire town of Mar Pacifica from the world, but she had been hoping that there would be enough to cut a swath of destruction all the way to San Francisco. It seemed like a waste to her to use such a mighty weapon against so few, when it could be used to slaughter thousands.

But she wasn't in charge . . . *Yet.*

One of the men appeared at her side. "Is the evidence planted?"

He nodded, obviously not liking taking orders from a woman, but the Chairman had personally put her in charge, so that was just too bad. "We have used the guards' rifles to shoot the anarchists. Their manifesto was left at the entrance for all to see. Masaharu has painted their symbol on the doors using the blood of the technicians."

"Excellent touch," she answered. Framing militant Actives had been Madi's idea. The Bolshevik-funded anarchists had been a constant, yet minor, thorn in the Americans' side for decades, though they had never dared an operation of this immensity. A few known agitators had been easy enough to find in San Francisco. Once the news of their taking over a Peace Ray reached the wires, a violent response against all American Actives would be inevitable. The more pressure that was brought against Actives, the more dissension it would bring, the better it would be for the Imperium. She had to admit his plan was remarkable in its simplicity.

She checked her mirror. Her Traveler had exhausted his Power getting Madi, the other Iron Guard, and a blonde woman back to their trucks. She was disappointed to see that she had lost one of her fellow Shadow Guard. Travelers were irreplaceable. The Chairman would be displeased.

They would be out of the kill zone in a matter of minutes. "Charge the tower," she ordered.

Sullivan had taken a beating, but he was still strong enough to carry both Delilah and Lance, one under each arm. Heinrich had Garrett, while Francis had thrown the surprisingly frail weight of John Moses Browning over his shoulders in a fireman's carry.

Behind them, a butler's limbs were torn off, one by one, and smoke from the destroyed Summoned obscured the first floor. Faye brought up the rear, carrying Browning's shotgun. She blasted a rushing undead in the knee, then slammed the kitchen door shut just as it slid into the wood with a crash.

Heinrich took the lead, Garrett's arm thrown over one shoulder, his shoes dragging limp, leaving blood splatter across the pale tiles. Heinrich kicked open a door and started down. Faye was stronger than she looked, and shoved a table against the door as the zombies crashed into it.

"*Schnell*! Hurry!" Heinrich shouted. Francis stumbled after them, his arms slick with blood. Browning wasn't moving. Francis was so scared he could barely breathe.

Madi was in no shape to drive, so he sat in the passenger seat of the truck as the Shadow Guard took them up to their maximum speed of fifty miles an hour. He'd made Hiroyasu, that cowardly bag of piss, ride in the back. The handful of surviving men probably wouldn't make it to the other truck in time, and that was if the undead didn't lose it and pull them apart, but that was too bad. They hadn't particularly impressed him, so no great loss. The Peace Ray would take care of the evidence. He could always recruit more.

The Grimnoir had managed to hurt him bad. Every one of his kanji was earning its keep now, forcing his heart to keep pumping, moving oxygen to his brain, and knitting together broken blood vessels. He was starving. Getting hurt always made him hungry. *I could really go for a good meatloaf and a cold Coca-Cola . . .*

The Healer stirred, came awake, and screamed her heart out when she saw him. She started thrashing, which he found annoying, and the driver jerked the truck when she struck his face. So Madi reached over and knocked the hell out of her with the back of his hand. Her face struck the dash. "That'll leave a mark," he said. "Keep squealing in my ear and I'll pop you a good one next time."

She folded her arms tight and seemed to shrink into the seat, trying not to cry. "What are you going to do with me?"

"You'll be lucky if it's *with* you and not *to* you," he snorted. "You can start earning your keep by fixing the hole in my heart. You got any Power left after that, I've got one lung full of blood."

Her eyes grew defiant. "I'll never help the likes of you."

She had a spine. He could appreciate that. "Bitch, you heard of Unit 731?" That scared her. Everybody had heard about them. "Yeah . . . You know what those weirdos would give to have a Mender to experiment on? Especially a soft little thing like you . . ." He rubbed one hand down her bruised cheek and she flinched away. "So, unless you want them carving on you, you'll do what I say."

He gave her a second to think about it while he checked his watch. They should be clear of the blast. "Toshiko, light 'em up."

"It will be done," she responded from fifty miles away. "Accelerators are at full, but that's barely seven percent of maximum. Lazy Americans can't be bothered to even maintain their equipment. Firing in two minutes."

"It'll do," he said.

"We are on our way out." There was relief in her words.

He couldn't blame her. The Imperium's recent experiments into ray technology showed that the very air around a beam could kill or sicken you. Some sort of invisible poison got in the atmosphere and it would actually damage your cells. He'd once seen Unit 731 tie a bunch of prisoners to stakes at various distances along the path of a small beam, and they timed everyone to see how long it took them to die, either burned immediately or throwing their lungs up and dying covered in black blisters. It hadn't been pretty. But he wasn't worried about that now. He'd got himself a new pet Healer.

***

The stairs were steep. Sullivan's big boots could barely find purchase on the narrow stones. The muscles in his arms were burning almost like the magical fire on top of his chest. He had Delilah clamped under one arm, and he hoped that she would hang on. She'd lost so much blood that he was terrified to even look at her. Lance was short, weighed a ton, and was completely unconscious, and therefore useless. His auto rifle was still banging back and forth on its sling against his back, but he was too worried about zombies following them down to drop it.

An electric-battery torch had been stashed at the top of the stairs, and all he could see was a narrow pale beam swinging back and forth ahead as Heinrich led them into the bowels of the earth. Delilah cried out in pain as he slipped and hit the damp wall. "It'll be okay, baby. We're gonna make it," he whispered.

They kept going. Behind him someone tripped and cursed. They needed to stop and tend to the wounded. Keeping Delilah moving was a death sentence, just as surely as stopping and waiting for the Peace Ray to end them. They had to be a couple hundred feet under the ocean cliffs by now, and he didn't know if that would be enough. "How much further?"

The rich kid, Francis, was a few feet away. "Almost there," he gasped.

Not good enough. If this ray had a fraction of the energy as the one they'd hit Berlin with, there wouldn't be near enough dirt overhead to save them. They hadn't called it the Peace Ray then. The Brits had christened it Tesla's Sickle, but his boys weren't poetic. They had simply called it the Death Ray. Kinetic energy had shattered everything around the impact zone and turned the Reichstag into a blackened pit, but it was the wave of carnage that had radiated out from it that had done the real killing. Sullivan had seen the bodies like broken charcoal statues frozen wherever they'd been when the destroying angel had come. One snap of light and a whole city had died.

The heat alone would be enough to steam them like lobsters in this tunnel. "Move faster!" Sullivan bellowed to nobody in particular.

There was a noise ahead, water crashing against stone, and behind, the hate-filled screams of the dead, and under his arm, a rasping breath as Delilah's life slipped further away, and over everything came the crackling hum as the Peace Ray hit, light filled the universe, and for the first time in many years, Sullivan prayed for a miracle.

The Peace Ray discharged at fifteen minutes after two o'clock in the morning. It was not an impressive sight from Lick Hill, even if any of the crew had been alive to appreciate it. In fact, with the warning klaxons disabled by the Shadow Guard, the only sign of the impending destruction was a single match flicker of white as particles were hurled up a thousand-foot copper spiral to a terrible velocity and flung to the west.

The simple fused dynamite explosion at the base of the tower a moment later possessed not even the tiniest glimmer of the Peace Ray's power, but it would leave a few steel girders twisted, delicate Cog-designed electronics shattered, and the costly weapon disabled.

But by the time that was done the Peace Ray had already struck the small coastal town of Mar Pacifica. Only the undead were walking at the impact point, their skeletons briefly visible through their flesh like a perfect X-ray frozen in time before being swept away in cleansing fire.

Even at only seven-percent power the flash was seen as far away as Sacramento.

Toshiko

Chapter 17

It seemed like a good idea at the time.

—William M. Jardine,
United States Secretary of Agriculture,
after the Magical Weather Alteration Board backfired and resulted in record droughts across the Midwest, 1927

New York City, New York

CORNELIUS GOULD STUYVESANT awoke to grim news. One of his servants had roused him before dawn, jabbering on so excitedly that he'd been forced to pick up a lamp from his bedside and hurl it at the man to get him to slow down. The crash had startled his mistress awake.

"Mar Pacifica?" he'd asked. "Destroyed?"

"Completely *gone*," his retainer had said, holding his handkerchief against the swelling lump on his forehead.

"Has there been any word from my family estate?" Technically, it wasn't his anymore. His son had left it to his grandson in his will, and the willful, disobedient young man, who reminded Cornelius so much of himself at that age, would have nothing to do with him.

"No. The whole area was burned instantly. They say there are hundreds dead."

It took him a moment to organize his thoughts around that. He could not possibly care less about hundreds dead when there was only *one* person that mattered in Mar Pacifica. He threw off the sheets. "Egads, man! Awake my staff. Awake my guards!" He'd lumbered out of his bedroom suite, screaming orders at his subordinates, temporarily forgetting his self-imposed quarantine. "Get my Healer! Call the President!"

His staff had quadrupled in number since his encounter with Harkeness, and he'd made all of them wear surgical masks. A sea of white masks watched him as he strode down the hall, ranting, still in his silk nightclothes. He'd risked his health, his good name, and his very life to curse the man that had brought division into his family. So soon after Pershing's death, could it be possible that it had all been for nothing? Could his once favorite heir be dead? This was not what he'd intended, not what he'd intended at all.

He had to make haste for California. He had to see with his own eyes. It was a good thing that he had the world's fastest airship at his disposal. "Fetch the *Tempest*!"

San Francisco, California

THE PALE HORSE stood on the flat hotel roof, along with about two dozen others, watching the smoke rise from the south. It was a tall enough building that it afforded him a good view of the blackened horizon. The sunrise was hazy and the sky to the east was the color of dark wine.

"Unbelievable," Isaiah muttered from his side.

"Believe it," Harkeness answered with a heavy heart. "Let this strengthen your resolve, old friend."

He had met his associate the previous day at the air station. Isaiah had a valid reason for being in the area, and with Pershing dead, Harkeness could not resist a visit himself. He had family in the area to call upon. The two had discussed their best options over a glass of wine late into the night. There was one final obstacle to overcome, but it was a decidedly difficult one, and one glass of wine had turned into several, and he'd retired, exhausted, far too late. Only a few hours later, a brilliant beam of light had pierced the curtains of his room. It had been so bright that at first he'd thought someone had discharged a pan of flash powder next to closed eyes. It had awakened the entire city.

And the dawn had brought this. A fog of ash hung over the land. Fires still burned in the distance. He could taste the smoke, and it filled his heart with a bitter regret. He had not intended it to be this way.

"What could it have been?" a fellow traveler asked another.

"Perhaps a comet fell to earth," a stately older woman replied. "I've read of such things."

"Balderdash," said a man with thick whiskers. "It's an act of war!"

"But who?" someone else sputtered.

"The Kaiser has come for his revenge, I tell you!" the man shouted.

There was very little panic. He'd come to marvel at how pragmatic Americans were. Harkeness did not join in the conversations of the other hotel guests. He recognized the work of a Peace Ray, and knew that there was only one within range. The sheer audacity of the operation impressed him. The fact that it had happened to destroy one of only twenty Grimnoir safe houses in the country narrowed down the list of culprits even further. He did not need to share his thoughts with Isaiah since he could tell that the man was Reading them anyway. He made no effort to disguise them. It was quicker that way.

What now? Isaiah sent. *We'll have to find another way to track down Southunder.*

He was right. Timing was essential. For as impressive as the scorched hills were in the distance, the Peace Ray paled in comparison to the awesome destructive might of the Geo-Tel. Once the Chairman had it in his grasp, there would be no hesitation. It would be used and that would change everything.

Harkeness pulled something out of his coat pocket and held it up for Isaiah to see. The gold and black ring appeared dull in the red light. *There is one way.*

Southunder is too suspicious. That's why Pershing picked him.

The Pale Horse nodded. Southunder was a sly one, but he was also loyal to a fault. He'd had a falling out with the Society, but he had a problem with their leadership, not their mission. He would always be faithful to that. *He will answer the call.*

It's too risky. Isaiah shook his head. *Spook him and we'll never find it.*

If that is the worst that happens then we just have to wait for the Chairman's Cogs to reverse-engineer the final piece.

Isaiah gave a sardonic laugh. A few other guests scowled at him, and someone muttered something about *impertinent* negroes. He paid them no mind. He'd endured far worse in his life. *I'd prefer not to die of old age in the time it'll take Unit 731 to decipher the genius of the greatest Cog that's ever lived. Tesla may have been crazy, but that man sure could build some mighty things. Why are you suddenly so rash? It isn't like you. You are normally the patient one . . .* "Wait . . ." Isaiah said aloud, Reading deeper. *You lost someone out there? Why didn't you say so?*

He clenched the Grimnoir ring in his bony fist. *It was a small sacrifice to pay for our duty.*

It's a shame when you outlive your own descendants. I'm sorry.

Harkeness frowned. *Damn you and your pity. Let's finish the mission. Call for Southunder. He will come.*

"Very well . . ." Isaiah said, turning to face him. "We can—" He grimaced, raising his hands to his head as if a terrible headache had come upon him. Harkeness could see inside his friend's body, all the inner workings, blood moving, organs working, bone, pressure, even impulses of the nervous system, but he saw no reason for the pain, and knew that it came from Isaiah's Power. That he could not see. Harkeness took him by the sleeve and led him away from the crowd.

"What is it?" he whispered.

There is a place. It has been ringed with focal spells. They're calling for help. "Pershing's knights. Some of them are alive . . ."

Harkeness looked back to the distant wastes and felt a flicker of hope.

Mar Pacifica, California

"Faye? Can you hear me?"

It was pitch black, so completely dark that even her grey eyes couldn't see a thing. The air was wet. The ground was damp and slick and cold under her side. Hands were on her arm. "Francis?"

"Yes, it's me. Are you injured?"

Her head really hurt. When the blinding light had come down the stairs, she'd fallen. She couldn't remember much after that. Her hair felt sticky and there was a huge throbbing lump on the back of her head. "I'm okay, I guess." She resisted the urge to sit up, because she had a fear that she'd hit her face on something. It felt tight and scary in the dark.

She checked her brain map and recoiled in shock. Other than a few separated spaces of air and salt water, everything else around them was solid rock as far as she could feel. The tunnel had collapsed behind them. They were in a tiny cave. Waves crashed right below. She backed out of her head, brought her knees up to her chest, and held them there as she rocked back and forth. She didn't like being somewhere she couldn't Travel out of.

There was a rustle in the dark as something heavy crawled toward her and Francis. "How's the kid?" Lance asked.

Francis sounded relieved. "I'm glad you're awake, Lance."

Hearing his gruff voice made her feel better. The last she'd seen of Lance, he'd been falling from the ceiling. "Fine," Faye answered. "What happened?"

"Hell if I know," he grunted. "I'm in bad shape. Feel like I went twenty rounds with Jack Johnson. Status, Francis?"

"Browning is the worst. He was wearing one of those tight-woven silk vests he'd been working on, so the bullet didn't go through, but I think a bunch of his ribs are broken. He's having a real hard time breathing."

"Doesn't Jane have any Power left?" Lance asked.

Francis swallowed so hard that Faye could hear it. "Jane's *gone*, Lance."

Another voice came from Faye's other side. "Madi took her." It was Mr. Garrett. He sounded so sad that it broke Faye's heart. "We've got to get her back."

"We will, Dan, we will. You injured?"

There was a long pause. "I'll live." She couldn't see him in the dark, but there was something wrong with the way he sounded. Mr. Garrett was in a lot of pain, and she couldn't tell if it was his body or his heart that was more hurt.

There was a thump from above. "The stairs are blocked." Heinrich said. "I tried to Fade through the rocks, but I'd run out of Power before I made it very far."

Faye could have told him that. All the rock around them was making her real nervous. "Where's Delilah?"

"Over there," Lance said moving in the dark, not realizing that it was so dark that it didn't matter. "Sullivan's got her."

"Is she—"

Lance cut her off. "Don't you mind her, Faye. She'll be just fine, so don't you worry." He was a terrible liar. "We need to figure out how to get out of here. Anybody got a damn light?"

"Broken," Heinrich said. There was a tiny flicker of flame as he tumbled open a lighter. "This is all I've got." It was so feeble that Faye could barely see Heinrich, let alone anything around him.

"There were some crates stashed down here with supplies," Francis said. "But the roof caved in over them."

"Never a Torch around when you need one," Lance muttered. "I already used my ring. If there's anyone else in the Society within range, they'll come, but I don't know how long that'll be. Command was supposed to be sending somebody to replace the General, and if we're lucky, they might already be in San Francisco, but they might not."

"If it was a full-power blast from the Peace Ray, then San Francisco's gone," Heinrich said. "But I doubt that, since we're still alive."

"Ideas?"

"We wait for low tide and some of us swim for it," Heinrich said. "We go for help to get the wounded out."

"I don't think Browning's got that long," Francis said. "The water's still high. I can swim for it now. I'm a strong swimmer."

"And you'll drown or get smashed on a rock," Lance said. "No."

"What is this place?" Faye asked.

"It's been here forever. Everyone from pirates to bootleggers has used it over the years," Francis said. "My father had Mexican booze brought in this way and sold it in the city. It wasn't like we needed the money, but I think he just liked the excitement. When the tide goes out you can bring a little boat right to the rocks outside and wade up here. I can make it now, Lance," he pleaded. "It's only partially submersed. There are plenty of spots to come up for air. I used to play down here as a kid."

Faye went back to her head map. The way out to the ocean was filled with crashing water. There were no spots to come up for air. Either it was a lot tighter than Francis remembered, or he was lying, willing to risk almost certain death to try and get help for his injured friends.

"I don't know . . ." Lance muttered, tempted to believe his young friend. "Hang on. Let me check on Browning first. If he's got time, we'll wait for low tide, if not, you can go for it and risk your fool neck." Faye noticed that he didn't mention needing to check on Delilah and that filled her with dread.

"You did the best you could . . ." Lance had told him softly. "I'm sorry . . . I've got to check on the others."

Sullivan held Delilah in his arms and rocked her back and forth. "No . . ." he finally said aloud, long after the Grimnoir had left his side. *I failed her.* He began to weep.

When the light had come he'd fallen along with the others. The energy of the Peace Ray had briefly snuffed out consciousness like a candle before a gust of wind. He'd come to, not sure if seconds, minutes, or hours had passed, and found Delilah at his side, one arm thrown over her protectively. Her breathing had grown much weaker.

In the pitch black it was impossible to check her wound. Her skin was clammy and cold to the touch. He'd left a pack of matches in his room and cursed himself for not picking them up when he'd grabbed his guns.

The Grimnoir had begun to stir and he'd screamed for help, for a light, for anything. The German had joined him first and produced a small cigarette lighter. The flickering light had revealed a grisly wound. The ninja had opened her up from belly button to pelvis and her insides were exposed like a tangle of purple snakes. They were kneeling in a puddle of blood.

He'd pulled the trench knife from his belt. There was no time. "What are you doing?" Heinrich had hissed.

"I need your coat," he'd answered. The German had been splattered with the Greater Summoned's blood-oil. The light vanished for a moment as Heinrich complied without question. Lance had joined them a moment later, realizing immediately that he was attempting the same thing that he and Browning had tried to save Sullivan's life.

Sullivan had been meticulous as he'd cut perfectly straight lines into her abdomen. The design was perfect. The healing spell a copy of the one on his own chest, a proximity to the geometric thing that was the living Power, and then he'd burned the second triangle over it with the smoking oil from Heinrich's coat. Then they'd waited.

Nothing had happened.

Heinrich left to check on the others. Lance had a box of matches and struck one to replace the light. He burned it down until it hurt his fingers, and then he did another, and another. Finally they sat there in the shadows. It was there in the dark that her breathing had become weaker and weaker, until it sounded like a bare snore.

Now Sullivan was alone, holding Delilah tight against him. While his mark was burning, repairing his body, hers was as cold as the cooling space inside her chest. *Why? Why didn't it work?* He had done everything right, but his magic was weak. He was useless. He knew more about magic than almost anyone else in the world, but even then, he was blind, stupid, a helpless child playing a man's game.

He'd actually seen the Power, not as some nebulous idea, but as a creature that lived and fed through them, but he didn't understand it, and his failure was going to end the life of the only woman he'd ever had feelings for.

"Please, baby, please hang on," he whispered. "If you can hear me, you need to touch the Power. I drew the spell for you. It'll start fixing you. Come on. Reach for it. Please. Please. You can do it."

Not like this. I need you. I love you.

Delilah stopped breathing.

And just like that, it was over.

A dam of rage broke loose inside of him. Sullivan lifted his face and screamed at the darkness.

The sound that came out of Mr. Sullivan was so terrible that Faye cringed, half expecting the rest of the cave to collapse around them and she knew that Delilah was gone. His voice finally broke after what seemed like forever. The sound tapered off to a hoarse wheeze and then nothing.

Delilah had always liked the sunshine so much. It didn't seem fair to die in the dark, in a wet hole far underground. She crawled toward Mr. Sullivan, but a hand fell on her shoulder. "Leave him be, Faye," Lance said gently.

"You lied. You said she'd be fine," Faye shouted.

"Yes, I did," he responded sadly.

"What about Mr. Browning? Is he going to be *fine* too? And what's wrong with Mr. Garrett? Is he going to live like you said Delilah would?"

Lance sighed. "Quiet down, girl. You want the truth? John hasn't long unless we get him to a Healer or a real hospital. Dan's hurt bad, but I don't think the bullet that went through him is the worst of it. You go over there to Sullivan and he'll take your head off right now."

"How do you know that?" she spat.

"Because I been where he is before is why. That burned house, where we met? That was *my* house, Faye. The last time the Imperium found us I lost my wife and I lost my baby daughter."

She thought back to the charred timbers and the feeling of sadness in those ruins. "I didn't know."

"How could you? Listen, Faye. That's the life of a knight of the Grimnoir. It's pain and loss and suffering, but we keep on going, no matter what. Your Grandpa understood that. We're a dying breed. There's fewer of us every day and nobody in control seems to care, and there's gonna be even fewer if we don't get John and Dan some help soon."

She could hear Mr. Sullivan sobbing and it seemed extra sad to hear somebody that strong break. "What are you going to do?" she asked.

"Francis seems to think he can make it. If he goes now he could maybe get a boat back here by the time the water goes down and we can get everyone out. Or I can send a young man to drown in a futile gesture to save an old man's life . . . John's got a few hours in him, but that's it. I hate being in charge, but I'm the senior man, so I get to make that call."

Don't kill Francis. He's nice. "Can't you get a bird or a fish or something?"

"Too much rock. My Power can't see through it."

"Mine either," Faye muttered. "I could Travel up top in seconds. It isn't that far, but farther than I can feel, so I'd probably die . . . If only I was like Heinrich and could walk through walls, then I wouldn't have to worry about getting stuck."

"Hmmm . . ." Lance said. "That gives me an idea. Heinrich!"

He crouched next to them a second later. "*Ja*? What do you need?"

"Can you Fade with another person? I mean, can you take another body through solid objects with you?"

He was quiet for a moment. "I have done this before. It is very draining. I can only do it briefly, but it is just like taking the clothes on my back or a firearm, but the more mass I have to Fade, the faster it uses up my Power. If I run out while embedded in something . . . well, I've seen it happen to others. The matter becomes fused together. It is not pretty."

She understood what Lance was thinking. "I can Travel with more than one person!" Faye clapped her hands with glee. She wasn't exactly an expert at it, since she'd done it exactly once, and that had been in a moment of panic. "If I was all . . . fadey . . . I wouldn't be worried about getting stuck in something when I Travel. I could go further than I could see, and not die!"

"What do you think?" Lance asked Heinrich.

"It makes sense," he answered. "What's the worst that could happen?"

Lance grunted. "Besides getting stuck together into a big lump of meat or maybe somehow screwing up and getting embedded in solid rock? I don't know." Lance said. "So it's either drown Francis, let John suffocate in his own blood, or kill the two of you . . . I got to do the math here. It was a stupid idea. Forget it."

There was a flicker as Heinrich thumbed his lighter. He held it close to her face. He was looking into her eyes, studying her. "Can you do this thing, Faye?"

"You didn't trust me before. Do you trust me now?"

He shrugged. "There are easier ways to betray someone than a suicide trip through a cliff." He grinned. "Poor Lance, trying to be responsible with such impulsive young people under his command. How much time will you need?"

"No," Lance interrupted. "John wouldn't want you to do this."

"I can go super fast. I can probably do it in two, maybe three hops. So, figure five or six seconds."

"I am good for double that," Heinrich said. "You do not appear to weigh much." He closed the lighter and then took her hands in his. "Please try not to kill us and do not let go."

"No way. Too dangerous. That's an order, damn it."

"Lance, don't be such a wet blanket." She would have to push extra hard. When she'd Traveled with Francis, she'd gone a much shorter distance than she'd expected for the amount of push she'd given it. It was terrifying to think about Traveling into the unknown. "Ready?" Faye asked, but there was no need, as her body suddenly felt very tingly. It was like she was made out of fog. With a shock she realized she was sinking *into* the floor. It tickled.

Faye grabbed her Power, more than she ever had before, and was surprised how much there seemed to be there, just waiting for her to use.

"Sto—" Lance had begun to bellow but then everything around her and Heinrich was solid, like being buried in the ground, only they weren't in the ground, the ground was *in* them. It was like her body was made of little tiny bits and Heinrich had spread those bits out wider, and the tiny bits that made up the ground were passing in between her bits. There was no air, no light. They were stuck in the cliff! Panic hit her like a club and she nearly let go of Heinrich and killed them both.

Go! Her head map was useless, and she grabbed all that extra Power that she'd always been afraid to mess with and hurled them both straight up.

Too far! She shrieked as they appeared in the sky, tumbling through the air, suddenly falling. The light was blinding and she blinked as they spun. Heinrich released his Power and she could feel that he was holding onto her hands so hard that she thought the bones would break. He was screaming something but the wind was rushing by too fast and all she could hear was it beating her ears.

She could barely see from all the sudden sunlight and the wind making her eyes water, but the ground was *way* down there. The earth curved in the distance and green and brown and blue and there was a charred black half-circle directly below that terminated against the ocean.

Have to get to ground. When she came out the other side of a Travel, she was always going the same speed as she was going before, and she didn't went to hit the ground and explode like an egg that had fallen out of a bird's nest. Her hair hit her in the face as she focused and—

There. She was staring up into the blue sky, Heinrich above her, his eyes impossibly wide, his mouth in a perfect *O* as he screamed. The rotation continued and the ground spun up to meet them. *TOO FAST!*

She felt Heinrich's Power shimmer down her arms. His body went grey and blurry and she sure hoped she looked the same. She squeezed her eyes shut as they impacted the ground, but there was no splat, no explosion of guts all over the place, and opened her eyes to blackness as they sunk through dirt. She felt like they were gradually slowing, like they were sinking through thick water.

The head map didn't let her down this time. *Clear.* They were right beneath the surface, descending gradually, and she Traveled just as Heinrich's Power gave out.

They flopped into a pile of hot ash and crackling branches.

The map showed that the world immediately around them had been scoured clean of life. Trees trunks were laid sideways, all of them cleanly pushed down by a single wave. Fires were still burning on the hillsides. Everything was black and nearly as scary as the place with the big magic jellyfish.

Heinrich groaned as he gradually let go of her hands. "Never never ever never again will I do anything like that ever again," he said, sitting up, coughing as he inhaled a lungful of smoke. "Never!" He made it to his feet, managing a few steps before stumbling off balance and landing on his butt in a puff of soot. "Never!"

In the middle of the wasteland, Faye began to giggle.

Chapter 18

Among the many misdeeds of the British rule in India, history will look upon the act of depriving a whole nation of magic as the blackest.
—Mohandas Karamchand Gandhi, 1930

Mar Pacifica, California

SULLIVAN did not know how much time had passed in the dark. Delilah's body was cold next to him. Her blood coated him and had dried, sticky on his hands, clotted and pulling at his arm hair, but he would not leave her side. He only partly heard the others over the crash of the ocean. Someone had come to speak to him, but the words had been uncertain, his memory vague. Browning was coughing, dying. Dan was getting worse, but there was nothing he could do about it. He was useless.

Madi had been right. He was *weak*.

No longer distracted with trying to protect the others, his mind turned inward, focusing on his own pain. He'd broken super-hardened bones, torn flesh, bruised muscles, yet the magic design on his chest had managed to keep up. It had burned Power to keep him alive. Even now he could feel the hot itch as his body mended itself far faster than normal.

But why hadn't it worked on Delilah?

He moved back and forth between wakefulness and fitful sleep. His dreams were terrible, and he relived Delilah's wounding, over and over. He saw the assassin's steel wrench out of her body, and he questioned what he could have done differently, what he could have done better. If only he'd been quicker, faster, stronger, smarter.

Anything. If he'd been able to defeat the Greater Summoned faster, then she would never have come down to help, and he drifted off, hating himself for not accomplishing something that whole squads of Actives had failed at during the Great War.

He awoke once to the noise of chattering teeth and talking. Francis had tried to swim for it when the tide had gone out, only to find that more of the cave had collapsed toward the entrance and he couldn't squeeze through. He'd nearly drowned, and surely would have if he'd gone earlier. There was some talk about Faye and Heinrich disappearing after trying something stupid, but he tuned it out and went back to his stupor. They were dead too, and that was probably his doing as well.

Damaged goods, Delilah told him in his sleep. *You understood me, Jake. You were the only one.*

Sullivan found himself walking along the top of a trench at Second Somme, the Power visible around him in the land where the dead went to dream. He knelt in the dirt and studied the mysterious being and the geometric patterns that made up its body. It eluded him. There was no way to bring her back. The Chairman was there, reclining on a throne made of barbwire and human bones. He did not mock Sullivan. He understood such pain.

Delilah was dead and it was his fault. The dreams told him that he deserved to die for his mistakes. He deserved to be the corpse, not her. The Chairman told him that ritual suicide was the appropriate response for such weakness, for such total failure. At one point he awoke with his pistol in hand, the safety off, the muzzle pressed against his temple. *No. Not like that. Never like that.* He unloaded the 1921 before putting it back in the holster.

You don't even have the balls to do that right, his brother's voice whispered in his ear.

Delilah's ghost came to him once. She didn't speak. She just pointed at him, accusing him, and after a while it faded, but the afterimage swam on inside his eyelids. He'd not realized how much damage he had taken in the fight, he knew that he was hallucinating, but he could actually feel his skull mending from where Madi's fists had left it cracked and his brain swollen.

They'd lain together—was it last night? The night before? Weeks? Just like back in New Orleans where he'd saved her from herself, until he'd thrown that all away for a moment of stupid charity trying to protect some kid he didn't even know. There had been letters he'd written her from Rockville, but he'd never gotten a response. Not a single one. He didn't know if he'd ever have worked up the courage to ask her why, but it didn't matter now. She was lost forever. Dead in a cold black hole, her spirit surely stuck between hell and the Pacific Ocean.

Back in the land where the dead dreamed, he watched the Power. It had surely fed well when Delilah had died. The Power made a certain kind of sense. The day of the Second Somme it had feasted, growing fat, and he knew that with the deaths of all those strong Actives, thousands more of the children born on that terrible day in 1918 had been born with the gifts farmed from his dead friends and enemies. The new Actives, teenagers now—had it really been that long?—They too would increase their Power, until they died, and the cycle continued, until . . .

Until what? Until everyone in the world had magic?

He wondered where the Power had come from. It certainly had not been born on this world. The Chairman had said it came from someplace else.

"It was pursued," the Chairman said from behind him. "Chased from the other place. We are its refuge. We are its hope." Sullivan did not bother to turn. He knew that this was not another dream of a swollen and fevered brain. His enemy was actually speaking to him from the other side of the world. He was glad for the company.

"Why are you telling me this?" Sullivan asked.

"Because you impress me. Because there are very few people that I can discuss such things with who would understand, and these things I tell you will give you no advantage in your struggle against me." The Chairman stopped beside him. Today he was dressed in an elaborate military uniform, resplendent with braids and medals and gold. The only thing that was not flashy was the well-used sword at his side. It was remarkably utilitarian. The Chairman saw Sullivan taking in the flash. "I was at a parade," he explained. "As I was saying, it fled its old world, as it fled the one before that. You are correct, Mr. Sullivan. It feeds on us. It needs us, and we need it. We increase it, but as we grow dependent upon it, we must also defend it from the thing that preys upon it and has pursued it across the stars."

"What's it running from?"

The Chairman's expression seemed sincere. "When the Enemy comes, you will know. The Power wants me to cleanse this world of weakness. Only the strong will be able to defeat the Enemy. If the world is not ready to stand before the Enemy, the Power will flee, and the Enemy will consume us all in its hunger, then the cycle will begin anew."

He was in no mood for the Chairman's bogus religion. "Sounds like a load of bunk . . . Why didn't the healing spell work?"

"This, I will not tell you. You have chosen to stand in my way. It would be folly for me to help you become stronger." Sullivan turned back to the Power. The mystery of his failure taunted him. The Chairman cleared his throat. "I will tell you this. When one is so very close to death, they have to *want* to come back. Perhaps your lady believed she would be happier in the next place."

He nodded slightly. Every moment of Delilah's life had been an uphill fight. From her drunken, abusive father; to her miserable poor upbringing; to a life on the streets; to petty crime, abandoned by everyone she'd ever loved . . . She'd had to fight for evey scrap that had fallen from life's table. Maybe he was right. Maybe she'd gotten to the end and saw something on the other side that was better . . . She'd sure earned it. "Thank you, Chairman."

The leader of the Imperium gave a slight bow. "You are welcome, Mr. Sullivan."

He spat on the ground. "But I'm still gonna kill you. I swear to God Almighty, I will. I'll kill you and every fool that follows you, including my own brother, for Delilah and every other decent person you've ever hurt."

"I would expect no less. I look forward to our meeting."

Sullivan awoke in the tiny sea cave. There was an excited commotion from the other side as a brilliant light scalded his eyes. Faye had returned somehow. His body ached from the damp, but his injuries were mostly healed. His head was clear for the first time. If he could not live for the future, he could live for revenge. He knew *exactly* what he had to do. If he lived long, there would be time for grief in the future, but now he had duty. He found Delilah's face in the dark and kissed her gently on the cheek. "Goodbye, girl. I'm sorry I let you down."

❖❖❖

Francis almost had a heart attack as yellow light filled the cave. At first he thought that it was the Peace Ray firing again, but as he lowered his shaking hands, the light resolved into the single circle of an electric torch.

"I did it!" Faye shouted. "I made it, Mr. Rawls! Good job . . . Yes, I know I don't need to shout!" she said, still yelling.

"What the hell?" Lance asked. "How'd you get down here?"

Faye put the torch down and went to John Browning's still form. "No time to explain." She grabbed Browning's hand and they both disappeared.

"So . . . I guess that means she made it?" Francis rasped. He was dying of thirst, and wished that Faye had dropped off some fresh water with that lamp. "I thought this was out of her range?"

"She just keeps getting better faster," Lance said proudly. "That girl's got scary lots of Power. Best Traveler I've ever seen, and getting stronger every d—"

The Traveler reappeared and Francis flinched, having never realized that her grey eyes actually reflected light in the dark like a cat. "I'll explain in a minute. I met the nicest old Grimnoir! He's a Reader, and he's putting the picture of *up there* right in my head!" She latched onto Garrett's leg and took him next.

"What happens if she runs out of Power while jumping back and forth?" Francis asked nervously. "She doesn't seem to be slowing down any . . ."

"I don't know. You probably don't want to go last though." Then Faye appeared, put her hand on Lance's head, and they were both gone.

Francis felt the cold tug of fear in his gut. He didn't like the idea of magically zipping through a whole bunch of rock, especially in the hands of somebody who was so carefree, no . . . *reckless* and—He actually screamed as Faye landed beside him and the next thing he knew, he flopped harmlessly into a pile of ash.

Faye grinned at him. She was covered in soot from head to toe. Her wild hair was a mess of tangles and blackened sticks. She was completely in her element. This was no longer the scared little girl that they'd found such a short time ago. This was one shockingly gifted Active. "You can thank me later!" she said as she vanished.

Francis stood shakily. He still felt nauseous from swallowing and vomiting all that seawater. Everything around him was blasted and black. It took him a moment to realize that the ashen lump nearby was all that was left of the mansion he had grown up in. The sky was dark with smoke, and the afternoon sun was angry and red overhead. If he hadn't been already so emotionally drained, he might have started crying.

In the light, he could finally see how bad his companions looked. Browning was pale as death, nearly blue even. He had been placed onto a stretcher by a few men in long yellow slickers and they were putting him into the back of a truck. Garrett didn't look much better. Madi's bullet had passed through his left arm, leaving a hole that you could put a finger through. He'd become feverish and incoherent over the last few hours. Lance was covered in black and yellow bruises and his beard was matted with blood.

Faye reappeared, this time with Delilah's body. Francis had to avert his eyes. "Sorry, Mr. Sullivan said that she came up before he did. I'll be right back." Lance limped forward and draped a wool blanket over the corpse as Faye left.

There were several dirigibles in the air. A flight of biplanes tore past. Dozens of cars and even a few tractors were on the nearby hills. Cameras were snapping and film reels rolling as newsmen recorded the destruction. His home had been isolated, but there had been a lot of other nice houses in the area, and a small town on the other side of the forest now looked like a box of spilled matchsticks. The village was flattened except for a handful of broken buildings. The only things moving were the searchers.

A man in a cowboy hat approached and offered him a canteen of water. Francis sucked it down greedily. Cold water spilled down his neck. "How long were we down there?" He gasped when he was done.

"A day and a half," the man said. "We've been combing this place the whole time. We've got a couple thousand volunteers and the Army tearing it apart, but y'all are the first survivors we've found here in the black circle." His eyes were bloodshot. "Everybody else for miles is dead. Then at the line, it just quit killing. We've got hundreds of people with burns and injuries outside the circle, but not a single one killed."

Francis had no idea how many people had lived in the area. The very thought sickened him. Sullivan and Faye appeared. The volunteers didn't so much as flinch from the display of magic. They'd seen too much already. Sullivan had his Browning Automatic Rifle over one shoulder and was still wearing the canvas vest filled with magazines. The haunted look in his eyes frightened Francis.

An older black man took Francis by the arm and led him to the back of the truck. His voice was low so the volunteers wouldn't overhear. "Come on. We need to get you knights out of here."

He was familiar, but it had been a long time since he'd seen a member of the Grimnoir elders. "Mr. Rawls?"

He held up his left hand, showing his Grimnoir ring. "It's been a long time, Mr. Stuyvesant. And I see that you are a grown man now. Please, call me Isaiah. Come, get in. We have much to discuss."

Faye was excited, near giddy. She'd been the one that had saved everyone. She'd been the one brave enough to Travel through the cliffs. She'd been the one that had found Mr. Rawls and led him to the spot where the mansion had stood. If Mr. Browning and Mr. Garrett lived, she knew that it was because of her. She was as big a hero as the brave adventurers on the radio programs. She'd never seen a motion picture, but she assumed that she was at least as brave as those people too. She knew that Grandpa would be proud.

If she could squeeze any more pride inside she figured she would burst. Her Power was stronger than she'd thought. It hadn't let her down. It was still there, as much as ever. It wasn't just a well that she could dip a bucket into. It was a *river.*

They'd all been loaded up into the back of the big farm truck and it rumbled through the ash heading north, kicking up plumes of smoke from under the tires, going back toward the city. She was pleased to see that so many folks had shown up from all over to help. Farmers had used their tractors to drag broken trees off what had been the road. They passed an Army bulldozer pushing up dirt, looking for bodies inside what had been a house. After that was another truck like theirs, only all the charcoal things stacked into the back of it had once been people and that made her real sad. The Peace Ray had burned them all.

There were two new Grimnoir. Both of them were old men,

nearly ancient by her standards. Mr. Rawls was the first black man that she'd ever actually spoken with and he seemed really nice. He was a Reader, like General Pershing, only he had a whole lot more Power. His hair was white and his skin was dark as night. His suit was covered in ash, and the fact that he'd jumped right in to help look for survivors made her like him even more. He wasn't afraid to get dirty. She was willing to bet that he was a very nice grandpa to his grandchildren.

The other one was named Mr. Harkeness. There was something about him that didn't sit right with her. He was old too, but he'd dyed his hair black, like he was trying to disguise his age, but he was too dried out and wrinkly to be vain. His eyes were cold, his face narrow, and he talked funny. He was European, not from the warm, loud, laugh-a-lot side of Europe like Grandpa and his family, but from the cold, harsh, serious side of Europe. Mr. Browning and Mr. Garrett were on litters in the middle of the floor, and he was kneeling between them, checking their vitals.

"Are you a Healer?" she shouted hopefully over the engine noise.

"Something like that, child. Not nearly that strong though. Please, let me be."

Mr. Harkeness had seemed sullen ever since she had first spoken with him. The very first question out of his mouth was if Jane was alive. When she'd told him that Mr. Madi had taken her away, he had given her the sternest glare, like he held her personally responsible for her friend's loss. That wasn't fair at all. She'd killed an Iron Guard and shot Madi and a couple of zombies and kept Francis from getting squished and kept Mr. Sullivan from getting a bullet in the back of the head. She'd done her very best and she wasn't even officially a Grimnoir yet. She'd like to see the fancy-pants European do any of that.

Her friends were all staring out at the destruction, bouncing back and forth in the rusty truck bed, all except for Mr. Sullivan, who was watching something else, something far away in the distance, where only he could see. Delilah's body had been wrapped in a blanket and he knelt next to it, protectively. She'd sworn to kill Mr. Madi, but she figured it was going to be a race now between the two of them as to who got to kill him first. Mr. Sullivan looked real mad. The truck bed smelled like manure, and that made her feel a little more comfortable, like home. Either way, as long as Madi died, that would make Grandpa and Delilah happy in heaven. Maybe they would kill him together. That seemed fair.

A bunch of volunteers waved at them as they went past. They looked glad to see someone alive and that gave them hope to keep digging with their shovels. Lance was talking to Mr. Rawls, telling him about what had happened. Apparently Mr. Rawls was the one who had been assigned to come out here and take General Pershing's place.

"It seems like we've done this once before, doesn't it, Mr. Talon," Mr. Rawls said sadly, putting his arm over Lance's broad shoulders. "Only this time, the toll was much worse."

Lance caught Faye giving him a curious look. "Last time the Imperium found us, they burned my house down. That was three years ago, in the attack where Black Jack got cursed. Isaiah and Kristopher here were some of the knights sent to reinforce us," he explained. "We tracked them down and killed the lot of them, but we lost some good men in the process."

"Poor Jane, always so gentle and naïve. She volunteered to stay and minister to Pershing. I told her it was too dangerous. Pershing was always getting into trouble. Look where that got her. And my granddaughter took a liking to this one," Mr. Harkeness muttered, poking at Mr. Garrett's belly. "Girl never had any sense . . ."

That made Faye angry. Mr. Garrett was a very nice man. He was unconscious so she felt the need to stick up for him. "Jane loves Dan a whole bunch."

Harkeness snorted. "And this lump told me he'd protect her, keep her safe. Fat lot of good you all did."

Heinrich was sitting across from Mr. Harkeness, one leg dangling over the side. When he lifted his face, Faye saw a look very similar to the one he'd had when he'd shot her in the heart with his Luger. His voice was totally flat. "Say that again, *Scheisskopf,* and see what happens."

"That's enough, Kristopher," Mr. Rawls barked. "These knights have been through too much." Mr. Harkeness frowned, and went back to his work. "It isn't their fault your granddaughter was lost."

"We will get her back," Lance vowed. Heinrich and Francis nodded, so Faye did too. Sullivan was still staring off into space.

"Sadly, there are more important things at stake than the life of a single Grimnoir," Mr. Rawls said. "General Pershing was keeping me informed about the Geo-Tel situation. We must secure the last piece before it is too late . . . You were Pershing's men. Who did he entrust with the location?" There was no response. Faye looked around. She knew, but she didn't think she was supposed to say. "Look, I know he kept it secret. The General was paranoid, for good reason, but he's gone now. The elders have sent me to fill his shoes, and they're some mighty big shoes to fill, believe me. I rode with him before most of you were born. I was a young Buffalo Soldier under his command, before either one of us was recruited by the Society. I feel his loss as much as anyone, but you must understand how important this device is."

"Oh, I think we do," Francis said, gesturing at the scorched earth all around them. Buzzards weren't even circling, because everything dead was too crispy to eat.

Mr. Rawls' laughter was genuine. "This? Francis, my boy, this is *nothing*. The Geo-Tel cut a swath through Siberia that you can't even imagine. I was one of the knights of New York, and we came this close"—he held up thumb and forefinger nearly touching—"to losing the whole east coast. When there were many pieces scattered and unknown, then Pershing's way made sense, but now there is only *one*. The single most important mission of the entire Society is to find it."

"And destroy it," Lance said.

"Of course. The elders were foolish when they thought they could keep it to maybe use it themselves one day. We should have smashed it to bits back in '08. If the General confided in any of you, we must know. The world depends on it."

The truck reached the edge of the blast zone. The black ash just stopped in a perfectly straight line. On one side was death and on the other there was yellow summer grass, seemingly undisturbed. Police cars were parked on both sides as the road reappeared. Soldiers hurried and moved wooden barricades out of the way as the driver shouted there were survivors to take to the hospital.

The gear box ground as the truck rolled forward. A police car got in front of them and turned on its siren. Reporters tried to take their picture as they went by but the Grimnoir kept their heads down. The group was silent, and Faye thought about raising her hand, but she hesitated. General Pershing had shown her exactly where to go to find Southunder.

"The only thing standing between the Chairman and the deadliest device ever conceived is a single Grimnoir, who probably doesn't even know that his old companions have all been slaughtered. We must get to him before it is too late." Mr. Rawls pleaded, "You are not betraying the General, you are fulfilling his final mission."

Sullivan started to laugh. It was a low chuckle at first, but then it turned into a full belly laugh. He was at the rear of the truck, and the shocks creaked under his weight as he turned. "You all are too rich." He had to wipe his eyes with his sleeve. "Damn near as self-righteous as the Chairman."

"Pershing told *you*?" Mr. Rawls said incredulously.

"Because he knew better than to trust anyone else. Yeah, I know how to find Bob Southunder."

"You must tell us then."

"Pershing gave me a job. I intend to do it. I'll find Southunder and the last piece. That's my duty. Not yours."

"You can't hope to do this on your own. You're just mad with grief, son," Mr. Rawls said.

"Maybe. But that don't change nothing."

"If the Chairman finds out where it is, he'll send his Iron Guard against you," Mr. Harkeness said coldly.

"I'm counting on it. And when they come, I'll be there, waiting," Sullivan stated. Faye could tell he meant it. If there was anything she knew about Mr. Sullivan, he was a man who kept his promises or who'd die trying.

Mr. Rawls was upset. "This isn't a game. Tell me where Southunder is. That's an order, Grimnoir."

Sullivan paused, took Pershing's ring from his pinky and tossed it into the truck bed. It rolled to a stop next to Mr. Browning. "I never took no oath."

Mr. Rawls' thick white eyebrows scrunched together as he glared at Mr. Sullivan. Faye could almost feel the Power crackle through the air around them. If Sullivan wouldn't talk, then he'd just pick the truth out himself. She'd felt how strong Mr. Rawls was. He'd been able to talk to her mind through hundreds of feet of solid rock.

But Sullivan was stronger than any old ocean cliff. Unbreakable. He closed his eyes as Mr. Rawls tried to force his way into his head, a look of terrible concentration creasing the big man's square face. "Get out of my *brain*," Sullivan said. She turned to Mr. Rawls; sweat was rolling down his face and veins were popping out in his forehead. The whole truck creaked as Sullivan stood up. He calmly drew his .45, took a magazine from his pocket, stuck it into the grip, and racked the slide. Raising the gun, he aimed it at Mr. Rawls. "I said, get out of my brain or I spread yours all over the road."

The Reader gasped as he let go. "What are you?"

"Angry." Sullivan put his gun back into the military flap holster on his belt. He turned to Heinrich. "See to Delilah. She'd want to be buried in a place with a pretty view. Have somebody say some words. I think she'd like that."

"I will," Heinrich promised.

He addressed them all. "I can't come with you to save Jane. Tell Dan I'm real sorry when he wakes up. Maybe we'll meet again and maybe we won't. Faye, thank you kindly for getting us out. Delilah told me she took a real liking to you." Sullivan nodded at her, and Faye felt herself blush. "Good luck."

"What're you gonna do?" Lance asked.

"My duty." Sullivan nodded once and stepped off the back of the speeding truck.

Chapter 19

It was during my wandering time that I first met an American. The black ships of Commodore Perry had recently arrived in Nippon. These foreign barbarians did not ask the shogun for permission to open trade; they demanded it from the decks of their warships while ringed in cannons under a cloud of coal smoke that blotted out the sky. There was an assumption of this absolute right. The strongest does not ask, cajole, or beg. It is the duty of the strongest to command and the weakest to obey. I had long made my way by selling my sword, and whatever lord I served inevitably became the strongest, so I was well acquainted with this concept at the individual level. Yet, it was the Americans that opened my eyes to the greater possibilities. As the strong lord must rule over the weak peasant, so must the strong nation rule the entire world. I owe them a great deal as I have tried to apply this lesson ever since.

—Baron Okubo Tokugawa,
Chairman of the Imperial Council, My Story, 1922

280 miles west of San Francisco

MADI SAT CROSS-LEGGED on the floor of his cabin, attempting to meditate. He could feel the ship rocking. It had taken him forever to figure out how to sit like the other Iron Guards. He wasn't exactly a limber man, but he'd decided a long time ago that anything they could do, he'd do better, and now he could sit as still as a statue for hours. At the Academy, old master Shiroyuki would come by and crack him on the spine with a bokken anytime he started to slouch. The old bastard had been big on posture.

Thinking of the old master made him smile. That was his problem with meditation, thoughts just kept coming, and now he was remembering Shiroyuki and his big ridiculous samurai mustache. He'd hated Madi. Not only for being the first white man accepted into the brutal Iron Guard training, but also because he had come to Japan as a prisoner of war.

He'd been part of AEF Siberia, the Polar Bears, they'd been called in the news. It had been a shitty mission to a cold unforgiving place, mostly to protect American business interests while the Bolsheviks were getting their asses handed to them by the Japs. He'd gotten separated from his unit when his chicken-shit commanding officer panicked and ran. It was an empty feeling, waiting at your post for relief that never came. It had taken three weeks on foot through the coldest damn forest in the world, but the Imperium troops had finally captured him, though he'd killed a whole mess of them in the process.

They'd dragged him behind their horses for miles but he'd refused to die. Then they tossed him into a deep dark hole and quit feeding him, but he'd lived off of rats that he'd crushed with his Power. One day a new commander showed up and had marveled at the one-eyed Heavy chained in the hole. Apparently the weeks he'd spent evading and murdering them had earned him a reputation as some sort of great white freak show. He was the biggest man any of the Japs had ever seen and he was the only American in the camp, so the new commander had logically decided it would be fun to watch him fight a bunch of the captured Russians for his amusement.

That part had been fun. He'd never had any qualms about killing. It was really the only thing he was good at. The regular Russians were easy to beat. He could snap most of them in half. The Siberians were different. Those boys were tough, and he picked up a bunch of scars giving the Japs their show. Afterward, they'd put him back in the hole, only this time the commander had sent down food, honest-to-God real food. It was mostly rice, but after eating raw rats, rice was good.

That had gone on for another month, until Madi had damn near depopulated the entire camp of other prisoners. When they'd run out of Russians, they'd tossed in some Chinese, five at a time, and when they ran out of those, they'd thrown him in the arena with an angry bear. The bear had been easy. A ten-second surge of Power had turned it into mush.

He'd tried to escape, a couple of times in fact. The first time they'd beaten him senseless with rifle butts, but the commander had told them to let him live. He was intrigued by the Heavy at this point. The second attempt resulted in the death of nearly a dozen of the camp guards and he'd gone down fully expecting to get his head chopped off, but instead he'd woken up chained back in the hole, the commander sitting on a stool across from him.

Madi could remember it like it was yesterday.

The man studied him for a long time before speaking. The commander spoke English, even if he was damn near impossible to understand the way he tried to shout half the words. "Why you still alive, Heavy? Why you not dead while everybody else dead?"

Madi didn't need to think about that for very long. "Because I was stronger."

The commander had nodded real slow, like that was the wisest thing he'd ever heard, then he had passed Madi a dirty envelope. "My men capture this." Inside was a typed letter on AEF stationery and he even recognized his old captain's signature. The letter was real matter-of-fact, about how Sergeant Matthew D. Sullivan was AWOL and a no-good deserter and a coward. That had really left him steamed, since the only reason he was in this Jap prison was because his old captain had been yellow and run at the first sign of an advance. He'd been the one who'd left Madi at his post to be overrun. Madi had survived the Second fucking Somme. What did Captain Cocksucker know about cowardice?

"You read this?" Madi asked, disgusted. The Jap nodded. "Liars. I've never run from nothing in my life."

"Your people dishonor you."

"Ain't the first time. Got my brother killed in France. Tore half my face off and they didn't even bother to fix it all the way . . ." The women told him he was good-looking before the war, but now, it didn't matter what they said to his torn-up face. He saw their disgust with his good eye. "What did I get? Nothing," he'd spat. Jake had been the one who'd gotten all the fancy medals and the recognition and the praise after the war but his little brother had never cared about that kind of thing. He sure had, but all he'd ever wanted was some respect, but they hadn't given him shit. "Then when I get captured 'cause of some yellow officer they blame it on me." He threw the letter on the ground, planning on using it to wipe his ass later.

"You are great warrior," the commander stated. "My men told stories of how hard to catch you it was in the forest. How you killed many men. You put fear in their hearts. It is hard to make Imperium man fear. You strong. Strongest should be most respect."

"Hell with 'em," Madi agreed, really studying the commander for the first time. He was tall for a Jap, otherwise nothing special to look at, but he emanated a quiet confidence. Madi could tell he was some sort of Active by the way he carried himself.

"Yes. You think you strongest? Prove it. Make pact. We fight. You beat me, you free go."

He'd had a good laugh. "No shit?"

"Shit not. I am Rokusaburo of Iron Guard. You beat me, you free. I beat you, you serve me."

He figured that the Jap would last even less time than the bear in the blood-soaked little field they'd made him fight all those Russians in, and the next morning they'd led him out there. The whole Jap battalion had shown up and was standing in a big circle, watching, excited. They had bayonets mounted and he was no sucker. When he won over the crazy little man, they were sure as hell gonna stick those long bayonets in him, no matter what, but maybe he'd get to squish a Nip officer in the process. Rokusaburo had been waiting in the middle, shirtless, his body covered with strange intricate scars. He bowed.

The little man *destroyed* him.

Afterward, when he'd regained consciousness, Rokusaburo had come to him again. "What were all those burns on you?"

"Kanji, to grant me more Power. Iron Guard unbeatable. Iron Guard strongest of all."

"Then I want to be an Iron Guard," Madi told him.

To his credit, Rokusaburo didn't laugh. He'd only given him that same slow nod, and Madi's education had begun.

Back in the present, Madi's nose itched, but he decided not to scratch it. It was probably from that damn incense that was stinking up the ship's cabin. He might be lousy at meditation because he couldn't stop thinking, but he could control his body. What had gotten him thinking? Oh, yeah, that asshole, old master Shiroyuki.

Rokusaburo had gotten him into the Academy. Madi had forsaken his country, his old ways, and sworn allegiance to the Imperium, but he'd felt no loss. He felt no loyalty. All his homeland had ever given him was pain and betrayal. They'd used him, hurt him, killed the only decent folks he knew, then called him yellow and left him to rot. The Imperium at least appreciated strength.

Shiroyuki had been hard on him. The old bastard had taught him and tried to have the other students kill him. He was always extra hard on the big white one. While the Chairman preached that he didn't care where an Active was born, Shiroyuki was old school, real proud that he came from the same ancient samurai family as the Chairman himself, and hated the round eyes. He'd tried to break Madi every step of the way.

The fact that Madi never quit and was strong enough to just keep accepting kanji infuriated Shiroyuki. To bind with a new mark you had to go right up to death's door, and each one you got, the harder it was to come back. The other students began to respect him at five, and then fear him at eight. The Chairman took a personal interest in Madi's education, realizing how valuable it would be to have an operative able to move seamlessly in America. Plus, he was a sort of vindication of the Chairman's beliefs, of his vision for a perfect world, ruled by the strong and the wise. The Chairman had taken him under his wing, showing him the dark secrets, the truth of the Power. Madi did not just follow. He *believed.*

Then old man Shiroyuki had dared to publicly disagree with the Chairman, saying that only the superior Nipponese should be Iron Guard. The Chairman had replied with his usual wisdom that the Power lived inside their bodies where all blood and bone was the same color. Shiroyuki had been chastened, dishonored, and when he was no longer in favor, Madi struck. He'd waited until he had received his tenth kanji before challenging the old master to a trial by combat. He had been honor bound to accept.

He'd ripped Shiroyuki apart like he'd been one of the Russian prisoners in Rokusaburo's camp. The memory of the old man's arms coming off in twin fountains of blood and the samurai screaming through that ridiculous mustache made him grin. He opened his eyes. "Hell with it." The Chairman was a big fan of meditation, but reaching inner peace wasn't exactly his thing. The Chairman taught that with proper clarity you could actually converse with the Power. Madi didn't know about that, but if the Chairman said that's how it was, then that's how it was. Unlike the people he'd sworn allegiance to before, the Chairman never lied.

There was movement in his bunk. Toshiko was awake, watching him. She'd pulled the sheet up to cover herself, feigning modesty. The Shadow Guard was such a tease, but damn if her academy hadn't taught her in *all* the arts of espionage. He could barely feel anything anymore, but he had felt *that*. He realized she'd been counting his scars. "How many kanji have you taken?"

"Thirteen." He rose, retrieved his shirt and threw it on. He still ached from all the wounds the Grimmys had inflicted on him, but that Healer bitch had done as she'd been told and fixed him up, and he'd only had to smack her in the face a few times to get his point across. "More than any other man in the world."

She either really was impressed or she faked it good, he never could tell with a Shadow Guard. They were such trained chameleons that you never could tell where the real person began and the act ended. They were spies and assassins that could be whatever you wanted them to be. "Even more than the Chairman?"

He snorted and buttoned up his shirt. "The Chairman don't need no marks on him. He just goes right up to the Power and takes whatever he wants. Us mortals need the kanji just to keep up." He knew it was true. The Chairman was the greatest of all. He wasn't just strong, he was smart too. He even painted, and wrote poetry that Madi didn't really get, but all the other Iron Guard always kissed the Chairman's ass and told him how great it was. If the Chairman wrote a haiku, you could damn well better believe it was the best haiku ever.

Toshiko dropped the sheet. "I bear five." Her kanji were much smaller, more discreet, almost graceful. The Shinobi Academy magi were artists compared to the Unit 731 butchers with their glowing red-hot branding irons. She fingered each one reverently. "Hearing. Stealth. Strength. Sight. Vitality."

"Yep. I see 'em," not that he was looking at her scars as he shrugged into his shoulder holster. "Get dressed. Our ride will be here soon. I'll grab the prisoner."

"You really believe that soft thing will be of use?"

Madi shrugged. "We'll take her to Nippon, break her and rebuild her. If she sees the light, then sure . . ." An old Iron Guard had been patient and shown him the true way once and he owed Rokusaburo his life for it. Too bad his blood brother had killed his spirit brother, but he'd already balanced those scales. "I figure I'm doing her a favor."

Toshiko sneered. "And if she does not see it that way?"

There were schools all over the Empire for training Actives, and not just for volunteers either. The Chairman's instructors had ways of making people catch the vision. Those deemed unfit were used in the experiments. "Then she goes to Unit 731."

"Throw her overboard and let the sharks take her," she suggested. "It would be more merciful."

Madi slid down the ladder into the hold of the ship. His boots hit the steel grate and he started down the corridor. He had to duck to keep from hitting his head on the pipes. The crew averted their eyes and got out of his way. They were loyal Imperium subjects, and they knew not to keep an Iron Guard from his business.

They'd boarded the cargo ship and made it out of the harbor before the authorities had locked down the coast. Officially they flew the flag of the Free City of Shanghai, but this was the same vessel that had brought in his reinforcements. Shanghai was only free as long as it was convenient for the Chairman for it to stay that way.

The emergency radio broadcasts that morning had been priceless. His ruse had worked. Word had already leaked to the press about the anarchist propaganda scattered at the Peace Ray. All the known commie-backed agitators were getting rousted as the real culprits sailed away. They were going to be picked up by an Imperial airship and rushed home, and by the time he'd be soaking his feet in Edo, the American Actives would be feeling the heat. If he was really lucky, there would be a crackdown. Anything that caused dissension in the enemy's ranks would only swell the Imperium's own.

The corridor stunk of diesel and body odor. The paint was peeling and the tub rusting, which normally would be unacceptable in an Imperium vessel, but this one had to keep up appearances as being a low-class merchanter. Madi found the door and spun the wheel. It creaked violently as he pulled it open.

The Healer was on the floor. She closed her eyes as blinding light spilled into the tiny cell. She was pathetic. Filthy, her clothes ripped, her wrists bound behind her back with cord. *I wonder if this was how Rokusaburo saw me?* Probably not, because he had at least been tough. This Grimnoir girl was soft, and the only reason he'd thought to bring her along was the sheer rarity of Healers.

"Get up," he ordered. She whimpered, so he kicked her in the leg. Not hard enough to hurt, but hard enough to let her know he was serious. "Get your ass up or you'll really feel the boot." He reached down, grabbed her by the arm, and jerked her off the floor. "We got a flight to catch."

"Where are you taking me?" she asked, grimacing against the pain.

He thought about backhanding her, but it was a fair question. "Nippon. From there, you'll go wherever the Chairman thinks is best." She limped along as he pulled her into the corridor. "If you're lucky, you'll stay at an Edo school to serve. If you piss us off, you're going to Manchukuo. Trust me, sister, you don't want that. You're too pretty and those mutants are awful lonely." There still was defiance in her eyes. He could see her thinking about how she would never serve the Imperium, but she was smart enough not to say it out loud. "Fine, we'll see how tough you are when the branding iron comes out," he said as he dragged her along.

Toshiko, Hiroyasu, and the others were waiting for them on the deck. The sea air felt cool on his skin. In the distance to the east, a black shape was growing. It was the Chairman's new flagship, fresh off the UBF assembly line, heading home for the first time, the most advanced hybrid dirigible ever developed, and the Chairman had it diverted to pick up his star Iron Guard so that he could return home in honor.

"It's beautiful," Toshiko muttered.

It really was. Madi was no expert on airships, but he'd ridden on one of the new Kagas, which were more like battleships suspended under three armored hulls, all business. This was nowhere near as big, but it was much sleeker. The flagship was like something off the cover of those science fiction pulps. It also had three separate hulls, like long grey cigars, but the outer two were angled inward at the front, and the whole thing was covered in a housing of rooms, balconies, and glass enclosures, giving it an overall triangular shape. It was driven by twenty roaring engines, both lifted and fueled by hydrogen, and it would be crewed entirely by Actives.

The Imperium had not developed its airship technology as rapidly as the Americans, and when Madi had heard that their new flagship would be built by UBF, he'd been offended, but those thoughts were forgotten as he saw the gleaming beast coming toward them. Their Cogs would catch up. They'd even improved on UBF's original Kaga design by adding hydrogen-powered Peace Rays. It was only a matter of time until the Imperium was able to produce marvels like this at home but, in the meantime, the Chairman would ride in style.

"*Da-nippon teikoku kaigun Tokugawa.* It is called the *Tokugawa*, in honor of the Chairman's family name," Hiroyasu said reverently.

"I thought you didn't name a ship after somebody until after they died?" the Grimnoir Healer said. "Maybe we'll get lucky?" Toshiko slapped her to the deck for her insolence.

"He's immortal," Madi said. "We didn't feel like waiting around."

The four-engine amphibious PBY Silverado biplane had flown west until the Presidio, then San Francisco, then finally the blackened coast had been lost. Sullivan watched out the rear window of the cargo plane until the final line of land disappeared, then moved forward to take his seat amongst the cargo headed for Pearl Harbor.

The Silverado would normally have an eight-man crew, but none of the guns were mounted, so there were only four—the pilot, co-pilot, navigator, and engineer—and all of them had been specifically instructed by Major Arnold not to talk to the large man in civilian clothes. There were a few other passengers, soldiers being transferred to Hawaii, and they hadn't gotten the message.

"Where you headed?" the private sitting across from him asked, having to shout over the thunder of the props.

There were two soldiers. They had to be fresh out of training. Had he been that young once? He had lied about his age and volunteered for the First when he was seventeen years old, so it was sad to say that he probably had. "Nowhere you need to know about,"

Sullivan answered in a tone that suggested he just wanted to be left alone. He went back to looking out the port window and the soldiers returned to their conversation.

Pershing's memory had directed him to a man at the Presidio. The base had been on alert, and soldiers had been scrambling. The men at the gate had regarded Sullivan—dirty, coated in dried blood, clothing in shreds—with suspicion, glaring at him over the muzzle of a Colt Potato-Digger machine gun that had been thrown down behind a bunch of sandbags. He was glad that he'd detached the barrel from the '29 BAR and stashed it in his bag or they probably would have shot him. When he said that he had a message for a Major Arnold, they had sent a runner.

The major had taken him aside as soon as he said that Black Jack Pershing had sent him. Sullivan had repeated exactly the code words that had been left in his head. "It's time to see the Pirate."

"How's the weather?" the major had asked in return.

"Getting hotter," Sullivan had responded as instructed. "That's why we need the Weatherman." The major's expression had turned grim but he had immediately given him a place to clean up and had sent someone to fetch him some food and a change of clothing. Thirty minutes later he'd showered, sucked down some bacon and eggs, along with a pot of coffee, and reported back to Arnold, who was busy coordinating men and supplies to the damaged area around Mar Pacifica.

When they were alone, the major had locked the door of his office and bid Sullivan to take a seat. "I don't know what this is about, but I promised an old friend that if this day came, I'd help. I've got a Silverado leaving for Hawaii in twenty minutes. You'll be on it." He reached into his desk and pulled out an envelope that had been sealed with wax. "I'll instruct the Silverado to follow these orders, but they will not help you in any way other than to take you to your destination as part of a *training* mission. They will not cross into Imperial territory. They're a good crew, and they'll keep their mouths shut. I assume you know what to do next."

"Yes, sir," he answered, taking the envelope.

"Good, because I don't. The General could be a cryptic man at times. I'm assuming this has something to do with the Peace Ray."

"Yes, sir." Sullivan had picked up a morning paper on the way here and read the lies. "Only it wasn't no anarchists like they're saying. It was the Imperium."

"That's not my area, mister . . . I don't decide who to bomb, they just tell me where to drop them. But off the record, I'd say you're probably right. The anarchists they're laying this on couldn't find their own ass in the dark. I've been pressing to deal with those Imperials for a long time. But there're too many politicians, making too much money off them for that to happen."

Sullivan nodded. That's why Pershing had given this man a piece of the puzzle. "What's gonna happen?"

"Nobody wants another war," the major said. "I'm afraid people will believe whatever they want. I think they're fools. War's coming, no matter what we say. All I can do is make sure my little corner of this machine is ready to fight." There was a knock on the door. "Now if you'll excuse me, Mister man whose name I probably don't want to know . . . duty calls."

Sullivan had returned his salute smartly. *Duty calls.*

The view out the window of the Silverado was breathtaking but his thoughts were elsewhere. Huge fuel tanks hung pendulous between the wings, pontoons even larger were below that. The ocean was dark blue as far as the eye could see. A dark shape came into slow focus as they drew near. It was an airship, and one of the biggest he'd ever seen. It was so far away that it was hard to make out details.

"What is that thing?" one of the soldiers asked.

"That? I read about that in the paper yesterday. That's the Imperium's new super airship. That Stuyvesant made a pretty penny off that pig, I'd bet," the other answered smartly. "It's heading from Michigan out to Japan. I read the whole article."

Sullivan watched the huge craft in the distance. His scalp prickled at the sight of the rising sun painted large on the outer hulls. These were the bastards who'd robbed him of Delilah—not the same bastards, but they worked for the same madman. Not that being angry did him a lick of good. The Silverado was unarmed, and that monster sure as hell wouldn't be. Major Arnold's men weren't about to start an international incident just because he was in a foul mood.

The biplane was parallel to the distant dirigible, but they were easily passing it and he realized that it was stationary. There was a glint of light reflecting off something metallic below it, and it took him a moment to realize that they were hovering over a ship. The Chairman's airship dwarfed the tiny vessel.

Why were they tethered to a cargo ship? Airships had to gas up, same as anything else, but why do it at sea when they'd just passed over land? "Soldier . . . that article say if it ran off diesel?"

"No, siree, that thing's engines run off the hydrogen in its bags. UBF says it could fly nonstop all the way around the whole world if the wind was right. The crew has like a dozen Torches to watch for fire and its own Weatherman and—"

What else could they be picking up from a ship off the coast of San Francisco? That was brazen, even for his brother. There might not be anything he could do about it, but maybe somebody else could. Sullivan stood and lurched into the aisle. He caught the engineer midway up the cabin and grabbed the airman on the shoulder. "I need to use your radio."

San Francisco, California

FAYE WAS SWEPT up in the confusion as much as everyone else. Reporters had tried to take their picture when they got to the hospital, but Lance had swept her under his arm and gotten her inside with his wide-brimmed hat pulled down low over his face. "Last thing we need is for people who think we're dead to know we're not," he'd muttered. As Francis had gone by, the cameras had mysteriously broken and they'd retreated from the cursing reporters.

The hospital had been packed with injured. Several local churches had been pressed into service for the less serious burns and she heard that medical people were being brought in from all over the country. Heinrich told her that someone named Doctor Rosenstein was flying in from Chicago and that he'd personally see to Mr. Browning if they couldn't find a Healer.

The regular doctors had taken Mr. Browning away as soon as they arrived. Mr. Garrett had been taken to surgery. Lance had yelled at them about something, until they agreed to not sedate him while they tried to tend to his injuries. He also refused to part with his six-gun. "If the police talk to you, you were a guest at Francis's house. Don't say *nothing* else."

"I'll see to her, Mr. Talon," Isaiah assured him. "Please, go get yourself tended to. Please, Faye, have a seat with me. My back is killing me." The two of them sat down on a bench in the hallway. Mr. Rawls took a handkerchief from his pocket and cleaned his glasses. He looked tired, all covered in soot. Many of the other people in the hallway were also covered in ashes, so they fit right in.

Francis saw an older doctor pass them at a quick walk. "Excuse me, sir, do you have a Healer available?"

The doctor paused long enough to give an exasperated laugh. "Young man, don't be absurd. You couldn't afford a Healer."

Francis's face turned red. "I'll have you know I'm Francis Cornelius Stuyvesant the Second! I could write a check and buy this hospital!"

The doctor took in Francis's bedraggled condition, snorted, and spun on his heel. "That's a new one, usually people around here insist they're a Hearst," he called over his shoulder as he hurried along to more pressing business.

Francis's hands curled into fists and he went after the doctor, still demanding to be heard. "When I buy this place, the first thing I'll do is fire you!" He disappeared into the mob.

Faye sighed. It had been a very tiring day. Mr. Rawls patted her gently on the knee. Harkeness had sulked away as soon as there was a crowd. "Your friend isn't very nice," Faye said.

"Kristopher is having a difficult time, I'm afraid. The loss of his granddaughter is weighing on him greatly. We have no idea which way they went and they have a long head start on us."

She could understand. She couldn't bear to think of what that bully Mr. Madi would do to poor delicate Jane. "Mr. Harkeness said he's something like a Healer, but he couldn't help Mr. Browning or Mr. Garrett. What good is he?"

"He has some minor Power where he can stop the spread of disease. He kept their wounds from becoming infected. There are degrees of Healers, and in that family, I'm afraid that his descendents inherited far more Power than he has," he sighed.

"You sound really tired, Mr. Rawls."

"I am, dear. The elders sent me to secure the Geo-Tel"—he gestured around the dazed and ashen crowd—"and none of you know about it, so I've failed. Pershing took it to his grave, but I think he underestimated the Chairman. He will find it unless we can destroy it. You see this, Faye? Imagine this a thousand times worse. Why, a single firing of the Geo-Tel could destroy all of California. America would fall, Europe would fall, and the whole world would surrender to the Imperium's horrible ways."

"That's terrible." Her heart ached at the sight of the people suffering. A little boy was crying, tears cutting paths through the dirt on his cheeks, and it reminded her of how her brothers had looked, tears tracking mud through the dust that had caked onto their faces when the soil had gotten all dry and the wind had blown it all away. Only this time it wouldn't be big clouds of dirt covering the sky, it would be ashes from all the beautiful cities burning. "I promised to kill the Chairman."

He shook his head. "Poor child. You don't realize, but we've tried, many times. He simply will not die. We've burned him, shot him, stabbed him, blown him up with bombs on many occasions. The Grimnoir have sent men to poison him, but he doesn't need to eat or drink, we've tried to capture him in his sleep, but he doesn't sleep. We once had a Torch scorch his flesh away in a pillar of fire, and he walked out, his clothes burned off, but he was fine. A Grimnoir knight once blew up a bridge while a train he was riding in was passing over it. The whole thing fell five hundred feet into a ravine and the Chairman walked out without so much as a scratch."

"But there has to be a way!" Faye insisted. "I could Travel right next to him."

"Others have tried. Basically you can't get close unless he lets you and that only happens while he's killing you. He has a strange Power that lets him pull all the knowledge and life right out of someone, just by laying his hands on them. The elders discussed how to destroy him with our smartest Cogs. Perhaps a direct hit with a Tesla weapon could do it, but other than that . . ." Isaiah shrugged.

So if you can't kill him, that's why the Grimnoir put so much effort into messing up his plans . . . She had promised General Pershing not to share his memories with anyone else, but Mr. Rawls was right. The Chairman was too smart. He'd find the piece on his own, just like he'd somehow tracked down Grandpa. She'd barely known the General. Maybe his sickness had made it so he wasn't making the best decisions . . . and she felt like she could trust Mr. Rawls. He wasn't just Grimnoir, he was like a boss Grimnoir, and if she couldn't trust them, then she'd never be a proper knight like her Grandpa had been.

Faye looked around to make sure no one was listening in. She leaned in conspiratorially and whispered, "I know where it is."

Mr. Rawls smiled.

Mar Pacifica, California

THE *TEMPEST* made excellent time and he was in California before the smoke had even settled. Cornelius had commandeered one of the UBF Weathermen stationed at the Empire State Building and put him to work making sure that they'd had the wind at their back the entire way. It had left the Active exhausted, and it would probably cause erratic weather patterns across the entire nation in their wake, but it was a small price to pay.

They'd flown over the impact area and he couldn't believe his eyes. His son had insisted on building an estate on the rocky finger of land that had jutted into the ocean because it was so green and beautiful. Now it was wiped bare, under ash as thick as Michigan snow. The mansion was simply gone, timber and brick burned or hurled into the sea.

His hopes had been dashed. Nobody could have lived through that. Not even a Stuyvesant, and they had a talent for surviving anything. His once favorite heir was surely dead.

Oh, the way they'd fought. The boy had always been a rascal. While Cornelius could barely stand most of his heirs, brownnosers and sycophants the lot of them, young Francis had not been afraid to say what was on his mind, and he'd loved him for it. He was as much a contrarian at heart as the eldest Stuyvesant, and it did Cornelius proud to see that Stuyvesant fire in another generation.

Francis's father, Cornelius's least disliked son, had been a congressman and then ambassador to Japan. It was during that time that he had met John Pershing, and young Francis had taken a liking to the soldier. His father was too busy womanizing and collecting bribes to have given the boy a proper upbringing, so of course

Francis had gravitated toward the manly activities of horsemanship and shooting. Cornelius had approved at first.

It wasn't until after they got back to Japan that he realized how much nonsense Pershing had put into his grandson's head. Francis was preoccupied with frivolous things, like right and wrong. Apparently he'd seen some atrocity or another at an Imperium school and that had soured his outlook on profiting from the Chairman's wild spending. His son had no such qualms, and had arranged many lucrative deals, but Francis would have none of it.

Then his son had died. It had been right after an argument with Francis, where the young man had stormed out, vowing to have nothing to do with his family. They said that it was a suicide, but Cornelius knew that was a filthy lie. No Stuyvesant would ever lower himself to such a fate. He knew that it had to be the work of that vile Pershing. No, it wasn't enough to turn his favorite heir, the boy who was the spitting image of his own youthful vigor, against him. Pershing and his mysterious Society had surely killed his son as well.

So he'd sought out a Pale Horse. With Pershing's foul influence gone then surely Francis would see reason and come back to the family, but as he looked out the windows at the wreckage, he knew in his heart that he'd been wrong, terribly wrong, and he could never take it back.

There was a polite cough behind him, and he turned to see a surgical mask. It took him a moment to remember why everyone was wearing masks. "What? Can't you see I'm mourning, idiot?"

"Sir, we have received a message. There were some survivors. Someone claiming to be a Stuyvesant is at a hospital north of here."

He looked back at the house. *Impossible.* But it was hard to keep a Stuyvesant down. *Could it be?* "What are you waiting for? Fire up the engines!" he shouted. "Full speed ahead!"

Chapter 20

Gott in Himmel. Lassen Sie uns bitte sterben.

Translated: God in Heaven, please let us die.

—*Graffiti seen in Dead City,* 1925

San Francisco, California

HARKENESS WAS SMOKING a cigarette on the hospital roof when Isaiah found him. The Pale Horse had wanted to be alone with his dark thoughts. In a foul mood, he tossed the butt over the side and watched it fall.

"Good news," Isaiah said. *Pershing told the Traveler girl where to find Southunder.*

"Really? Her?" The old man had been getting desperate.

She's stronger than you realize. Pershing saw that. Isaiah joined him at the railing. "It is done. I've already made the call." *The Chairman will have possession of the complete Geo-Tel in a matter of hours. Pershing hid it right under his nose.*

If Isaiah felt any guilt for taking advantage of such an innocent, he did not let it show. The Reader had suffered so much at the hands of the willfully ignorant and evil that there was nothing he wouldn't do to accomplish their mission. "So that's it . . . All we can do now is wait."

And pray.

Harkeness nodded thoughtfully. There was no turning back now. But there never was, not after so many sacrifices . . . Jane had merely been the latest, an innocent girl swept up into their grand scheme, but if this worked, then her sacrifice wouldn't be in vain. The years of lies, the oaths broken, and the hundreds of lives he had taken would have meant something.

"I would join you in prayer, old friend, but I'm afraid that God will not listen to the likes of me."

Francis grimaced as the doctor ran the needle back and forth through the skin of his forehead, stitching the nasty gash back together. He'd bashed his head on a rock in the cave while thrashing back and forth trying to squeeze into the ocean. It had been the most frightening thing he'd ever done and he knew that he was lucky to be alive.

But he didn't feel lucky.

"No Healers, huh?" Lance asked from the other table. He'd broken at least one rib, and they were guessing that he might have cracked his hip. Lance looked like Francis felt.

"Once I convinced them who I am, it didn't matter anyway," he muttered. The one the hospital had on call was away in Hollywood tending to some starlet's sprained ankle and it was unknown when he would get back. "We can't wait around."

"I'm mobile," Lance said, trying to sit up.

"Hold still," the nurse ordered him.

He sighed and lay back down. They had to be careful what they said in front of witnesses. "John and Dan are out, but we've got Rawls and his man."

"Where do we start?" Francis asked, already knowing that it would be futile. Madi was long gone by now, which meant that Jane was as good as dead.

"We split up, probably groups of two, start chasing down leads."

"You aren't going anywhere," the young doctor working on Francis's head said. "Neither of you is in any shape and there are some government men outside waiting to speak with you."

"I already explained everything," Francis complained. He'd told the state police about how he'd been giving his guests a tour of his mansion's basement when there had been a bright light and a cave-in. Lance and John were both officially dead. They had fake identities, but he knew that as soon as word got to the police that both Browning and Garrett had bullet wounds, then their story was out the window. Right now they were victims, but they needed to get out before the authorities decided that they were somehow involved with the Peace Ray attack.

"One of them is from the Army," the nurse cleaning up Lance added helpfully. "He said he had a message for the survivors, but I told him he'd have to wait."

"What kind of message?" Lance asked suspiciously.

She shrugged. "Beats me, something about Imperial blimps. He was talking to that white-haired negro."

Francis was off the table, pushing past the doctor before she had even finished speaking. The iodine-soaked thread swung back and forth in front of his eye as he shoved the doors open.

In the hallway, a young man in an Army aviator's uniform was walking away. Isaiah Rawls was reading a typed note. He saw Francis coming. "Now stay calm, I—" Francis tore the note from his hand and scanned it quickly.

"Sullivan, you son of a bitch," Francis said, grinning. *The Chairman's personal airship!* This had to be it. The timing was too perfect. That had to be where Madi had taken Jane. "We can go after them right now." His pocket watch had been smashed on the rocks, but there was a clock on the waiting room wall. They had one hell of a head start, but if they hurried—

"No," Isaiah said sternly. He leaned in close so the other people in the area couldn't listen in. "It is too dangerous."

"What?" Francis couldn't believe his ears. "Are you daft, man? They've got my friend."

"Even if you could catch them, you expect to board the *Tokugawa,* defeat its whole crew, and get away? You don't even know that's where they are. All you have is the word of one untrustworthy Heavy that he saw it docked with a ship off the coast."

"It's more than we've got now," Francis spat.

"No wonder the elders sent me out here. Pershing's lack of caution has trickled down. You think it's wise to throw away the lives of an entire cadre of knights on a hunch? Listen to me carefully, Francis. We will get your Healer back, but we need to be smart. An overt attack on the Imperium's flagship would be war."

Francis didn't care who heard. He threw his hands wide and shouted. "Look around you, Rawls. This is war!" Dozens of eyes turned toward them. "Yes, it was the Imperium who did this!" The other patients and hospital staff began to mutter.

The senior Grimnoir appeared ready to explode. His voice was a barely audible hiss. "Calm. Down," Isaiah ordered, and Francis could feel the matching thoughts inside his head. "You will *not* go after that ship. That is an order. You took an oath, and part of that is that you'll follow the elders. There are plans within plans, and your half-cocked actions will have repercussions."

Francis was seething. "What are you so scared of?"

"The *Tokugawa* must not be harmed. There are bigger things afoot than you understand, young man. You need to trust me."

Before Francis could respond there was a commotion at the main desk. A group of men in suits and surgical masks were pouring into the waiting area, and in their midst appeared a fat, bellowing, bull of a man, sputtering and swearing. "Who's in charge of this fiasco? I demand to speak with the head!" He pulled down his surgical mask revealing a face that was red and sweating and shouted at the top of his considerable lungs. "Bring me my *grandson*!"

"Grandfather?" Francis asked in bewilderment. He turned back to Isaiah, but the Grimnoir elder had his head down and was retreating down the hall. "Grandfather Cornelius?"

"Francis!" Cornelius Gould Stuyvesant lumbered down the hall, past startled onlookers, and engulfed Francis in a hug. His belly was so large that his arms wouldn't close around Francis's back. "You're alive! Thank God, boy."

"What are you doing here?" he asked in disbelief, taking in the wall of surgical masks that were watching him. "I don't—"

"I've come to take you home, Francis," he said. "Oh my, look at that awful wound. What are you doing, getting stitches like a commoner? Howard!" He snapped his fingers. "Heal this man!" One of the masks stepped forward.

Francis grabbed Cornelius by the lapels and jerked him forward. Francis was much taller and stronger, and he swung the fat man around so hard that the security men reached into their coats for their pistols. "You've brought a Healer?"

His Grandfather was shocked by the rough treatment. "Of course. When I'd heard of the tragedy, I gathered all of my staff into my fastest prototype airship and came straightaway."

"Fastest . . ." he let go of Cornelius. "You have this ship here?"

"The *Tempest* is docked at the city terminal. It will need to be serviced but we could be on our way back to New York within a few hours. I—"

Francis pointed at the Healer. "Howard, right?" The man nodded. "Follow me. Grandfather, I'm going to need to borrow that dirigible."

Faye found Heinrich Koenig in the morgue. The room was empty of live people except for him, sitting the wrong way on a chair with his arms folded on the backrest, though there were plenty of dead people lying around. She was a little taken back by the number of shapes under white sheets.

Heinrich had heard the boots hit the floor when she'd Traveled in. He turned to regard her. The young man appeared very tired, with dark circles under his eyes. "Hello, Faye."

"Everybody else is getting patched up . . . I . . ." She hadn't wanted to be alone with a bunch of strangers, so she'd found the man who'd shot her in the heart instead, because at least she kind of knew him, but saying that out loud seemed silly. "What'cha doing?" she blurted.

Heinrich turned back to the sheet-covered body. Long dark hair hung loose from one end. "One last vigil, I suppose . . . I promised Sullivan I would see to her." He gestured at Delilah. "I know that there are more pressing matters, but there is something I must do."

Faye was confused. "Like what? We've got to start looking for Jane, so we don't really have time for a funeral or nothing." The arrangements for Grandpa's funeral had seemed to take forever, and that was even after he'd been burned to near nothing with the haystack.

He gave a sad little shake of his head. "Nothing like that. We must see to the living first, though I'm afraid that it is too late for Jane. No, afterward, I will dig Delilah's grave myself. I have much practice at digging graves."

She leaned on a big porcelain sink and waited for him to continue. There was a rusty drain hole in the floor and the idea of what it was for made her uncomfortable. Heinrich rubbed one hand over his face and she saw that he had his Luger sitting in his lap. "Why the gun?"

"Because sometimes when a Lazarus creates undead the effect can linger for awhile. Sometimes if the Active is strong enough, it can last for hours, and anyone who dies in that place could have their spirit trapped . . . When I followed the orderlies down here with her body, I thought that I felt a tingle of magic."

"You think Delilah could be a . . . *zombie*?" she asked, incredulous.

He shrugged. "Probably not, but if she is, I will deal with it on my own and spare her dignity. It is a terrible fate, and one that I would never willingly have fall on another. I have known of people waking up as much as twenty-four hours after their death, and they do not even realize it."

He sure does know a lot about zombies. "I heard that you grew up in Dead City."

The silence was long and uncomfortable. A sink was dripping. "I do not wish to speak of it . . ." he said.

"Okay," Faye answered, not really knowing what else to say. "Would you mind if I helped you . . . keep watch?"

Heinrich didn't answer then. Seconds passed into minutes and he had a faraway look in his eyes. Faye grew bored, and started counting the drips coming from the faucet, but Lance and Francis were busy, Mr. Browning was medicated asleep, and Mr. Rawls had had to leave to place a telephone call.

"It wasn't always Dead City. It used to be called Berlin," he said finally, sighed, and then it was like a ditch had broken and memories spilled out. "It seemed like a magical place to a young boy. My family lived on the outskirts. Father fixed pianos, and he would often bring me along with him into the city. Many of the pianos were in old churches and schools, and while he worked, I would play. I would climb the towers, find the crawl spaces in the walls. Those places became my kingdom, and I was the valiant knight that defended them. There were so many people, always moving about, and then the war came, and all of the men went to fight, including my father."

"In the Great War?" she asked.

"*Ja*. We did not know to call it that then. To a little boy, I only knew that I missed my papa very much, and there was not so much happiness anymore. Many of the other boys received letters, saying that their fathers had died, but I knew that mine would come home. Food was scarce, and we were often hungry. It got worse, but I got older. I took care of my family, even if it meant stealing the food we ate. Finally so many of our soldiers had died that the government could not keep up with the letters, and all of us wondered if the war would ever end."

"But it did end . . ." Faye said. She was no student of history, but she listened to the radio. Everyone knew the brave Allies had beat the dastardly Kaiser.

"Ah, yes, it ended in a flash of light. When I woke up, my home, my town, was rubble. Berlin was ruined, all of the old places crumbled, and in the center was nothing but a smoking hole. I spent days searching for my family, but they were all dead."

"I'm sorry," she said.

He chuckled. "Do not be sorry. They were the *lucky* ones. Were you ever taught in school what happened next?"

"I never went to school."

"Good, you're not missing anything . . . History is mostly lies. The Kaiser had grown so desperate that he had used his wizards to keep his soldiers alive. As they were killed, he had their spirits chained to their bodies, so that they could continue to defend the Fatherland. When the war was over, there were still nearly a million of these poor wretches. They could not die, but the process of this false resurrection had left most of them too dangerous to send back to their homes. The treaty left us bankrupt and unable to care for them. But the Kaiser had a perfect solution. He had a dead city, so why not fill it with his dead subjects? A great wall was raised around the ruins, and the undead were herded inside."

"What about the alive people, like you?"

"The survivors were supposed to rebuild. It was our duty. We were to be caretakers for these poor soldiers. When the wall went up, there were several thousand of us . . . at first."

Faye was aghast. "That's terrible. They just left you?"

Heinrich fingered the Luger. "Do you know what happens to the *untotten*? The undead? The pain of death is upon them still. They never heal from the wounds that sent them there. The pain never lessens. It only grows as does their hunger. Most of them keep their wits, for a time, but soon it becomes too much to bear. They lash out in a rage at anything available, including each other . . . We were caretakers at first, then we were merely . . . *food*."

She covered her mouth, but a little yelp slipped out anyway.

"Koenig is not my real name. It means *King*. That's what they called me after a while, because I was the last man alive in Dead City. I was the King of the Living. I survived by my Power, by my cunning, by my stealth. The old places where I'd hid and played as a child became my sanctuaries. I spent my days in the walls, in the tunnels, hunting for food, killing the undead that tried to hurt me and my friends. Then after several years, I couldn't take it anymore, and I Faded through the Berlin Wall and never looked back. I was fifteen years old."

And I thought that I'd had it rough . . . An Oklahoma shack might as well have been Francis's mansion in comparison. Faye reached over and touched Heinrich gently on the shoulder. "Why'd you stay so long?"

He watched Delilah's sheet for movement, but there was nothing moving there except bad dreams. "Because not all of them were mad. Many of the dead remained true to who they were in life. My family never got a letter from the front, but . . . he did come home, most of him. Together, we found a working piano in an old school. He played it every day. The sound gave the other sane ones hope. Finally, I made him stop, because the sound attracted the hungered. After that . . . he had nothing to survive for . . . but I stayed with papa until the end."

"Son of a bitch . . ." Harkeness said, peering through the corner of the window into the hospital room. "What's he doing here?"

If he links us to Pershing's death, it could ruin everything.

The Pale Horse watched Cornelius Stuyvesant as he followed his grandson, still shouting useless orders at his functionaries. He had come as soon as he had heard Isaiah's panicked voice inside his head.

Stuyvesant brought a fast blimp. Francis intends to go after the Tokugawa *with it. It must not be delayed.*

"I will not let him ruin everything," he muttered under his breath. Harkeness awoke his Power. To him it was a dark, malevolent cloud that swam in his lungs. He could still feel the connection to Stuyvesant, lips under poison fingertips, the beating of his heart, the electrical firings of his brain, the pumping of blood. They were inevitably connected by death magic. He'd never thought that he would need to do this to the pathetic old man, but they could not afford the interruption. Not now. The Healer might slow him, but nobody could stop the full focus of his Power at this range. "Reap the whirlwind, you bloated fool."

Dan Garrett moaned as the hole in his arm hissed and steamed. Visible bone was coated by rolling muscle and sprouting veins, then finally by bright pink skin. The Healer's hands were glowing as he took them away. He paused to wipe his sweating brow on his shirt. "Next?"

"Browning is on the third floor," Lance said. "Come on."

"That's the one with the punctured lung?" the Healer asked. "Very well."

"Hold on there, Howard," Cornelius ordered. "How much Power do you have left?"

The Healer was a surprisingly tubby man with bushy sideburns. "Truth be told, not much, sir. After this I'll need to rest for a few hours before I give you your daily checkup, especially after I help this other man."

"Then you will do no such thing," the richest man in the world commanded.

Francis had known that this moment was coming. He could only keep up the momentum for so long before his grandfather's inherent stubbornness was sure to raise its ugly head. He looked around the room to see who was going to be witness to the coming argument. He had the surly Lance, and the semiconscious Dan, neither of which would be of much assistance, one hospital doctor, and then six of his grandfather's functionaries, hangers-on, and bodyguards. It was standing room only.

"Grandfather, could we speak in private?"

He thought about it for a moment, then snapped his fingers. "Everybody out!"

"But I work here," the doctor said, but a guard grabbed him by the arm and yanked him effortlessly through the door. Lance helped Dan from the room. His friend was obviously disoriented. It was too bad, because he sure could have used Dan's Influence right then. The last one out was the Healer. He closed the door behind them, leaving Francis with his grandfather. The only remaining witness was a white skeleton that was bolted to the wall.

"Why are you here?" Francis asked.

"I told you. I was concerned for your safety. You are family."

Francis shook his head. "That's not what you said the last time we spoke."

Cornelius lowered his gaze, studying the shine on his shoes. "What would you have me do? Apologize? That's not my way."

He laughed. "An apology? You think an apology makes up for all the terrible things the Imperium has done? That you've helped them do so you could turn a coin?"

"Don't you dare lecture me, boy!" Cornelius shouted so loudly that it seemed as if the windows shook. "It is a competitive world, and if I didn't do the job, then somebody else would have. I did what I had to do. I always make sure the family interest comes first. Your father understood this, why can't you?"

Francis ripped the skeleton off the wall with his Power and hurled it across the room. Cornelius cringed before the sudden fury. "My father was a coward. He saw what the Chairman was doing to people, and he looked the other way. I saw children being butchered because they weren't up to snuff! I saw people, horrible distorted people, broken and re-formed by magic! They kept Actives in cages like animals while they tortured them!" A bottle came off the counter and shattered against the far wall. "My father killed himself with opium once he knew I'd found the truth. He died rather than face it. He was a filthy *coward*!"

The door opened and his grandfather's guard stuck his head in. "Is everything—"

"Be gone, you oaf," Cornelius said. The door closed. "Francis, the world is what it is. The best you can hope to do is read the current so that you don't end up dashed against the rocks."

Francis did not have time for this. "If you really consider me family, then you'll grant me this one thing. I need—" he stopped, scowling. "What's wrong with your nose?"

"What?" A thin trickle of blood was streaming from Cornelius's nostrils. He touched it, and his glove came away red. "Why . . . Why . . . I don't rightly . . ." The trickle of blood turned into a torrent, rolled down his chest and splattered across the floor. He took a step, and Francis caught him as he fell, calling for the Healer.

Howard scrambled in, hurrying to his meal ticket's side. The rest of Cornelius's entourage was right behind, staring over their masks. His grandfather began to convulse in his arms, splattering blood across them both. "What's wrong with him?"

The Healer's hands turned to molten gold and he placed them against Cornelius' chest. "He was recently cursed by a Pale Horse, but I'd seen no sign."

"What? That can't be." *Just like Pershing.* "Why?"

"Nobody knows," Howard said. "Let me concentrate."

After several seconds of direct Power, the shaking stopped, and Cornelius began to breathe again, exhaling great rasping gusts that stank of corruption. The calculating part of his mind said that he should only feel disgust at watching this man die, but all Francis felt was alarm. Howard removed his hands and they returned to normal. "I can't believe it . . ." he said, shaking from the exertion. "It's as if everything is going wrong at once. Give me a moment to regain my strength."

His grandfather's hand closed around his sleeve. "Francis," he heaved. "Listen."

"Save your strength, Grandfather," he cautioned.

"No . . . Curse him. If this is to be my death bed, you must know . . . the truth . . ." When he opened his eyes, Francis cringed at the sight of the blood tears flowing from them. "I . . . I had Pershing cursed . . ."

What? He couldn't believe it. He'd known his grandfather was a crook, but he'd never . . ."Why? Why would you do that?"

"For you . . . To avenge your father . . . Forgive me." He spasmed as a terrible cough shook his ribs. Howard gritted his teeth and laid his hands back on Cornelius. "Oh, please, I did it for you . . ."

Francis couldn't respond. The words would not come.

The Healer rocked back. Visible heat waves bent the air around his hands. "I can't . . . It's like the Pale Horse is counteracting everything I do . . ."

The Power had bought him another few seconds. Cornelius dragged Francis close. "The Pale Horse . . . He made me do him a favor . . . Mod-Modify the Chairman's ship . . . Nonsense design . . . Nothing . . . He used me . . . as a fool . . . I'm a fool . . . But I did it for you." He closed his red eyes and his breath was coming in rapid, shallow gasps.

"Can't you do something?" Francis shouted, turning to the crowd. "Any of you?" But there was no answer.

Cornelius's eyes flashed open, and he spoke with force, making sure he would be heard by all. "Francis Cornelius Stuyvesant . . . you are my heir. You're the only one worth . . . a bucket of warm piss . . . in . . . in the whole lot. Howard, Raymond, Kirk, all of you . . . as my witnesses, Francis is my sole heir. Take it all . . . as an . . ." His voice trailed off to a whisper and Francis had to press his ear against his bloody lips to hear his last word. ". . . *apology.*"

The richest man in the world died in his arms. Francis took a moment to gently lower the heavy body to the ground before rising and stumbling over to the sink. He turned it on, as hot as possible, and washed his hands, then scrubbed his face until his skin was raw. He tore his shirt off and threw it on the floor. The scalding water felt good as it sent the blood down the drain.

Pershing died because of me. Father killed himself because of me. Mother drank herself to death after father's death, also my fault. Grandfather died, making a deal with the devil, for me . . . The Peace Ray was fired at Mar Pacifica because it was my home . . .

He had to steady himself on the sink. The UBF men were all watching him. None of them wanted to remove their masks now. The water dripped down his face and he watched it run in a stream from his nose. They'd always said he'd inherited his grandfather's nose. One of the retainers stepped forward and cleared his throat. "Sir, I'm your grandfather's senior attorney. There will have to be an immediate—"

"Shut up," Francis whispered.

"Sir, really, there will be an inquiry, and the board will—"

What would Black Jack Pershing do?

Every loose item in the room rose a foot off the ground before dropping in a terrible clatter. "I said *shut up!*" he screamed. They did. He pushed away from the sink and used a towel to dry his face. When he spoke again, his voice was as calm as he could make it. "You heard the man. I'm in charge. Now I want *my* airship ready to fly immediately, with fuel enough for a transoceanic voyage. Which one of you is in charge of security?" A Brute raised his hand. "What kind of weapons do you have aboard?"

"Other than sidearms? A few Springfield rifles and a Thompson," he said hesitantly.

"Not good enough," Francis snapped. "Go down to the local outfitters. I want trench guns, accurate rifles in heavy calibers, automatic rifles, and machine guns, lots of machine guns. And ammo, piles of ammo . . . and explosives . . ."

"Uh . . . Explosives, sir?"

"Dynamite, or something better if they've got it," Francis snapped. "Take my friend Heinrich, he'll know what to buy. If you're useless, leave now; if you're willing to go kick some Imperium butt, come with me. This is going to be dangerous and most of us will probably die, but if you do . . . Grandfather was bound to bring an accountant. Which one of you is the accountant?" A tall man raised his hand. "Any volunteer who dies. Make sure his family receives double, no, triple his salary every year for the rest of their lives."

"Can do," the accountant promised.

Francis scowled at the group. It would have to do. "Let's go . . . And take those stupid masks off."

After telling his story, Heinrich had gone back to his stony morgue vigil. Faye watched him quietly. She had not liked the German at first, but she decided that that was just because he had shot her to death. He was nice too, in his own way.

Each of the Grimnoir had his own burden. All of them had been beaten by the world, but rather than give in, they'd committed to making that world a better place. She really did fit in here, and she amended her promise accordingly. She would kill the Chairman, not just for revenge, but because as long as he was around, the world was going to stay a bad place, and maybe even get worse. She was sick and tired of mean people hurting others, and she was going to put a stop to them.

It felt good to put everything into black and white and to pick a side. It filled her with a sense of purpose.

Heinrich shifted imperceptibly in his seat. He was listening to something. "What?" she asked, but Heinrich rose quickly, Luger in hand.

"Faye, Travel away. Right now. You do not need to see this."

"What? Oh, Heinrich, no. It can't be."

"Please, just go, Faye. Leave this to me." He approached the table, gun extended.

She slid off the edge of the porcelain and prepared to Travel, her heart heavy. She felt hot tears rushing involuntarily to her eyes. Delilah had always been so good and beautiful.

A pale hand shot out from under the sheet, grabbed Heinrich's wrist, and Faye screamed.

Chapter 21

The white men were roused by a mere instinct of self-preservation. The negro during Reconstruction was threatening enough, but negroes with powerful magic were an inconceivable threat. At last there had sprung into existence a great Ku Klux Klan, a veritable empire of the south to protect the Southern country, to keep the magical negroes in check. Active Magicals, because of their chaotic nature, must be kept under constant scrutiny, especially those of untrustworthy races.

—Woodrow Wilson
History of the American People, 1910

Banish Island, Micronesia

THE PBY SILVERADO landed right on the ocean. The water thumped against the pontoons and water splashed rainbows over Sullivan's window. The propellers kept on turning, dragging them through the crystal waves.

"We've arrived," the Engineer shouted, touching him on the shoulder as he moved down the aisle, apparently unsure if he was awake or not.

Sullivan lifted his hat from where he'd been using it as a makeshift pillow. "Thanks," he responded, stifling a yawn. His ears had popped on the way down. "That was a nice flight," he lied.

"Whatever, pal. Looks to me like you're vacationing in tropical paradise, and we've got an extra five hours ahead of us to swing around a bad storm front that's coming in." It had been a terribly long flight. Sullivan had managed to sleep through most of it. His dreams had consisted of strange geometries, pieces of Power stacked and fitting together over and over in an endless procession like some sort of children's game, and in each dream, he still did something wrong, and Delilah still died.

After they'd dropped the other passengers off in Hawaii, they'd landed at two other islands to refuel, one of which had been flying a Dutch flag. He had no idea how long it had been since they'd left the Presidio, but he'd slept a lot. When he was awake, his thoughts would drift back to the Power, trying to remember it all. Looking at the surface of the being was like looking at a map divided into millions of shapes that were all locked together. He used a grease pencil to draw the strange geometries on the fuselage next to him, wiping them away each time as he decided they weren't quite right.

The Grimnoir had thought of them as words, the Imperium as kanji. They were both wrong. They were constructs. Avatars of the Power. If he could just learn how to make them perfect, to meet all the unknown requirements, then he could tap into those spells too.

The part of the Power he'd paid the most attention to was the section relating to his own, one end of an almost hexagram. He'd tried to draw that bit during the flight, and he must have gotten something almost right, because at one point outside of Guam, just as he finished the shape, gravity's pull had shifted, and the Silverado had dropped several hundred feet in one violent jolt. He'd quickly wiped the mark away while the crew struggled to keep them from falling into the sea. There were probably smarter places to experiment with physics-altering magic than on an airplane.

Now he was here. "Well, maybe not a nice flight, but it sure was long."

"Big ocean, slow plane. Meet me at the back hatch once we come to a stop." The engineer moved on and Sullivan tried to rub the feeling back into his cramped legs. The seats hadn't been designed for a man of his stature.

A few minutes later, the only motion he could feel was the rocking on the gentle waves. The tingling had subsided in his legs enough to move, and he slung his backpack over one shoulder. The Browning bullpup was still disassembled inside as well as over a hundred pounds of gear. He used just enough Power to carry it easily with one hand. It was burning hot inside the Silverado, so he'd stuffed his coat in the bag.

The entire rear of the plane was a ramp that lowered with a mechanical clank. Brilliant sunlight reflected off the ocean and the distant sand. He slid a pair of round sunglasses from his shirt pocket over his eyes. One of the departing soldiers had forgotten them when he'd gotten off at Pearl Harbor.

The engineer kicked a tiny rubber raft off the ramp and into the water. "It ain't got no style, but it beats getting wet." Sullivan climbed down into it, and nearly toppled over as it flopped about. "Don't fall in, buddy. I hear these waters is filled with sharks."

"Good. I wondered what I was gonna have for lunch . . ." he said as he took up the little oar.

The engineer spooled out the rope that was tied to the raft. "I'd wish you good luck, fella. I don't know what kind of secret type mission you're on, but we saw a mess of Nip vessels out there. They ain't supposed to be out this far, so keep your head down."

"You too, and tell the major thanks." Sullivan started paddling. The ocean was so clear that he could see fish swimming around the oar every time it bit the water. The beach wasn't very far, but it was hot, and his shirt was clinging to his back by the time sand ground against the bottom of the raft. He climbed out, managed to not get his boots too wet, tossed his bag onto land, and waved at the engineer, who immediately started hauling the raft back. Between the incoming storm and the Japanese navy, they didn't want to stick around to admire the view.

And it was a nice view. If he hadn't been on a mission of revenge and murder, all those funny trees swaying in the wind would be downright peaceful. But he hadn't traveled halfway around the world for peace. He'd come to smash the Geo-Tel and then wait for his brother to come looking for it, even if he had to call Madi up and give him the coordinates himself.

Behind the trees the land rose into black rocks. The whole east side of the little island was an old volcano that had fallen in on itself. According to Pershing's memory, there was a little village in the cove created by the volcano, and that was where he'd find Southunder. Supposedly the natives were friendly enough. There were some missionaries, and traders used this place to refuel and tie up in bad weather. That was about it. So he didn't figure he'd end up on a head-hunter's necklace like what always seemed to happen to the folks who wandered the South Pacific on the radio serials. On those shows there was always a hero to come along to rescue the damsel from the cannibals' stew pot.

Too bad I ain't no hero. If I were a hero, then my leading lady wouldn't have died in a hole in the ground. He scowled, picked up the backpack, wished he'd bummed a smoke off the crew, and started inland. The Silverado revved up its engines and headed back out to sea, driving up a plume of salt mist as it leapt into the air. The trees were thick, but he figured the fastest way across the island would be a straight line, the whole thing wasn't even a mile across. It felt good in the shade but after fifteen feet of clomping through the bushes, he realized that he didn't know if there were poison snakes in all that ground cover, so he backed out to walk along the beach. At least the snakes where'd he'd grown up had the common decency of having a rattle on them.

Either the island wasn't as sparsely populated as the General had remembered or somebody had seen the Silverado and come to check it out. Within ten minutes he could hear the kids in the jungle watching him. He waved, and tried to smile, real friendly like. He hadn't shaved in days so his face was dark with scratchy new beard, and he wasn't exactly the nicest to look at to begin with, but he didn't want to get off on the wrong foot with these folks. They were his key to finding Southunder. That's why his shirt was untucked to conceal his .45.

"Hey, you guys speak English?" The kids were little and brown, or at least the ones he saw were before they squealed and ran away. There was no way he could have kept up with them on their own turf. A minute later he found a narrow footpath and turned inland. Weird, colorful birds shrieked at him.

The village was bigger than Pershing remembered. Where there had been a handful of tiny huts on stilts with big leaves on top, there were now several wood buildings with tin roofs. The missionary's shack had turned into a white house with a little steeple. He could smell meat cooking on the smoke coming from the largest building and his stomach rumbled involuntarily. An unseen dog started barking.

The kids had raised the alarm. There were several adults watching suspiciously from the steps and doorways. The men were dark-skinned, with curly black hair, and contrary to the radio, nobody was wearing a grass skirt. He noted that half of them happened to be armed. The guns were old, but looked to be in good working order. The only woman he saw was busy herding kids inside and he took that as a bad sign.

Sullivan waved slowly. "Hello." Nobody answered. One of the men spit on the ground. Another one had been interrupted in the act of butchering a hanging pig. He wiped his machete clean on the grass. "Nice place ya got here." There was a rustle in the underbrush to his side.

"What do you want?"

Sullivan turned slowly, glad to hear somebody speaking his language, but not liking that he'd walked right past somebody who'd probably been waiting in ambush. The man was young, surprisingly white, with reddish-brown hair and a goatee.

"You sound like an American . . ."

"Yeah, I'm American," he answered, coming out of the jungle, and calmly pointing a pistol at Sullivan's chest. "The gun's Belgian."

He nodded. "Yep, I can see that . . . Saive GP32 9mm machine pistol. Nice piece."

The young man smiled a little, but the gun didn't move. "Yeah . . . It was based on Browning's last design."

Sullivan would have loved to whip the machine gun out of his bag and show the kid that he was wrong, but he had no doubt he'd catch a bullet if he tried that. "I'm looking for somebody."

"Strange place to be looking." The kid stepped onto the volcanic rock, still covering him. Sullivan knew that little buzz gun had a cyclic rate that could rip an entire magazine into him before he could even move, so he was a very obliging guest. "I'm guessing you came in on that PBY Silverado."

"You know your planes."

He nodded. "You know your guns. Who're you looking for?"

Might as well cut to the chase. "Bob Southunder."

"Never heard of him," he answered. "So you best go away."

He was obviously lying. "You sure?" Sullivan put his hand out at about shoulder height. "About yea tall. He was losing his hair. Probably in his fifties now. Controls the weather. Hates the Japanese."

There was a click as a hammer was cocked behind him. Sullivan felt the steel of a barrel press against the back of his head. "My friend said he don't know nobody by that name."

The second had come up from the jungle on the other side of the path. These boys were good and quiet. "Two Americans . . . Boy, I must have landed at the embassy by mistake."

"Naw, that's five hundred miles thataway." The kid jerked his head.

"Best start swimming," the other one said.

Sullivan wasn't in the mood. "Listen, assholes, I didn't fly around the whole damn world to get turned away. Take me to Southunder before I get mad."

"Can you believe the nerve of this chump?" the one behind him said in a deep voice. "Pirate Bob Southunder ain't real. He's a story that Jap sailors tell to explain whenever one of their ships don't come back. He's like a . . . a . . ."

"Sea monster," the first one finished.

"Yeah."

"So you two ain't pirates?"

"Of course not. We're . . . legitimate businessmen."

Sullivan snorted. "Oh good, for a minute I thought you were going to try and convince me that that was your church." He turned and waved nonchalantly toward the little white building just enough to remove the gun from the base of his neck. "But y'all didn't look like priests, either."

He could feel the gunsel at his back automatically follow his pointing finger, and then Sullivan Spiked outward. The Power left him in a circular wave, bending gravity away violently. The kid went into the jungle, almost like he was flying. The other dropped straight back, hit the end of Sullivan's range and tumbled, off balance, into the sand.

Sullivan followed him. Gravity returned to normal and the pirate struggled to his knees. The thing that had been pressed against his neck turned out to be a British Webley .455 revolver and Sullivan kicked it right out of the man's hands. The kid had bounced off a rubbery tree, and was coming back up with that Belgian buzz saw, so Sullivan concentrated, reversed gravity, and dropped him into the air in a cloud of white sand.

The villagers were interested now, and several were heading his way. The one with the machete was in front, looking pissed. Behind him was a man with a rifle that had been ancient before the Great War, and Sullivan got ready to Spike the whole damn village into the ocean. "I need to talk to Southunder. Don't make me hurt you."

The native with the old rifle said something fierce and Sullivan didn't need to speak the language to know that he'd just been told to go screw himself.

"That'll be enough," a calm voice called from the largest building. Immediately the villagers stopped and lowered their weapons. A man walked out onto the porch, shielding his eyes from the sun. "What do you want, Heavy?"

Sullivan recognized the Grimnoir from Pershing's memories, though he was more than twenty years older now. He was a little thinner, had lost the rest of his hair, but the main difference was that he'd gotten a better tan. "Pershing sent me."

For a legendary buccaneer, he wasn't much to look at. No big hat, no beard, no parrot or even a wooden leg. He was a completely average-looking man, small of stature and wearing simple work clothes stained with engine grease. Southunder paused to take a drink from a cup made from half a coconut. His manner was deceivingly mild. "I figured that from the way you were beating on my men . . . You hurt, Barns?"

The younger one came out of the jungle, glaring at Sullivan. "I didn't know he was a Mover," he said, shoving his machine pistol into a shoulder holster. It was a dual rig, and he had a matching gun under his other arm as well.

"Gravity Spiker," Sullivan corrected.

"Mr. Parker?"

"I'm good," the other pirate answered as he picked his Webley off the ground and blew the sand from the cylinder. He was dark-skinned, probably a mulatto, and was a big man, not fat but bulky through the chest and arms, though not nearly as large as Sullivan. "Only thing hurt's my feelings."

Southunder sighed. "Sad day for pirates everywhere. So Pershing sent you, huh? How is the old coot?"

"Dead," Sullivan answered. "Killed by a Pale Horse."

Southunder didn't seem surprised. "And the others?"

"The Portagee was murdered by an Iron Guard, same with Jones. Christiansen got torn apart by a demon. The Chairman got their pieces."

"So ends the knights of New York . . ." Southunder thought about it for a long time. He tossed the coconut off the porch and into the bushes. His men exchanged confused glances. Apparently this was all new to them. "Well, I figured this day would come." He turned and walked back into the building. "You ate lunch yet?"

Sullivan consumed all the fish they put in front of him, and figured he would keep doing so as long as the Japanese girl kept putting more on the table. She batted her eyes politely when he thanked her for the fifth plate, and returned to the kitchen. He'd told his story quickly and quietly, and now he was just plain hungry.

Bob Southunder studied him with cold blue eyes. Sullivan could tell that he was a calculating and intelligent man, the kind of man who'd grown impatient with governments and secret societies and had decided to make war on the Imperium by himself, but he was also a friendly enough host. "You sure eat a lot."

"So I've been told," he answered.

He watched Sullivan's hands. "Where's your ring?"

"Don't have one. Never took the oath."

Southunder nodded. "I would've figured otherwise. You've got Grimnoir written all over you."

He didn't know whether to take that as compliment or not, so he just grunted and kept eating.

The building was mostly an open space, sort of a village common room, and a long rectangular table made of planks filled most of it. More people had poured in after he'd arrived, taking up the other spots, and then filling in along the wall once the chairs were taken. Apparently his arrival was interesting. The people were made up of every race he could imagine, and were aged from teenagers to old men, but most of them looked to be of fighting age and in fighting shape. The only women present were the ones who kept bringing food from the kitchen. Apparently piracy was man's work.

Southunder hadn't lived this long in the shadow of the Imperium by trusting strangers. "I'd of figured Black Jack would have sent at least a knight . . ."

"John Moses Browning was supposed to have given me the oath, but he got hurt, and I had to leave in a hurry."

"*The* John Browning?" the kid named Barns asked from a few seats away.

"Yep," Sullivan said. The serving girl refilled his cup with some pungent rice wine. He kept catching her staring at him.

"You're pulling my leg."

Southunder waved him away. "He's not. We're old friends. How bad was he?"

Sullivan told them the story of the Peace Ray. The other conversations in the room tapered off to nothing, and soon everyone was listening in. When he got to the part about Isaiah Rawls trying to Read his mind, a look of disgust crossed Southunder's face. "He was one of the knights of New York too, but . . ." he paused. "Never mind, it isn't right to speak ill of someone who isn't around to defend himself. Let's just say that I'm not surprised he ended up in the leadership. He was a sneaky one. The Society always liked doing things in the least straightforward way possible. Maybe that's why they never liked me much. What was the other one's name?"

"Harkeness," Sullivan answered. "Why?"

"The name's familiar. I think he was one of the European Grimnoir that argued with Black Jack when he wanted to just break the cursed thing and be done with it. There were a bunch of them. They were one of the founding families. Leave it to them to be too proud to listen to reason, thinking that they were smart enough to use Tesla's mad device."

"How about we go smash the damn thing right now then," Sullivan suggested. "Everybody wins."

Southunder smiled. "Because I don't know if I believe you yet. For all I know you're an Imp spy, trying to get me to take you to it, so you can cut my throat and take it back to your master."

He wasn't the easily offended type. "Fair 'nuff." Sullivan looked around the crowded room. There were a few Japs within earshot, and he had no doubt the Chairman would pay a fortune to anybody who ratted them out. "You want to talk about this alone?"

Southunder chuckled. "This is my crew. We've been through hell together. I trust these men much more than I trust you, stranger." He turned in his chair, looking for someone. "Ken, come here, please."

A young Jap leaning against the far wall set his food on the windowsill and came over. His face was creased with scars and half of one ear was missing. "Captain," he answered gruffly.

"Show Mr. Sullivan here how much love you've got for the Imperium."

The Jap bowed his head a bit and unbuttoned his shirt. When he opened it, even as hardened as Sullivan was, he still cringed. Despite all the things he'd seen, he hadn't seen anything like this before. Every inch of his chest and stomach had been burned or cut, and was now covered in twisting black and grey scars.

"That'll be all," Southunder said.

"Yes, Captain," the Jap said as he pulled his shirt back on and returned to his lunch.

"Ken was one of the lucky ones we freed from a slave transport. See, his family didn't like the way the Chairman was running things, so he was *volunteered*. They started working on him when he was a little boy, but the kanji just wouldn't take, and they kept on burning until they ran out of skin. He was lucky he was born Nipponese, so failing out of school didn't get him turned over to Unit 731. If he had been a Chinaman or anything else, they'd still be experimenting on him. Mr. Parker?"

"Captain?" the muscular man responded from a few spaces away.

"Tell our guest what happens to the *gaijin* prisoners."

"I was on a ship running guns up the Malaccan Straights to the rebels fighting in Siam. We were boarded and taken inland." His accent reminded Sullivan of his time on the New Orleans docks, that cross between French and English that he'd never gotten used to. "There was a 731 camp there. The Cogs were doing surgery, cutting pieces off of people's insides, just to see how long it took them to die, givin' them diseases to see how fast different plagues killed different colored folks. They'd build whole little towns in the camps, fill them with folks, whole families, and then turn containers of plague fleas loose on them, just to count how many got sick. I was lucky, 'cause I was strong, so they used me to move the bodies to the pits where they fed them to the *things* they'd created. That's where I was when Captain Southunder and the *Marauder* bombed them bastards to hell."

The young one named Barns laughed. "He never gets tired of telling those stories. Scares the piss out of the new guys, so they make extra sure not to get captured."

"How'd you get here, kid?" Sullivan asked.

It was obvious he didn't like being called "kid." "I'm a pilot. Barns is short for Barnstormer. I like shooting down Jap planes."

"Everybody needs a hobby."

"Pays good too." Barns grinned and took a swig from a bottle of mystery booze.

Southunder shook his head at Barns, giving an exasperated look that told him that the kid had a story, and that he wasn't helping make the point. The old pirate turned back to Sullivan. "I could keep these men talking all day. Most of us have been wronged by the Chairman somehow, so don't you worry about my men's loyalty."

"That how you do most of your recruiting? Men who hate the Imperium?"

"Some. Any man who's willing to stand against the Imperium is welcome here. I don't care if they do it for the money, revenge, or just because they like to burn things. I've got a gang of misfits, deserters, and outcasts. I split anything we capture evenly with my men and we sell it in the remaining Free Cities or wherever people are buying. Don't get me wrong. There's money to be made but it's more satisfying when you pry it from scum. Any Imperium ship on the water or the sky that goes anywhere without heavy escort is mine for the taking, anywhere along their frontier. They've hunted us for years, but we're too smart, and we've given them a few black eyes."

Sullivan glanced around the room. "You've got, what? Thirty men? What do you expect to accomplish?"

"Oh, we won't quit until we're dead or we've killed them all, Mr. Sullivan." Southunder was a soft-spoken man, but Sullivan could tell that there was steel beneath those quiet words. "Every last one."

"EVERY LAST ONE!" the entire room bellowed in unison, banging their cups, stamping their feet, or hitting their rifle butts on the floor.

Sullivan decided that these pirates were okay with him.

Imperium flagship *Tokugwa*

THOUGH THE *TOKUGAWA* could certainly defend itself, it was not a warship. It was more like a floating palace. Madi had been amazed by the sheer opulence of the craft when he'd first come aboard and even after a couple of days he was still finding new things. Much of it was still bare, since the Chairman would use his personal favorite artisans to place the finishing touches, but the rooms and open spaces were majestic. There were paths lined with black soil where plants and even trees would be lovingly placed. It would be an appropriate vessel for the greatest man alive.

There was no other airship like it. All three giant hulls were mostly covered in structure and buildings. The top of the *Tokugawa* looked almost like a traditional ship, flat, and interspaced with structures, some as large as four-story buildings. The first and second hulls were side by side, with all of the engine and power-plant sections between them, and the third hull was evenly spaced below them. All three were angled, and the bags nearly touched at the front, so that the craft was shaped like a wedge, while the rear was mostly open and covered in powerful propellers. It was the greatest vessel ever created.

There was only a skeleton crew of three hundred men, sent specifically to Michigan to pick up the *Tokugawa* and bring it home. Once they reached Japan the crew would be brought up to full strength, and the Chairman would make this his new mobile command center.

The training dojo was in the very bottom of the ship, suspended alone beneath the third hull, so that nothing would impede its view. The wood floor had been polished until it gleamed and he could still smell varnish and sawdust. With the armored shutters open, the glass walls let in all of the sun and it seemed like he could see across the entire Pacific from here. The ceiling was thirty feet tall, and the dojo was a hundred feet long and eighty feet wide.

Twenty men had gathered to watch him practice. It was a great honor to spar with an Iron Guard. It was even rumored amongst the troops that if you could hurt one, the Chairman would give you a personal blessing. Rule number one, respect strength.

Madi's stance was wide, the wooden sword at his side hung loose and ready in his hands. "Again," he commanded.

He was sparring against six of the crew at one time. All were volunteers, hoping to impress the Iron Guard. Four were Imperial Marines, wearing a single kanji, but hardy fighters anyway. Two were

Actives, a Torch from the damage control team, and the lieutenant in charge of security was a Massive, like his old master, Rokusaburo. He was really the only one Madi was concerned with.

The Marines charged while the Torch circled, looking for a shot. Madi took the first two down with single clean strikes, quicker than the eye could follow, driving one to the ground so hard that he felt bones break. One almost caught him with the edge of a sword, but he hit that one with a quick surge of Power and now down for the Marine became straight into the air. The Massive swung, but Madi dodged back with the speed of a man a fraction of his size, and before the sword could come back, he threw several extra gravities on it. The lieutenant grunted, trying to lift the katana that now seemed to weigh a hundred pounds, and Madi hit him with a slash that would have cleaved even his superdense body nearly in half.

The one he'd put into the air landed flat just as the Torch engulfed him in fire. Madi dove and rolled through the heat, feeling it prickle his skin as the magic kanji protected him. The Torch scrambled back as Madi rose, but the Iron Guard was too quick, and the crack of his bokken against the Torch's shin might have been heard at the opposite end of the ship. He hit the ground and Madi kicked the Active across the floor with his bare foot. He pulled it, since he didn't want to kill any of the damage control crew on a vessel filled with hydrogen, but the man still slid ten feet.

Madi spun the sword and surveyed the damage. It had taken five seconds. All of his opponents were down, but most were game enough to struggle back to their feet to bow. The Torch was hobbling on a broken ankle, trying to hold back tears, and he even managed a deep bow, only to fall over on his face. The only one who didn't was the one with the broken collarbone, and even Madi couldn't rightly fault that.

"Healer!" he barked. The blonde Grimnoir was shoved forward onto the hardwood by one of the watching soldiers. They'd cleaned her up, fed her, and put her in a white kimono. At least she was easy on the eyes. Asian women were good and all, but too skinny for his tastes. "Fix 'em." She hesitated, until one of the men guarding her gave her a good smack on the back of the head. She lowered her tired eyes and went to work. *That's better.* He turned back to the crowd. "Eight men this time!"

The wounded were helped off the floor to make room for their replacements. The Marines picked up the dropped bokkens and two drew bo staffs from the rack. *Good. Now they're using strategy.* "Again!"

Ten seconds later they were all down. One man actually hit him in the lip hard enough to draw blood with the end of a staff before he broke his arm and Powered him across the room. He'd been distracted by the tremor in the airship's frame. They were changing course. The sun was shifting in the glass. They were turning south.

"Good shot," he told the young man who was being picked off the floor by his companions. Madi bowed, and the smile on the Marine's face told him that he'd remember the honor for a lifetime. A blue-uniformed flight crew member arrived a moment later with a message. He read it as he licked the blood from his teeth. The final piece of the Geo-Tel had been revealed. Naval units were closing in on the island now. It had been right under their noses, just like those slimy Grimmys. A submarine with Shadow Guard was ready to move as soon as the Finders pinpointed the exact location. Madi swore under his breath. It figured. He'd personally recovered every other piece. The last should be his honor to claim, not some candy-ass Shadow Guard.

But as he continued reading, his mood improved. The *Tokugawa* was to rendezvous with the *Kaga* carrying . . . the Chairman! The device would be reassembled aboard the new flagship. His lips parted in an unconscious bloody smile. He might not be the one to claim the last piece, but he'd be present for its firing. He would be there, at the Chairman's side, for the birth of a whole new world. A world ruled by strength and wisdom instead of weakness and corruption. *Perfect.*

"This time all of you who can stand." Madi turned back to the troops and raised his sword. "Again!"

Madi

Chapter 22

Billy Clanton and Frank McLowry commenced to draw their pistols at the same time Tom McLowry jumped behind a horse. I had my pistol in my overcoat pocket where I had put it. When I saw Billy and Frank draw their pistols I drew my pistol, I knew that the McLowry brothers had the reputation of having wizard's magic and I aimed at Frank McLowry. The two first shots which were fired were fired by Billy Clanton and myself. He shot at me, and I shot at Frank McLowry. I do not know which shot was first; we fired almost together. Morgan then shot Billy Clanton. The fight then became general. After several shots were fired Ike Clanton ran up and grabbed my arm. I could see no weapon in his hand and thought at the time he had none, and so I said to him, "The fight has now commenced. Go to fighting or get away." At the same time I pushed him off with my left hand. He started and ran down the side of the building and disappeared between the lodging house and the photograph gallery. My next shot struck Frank McLowry in the belly. He staggered off on the sidewalk but was still able to pick up a horse to throw at us. Virgil was struck by the flying horse before Holliday, who had the shotgun, fired at and killed Frank McLowry. Tom McLowry was unarmed. It made no difference, for his kind does not need a pistol to kill, and I shot him in the head.

—Testimony of Wyatt Earp,
Tombstone Epitaph, 1881

UBF *Tempest*

"CAPTAIN, I've found them again," the teleradioscope operator said.

I wish they'd quit calling me that. Francis walked over and looked over the UBF employee's shoulder. All he could see were green lights moving up and down, some fast, some slow, and some not at all. They'd tried to explain to him how the machine worked, but it was all about electrical resonance against metallic objects and the frequency and speed of return and traversing whatnots and so forth, and it just made him want a drink really bad. "Where?"

"About a hundred miles further south than we expected. They've changed course. I think they're heading for the Marianas."

That didn't make any sense, but at least they weren't getting any closer to Japan. That had been making him really nervous. "Driver!"

"Uh . . . It's *Helm*, sir," replied the man stationed at the very front of the glass bubble cockpit. Francis was still trying to learn the volunteers' names.

"Very well, Mr. Helm," he said, and couldn't figure out why that caused Lance to snicker. "Follow that blimp."

Lance was sitting in one of the vacant chairs in the command center, with his boots up on a bank of sensitive electronics. "You've really got no idea what you're doing, do you?" At least he was decent enough to lower his voice so the men wouldn't be able to hear them over the engines.

"Frankly, not even the slightest." He took a seat at the empty communications station. Most of the seats were empty in the command center. Less than a quarter of the *Tempest*'s crew had volunteered to stay, and that was only after he'd promised some very hefty bonuses.

Two security men had stuck around, and one was a Brute. Grandfather's Healer had told him politely to go to hell, but at least he'd convinced the man to stick around San Francisco long enough to help Mr. Browning once his Power had recovered. The only other functionary who'd stayed was, surprisingly enough, Mr. Chandler, Grandfather's accountant. All the rest had assured him that they would see to company business, and he had no doubt that they were currently maneuvering to get the UBF board to somehow get rid of him before Grandfather's body was even cold.

So he had a handful of barely-mended Grimnoir knights, a drastically undermanned and unarmed prototype ship, and no clue what he was doing. He'd broken a direct order from a Grimnoir elder and would probably be cast out of the Society he'd devoted his life to, if he lived that long. And he still hadn't even really come to terms with the fact that he was now, theoretically, the richest man in the world.

"Mind if I make a suggestion?" Lance didn't bother to wait for the reply. "If we're going to try this, then we need every advantage we can get. The *Tokugawa* is probably still running a skeleton crew, but that means they'll have five times as many men, and at least one mean son of a bitch of an Iron Guard. They won't be expecting this, but they will have men on watch, and they'll probably be doing it from behind mounted guns, which we don't happen to have. So how about we use that radio bouncer to keep track of 'em, and not get into visual range until dark?"

Francis sighed. "How about I just make you captain?"

The grizzled knight thought about it. "Do I get to wear the fancy hat?"

"You figure out how to get Jane off the *Tokugawa* alive, I'll have your old cowboy hat gold-plated."

Banish Island, Micronesia

PIRATE BOB SOUTHUNDER, Scourge of the South Seas, Terror of the Marianas, killer of men, sinker of ships, and general pain in the Imperium's rear took the time to pass out treats to all the village children like some sort of kindly South Pacific Santa Claus before joining his men on a mission.

"Where'd you get Mr. Goodbars?" Sullivan asked, as Southunder gave a candy bar to a kid, patted him on the head, and sent him on his way.

"They were on an Imperium cargo ship, believe it or not. Why? You want one?"

"Sure." As a general rule, Jake Sullivan never turned down anything free. The two of them walked up the forest path toward the remains of what had once been a mighty volcano. There were five heavily armed pirates right behind, and he was sure that was no accident. He'd not yet earned Southunder's trust.

The pirate had refused to talk further about the Geo-Tel yesterday. He'd slept in the village as a guest, but he'd seen the occasional flashes of cigarettes glowing in the jungle from the men assigned to watch him all night.

He'd woken up with one of the Japanese serving girls crawling onto his sleeping mat, but he'd turned her away as politely as he could without her speaking hardly any English. "No like girls?" "No. Like girls just fine." "No like me then?" "No. You're nice." "Oh. Have girl already." " . . . Yeah . . . something like that." She'd left him alone, and he'd gone back to staring at the tin roof, hating himself because he'd finally fallen asleep again only to catch himself dreaming of Delilah's body, her soft skin pressed against him, his lips on her neck, and he had awoken again, cursing himself as a selfish, pathetic failure of a man. He'd lain there awake until the sun came up.

They'd eaten breakfast in silence: more fish, fruit, and wild boar. None of the pirates commented on the .45 on his hip or the automatic rifle he'd reassembled. They might not trust him yet, but anybody worthy of sharing your hospitality should be worthy of helping to defend it. The men had been excited. Something was happening. After breakfast Southunder had invited him on this walk.

"Are we going to destroy the Geo-Tel now?" he asked.

"It's not here," Southunder answered.

"I don't care where it is, as long as it gets broken into a million pieces and burned. Are we going to go get it then?"

"I've kept it safe since you were wearing short pants, Mr. Sullivan. A few more hours won't kill you."

"Nope. But if the Chairman gets it, he'll kill the whole world."

Laughter always seemed to come easy to Southunder. "Truth be told, I'll be glad to be rid of it. I would have gone last night but my ship was still getting patched from our last job. I didn't dare keep it with me, because if they found me, they'd find it. No, not even Pershing knew exactly where it is for exactly that reason. I'm the only one who knows. It's well hidden. We'll dig it up later."

Sullivan stopped walking, right in the middle of the trail. The men following paused, uneasy. "You *buried* it?"

"Well, of course. I'm a pirate," he answered.

Sullivan shook his head and went back to walking. "Pirates and buried treasure . . . I can't believe this. So where are we going?"

"We have a train to catch, and you wanted a chance to earn my trust . . ."

⁂

The dirigible was sleek, of a design that he'd never seen before. It was a single hull, with one lightly armored bag. It was a hybrid, with two lifter wings folded in so that it could fit inside the hollow formed by the partially collapsed volcanic cone. There were four engines, big gleaming things with propellers longer than he was tall.

Sullivan walked under the cabin, dodging between the tie ropes as the crew let it gently rise. There was no top structure. Everything was under the gas bag, like they used to build them. It was remarkably streamlined for such an older design. Even the front of the cockpit was a circular mass of glass and aluminum struts with not a square edge to be seen. The cabin stretched from the very front to the very back, so seamlessly melded with the gas bag that it might as well have been one piece. It might have been old, but it was well cared for. The brass fittings gleamed. Every inch of hull was freshly painted: light grey underneath, dark blue on top.

On closer inspection, none of the parts seemed to match. The exhaust pipes on one side were different than the other. Two of the engines were different designs. As he studied it, he realized that the whole thing had had so many parts replaced from scavenged or captured vessels, it was hard to tell where the original ship began.

"Isn't she beautiful?" Southunder asked. "It's an actual Zeppelin, not some poor Stuyvesant UBF knockoff, but handcrafted by the finest airship Cogs there's ever been."

"It looks old . . ." Sullivan said.

"Aged. Like good cheese," Southunder agreed.

"It don't have much armor."

"Two hundred feet of raw speed. I could cover every inch in dreadnought plate, and it wouldn't help us beat the entire Jap navy. We strike quick and get out. The bag is divided into locking cells. We could lose three quarters of them and still limp it home."

"Hydrogen?" Hydrogen blimps made him nervous.

"Not a lot of helium out here," he said. "Don't worry, I've got a Torch."

A Torch, as in *one*. And if they lost their man who could control fire and *then* took a hit from an incendiary round . . ."It don't have many guns . . ."

"We don't slug it out with Kagas, Sullivan. Twin pom-poms in the nose and two more in the rear, one of our mutual friend John's big fifty-cals on either side to keep the fighters off, and a few rail-mounted light machine guns, plus we've got two fighters onboard, top of the line Curtiss R5C Raptors, most maneuverable biplane in the world."

Some of the Japanese navy ships carried like *thirty* fighters. After seeing what he had to work with, Sullivan came to respect Southunder even more. The crew was leading the dirigible out from its hiding place and into the sun. They were going on a mission.

"Pershing ever tell you why they ran me out of the Society?" Southunder asked. Sullivan shook his head in the negative. "They said I was too impulsive, too reckless."

"You use a twenty-five-year-old zeppelin with a few guns on it to harass the most powerful navy in the world . . . They might've had a point."

Southunder ignored him. "Pershing saw it too. He saw that times were changing for our kind. Something big is coming, and the world is going to be one way or the other, and I don't want it to be the Chairman's way. Too many folks think that they can keep the world from changing . . . I've got a wife who I only see when I bring in loot to sell in the Free Cities. We've been married for thirty years, and I've got kids and grandbabies. You got a wife, a family, Sullivan?"

"I got nothing."

His voice was so gentle that it was hard to hear him. "I don't want my grandkids to grow up in a world run by a bunch of fascists, or socialists, or progressives, or anarchists, or communists, or eugenicists, or any sort of *ist* or *ism*. When I get those types, the men who just need to control everything, to tell everybody else what to do, I stick it in and break it off. I'm fighting for freedom." Proudly, he gestured around the cave at his men. He loved them like a father. "We ride the air and plunder the seas. We're the last free men and I'll die a free man."

"Amen," Sullivan said.

"There's an Imperium dirigible train that's gotten out of their convoy routes because of the bad weather north of here. We're going to take it, and you're going to show me you mean business." Southunder raised his hand and gestured at the name on the side of the dirigible. "Mr. Sullivan, I give you the Free Ship *Bulldog Marauder*, best damn dirigible there's ever been."

Imperium Submarine J-47 *Flower of Carnage*

THE IMPERIUM CAPTAIN watched the dirigible rising from the side of the volcano through the periscope. He was normally lord of this vessel, but in the presence of a Shadow Guard, he had to defer to his betters. Having four of them aboard made him deeply uncomfortable. He moved aside so the elite soldier could look through the glass. "We could surface and engage with the deck gun before they are in position to return fire."

"No," the Shadow Guard commanded.

The darkened sub stunk of diesel fumes and polluted air. They'd been recycling the air for hours. The Shadow Guard's Finder had already vomited all over the deck twice, and the stink was annoying the captain. He had no patience for seasickness. Their orders were specific. He had not been told what they were supposed to be retrieving, but awareness of their presence could cause its destruction. They had been ordered to maintain complete radio silence and only communicate through the Shadow Guard's magic. The waters ran clear here and he knew that his submarine would show up like a vast black shadow so close to the surface. He shouted orders. The dive bell sounded.

The Finder was sitting cross-legged on the grate, eyes closed, deep in mediation. The captain had never seen one such as this. He had removed his loose shirt, and his torso had been crisscrossed with kanji. The captain wore two, as befitted his rank, so he knew a bit about such things, and he could see that none of the Finder's kanji were based in the physical geometries. Rather, all seven of his were attuned to increasing his Power's sensitivity.

The schools had taught him about Finders. They could feel and see through the disembodied spirits that inhabited the shadow of this world. A truly powerful Finder could actually become a Summoner, capable of bringing in servants from other planes and giving them life here, but this Finder was different. He was like a perfectly tuned tracking dog. He imagined that such sensitivity would drive one mad.

Finders were limited by such things as range, and certain

materials or spells could thwart them. The disembodied were easily distracted, but looking at this particular strange specimen, he knew that nothing brought within his range could possibly hide. It was if he'd been specifically bred for this kind of mission. Apparently his submarine's job was just to get this man within range of whatever it was he was seeking.

It seemed to take forever, but the captain was used to being patient. It came with the assignment. The heat from the burning kanji permeated the sub. It was like being next to a bank of electric heating coils. The Finder opened his eyes and let out a long exhausted breath. The Shadow Guard leaned forward eagerly.

"I have it."

Free Ship Bulldog Marauder

THE DIRIGIBLE TRAIN was floundering. The lead blimp's engines were disabled, and the other three were crowding into it. Four individual single-hulls had been close tethered together in a line when the *Bulldog Marauder* had appeared, and now it was all a jumble of crashing aluminum and fabric, like a herd of injured animals being circled by a cunning predator.

Most of the locals hated the Imperium, so there was always constant radio chatter reporting where their shipping was. They'd tried to trap Southunder a few times with decoys, cargo ships armed to the teeth, but he had a good nose for such things, and seldom had been caught unaware. They'd come up from behind, doing a steady eighty knots with horsepower to spare. Once the captain had made the call that it was a legitimate target, he'd used his own Power to alter the winds. Sullivan had never seen a Weatherman work before. There wasn't any flash or anything fancy. It was methodical. First they reached out and understood how everything was functioning within their range. Then they had to coax bits of it to work just right. Standing at the very front of the cockpit with his hands pressed against the glass, it had taken Southunder ten minutes to alter the currents until the wind was at their backs.

Once the Imperium train had spotted them, black smoke had puffed from their engines as they cranked up the RPMs. Southunder counteracted that so that the wind slammed right into the nose of the lead dirigible, slowing it, and rocking the crew. Within minutes they were passing through the oil vapor. Then they closed at terrific speed.

When they had gotten into range, a heavy machine gun had opened up from the rear dirigible. Southunder had calmly ordered the pom-pom gunner to silence it, and four solid one-pound shells later, it was done, leaving the cargo blimp's back end a mess of tattered fabric and broken railing and the black dot of the gunner tumbling toward the sea. "We can't use the bursting shells on the hydrogen ones," Southunder had explained calmly. "Can't sell burned cargo."

They'd dropped altitude then, diving beneath the train. They needed to get alongside to board and this route exposed them to the fewest guns possible. Pirates armed with scoped rifles were tethered to the outer catwalks and they fired at anything that moved on the train above, and when they had a clean shot, they started shooting at the lead dirigible's engines.

"This is the dangerous part," Southunder had said. "We've got a very powerful Torch on the crew, and can control any fires that break out if we're in range, but sometimes they'll go suicidal and ignite the whole thing while we're right under them." He'd smiled, trying to be reassuring. "That can get exciting."

Within minutes the engines had been destroyed and the blimps had started to blunder into each other like blinded whales. Southunder had spun his finger, the wings had been turned accordingly, and the outer engines were pointed straight down, driving them right toward the jumble of crashing behemoths.

"Now all we have to do is pull up alongside while they're shooting at us and board," Southunder told him. "Piece of cake."

Barns was the helmsman, and he frowned as he pulled back on the controls. "By piece of cake, Capitan Southunder means that it's just like elephants fucking while going a hundred miles an hour swinging on a trapeze . . ."

"Don't forget the elephants are filled with explosive gas," Sullivan responded. "Where do you want me?"

Southunder jerked his head. "Take that ladder up top. Boarding party is in position."

"Aye aye, Cap'n." Sullivan said. He'd always wanted to say that since he'd first read *Treasure Island* as a kid. He made sure all the pockets on his canvas vest were closed and that his automatic rifle was tightly slung, then started up the ladder.

"Sullivan," Southunder called after him. "Just so you know, we'll pick up the last piece of the Geo-Tel on our way home. It's not far from here. I just thought we'd kill two birds with one stone this way."

"About damn time." Sullivan climbed up through a hole onto the next deck. Ten men were crowded into the tight space, packed between hot pipes in two teams of five. It was dark except for a pair of red light bulbs. He had to crouch to keep from hitting his head. They were armed with a variety of weapons, everything from old Bergman subguns with snail drums, to Winchester trench shotguns, to stolen Jap guns he didn't recognize, and even a Mauser broomhandle machine-pistol with the shoulder stock. Beyond that they all had little axes or big knives on their belts. Parker was in the lead armed with a double-barreled shotgun that had been sawed off just ahead of the forearm.

"My team heads fore. Ken's team heads aft." Parker leaned around to see through the columns of ready pirates. "Ori, don't let us all burn to death, right? If these things catch, we don't have much time 'fore we're all cooked."

He had to be addressing the Torch. Sullivan turned. He had not seen the other Active tucked into the back of the room and he was surprised to see the serving girl from the previous night. "Okay, Mr. Parker. No fire." She waved shyly when she saw Sullivan looking at her, then decided to study her feet.

"*That's* your Torch?"

"Sullivan, meet Lady Origami, or at least that's what we've taken to calling her since she didn't have a name."

"Twenty seconds!" Southunder's voice came up the ladder. "We're mid-starboard side, second vessel!" Parker started to count out loud. Sullivan took a deep breath and let it out through his nose. Two men held massive steel grappling hooks attached to long spools of rope. When he got to three, the Jap named Ken jerked up the locking bar, and at one, he shoved. Sunlight flooded in as the pirates charged out, screaming. For a second it reminded him of the trenches in France, but then the moment was gone, and he was bellowing along behind the others, running up the steel grate, coming out the very top-front end of the *Bulldog Marauder*'s cabin.

The hooks sailed through the air, both of them catching on railings on the Imperium ship. Barns was good. Sullivan only had to leap across a few feet of empty space before he was on the enemy's craft. He didn't have an assignment, so he followed Parker's team down the catwalk. Gunfire erupted just around the curve of the hull, out of sight, but was answered with a thunder of two 12-gauge shells.

The pirates moved down the railing, shooting anyone that appeared ahead of them. As they reached a door to the interior, Parker signed for some to enter and clear it. They were followed by screams and the rapid chatter of a subgun. Parker kept going, so Sullivan followed. At the very end of the rail, a soldier in a brown uniform came tearing out from behind a spotlight, swinging a sword. He was screaming some war cry, and Parker shot him right in the face, dropping him clean. The pirate took cover behind the spotlight. Sullivan crouched next to him.

"See that bridge?" Parker asked as he broke open the shotgun and pulled out the spent shell. "We need to cross it and get to the next blimp."

Sullivan peeked around the spotlight. The knotted mass of cable and short planks might have been a bridge at one point, but after the dirigibles' crashing together, it was just a mess now that he didn't particularly want to try to climb. A group of Imperium soldiers was running down the other catwalk, coming their way. "Company," Sullivan said as he leaned out and shouldered the BAR. He lined up the peep sight, put the front sight on the lead man and squeezed the trigger. Bullets puckered the soldier's chest, sailed through and struck the man behind him too. Both went down in a spray of blood. He worked the rifle over the rest as they took cover behind the pylons.

Parker had to shout to be heard over the rushing of wind and the return fire. "We didn't expect this many. First blimp must've been transporting troops."

Sullivan analyzed the situation. There were lots of them, few of him, and they had more guns. The glass shattered next to his head as he ducked lower. They were all along one side of the blimp railing. It was far, but he figured he could do it. This would be tough, but he wouldn't need to hold it too long. The world faded to its physical bits. The lightness of the hydrogen offended him in an abstract way, but most everything was just matter when you got down to it, and everything answered to gravity. He Spiked.

For the Imperial soldiers on the lead blimp, down suddenly changed direction, and they found themselves falling away from the cover of the pylons. Many of them caught themselves on the railing, but the unlucky bounced off, spinning away into the empty sky. Sullivan cut his Power and those hanging by their fingertips fell to the grating where there was no cover.

Sullivan rose, firing the BAR, working it right down the opposite deck. The rate of fire was slow enough that he just gently worked it from body to body. It was a massacre. He dropped the empty mag, smoothly reloaded from a vest pocket, and put a single round into the last man still crawling.

"Damn . . ." Parker said, peering over the perforated spotlight. "You get them all?"

"No," Sullivan said. Somebody had been out of his range and had ducked beyond the curve of the hull. It had been an officer, and it sounded like he might be screaming someth—

THOOM.

The explosion was muted as the officer committed suicide, but whatever device he'd touched off had been incendiary, intended to take everyone with him. Sudden fire licked around the curve of the bag, bright hideous orange, and it just consumed everything. The canvas began disappearing like dry grass, leaving a hideous skeleton of aluminum in its wake, and the fireball was coming right at *them.*

"Ax," Sullivan said as he yanked the little hatchet from Parker's belt. He ran down the grating, toward the fire, and slid to a halt at the end of the catwalk. The bridge was attached by rope running through several steel grommets. He started chopping, slicing through the rope with such fury that sparks rose from the plate. *Wouldn't that be funny if a spark blew up this blimp while I was trying to—damn it—cut faster.* He kept swinging with speed born of desperation.

The wall of heat struck him, sucked the moisture from his eyes, burned his skin. The lead dirigible was curling into itself, forming a U, as the heaviest bit was in the center. Flames washed over his body as the last rope snapped free. He stumbled back with his shirt on fire, dropped the ax, and beat out the flames. The burning blimp spun downward, falling slowly, like the bright petals of a flower falling from a tree, and Sullivan swore as he realized his hair was on fire too.

He made it back to Parker just as he saw that the skin on the nose of his dirigible was smoking. "Aw hell . . ." Simultaneously tiny bits of hissing fire appeared all down the visible seams. They were at the wrong damn end to make it off this one. The entire nose instantly disintegrated in a jet of orange flame.

And then it just stopped.

Sullivan looked around in disbelief, somehow still alive. Parker was slowly uncovering his eyes. The fore section of the blimp was hanging in ragged tatters, beating in the breeze, and he could feel them tilting as they lost altitude. The Japanese Torch dame was coming down the railing toward them, her eyes glowing and hair whipping in the wind.

"Fire good!" she exclaimed, lowering her hands. The lights died and her eyes returned to normal.

"No, sweetheart, you're good," Parker shouted.

Sullivan couldn't agree more.

The crew of the *Bulldog Marauder* was efficient. They quickly searched the damaged dirigible's cargo hold, found a few chained slaves and some valuables, loaded them into the less damaged remaining blimps, and cut away the damaged blimp so that it could sink in the ocean. Southunder left five men to drive the remains of the train south to be sold in one of the Free Cities of New Guinea, where the resistance would surely appreciate the supplies. The slaves, mostly Chinese, were put to work with the promise they'd be set free as soon as they landed.

Sullivan joined Southunder in his stateroom, which was little more than a closet with a table sandwiched between armored bulkheads. He was getting tired of always having to duck to avoid hitting his head. There was a map on the table.

"I buried the piece on this atoll." Southunder stabbed his finger into the map. "It's in a chest, wrapped in enough cold iron to give any Finder fits, then sealed in wax. I put every ward and glyph in the

Rune Arcanium on it, then I booby-trapped it the old-fashioned way with spike traps and a bunch of dynamite that's probably unstable as hell by now."

Sullivan studied the map. The atoll wasn't that far from Banish Island. They'd probably flown over it to catch the train. "We should've went there first."

"Not if we wanted to catch that train ahead of the storm front. I can steer the weather some, but I can't board dirigibles in a hurricane, and I wasn't about to let that cargo get away. I've been keeping watch over that blasted thing for twenty years, and unescorted trains are rare. Tesla could wait a few hours . . . No need to risk the traps, so we'll just stand off and blast it with the pom-pom guns until the dynamite goes off. Then we'll go down and pick up the pieces."

"So you decided to believe me then?"

He shrugged. "You strike me as an honest man."

There was a sudden pounding on the bulkhead. "Captain! Come quick!"

Southunder was surprisingly nimble. Sullivan had a hard time catching up as the captain ran down the passage and slid down a ladder to the command deck. By the time he got up to the control bubble he could see exactly what the commotion was about. To the north was a wall of black clouds, crackling with lightning, but more terrifying was what was to their west, several large Imperium airships, and even to Sullivan's untrained eye, those did not look like cargo ships.

"There shouldn't have been any navy in this area," Barns said. "Could they have gotten here already from the train's distress call?"

"Damn it. Kagas." Southunder muttered. There was a large brass telescope mounted at the front of the cockpit and he swiveled it toward the ocean. Sullivan followed the direction it was aiming and noticed more black specks on the ocean, surface ships. "That's not why they're here."

There was a terrible sinking feeling in the pit of his stomach. "Is that the atoll?"

Southunder pulled away from the telescope, his face ashen. "Well, looks like you were right."

"Hate to say I told you so," Sullivan muttered.

The black ships were getting closer. Tiny dots dropped from

their bellies as they released their parasitic fighters. "Orders, Captain?" Barns asked.

Southunder steadied himself against the telescope. Pushing for the atoll would mean certain death. If the fighters didn't get them, the heavy antiaircraft guns on the surface ships would. "Run for the storm."

Chapter 23

We've been warned about magic since the days of Adam. Wizards from Canaan and Babylon were always there to lead man astray. Why should now be any different? What if what we're seeing in these times is a quickening of mankind, tempting us to stray one last time before the last days? This is nothing new. The serpent has just got himself a fancy new suit. Join with me, brethren, and demand that Washington round up these heathen wizards once and for all!

—D.W. Griffith
At the first screening of his blockbuster film
The Death of a Nation, 1918

UBF *Tempest*

LANCE JOINED FAYE on the observation bubble at the top of the airship. She'd been up here for hours, watching the distant angry clouds and now enjoying the orange sunset. This was the first time she'd ever flown and the first time she'd ever been over the ocean. She liked the view, and she didn't really feel like being around the others. For the first time in a very long time, she just wanted to be all alone.

"Hey, kid," Lance said as he limped over and leaned on the rail next to her. Faye was leaning way forward, with her forehead against the cold glass, so it felt more like she was outside, flying . . . *Flying.* Now that would be a neat magic to have. She wondered if anybody could fly?

"Hi, Lance. Do you know anyone who can fly?"

"We're in an airship right now . . ."

"No, silly, I mean, like a magic bird."

He thought about it for a moment. "Well, I sorta do, when I put part of my consciousness inside a bird. It's overrated. Lots of flapping . . . I came to ask you a favor, a real hard favor, and I won't blame you if you say no."

She figured she already knew what it would be. Faye might have been young, but she wasn't stupid. The *Tempest* was going to try and sneak up in the dark on the *Tokugawa.* If they were spotted, they'd get shot down. There was only one of them who could go over there and find Jane without having to actually make the ships touch. "Get me close enough and I'll get her."

Lance nodded thoughtfully. "I knew you would. You're a brave girl . . . but don't tell Francis, it'll scare him to death, and the poor lad's already a little addled, and especially don't tell Dan."

She hadn't spoken to Mr. Garrett on the trip. For someone whose Power was based on words, he sure seemed to be saving his up. "He wants to go get her himself."

"Yep. Can't say I rightly blame him," Lance said thoughtfully. "You still got your Grandpa's ring?" Faye pulled it out of her pocket and showed him. It was too big and kept slipping off her fingers, but she'd never lose it. "Put it on," Lance said gruffly. She complied. "Right hand, I'm making you a knight, not proposing, damn it."

"Really?" She put the ring on her right hand.

"Yeah, really." He looked at her for a long time. "John figured you were too young and that you hadn't been taught near enough, but I figure you're gonna need all the help you can get. John's gonna kill me." He cleared his throat. "Do you, Sally Faye Vierra, agree to take the oath of the Grimnoir knight—"

"Sure," she answered. "Is that it?"

Lance rolled his eyes. "No, that ain't it. Christ almighty . . . where was I? That you will swear before your God that you will stay true to that which is right and good, that your magic will be used to protect, never to enslave, that your strength and wisdom will be used to shield the innocent, that you will fight always for liberty even though it may cost your life, that the Society will become your blood and its knights your kin, and that you will heed the wisdom of the elders' council."

Technically, it seemed like they were violating the heck out of that last one, since they'd left Mr. Rawls and Mr. Harkeness in San Francisco, but she supposed that the other part about the knights being your family came first and Jane *was* in danger. "Okay."

"Do you willingly pledge your magic, your knowledge, your resources, and your life to these things?"

She had plenty of magic, so much that she was starting to think that maybe she had more than anybody else, but not nearly so much knowledge, and no resources to speak of, but she didn't really mind risking her life. It was actually kind of fun. So it probably balanced out. "I do!"

Lance took his thumb and pressed it against her forehead. He pushed hard, leaving a pink indention in her skin, making a simple design. She felt her Power perk up, almost like it was excited, and then the feeling was gone.

"Sally Faye Vierra, you are now a knight of the Grimnoir Society . . . On a personal note, don't screw it up."

Grandpa's ring shrunk just enough to fit her finger perfectly.

Imperium flagship *Tokugawa*

MADI WAS SO EXCITED he could barely contain himself. The *Kaga*, first of the Imperium's super warships, had just maneuvered alongside and the docking had been perfect. Ropes had been launched across and tethered between the two giants, and the canvas-and-silk covered bridge had been rolled across and unfurled. The Weathermen were burning Power to keep the air perfectly calm as the Chairman strolled across.

The crew had assembled and stood in perfect formation. They snapped to even tighter as the personal bodyguard walked from the bridge onto the *Tokugawa*'s deck. The soldiers were dressed in black with the traditional red shoulder sash and belt. They formed two lines, and at a command, lifted their Arisaka rifles as one, creating a roof of bayonets for the Chairman to walk under. They stomped their feet in unison. "Strength forever! Imperium forever!"

He could tell that the Chairman was eager by how he was walking with a purpose, though as usual his face betrayed none of that. The man never seemed to hurry. Everything was always done in the proper time, but even he had to be a little excited to fire up the Geo-Tel. The last message they'd received had said that the Shadow Guard sub had recovered the final piece, and that they'd used a magic portal, just as he and Yutaka had done, to send it directly the Chairman.

Okubo Tokugawa paused at the end of the ramp and took in the assembled men and the lofty hangar. He breathed in deeply, smelling the recent construction. "I *like* it," he said simply, and the men were happy. The Chairman was followed by several men in long black coats, Unit 731 Cogs, and they were carrying the pieces of the Tesla device. Behind them came another two hundred men to supplement the *Tokugawa*'s crew, handpicked from the finest in the Imperium navy.

Madi barely moved as the Chairman stopped right in front of him. Madi seldom wore an Iron Guard uniform, but this was a special occasion. His chest was covered in medals and commendations, and he'd even kept the stupid little one the AEF had given him, only it was below all the Imperium honors. *Is my uniform perfect? I should have ironed it better. Damn it.* He couldn't help but be nervous. The Emperor was supposed to be a god, but Madi had seen him. He was just some pathetic Normal, a figurehead. The real leader of the most powerful nation in the world was right here, close enough to smell his breath.

The Chairman looked over at the Healer standing at his side. The blonde had her head down, afraid to look at him. "What is this?" he asked.

"A gift. She is a Healer, captured from the Grimnoir. I thought you could find a use for her."

He studied her for a moment, sticking a finger under her chin and lifting her face. She didn't speak Japanese, but she understood what was happening. "Yes. She will do." He returned his attention to his Iron Guard. "Madi, I am sorry for the loss of Yutaka. You worked well together for many years."

"He was strong," Madi replied, "and his death was avenged."

The Chairman nodded. "Excellent work, my son. Intelligence shows that your operation has inflamed the American public. Their government is in an uproar. There has already been violence against Actives."

"Thank you, Chairman."

"You have shown great initiative. Some doubted your loyalty, but I never did. I saw in you a heart that was pure. You took the life of your own flesh and blood in my service. I am pleased. From this point forward, you are to be First amongst the Iron Guard until you perish or I discover someone stronger."

He'd never been so humbled. Madi dropped to his knees and bowed clear to the floor. This was the greatest moment of his life.

"Rise, First Iron Guard. We have much work to do." Madi rose quickly. "Keep our heading toward Edo. The *Kaga* will accompany us." The Chairman turned to one of the Cogs. Madi recognized the little man as the 731 officer who had given him his first kanji. "Shiro, take your men and prepare the device. I want it ready to fire immediately. I do not wish to step foot on the soil of my home until I can do so as the conqueror of the world. Is that understood?"

His initial thoughts had been right. The Chairman had been waiting for this since 1908. He would waste no time. The targeting marks that had been carved in America were still there, undiscovered all this time. He'd checked them himself on one of his early assignments. They were intricate designs carved right into the bedrock beneath a New York subway. The Geo-Tel would provoke the Power, and it would be drawn toward the Tesla-designed geometries. Their greatest threat would be crippled in one strike. Every other country in the world would fall right into line or risk having a spy scratch a mark under one of their cities. The war would be over before it had even been declared.

It didn't matter where the device itself was located. It was truly a global super-weapon. The initial test-firing had been from Tesla's lab, but the Power had risen up and burned a thousand miles around where Imperium scouts had put the targeting mark in Siberia. If it hadn't been for those damn Grimnoir, the device would have been in the Chairman's hands decades ago.

In a shallow, selfish way, Madi was thankful for those Grimnoir who'd captured the device. He'd only been ten in '08, and he'd been living in the area that would have been immolated. He would have died along with everybody else and never had the opportunity to become an Iron Guard. Fate had smiled on him, and since it spared his life by thwarting the Chairman then, it was only right for him to help put history right now.

The Cog bowed and scurried away with the others. The wizards still made Madi uncomfortable, but they had their uses, just like the Iron Guard, or even that madman Tesla. Everything was falling into place, all for the Chairman's inevitable reign, and Madi would be at his side until the end.

FS *Bulldog Marauder*

THE SKY WAS BLACK with rain. Clouds roiled and lightning crashed. The winds were blowing at terrible velocities, but Southunder's magic was cushioning them from the very worst.

"I think we've lost them," Barns said.

Sullivan was standing at the very front of the glass bubble, watching the energy. "We have to go after it."

"We don't even know where it is," Southunder said. He was sitting in his captain's chair, rubbing his eyes with his palm.

"They'll take it right to the Chairman, and one minute after he puts it together, America is *gone* . . . We need to at least warn them."

Barns turned around from his console. "Who'd believe you? I don't believe you, and I'm sitting right here."

Southunder rose. "I can at least alert the Grimnoir. They know people. Maybe they can . . . hell, I don't know, start evacuating . . . I still remember the spell, I just haven't done it for so long. Damn Pershing's orders! I never spoke to anyone, just in the off chance that the Imperium would find it." He went to the wall and pulled down a small round mirror. "Mr. Parker, go to the galley and get me some sea salt . . . It's been a long time, hiding, all for Black Jack, and all for nothing."

"We'll make it right." Sullivan vowed, even though he had no idea how.

UBF *Tempest*

Francis was biting his nails. The sun was down. They were on the outer edges of a bad storm. The teleradioscope was still getting a return telling them the approximate location of the *Tokugawa*. It was moving west again, heading for Japan. This was their last chance. They were moving along at full speed to intercept.

The boarding party was below. He wished he had more time, then he'd personally speak to every one of them, knight, mercenary, and *other*. The *Tempest* wasn't designed for such things, but Lance had told him that they'd land right on top of the giant *Tokugawa*, lower the ramp, and it would be just like parking at an airport. He had a sneaky feeling it wouldn't be that easy, and suspected that Lance concurred. Either way, he'd be joining them at the last minute.

Faye had joined them in the cockpit and was wandering around, looking at all the flashing lights, remarking on how pretty they were, and he felt a little nervous that she might start pushing buttons just to see what would happen. She was geared up for battle, armed with a short Auto-5 shotgun and wearing crisscrossed bandoleers of brass buckshot shells. Her hair was tied up, and Francis realized that he was staring at her, so he went back to trying to be a leader for the UBF men. He didn't like the idea of her going in with the boarding party one bit, but Lance had been adamant, they needed every warm body they could get.

Pain shot through his ring finger, as if it had gone molten. Lance had been talking to the navigator, and he jerked as his ring ignited too. He'd never felt one burn so hot. It was like a knight was trying to contact *everyone*. The signal was so strong that all the Grimnoir in the world had to be feeling it. He shouted at the nearest crew member. "Get me some salt!" Lance started clearing maps from the navigator's table.

"I don't think I would have took the oath if I knew it was gonna try and cook my fingers off," Faye said as she watched them make the circle. Dan Garrett had come running. The stubby man was so weighed down with extra ammo that he had a hard time climbing up the ladder. Heinrich Faded through the wall and took his place off to the side. Francis could see that Heinrich's wrist was still bruised and discolored from where Delilah's magically enhanced grip had crushed it in the morgue.

A minute later the circle was complete, and light from the shining disk filled the little room.

He did not recognize the Grimnoir in the circle. He was older, weathered, totally bald, with wrinkles around his eyes that suggested he was a man who spent a lot of time laughing and smiling, except those eyes were hard now and there wasn't an ounce of laughter left in him. "Attention all Grimnoir knights. This is Robert M. Southunder, once of the knights of New York."

"Former knight," came another voice with a French accent, and the circle suddenly shifted to another man that Francis had never seen. "A disgraced knight, turned to brigandry."

"The vagabond returns," said a grey-haired woman. She sounded English. Francis had never seen so many people communicating through a magic circle before. The background noises told him that there had to be many others listening as well. The Power drain to the creator had to be enormous.

"Stick it, Harriet," Southunder said as the circle flew back to focus on his face. "There's no time for your politics. The Chairman has the Geo-Tel."

There were collective gasps from every corner of the world.

"Preposterous!" bellowed someone else, a hundred other people started to talk and now the circle was spinning so fast that Francis thought he was going to be sick.

There was a brain piercing whistle. Faye pulled her fingers away from her lips. "Y'all shut up and let the man talk already, jeez-Louise."

The circle returned to Southunder. "Thanks. I can't keep this up for long. The Chairman recovered the last piece. Did we ever find where they'd marked New York?" There was a spinning chorus of negative replies. "Then we've got to assume that he'll fire it at the same place as last time. We need to evacuate the Eastern Seaboard. Contact the President, the Army, do whatever you have to do."

"Things have changed since you left, Robert," the Frenchman said. "Actives have no favor in the halls of politics. They will not listen to us."

"Then get off your asses and do something," Southunder barked. "Live up to your damned oaths for once."

Lance cut in. "Where is the Chairman?" Everyone knew he'd want to be there when it was used.

"I don't know. The device was in the Northern Marianas," Southunder replied. There was another voice from behind him, a deep rumble, and a large, beard-stubbled face pushed past Southunder.

"Lance?" Sullivan asked.

"Yeah, we're not far from you. We're tailing the Imperial flagship now," Francis said.

"He'll fire it from his flagship, sure as hell," Sullivan said. "That's his style. Give us your coordinates."

Francis signaled for the navigator, who had recoiled in panic from the glowing, levitating, magic circle. He really had to remember that not very many people got to see stuff like this.

The next face that appeared in the circle was more recently familiar. It was Isaiah Rawls. "It looks like I'm the senior member of the council listening, so it falls on me to do this. Stand down, knights. That is an order. Do not, I repeat, do not attack the *Tokugawa*."

"Are you mad?" Dan shouted. His voice made Francis reel. Dan was under such stress that he could barely control his Power. The anger in there was palpable, and Dan's emotions made Francis want to pull his .45 and shoot Rawls right between the eyes. "You couldn't stop us when we were going to do it for one person, let alone ten million."

"Let them try, Isaiah," the English woman said. "We've nothing to lose at this point."

"We have everything to lose." Isaiah was furious. "You must let the flagship continue toward Japan. That is an order."

Sullivan's voice was utterly cold. "Captain Southunder, could you please ditch all these other bozos and just talk to my friends?"

"Gladly."

Isaiah began to scream. "No, you mus—"

The circle spun back around to the sweating Southunder. "That's much nicer . . . but I can't hold this much longer. Location of the flagship?"

The UBF navigator read off a bunch of what seemed like random numbers to Francis, but Southunder just nodded, doing the math in his head. "We can be there within an hour if I mangle the winds from here to Australia."

"Us too," Lance said. "See you there."

As the storm clouds parted, they spotted the *Tokugawa* before it spotted them, which was easy to do since it was the size of a skyscraper flipped on its side, and was running with all of its lights blazing. It was a thousand feet lower than they were, but only a mile ahead.

"Will you look at that . . ." Lance whistled. "It's huge."

"Forget that," Faye said. "There's two of them."

Francis followed her pointing finger. Sure enough, there was another vessel ahead of the triangular *Tokugawa.* Once again her weird grey eyes proved superior to everyone else's. This craft was also wedge-shaped, but more bulbous. It was only running a few lights, so its overall size was hard to determine, but it had to be at least as big as the flagship. "What is that thing?"

Mr. Chandler, the accountant, had joined them in the control center. "I believe that is a Kaga-class superdreadnought."

"How do you know that?"

"Because UBF made a fortune selling the design to the Imperium," the accountant replied. "That's one of ours. I'm afraid your grandfather didn't really worry about the embargo."

"Weapons?" Lance asked hesitantly.

"Unknown. We just provided the basic hull, and they worked out the rest, but probably at least equivalent to a Great War battleship, and it has a hold that can fit, depending on the size, a whole bunch of planes."

Lance scratched his beard. "Define *bunch*, Mr. Chandler."

"Forty or fifty."

"That nice pirate captain has *two*," Faye pointed out. "Now, I'm not an expert or nothing, but that doesn't seem quite fair."

Francis bit his lip. If it had still just been a rescue mission, he would have called it off. It didn't make sense to trade a bunch of lives for one, even though they'd probably have to knock Dan out first and tie him down, but this was too big now. The Geo-Tel was on that thing. "Call the *Marauder.* Warn them and get their ETA. The battleship won't be able to shoot at us if we're tethered to the *Tokugawa.*"

Lance looked at him slyly. "You're sounding more like a captain already, kid. You want the hat back?"

"Not after it's been on your smelly head."

FS *Bulldog Marauder*

CAPTAIN SOUTHUNDER put the mirror down. The news had been grim. In twenty minutes they'd break the edge of the storm.

Sullivan held on to the wall of the stateroom as the dirigible was slammed back and forth by the wind. The creaking and flapping was making him nervous. It would really not be fair if they crashed before they even had the chance to get shot down.

"Two ships, which also means that the crew of the flagship will be reinforced with more men . . ." Southunder said slowly.

Not to mention Madi, who was probably capable of killing all of them by himself, but he didn't bring that up. Dealing with his brother was personal business. "What are you going to tell your crew?" Sullivan asked. They were pirates after all, and mutiny was a distinct possibility.

Southunder smiled. "Why, the truth, of course." He stood and walked from the room, not seeming to notice that the entire place was swaying violently back and forth and rattling like they were about to fly apart at any second. "Remember how I was talking about loyalty? Let's see if I was right, because I've already been wrong far too much for one day."

"I hope you ain't on a roll . . ." Sullivan muttered as he followed.

Most of the *Marauder*'s crew had assembled in the little galley. They were a motley bunch of toughs, armed to the teeth, outside the law, perfectly adjusted to killing, and they were about to be asked to go on a deadly mission to help a bunch of folks who not only didn't care about them, but didn't even know they existed.

Southunder stopped at the front of the room. Sullivan was expecting some big display, maybe a pep talk, like the kind General Roosevelt had given them before Second Somme. Fat lot of good that had done. Instead, Southunder sat on the end of a table and folded his arms. He didn't even raise his voice. "Well, boys, I've got bad news. We've got two Imperium ships. Both of them are bigger and have more guns than we do, with probably ten times the crew. There's probably going to be several Iron Guards on board, not to mention ninjas, and who knows what other kinds of terrible blood magic."

"What's the bad news?" Barns asked jokingly.

"One of the ships is a Kaga, which means that it is ringed in 37mm long-range cannons and a main ten inch gun. Rumor is that they might even have a Peace Ray. If that don't get us, the host of biplanes piloted by fanatics probably will. I won't lie. Our odds of survival are about none." He was completely honest.

"So we're running?" a muscular Polynesian with tattoos all over his face asked.

"No, Mr. Paonga, we're not. Because aboard one of those ships is a superweapon that is about to destroy a quarter of the United States, and once it falls, then the rest of the world will surrender. The Chairman will rule the world and everyone like us will be extinct within a year, tops. This job isn't about the loot, crew, I'm asking you to do this because it's the *right* thing to do. Stick with me and I'll do everything I can to make sure we make it through."

"This is madness," said the badly scarred Ken.

"I'd take volunteers, but we're either all in, or all out. There's no time to drop anyone off. We either fight together, or we run, and if we run, you'll have to kill me first. I can't promise we'll live, but we'll die free men, and our great-grandkids will tell stories about the bravery that goes on tonight."

There was a tiny voice from the back of the room. "I not have babies yet. Like to have babies someday." Lady Origami squeezed between the burly men. She had neatly folded a piece of rice paper into an intricate shape. She tossed it into the air, and the miniature blimp almost seemed like it would fly, but it burst into magical flame and was consumed instantly. "But only babies I make be from Imperium rapers if Chairman win. I fight with captain."

"I didn't join to prove I'm brave. I joined to make money . . ." Parker said, but then he smiled. "And to kill some Imperium. I'm in."

One by one the pirates added their assent. The last to speak was the young American, Barns. "Do I get to take a Raptor out and die in a glorious dogfight?"

"Yes," Southunder answered.

Barns grinned. "I wouldn't miss it."

Southunder nodded calmly. "Let's go murder some Imperium dogs then. Every. Last. One."

"EVERY LAST ONE!" All the pirates shouted together.

Sullivan followed Southunder back into the hall, figuring he could learn a thing or two about leadership from this man. "You didn't tell them that the Chairman himself would be on board . . ."

Southunder gave him a sad little smile. "They're brave, Sullivan, not suicidal."

Chapter 24

The Imperials have a war cry. Tennoheika Banzai. *It means something about the emperor ruling for ten thousand years. The emperor is a puppet, but the soldiers meant it when they bellowed it at the tops of their lungs. Their Actives would often charge numerically superior, entrenched positions, with complete disregard for their own lives, confident in the rightness of their cause.* Banzai!

—Captain John J. Pershing
Army Observation Report on the taking of Vladivostok, 1905

San Francisco, California

JOHN MOSES BROWNING was sitting up in bed. His chest still ached from the gunshot that had left him crushed and bruised, but he could certainly call his new, lightweight, woven-armor vest a success. He was getting far too old for this business. The UBF company Healer had stuck with his parting promise to Francis and had Mended him, but not nearly all the way, just enough to keep him from dying, the rotten weasel.

He had listened to Southunder's message along with most of the Grimnoir in the world. He knew Southunder well, so he knew that the man spoke the truth. Many thought that he had been run out of the Society because of his rashness in dealing with the enemy, but Browning suspected it had been more because of his outspoken loyalty to Pershing's cause to take the fight to the enemy, rather than to skulk in the shadows.

Something about that magic conversation had left him unsettled. He'd had a notebook in his pocket, as was his custom. It had been retained with his other things at the hospital, and he had sent for it. When the nurse had brought it, he had turned immediately to the last few pages, where he had carefully copied down the mad scribblings that Jake Sullivan had drawn on the mansion walls after his brief death.

He had never seen the Power represented as a single cohesive entity before, yet it made sense. His mind had always been attuned to making pieces fit together in perfect harmony, and this was no different. Given sufficient time, he had no doubt that a map could be made of where every single individual magical ability originated, and if that corresponding geometric shape could be drawn correctly, then those energies could be harnessed. It was exciting, but it would have to be a younger man's work, because he had no doubt that it would take a lifetime, and he'd been living on borrowed time for too long now.

But it was for another reason he'd turned to Sullivan's map. It was the interrelation of the various Powers. He'd long held suspicions that a sufficiently powerful Active could blur the borders between their own abilities into those areas that traditionally belonged to others. Sullivan was a perfect example of this, having moved beyond just altering gravity into the related fields of mass and density. If this new hypothesis was correct, then it was possible that with sufficient knowledge, any Active could do this, which was extremely exciting, but once again, not his purpose.

The Power's complete body seemed to be two overlaid triangles. Sullivan's drawing was two-dimensional, so that was all Browning had to work with. The bottom triangle was how the Power interacted with the physical world, the top triangle was how it interacted with the living world. The two combined into one great mass in the middle. Overall, it looked a bit like the Star of David. The physical triangle's three points were gravity, electromagnetism, and nuclear forces; the governing laws of the universe. Each of the Active magics that influenced physical realities was connected to coordinates within those areas.

It was the top triangle that had been more mysterious to Sullivan. This one appeared to interact with life, with three points ending in the biological, the mental, and then into one that Sullivan had left as a question mark, but that Browning's personal belief system logically attributed to the spiritual.

The coordinates in the middle were where Actives that seemed to overlap the two areas came from. Healers were such, near the middle, and Sullivan had gotten a good look at the geometric structures there that Browning had long erroneously thought of as stylized archaic letters. Healers operated in the realm between physical and electromagnetic. The other areas around that had also been mapped into their coherent pieces by Sullivan's fevered hand, and the close cousin to the Healer was the Pale Horse. They inhabited bordering areas. Both bent the laws of biology and matter to their will. One for good, one for ill.

And if one were to reason that a sufficiently strong Active, such as a Heavy, could wander into fields such as mass and density, then why couldn't he assume that a sufficiently strong Healer could wander slightly into the area of *causing* disease? Or even more important to the particular question haunting him . . . Could a sufficiently strong Pale Horse drift across the boundary and masquerade as a weak Healer?

They had never found the man who had cursed Pershing. Oh, how they'd looked. They'd torn the world apart, overturning every rock, but they'd never found the Imperium villain. But what if they'd been looking in the wrong place all along?

Browning summoned a nurse and sent for a runner. Even under a different identity, he was still a man of great means and resources. When the errand boy arrived he requested for him to travel to a bank to a specific safety deposit box to retrieve something for him.

The boy returned an hour later and gave Browning a wrapped package. He tipped the boy generously, sent him on his way, and then removed the Colt M1911 from the box. He loaded it with a seven-round magazine of 230-grain, .45-caliber ammunition, all of which had been designed by his hand, put the safety on, and placed the gun beneath his pillow. Then he activated his ring and called for the nearest Grimnoir to come to his aid.

There were only two other Grimnoir in the area, both oath-bound to respond, and whichever one came, they had some explaining to do.

UBF *Tempest*

FRANCIS WAS SO NERVOUS he could barely think. By hugging the clouds, they had gotten within half a mile of the *Tokugawa*. Both vessels headed due west, but the *Tempest* was traveling twice as fast. They would be attacking from above. The *Marauder* would be coming in from the left. *Was that port? Whatever, south*, he corrected himself. He had to try to remember to think in nautical terms. The other battleship was half a mile ahead of the flagship and they were trying to orient their approach so that the flagship blocked its shot.

"We've been spotted!" the driver shouted. "Searchlights." And as soon as he said that, a perfect white beam flashed across the window bubble, highlighting the crew's taut faces and clenched teeth.

"Weatherman, draw in the storm. Helm, full speed ahead!" Lance shouted. "Bounce this son of a bitch off their top deck if you have to, but get us down there now!"

Sparks rose from the still distant *Tokugawa* and Francis realized in an abstract way that those were giant tracer bullets heading right for them.

Faye was standing off to the side, shotgun over her shoulder, scowling, waiting for something. "You got it, Faye?" Lance asked quickly.

"Not yet . . . Almost . . ." She had her eyes closed.

"Wait, what are you doing?" Francis asked. "You're not going to—"

"Got it." Faye opened her grey eyes and disappeared.

By herself? "Damn it, Lance!" Francis shouted.

The front window shattered in a spray of glass. Sparks shot from the radio console as the tracers screamed past his head. Bullets puckered through the walls and the driver screamed in pain and lurched away from the controls. Foam from the torn seat blew around in the new wind like a snow flurry. Lance immediately shrugged into the chair and kept them on course. "It ain't like she's any safer here, kid," he said.

Imperium flagship *Tokugawa*

FAYE HIT THE DECK ten feet from the gunners. They were so focused on the blimp heading their way that they never even saw her coming. She tucked the shotgun butt tight into her shoulder pocket and welded her cheek to the stock just like she'd been taught. She lined the gold bead at the end of the barrel with the soldier's head and pulled the trigger.

The shotgun really kicked hard, and the muzzle rose, but she still saw his head pretty much pop open all over the place. The Browning shotgun was nice because you didn't have to do anything but pull the trigger and it just kept cycling itself. She brought the gun back down and shot the other one in the back.

These men might look different, but they were *exactly* the same as the ones that had killed her Grandpa, and killing them made her feel *good. Justified.* There was another big cannon throwing those red sparkle bullets at her friends, so she Traveled over there to give those bad men a piece of her mind. She did that by landing six feet away from the two gunners, blasting them both to bits, and then turning and nailing a third one in the chest who was running up with another can of ammo. He hit the railing, flipped over the side, and a belt of cartridges spilled and rolled out nearly to her feet.

"Serves you right, jerks!" She shouted at no one in particular. That was it for the guns on the rear end, but there were more popping away on the other side, probably at the nice old pirate's ship, so she pulled shells out of her bandoleer and started shoving them in the shotgun's magazine tube.

The *Tempest* screamed by overhead, a giant grey mass that looked sort of like two footballs stuck together with wings. She craned her neck and saw that the loading ramp was already open and Heinrich was hanging out the back end firing a loud gun that seemed to shoot way too fast. She waved, checked her head map, and picked a spot right in the middle of the next gun emplacement.

Faye Traveled, landed between three surprised young men in black uniforms, realized one was wearing one of those grenade things on his belt, so she reached down, yanked the pin out of it like Mr. Browning had shown her to arm the explosive and Traveled. She reappeared, landing in a crouch, balanced effortlessly on a railing fifty feet away as the soldier panicked, trying to get the grenade out of his pouch, but then it blew up, and bits of sharp wire blew him in half and maimed his two buddies. That gun was quiet and she'd saved ammo! *I'm pretty good at this.*

When they had just been here to rescue Jane, her job had been simple—find her friend and get her out—but with the big evil superbomb about to go off, her mission had changed. It was time to cause some *trouble.* She liked this new mission a lot more.

FS *Bulldog Marauder*

"SO IS THIS THE CRAZIEST THING you've ever done, or what?" Barns asked from the pilot's seat of the streamlined Curtiss biplane.

Sullivan was balanced, holding onto the struts, leather straps anchoring him to the plane so he wouldn't be torn off as soon as they dropped into the open sky. He thought about the question. He had done many things that would be considered crazy. Jumping from a moving airplane onto a moving dirigible thousands of feet above the ocean was probably near the top of the list.

The only thing under his boots was a narrow aluminum wing. Under that was nothing but darkness and lightning that seemed to go forever. When Sullivan didn't answer, Barns just kept shouting. It was more like he read his lips over the thunder of the already moving propeller. "Don't worry. Barns is my nickname, short for Barnstormer. Wesley 'Barnstormer' Dalton, best damn pilot you've ever seen."

I really hope so, Sullivan thought.

Barns revved the engine, and the whole plane protested against the hooks holding it suspended to the dirigible. Now Sullivan was totally deaf. Barns pulled a tight black mask down to cover his face, and then put on a pair of round aviator's goggles, making him look alien. Since Sullivan was dressed in the exact same manner, with a big black coat, mask, and goggles, they probably matched. Barns stuck out his fist and put his thumb up. Sullivan figured that the thumbs-up was some sort of aviation symbol, but from his reading of classical history, he couldn't remember if that meant the gladiator lived or died. He'd find out in a minute.

Southunder was driving the *Marauder* right at the *Tokugawa,* trying to maneuver in a way that kept the more lightly armed flagship between them and the dreadnought. The *Tempest* was hitting the topside, so their pom-pom guns were pounding shell after one-pound explosive shell at the side engines. The more they could damage its mobility, the easier it would be to keep using it as a shield.

Southunder was using his Power to drag the storm with them, wreaths of lightning crackled around their ship, and the only reason they hadn't exploded yet was Lady Origami.

Sullivan wasn't sure if he was going to be more scared out there riding on the wing of a biplane, or in here. A red light in the bay above them turned green, and Barns reached up and pulled a lever. The steel claw released and they dropped, screaming, into the night. He closed his eyes tight as his stomach fell through his pelvis and decided that he had his answer. This was definitely worse.

This was madness, but Sullivan was the most powerful Active on board, and this was the fastest way to get him to where he could do the most damage. The Curtiss Raptor was quick and the wet air made him feel like it was going to rip his skin off. He thought about increasing his density, but was terrified that might somehow mess with what Barns was doing, and that was the last thing he wanted to do.

They streaked across the sky, tracers crossed *X*'s ahead of them and Barns shoved the stick down hard. There was a small explosion next to one machine gun nest, and the pilot instinctively turned into that open space.

Something black zipped under them, and Sullivan didn't realize it was a Jap fighter until it was past. Barns was whipping the Raptor back and forth, getting them closer, moving like magic between the bullets. The kid had to possess some kind of Power, because no normal human was capable of these kinds of reactions. The Lewis gun mounted over the engine fired, ballooning red right through the propeller as the interrupter gear kept them from destroying their own prop. There was a flash of sparks and a Jap fighter that Sullivan hadn't even known was there burst into flames and fell from the sky. Barns pumped his fist in the air.

Then they were over the *Tokugawa* and it was as bright and wide as a city boulevard. Soldiers scurried about under them, shooting at them with small arms, and a hole appeared between Sullivan's feet. *Good as it's gonna get.* He uncinched the buckle and let the momentum tear him from the plane.

He fell like a stone, arms tucked tight against him, long black coat whipping in the wind, and though he was falling far enough to splatter him all over that blimp, he was just glad to get off that damn biplane. He Spiked, lessening the Earth's pull. He spread his arms and legs to catch more resistance, until his momentum slowed. Concentrating hard, he waited until he was close enough, then cut his magic, and dropped the rest of the way.

Already soaked to the bone, he landed on the metal roof of the superstructure, in a splash of collected water. Automatically opening his coat and unsecuring his bullpup auto rifle, he assessed the situation. On the opposite end of the *Tokugawa* the UBF ship was coming in hard. He ran the charging handle and raised the gun. Soldiers were running down the catwalk below him, ready to repel boarders. In all the confusion, nobody had seen him falling. They didn't even know he was here, but he could fix that *real* quick.

Even though it made the gun longer, he'd screwed the Maxim sound silencer onto the end of the BAR's muzzle. Rather than the slow roar he was used to, the gun sounded like a series of hissing cracks as he mowed down the Imperium troops. The men stopped, confused, unsure where the bullets were coming from. One of them turned and pointed at the black-clad figure in the goggles, but Sullivan calmly dropped him with a single .30-06 through the ribs.

But there were too many down there and more pouring outside every second. *Gotta keep moving.* It was time to take this fight out of the rain. There was a skylight ten feet away, so he ran over and jumped onto the glass as the soldiers below returned fire. He activated his Power as he hit and the roof beneath his feet shattered into a million gleaming shards.

Imperium flagship *Tokugawa*

"IRON GUARD, we are under attack! Spotters confirm two airships incoming, one single hull, one small double."

Madi walked across the red-lit command center. The captain did not speak. Technically the naval officer was in charge, but when the First Iron Guard was on deck, everyone addressed him instead. Madi listened for a moment, his magically augmented hearing discerning that the aft antiair batteries had opened up on something. They only had a handful of weapon stations up and running so far and those had been hastily installed with equipment brought over from the *Kaga*.

"Battle stations," he ordered. The alarm klaxon sounded. "Tell the *Kaga* to nail them with their Death Ray."

The radio operator chimed in. "*Kaga* reports no clear shot. They're hiding behind us." There was a slight tremor as an explosive shell struck their vessel. It was like an ant biting a horse.

"Tell them that's what the fucking rudder is for and move until they can get one!" he bellowed. "Captain, you have the bridge. Kill these assholes."

Madi moved quickly down the long hallway. He got into the elevator and cranked the down lever. He could still hear what was going on topside. One rear gun stopped, and then the next. The smaller machine gun positions on the outer hull were firing now. He picked up the vibration of an explosion and small arms-fire. "We've been boarded," he muttered.

He stepped out of the elevator into the engineering section, which was midway down the center of the craft, sandwiched between the first and second hull. He walked down the wide metal catwalk with two heaving gas bags the size of buildings on either side. This section's Torch saluted him as he passed. There were nine of that type of Active on the *Tokugawa*'s crew, three for each hull, so that there would always be at least one working each hull, twenty-four hours a day. It might seem like overkill, but Torches were one of the most common Actives, and no expense was too great to assure the Chairman's security.

The Unit 731 weirdos were clustered in the main workshop, fiddling around with the Tesla device. It had all been screwed together, and he recognized most of it, since he'd been the one to personally secure the pieces. The blueprints he'd snapped Wild Bill Jones's neck for were tacked to the wall. The bottom piece had come from Christiansen's cabin after Yutaka's Bull King had torn his guts out. The center came from that Traveling Portagee after he'd shot him with the Beast. One section was shiny and new, produced by the Cogs to make up for the small part that damn Traveling brat had kept. Only the top bit was unfamiliar, a round globe made of an unknown substance, crackling with purple electricity. The whole thing was only a foot long, which really wasn't very impressive considering it could blow up whole countries.

"How much longer?" he barked.

The Cog leader, Shiro Ishii, bent his neck in submission. "We will need another twenty minutes. The design is extremely complex."

"Well, we've been boarded by somebody, so get your shit together." He moved to the phone and pulled up the mouthpiece. It took the switchboard a minute to connect him to the marine command. "This is Iron Guard Madi. I want a squad protecting the Cogs in engineering and whatever Iron Guard are available. Now." He put the horn back in the cradle and folded his arms. He'd stick around here until the Marines showed up. Protecting the device came first. Then he'd go find those boarders and stomp the life out of them. The Chairman was more than capable of looking after himself.

He felt a prickling of his scalp. Madi wasn't sure it had something to do with the extra sensitivity granted to him by his kanji, or maybe because they shared the same type of magic, or maybe it was just because they were of the same blood, but he just *knew*.

It was impossible. He was dead. He'd beaten him to a bloody pulp and left him to be cooked by the Peace Ray. The Chairman had promoted him to First for having the will to kill his own brother in service to the Imperium. His very existence was an insult, a mockery, a *dishonor*. He didn't know how that little bastard had lived, but somehow he had, and he was here, on the *Tokugawa*, just to piss him off.

Jake was here.

The *Tempest* hit the top of the Imperium flagship so hard that they broke one of the landing skids. They bounced, the entire dirigible creaking as the skeleton bent, and then hit again. The top of the *Tokugawa* was mostly flat, like the deck of a traditional ship, with glass and aluminum superstructure rising all along the center. The shattered bubble of the UBF prototype skidded to a halt next to a two-story structure covered in antennas, some sort of rear control area for the back of the flagship. One of their wings crashed into the structure's pylons and snapped.

Francis rose from where he'd been flung behind the captain's seat. Not twenty feet away through what had once been the control room bubble, there were two Imperium men looking at him from a wide window in the building, apparently shocked by the sudden appearance of an American airship landing right on top of them.

Francis waved, and one of them hesitantly waved back. He used his Power to slam their glass. It crashed in a sheet, which he then whipped up into a tornado of slicing bits, and blood splattered their walls. *Don't mess with a Mover.*

"Everyone okay?" Francis shouted. There was coughing and some movement as the crew staggered up. Lance got out of the captain's chair, dusting broken glass from his beard. "Crew! Keep her running. We'll be back as fast as we can," Francis shouted, picking up an Enfield rifle and heading for the ramp.

The *Tempest*'s boarding party had already debarked ahead of them. Francis came running down the ramp, but there wasn't much to see. They'd landed on the very tail end of the *Tokugawa,* and he had to run around his own ship to see where they were going. He slipped and tumbled, since everything was slick with pounding rain, but he made it back up, and kept running.

Heinrich was in the lead. He'd picked up one of those new Solothurn 8mm attack rifles with the big curved magazine sticking out the side. It had a rate of fire so intense that it sounded like ripping cloth. Ahead of the Fade was the length of the *Tokugawa*'s top deck. It seemed to go on forever. The *Tempest* was absolutely tiny by comparison.

The UBF Brute had kicked in the door to the structure they'd crashed next to, and Francis followed him in. Except for the lacerated bodies from the men he'd telekinetically killed in the main room, the structure was clear. There was a ladder that led downward into the bowels of the ship between the three great hulls.

"If they need a workshop for that Tesla device, they'll be in engineering. It is in the center of the ship." Francis looked over and was surprised to see that the accountant, Mr. Chandler, had followed him and was holding a Thompson. "What? I was in the war, Canadian Army, Gordon Highlanders . . . UBF built this thing. I know how much every part of it cost *and* I took the tour."

Heinrich appeared, walking right through the wall as he changed the magazine in his Solothurn. The barrel was white hot. "There are more coming. There's little time."

They had to find this thing and find it fast. "One team up. One team down."

❖❖❖

Faye was jumping around like a madwoman. She figured the best thing she could do was just keep moving, causing trouble, and besides, the longer she stayed in one place, the more likely she was to get shot. It was harder to aim at something that wasn't there by the time you pulled the trigger.

Other Actives worried about running out of Power, but she didn't. It just seemed to be there, the same as always. She appeared behind a soldier in a brown uniform, stuck her shotgun in his spine and pulled the trigger. She was Traveling so fast now that by the time the action cycled, the spent shell ejected two hundred yards away as she landed right in front of another soldier and tripped him so he fell down a ladder and broke his neck.

Her head map was filled with information. There were hundreds of people moving. Thousands of bullets. She had to stay in motion.

One second she was in the flagship inside a room filled with dirt and windows like they were gonna try and grow crops and then she was outside in the rain where she hit a man in the head with her shotgun butt and watched him flip over the railing and then she was in a narrow little room filled with red light and shooting steam and there was one man in a black uniform using his Power to keep the hydrogen from catching on fire so she just shot him in the neck and then she was up in a room with a bunch of radios so she shot all of those folks too and then she shot the radios for good measure until her shotgun was empty.

Whew . . . She paused to catch her breath as she pulled more buckshot off her bandoleer. Her Power might not run out, but she was getting tired and this was about the fifth time she'd emptied the stubby shotgun. The Browning was smoking hot and her shoulder was going to have a really nasty bruise. Faye brushed an errant strand of hair away from her eye. She still hadn't seen anything that looked like her Grandpa's Tesla device, but as soon as she did, she was gonna smash it real good. She couldn't find it on her head map, because everything here was so filled with complicated mechanical devices that everything looked kind of the same.

Her head map warned her to move, so she did, not even knowing why, and a sword cleaved through the air where she'd been standing. There was a woman in front of her where there hadn't been anybody a second ago. She was dressed all in tight black, had red hair spilling over her shoulders, and was way prettier than Faye, and strangest of all, she had grey eyes too! "Hey, you're just like me!" she exclaimed.

The woman didn't respond, she just whipped the sword around to take Faye's head off, but Faye was too quick for that. The sword snaked chips from the wall and Faye appeared behind her. "Oh, so that's how it is?" Faye said as she pulled up the shotgun. But the woman was just as quick as she was and the buckshot blew twelve holes in the wall instead of meat. Faye instinctively ducked as the sword stabbed over her shoulder.

She appeared in an empty access tunnel two stories below, put her back to the wall, and kept loading the shotgun. *Could the redhead follow her?* Faye had never tried to use her head map to keep track of another Traveler before, so she wasn't sure. She realized her shirt was torn and blood was welling from her shoulder. The blade had been so sharp she hadn't even felt the cut, but she sure did now.

The woman appeared at the other end of the tunnel. "You're a slippery one," she said, "but no one escapes Toshiko of the Shadow Guard."

"Well, I'm Faye of the Grimnoir knights, and I wasn't trying to escape," Faye answered bravely. "I was just waiting for your slow ass to catch up."

The woman screamed, raised her sword, and charged. Faye lifted the shotgun and fired as the woman Traveled, appearing just behind the passing buckshot, and swung, but only raised sparks off the grating as Faye disappeared.

Faye landed at the opposite end of the tunnel. The woman was too fast, but maybe she was like everybody else and her Power had to run out sometime, just like Delilah had taught her. "Hey, Toshiko! That ninja suit makes you look like a fat cow."

The ninja raised her sword. Red light reflected down the razor steel.

It would be just like playing tag. "Catch me if you can, fat cow!" Faye taunted before Traveling as far as her map would take her.

Sullivan swung the barrel of the BAR around the corner and caught the lead crewman in the face. Cheek bone shattered, he stumbled back into his companions, and Sullivan followed, using his Power to tumble them down the hall into the far wall. These were in navy uniforms, so maybe they knew their way around this giant maze. He dropped the rifle, knowing the sling would catch it and hold it against his chest, as he drew his .45 and walked forward. He put one bullet into each head, but stopped at the last one. He grabbed the soldier by the throat with his left hand and picked him off the ground and slammed him against the wall.

He didn't know if the Jap spoke English, so he kept it simple. Wherever his brother was, that's where the Tesla device would be. "Where's Madi?" The sailor started to jabber something. Sullivan lowered the .45 and shot him in the knee. The sailor screamed. "English! Do you speak it?"

"Madi! Madi!" The man pointed down, said a bunch of other words, but Madi was in there, and he kept pointing in a downward direction. That would do. Sullivan slammed the sailor's skull into the metal bulkhead then dropped him. There was an interior stairwell around the next corner so he started down.

He paused at the next level, but then snapped back as a subgun barked, hitting the corner of the wall. Someone bellowed from behind the gun. "More ninjas!"

English? "Grimnoir?" he shouted.

"Sullivan? That you?"

"Yeah, don't shoot," he answered, coming around the corner. He'd forgotten about the black mask and goggles. He pulled them off and shoved them into his coat. Sure enough, it was the Grimnoir. Dan Garrett was in the lead, followed by Heinrich Koenig, a dark-haired stranger, and more people were coming up behind them out of the darkened passageway.

"One of yours?" the man with the Thompson asked.

"Proud to say yes on that one," Dan answered. "Sullivan, have you seen Jane?" When Sullivan shook his head, Dan lowered his. "Damn it. I've got to find her."

"Engineering is this way, I think," said the man with the Thompson. "Come on."

Heinrich grabbed Sullivan by his coat. "Listen to me, friend. There is something I must tell you. Something—"

"It can wait, Heinrich," Sullivan answered.

"No, it can't." The woman's voice came from the darkness of the hallway. She stepped forward into the dim light.

Sullivan blinked hard. "De-Delilah?" It couldn't be, but he recognized her shape in the shadows, but something was different, something was *wrong*. "How?" Had the Healing magic worked after all? But why wasn't she coming closer? He started to go to her, but Heinrich held on with all his might.

"Sullivan, please, I beg you. Listen to me."

He shoved the Fade off and ran for her, his heart leaping. Delilah stepped out of the shadows and—

She was dead . . .

It was obvious. He'd seen thousands of zombies during the Great War. The unnatural fire in her eyes, the way her skin hung loose over her face. She was dressed in a formless UBF coverall, but black blood had congealed all around the hole in her abdomen from the wound that had killed her.

Delilah stopped right in front of him. "I'm sorry," she cried, her voice trembling. Her skin was pale white, but blotted with black and purple bruises.

He encircled her in his arms. "It's not your fault," he whispered. "It's mine. Oh, God, forgive me. Please forgive me." Now that he was close, he could smell her. Her body was already decaying. "I didn't know. I never would have left."

"Jake. I'm gone. Let go of me. Please, let go."

He did so, uncomfortably stepping away. He wanted to die. "What . . . What . . ."

"The Lazarus magic got me. I died while it was still in effect. I think it was a fight between your magic and his, but his was stronger." She raised one hand and stroked his cheek, fingers hard and dry. "Heinrich was going to mercy kill me, but I told him who better to go on a suicide mission than somebody who was already dead?"

"Shhh . . ." he pleaded. "I'll find a way. There has to be a way to fix this. The Power—"

"No . . ." she answered. "You can't understand the pain, Jake. I'm using my Power just to keep it in check enough not to go crazy, and when I run out . . ." she sighed. "I won't turn into one of those mindless monsters, out of their gourd with pain. This is a one-way trip for me, baby. You have to let me do this."

"I can't."

"You can, because you're the strongest and best man I've ever met. Do this for me, Jake. Let me go. Be happy. Promise me you'll go on and live a long happy life, have lots of kids, and die of old age." She leaned in and kissed him gently on the lips, cold as ice.

He started to cry. "I can't."

"You can, and you will, because that's my dying wish, you selfish bastard." Her blackened lips cracked into a smile. She took his hand in hers, placed it on the center of her chest, where there was no heartbeat, and he died inside. "Now come on. I deserve to go out with a bang."

Heinrich was waiting for them, his hat down low, covering his eyes. "This way," he said softly.

Faye had jumped a hundred and fifty-two times in the last four minutes, she'd counted, and that damn ninja cow bitch had stayed with her every step of the way.

The two of them appeared at the very tip of the *Tokugawa* where the three balloons came together. Lightning crashed and rain pounded, as the other battleship loomed right overhead like a big black shadow. A single white biplane screamed past being chased by ten black ones, all shooting, and the white biplane exploded in a ball of fire. The old pirate ship had been shot so many times that most of its gas had leaked out, and it was gradually crashing into the side of the flagship. Her head map told her that men were dying all around her and a strange magic energy was building in the center of the ship, which could only be coming from the big, evil, magic superbomb.

Faye was gasping for breath. She'd lost her shotgun after using it to club a passing officer in the face, not that it mattered, since she'd gone through all her shells by that point. She'd been counting Travels, but she'd lost track of how many people she'd killed, shot, stabbed, maimed, pushed overboard, set on fire, or blown up. She was armed now with a meat cleaver that she'd picked up in the kitchen. It was still dripping blood from where she'd taken off a sailor's hand.

Toshiko had dogged her the whole time. The ninja was panting almost as hard as Faye was. Her magic kanji were burning so hot that the rain hitting her instantly exploded into steam. Faye had shot at her, but she was always one step ahead. She'd pulled the pins out of grenades and dropped them, hoping that Toshiko would Travel right into them, but she'd been too smart for that, and would always Travel outside the blast zone.

The ninja raised her sword in a salute. "You are the finest Traveler I've ever known," Toshiko said simply.

"And you're still a big mean cow," Faye answered, not that she was being honest. Cows were wonderful creatures. Imperium assassins, not so much. "Ugly and mean."

"Surely, you're almost out of magic by now?" Toshiko hissed. "I have direct lines to the Power, granted by the Chairman and his finest wizards. You have none. You cannot possibly outlast me."

Faye checked. She still felt the same as ever. Physically, she was bushed, but magically, she was fine. "I'm just getting warmed up."

"Let's finish this, child, so I can get to killing your friends . . ." Toshiko had an evil smile. "That gives me an idea. Let's see if you can keep up with me this time?"

NO! Toshiko Traveled. Faye checked her head map. *There.*

The ninja was in the control room of the pirate ship. She yanked her sword out of the driver's back in a spray of blood. The bald pirate captain was turning as she swung her sword at his face, but Faye crashed into her forearm. "No, you don't!" Faye shouted in her ear. Toshiko grinned savagely as she Traveled out of Faye's grasp.

Faye screamed as her clothing burst into flames. Some pirate woman had just set her on fire! "Not me, stupid!" she shrieked as she Traveled.

She caught Toshiko a short distance above, balancing on the slick top of the flaming pirate ship. The crashing rain dashed out the fire on her clothing. Her feet squished into the balloon fabric, once hard with gas, but now falling apart. They were about to hit the *Tokugawa.* Toshiko swung her sword, but Faye appeared behind her, trying to put the cleaver into her back. The two danced, steel swinging, both disappearing and reappearing so fast that Faye was only moving on unconscious instinct.

The ninja had been trained how to fight with a sword, and Faye hadn't, and the steel drove through her calf. She screamed as she toppled, sliding down the edge of the balloon. Hydrogen fire was licking up to meet her. She had to outwit Toshiko somehow, something *crazy*. She Traveled as she entered the flames.

Faye hit the metal engine housing on all fours. The giant propeller was screaming only inches away, a huge black blur that would destroy her instantly. Maybe Toshiko's head map wouldn't be as accurate and—

The ninja appeared on the next engine over and waved. "*Damn it!*" Faye screamed in frustration. Toshiko mouthed something, but she couldn't be heard over the roar of the propeller, but she just knew that she was going to go kill some of her friends. The Shadow Guard disappeared, but Faye was right behind her.

Lance was on the deck, hunkered down behind one corner, rain-water pouring off the edges of his big hat as he fired his Winchester at the approaching Imperium troops. Francis was off to the other side, smoothly working the bolt of his Enfield. "Look out!" Faye screamed.

But where was—and then she gasped as the sword hit her square in the small of the back. Faye rolled forward through the water. Toshiko stood over her, blade gleaming overhead, and the ninja was triumphant, knowing that she'd just struck a lethal blow.

"Faye!" Lance shouted, but Faye was already Traveling. She folded space and fell through, landing on her face in a puddle of water on top of the *Tempest,* only a few feet from where she'd taken her oath. Toshiko appeared, gloating. "You can't run when you can't feel your legs. I *felt* my wakizashi bite the bone . . . Pity. I have no doubt that if you were with us, you'd be the First amongst the Shadow Guard."

Faye was coughing, lying on her back. She reached around behind her and found the little Iver Johnson .32, her faithful little companion that she'd bought in Merced for ten dollars, the same amount of money that Grandpa had bought her for. The mighty sword blow had nearly cut it in half. Once again, her life had been saved by ten bucks. "Oh, that wasn't my spine, but you really messed up my gun."

Toshiko finally lost it. She screamed in fury as Faye Traveled.

Faye appeared, falling in midair, right in front of the astonished Lance. "*Shoot me!*" Faye screamed.

To his credit, Lance Talon didn't hesitate. He lifted the .351 Winchester and pulled the trigger.

Toshiko appeared behind her, still screaming, but according to the ninja's map, the area had been clear, safe, and a tenth of a second before, it had been. Time seemed to slow to nothing as Faye's head map recorded everything in the universe. The bullet traveled from the barrel, straight and true, and Faye only needed to fold space a tiny bit to get out of the way, and it was almost as if she could watch the bullet rotating as it passed through the air she'd inhabited, past Toshiko's descending blade, and right into the Shadow Guard's chest.

The bullet cleaved through her sternum, breaking and turning as it pulverized her heart, severed her spine, and flew out her back. The blood droplets and bone fragments seemed to hang suspended, intermingled between the raindrops, and then Faye reappeared off to the side. Time restarted. The ninja was looking at her, as if to say, how the hell had *that* happened, but then the lights went out. Lance hit Toshiko twice more as she fell, even though she was already dead.

"Told you so, cow . . ." Faye went to her knees, swooning from blood loss. She felt Francis' strong hands on her, and the next thing she knew, she was in his arms, and he was carrying her away from the gunfire.

Sullivan

Chapter 25

I must tell you, Kermit, of these three particularly remarkable Heavies amongst the volunteers. They come from brave stock, as their father had been with me during the advance on Kettle Hill. Though all three are exceedingly similar physical specimens, these Sullivan brothers could not be of more disparate temperaments. One is a simpleton, with the gentle soul of a child, yet a more diligent soldier you could not ask for. One is a killer of men, a force of calculated belligerence, I fear he is only obedient to his officers because a discharge would jeopardize his opportunity to murder more Huns. The last is a thoughtful young man, the quietest of the three. He shows great promise as a leader. Never before, in all my years of campaigning, have I come across such stalwart troops. I tell you, son, the three are a terror to behold in battle, and if I had a thousand more Sullivans, this war would already be won.

—General Theodore Roosevelt,
personal correspondence posted
before second battle of the Somme, 1918

Imperium flagship *Tokugawa*

MADI WAS WAITING at the end of the twenty-foot-wide catwalk. He had been joined by two other Iron Guards: the wretched Lazarus, Hiroyasu, and the stalwart Nobunaga, a Brute who was also the Chairman's champion sumo wrestler. Sumo was another weird Jap obsession that Madi had never gotten into. He found the whole thing kind of queer, with men pushing and slapping on each other in loincloths, but Nobunaga had been a tough guy before he'd picked up half a dozen kanji to increase his already formidable strength and vitality. Behind the three Iron Guards was the engineering section's Torch and twenty of the strongest Marines on board.

Of course, it was his brother that appeared at the far end of the catwalk first. Jake looked a little scary in the red light, the foreign invader surrounded by the giant heaving bags of gas, and for just a moment, it was like the bags were lungs and the *Tokugawa* was a great living creature. Jake was the disease infecting it and he was the cure.

"Maybe I *should* start writing poetry," Madi said.

"Huh?" Nobunaga grunted.

"Nothing . . ." Beneath the catwalk was a two-hundred-foot drop to the armored section that separated the two top hulls from the bottom one. There were a few ladders that went all the way down, but he had a feeling that anybody who went over this rail in the next few minutes wouldn't be taking a ladder. "Hiroyasu, fall back and animate the marines as they die. Marines, stay behind cover and use your rifles. Choose your shots carefully. Do not let anyone through. Protect the Torch. We don't want a fire in here. Nobunaga, on me."

Jake just stood there in the center of the doorway a hundred yards away, watching.

"Come and get me, Jake . . ." Madi whispered. The Geo-Tel had already been activated, and the Power was gathering, but his brother would be dead long before it fired, and he'd make sure this time.

A short, balding, pudgy, bespectacled man joined his brother in the doorway. The man scowled, as if sizing up the engineering section's defenses. Madi recognized him. In fact, he'd even shot him recently. Damn Grimnoir vermin, they were harder to get rid of than cockroaches. The man cracked his knuckles. He'd been a little woozy from all the hits he'd taken at Mar Pacifica . . . What had that lump's Power been?

And then he remembered. "Marines, cover your ears!" he shouted, but it was already too late. The Mouth had started talking. It wasn't a voice, it was a *Voice*. It was too big to come from a man, it came from a god. It didn't sound in his ears, it was like an ice pick driven through his skull and twisted around inside his brain. Madi ground his teeth together so hard that some of them broke. He had to steady himself against the railing to keep from falling.

His accent was off, the pronunciation was terrible, but apparently

Japanese wasn't this god's first language. "*Omaetachi wa kotei o shitsubou saseta. Watashi no meiyo wa hijyou ni kizutsuite. Watashi ga dekiru koto wa, mohaya jiketsu shika nai.*" Madi could feel his own will surging against the command, but behind him, he could hear the bayonets clearing their scabbards and a scream as the Torch turned his fire inward and burned himself to a crisp. *You have failed your emperor. I am deeply ashamed. The only honorable solution is immediate suicide.*

"No! Stop! It's a trick," but the blades flashed and his men died, gurgling and choking. The terrible Influence waned and his head cleared. Madi let go of the railing, having bent the pipe with his fingers. Only the Iron Guards had been strong enough to resist. Nobunaga had drawn his Nambu pistol, but Madi clamped down on his wrist. "No guns."

The other Iron Guard's eyes widened in understanding. With their Torch dead, they couldn't risk shooting in here. Madi turned back to his brother. Jake was still standing there in a big black coat. The Mouth was at his side. A blond man in grey appeared to Jake's left, and then he was joined by a female zombie to his right. The four walked forward together, side by side, ready to fight.

He could still beat all of them by himself without making so much as a spark, plus he still had an extremely powerful Brute, and already Hiroyasu was using his Power to raise the disemboweled marines. Jake and his Grimnoir were still dead, they'd just have to do it the hard way. He started walking. They'd meet in the middle. "Come on."

That had been one of the most impressive displays of raw Power that Sullivan had ever seen. Daniel Garrett hadn't just been fueled by his magic, but also by desperation, hate, and the burning desire to save the woman he loved. Dan was grey and shaking, sweat pouring down his face, and he looked like he might fall over.

"I didn't know you spoke Japanese," Heinrich said as he joined them.

"Just that one . . . been practicing." Dan grimaced. It physically hurt to channel that much Power at once. "I can't make people do something they wouldn't normally do, but these Imperium elites are so honor-bound, I figured it was worth a shot."

Delilah stepped up next. She was weaving as badly as Dan, but for an entirely different reason. "The Lazarus who . . . *made* me. He's inside. I can feel him. He's going to wake the dead."

The UBF Normals were hanging back. This fight was *way* beyond them. In fact, now that they were down to just Iron Guards immune to his magic and unable to use his guns, their Mouth was out of his league too. "Dan, why don't you take the others and go look for your girl."

"The Geo-Tel comes first," he stated with firm determination. "Jane would hate me if she found out I let a million people die to save her first."

"Come on," Sullivan said. The device had been activated. He could feel it within, like its dreadful magic was beating against his own inside his rib cage. They started walking.

Madi was dressed in some sort of red and black samurai robe, the traditional look thrown off only by the big revolver hanging in his shoulder holster. Next to him was a similarly attired, short, yet incredibly broad man with a round face and a top knot. "Look, they got a fat one," Heinrich said.

"That's not fat," Dan answered. "That's a sumo."

"Sumo-schmoo-mo," Delilah said. "I'm about to whoop his ass."

The others didn't realize it yet but he knew that his brother was too powerful to defeat, especially in a limited amount of time. "No matter what happens, get to that device." He dared not share his plan because he was worried that Madi could already hear them. Sullivan looked at Delilah out the corner of his eye. "I'll always love you."

"Just remember your promise," she whispered, and then she pushed her Power so hard that she seemed to grow. He'd never seen her do anything like that before. She was holding nothing back, running so much magic through her tissues that she was sure to destroy them when the magic wore off. There was no reason to hold back anything now.

Both sides charged.

Sullivan let loose with his magic the same time Madi did. Two conflicting gravitational fields collided between them. The air rippled like water. Delilah charged through the distortion, screaming. The sumo bellowed in return and hurled himself at her. He dwarfed her and kanji could be seen glowing through the open neck of his robe.

At the last second Delilah dodged to the side, extended her arm like a clothesline, and hit the Iron Guard in the throat. His head snapped back, momentum still carrying him forward, and his feet flew out from under him. The landing was hard enough to shake the entire catwalk.

Madi extended one hand and Delilah fell into the air. Heinrich leapt over the downed sumo and went at Madi swinging. Madi threw one mighty fist clean through Heinrich's chest as the German went grey. Heinrich came out the other side and slugged Madi in the back of the head. Madi didn't seem to notice it, but gravity changed again and Heinrich was slammed to the metal floor. He cried out under the crushing force.

"Fade out!" Sullivan shouted. Heinrich fell through the floor and Sullivan slammed his Power against Madi's field. The extra gravities were forced away from Heinrich, leaving the German hanging by his hands under the catwalk. The sumo was sitting up, despite Dan futilely punching him in the face. Sullivan roared and headed straight at Madi as Delilah rebounded off the railing behind him.

Sullivan slammed a big fist into Madi's jaw, then the other, then threw out a boot and kicked Madi in the stomach. The Iron Guard didn't even seem to feel it and one hand shot out and grabbed Sullivan around the throat. He dragged Sullivan in close, crushing off his air. "I'm the strongest there is. You understand me? The *strongest*! You'll *never* make it past me! NEVER!"

Sullivan used his Power, increasing his density, protecting his throat. "I know." The railing creaked around them. He Spiked hard, slamming as much force onto them as he could muster. Madi threw it back, just as he had in Mar Pacifica, but his eyes widened as he realized that Sullivan wasn't trying to crush him, but what was underneath.

"Jake!" Delilah screamed as a perfect circle of catwalk sheared away and the two of them fell.

They dropped like a pair of stones. Jake kept striking Madi in the face and Madi hit him back with bone-jarring force, but both of them were running as dense as iron. The armor-plate floor barely slowed their descent, and they ripped clean through the steel, crashing through beams and supports, tearing wires, and then ripping through the bottom hydrogen hull. They fell through the gas, in an empty, totally lightless space, kicking, punching, throwing knees and elbows, in a freefall brawl to the death. Sullivan held his breath.

Fighting through the pain, Sullivan flared his Power again. He didn't want to fall through the bottom of the dirigible. Madi must have realized the same thing, and together they slowed, but still trying to kill each other. The bottom of the hydrogen chamber barely impeded them, and then they were rebounding through more materials—aluminum, steel, copper, and finally wood. Sullivan threw his hand out and caught hold of something as Madi tore free and kept falling. His brother crashed through one last darkened floor, highlighted in a circle of sudden light but shrinking away. Madi flared his Power before impact and landed in a heap far below.

He'd ended up in some giant wooden room. There were other people down there, and a circle of curiosity was closing in on Madi's fallen form. Sullivan let go and followed. He landed in a crouch, boards splintering, reaching for the rifle slung on his back, but it was gone, torn free from its sling somewhere above. He reached instead for his pistol, and luckily it was still in its flap holster.

The Iron Guard came up off the floor, snarling. Sullivan was able to crank off four rounds before Madi threw a backhand that would have taken the arm off a normal man. The .45 went flying away. Sullivan stepped back, shaking his stinging arm.

Four holes began to drizzle blood down the front of Madi's torn robe. His brother stopped, looking around, realizing where he was. "Well, I'll be damned. Ain't *this* appropriate."

The room was huge and mostly bare, probably some sort of training room. The walls were glass, and beyond them was nothing but darkness. The floor was polished hardwood. He turned slowly. There was a mess of Imperium in this room, dressed in black uniforms with red accents and a big red sash. All of them were pointing guns at Sullivan, except for the ones that were ready to destroy him with the ice crystals collecting down their arms, or the jagged bones twisting between their hands, or the electricity cracking in their eye sockets, or the floating objects that they'd telekinetically picked up with their minds . . . He was in a room *full* of Iron Guards.

"Well . . . shit," Sullivan said.

"Ahem," someone gave a polite cough, and both he and Madi turned at the same time.

"Chairman!" Madi exclaimed, sounding embarrassed, just like back when Dad used to catch the oldest Sullivan brother doing something bad, like torturing animals or setting fires. He dropped to his knees. "Forgive the intrusion."

Heinrich was nowhere to be seen. Delilah was picking herself off the ground from where she'd crashed through the railing hard enough to break every bone in her body. So it was up to him. Daniel Garrett had hit the fallen Iron Guard with everything he had. He punched him in the face until he felt his knuckles break, and then he'd tried kicking him, but the huge Iron Guard slowly got up from the grating anyway. Dan stepped back, shaking his stinging hands.

The Iron Guard twisted his head and he could hear the vertebrae pop. His little black eyes were far too small for the size of his head, and they zeroed right in on Dan. The sumo growled.

"Sure you don't want to talk this over?" Dan asked. The bridge shook as the Iron Guard lumbered at him. *Guess not.*

Delilah shoulder-checked him out of the way. "Pick on somebody your own size!" The two Brutes crashed together; one dead, one alive; one huge, one tiny; but both of them *very* angry. They stood toe to toe, hammering each other.

Dan landed on his side with a grunt. The Iron Guard hit Delilah so hard that he felt the vibrations travel down her body and through the floor, but she didn't budge. Delilah responded by putting one hand on his shoulder, shoving herself into the air, and bringing her elbow down in the center of the sumo's head with a blow that could have killed an elephant. That staggered him a bit.

"Get the device!" Delilah screamed. "I'll hold fatty!"

Struggling to his feet, he saw Delilah throw a backhand at the Iron Guard's head, but he was too fast, too martially skilled, and he caught her arm while simultaneously bringing his other hand around. Delilah's forearm shattered, bone visibly ripping through the flesh. Dan gasped at the horrific wound. Delilah stepped back, looked down at the jagged bones sticking out of her forearm and the delicate hand dangling uselessly from the skin and tendons. No blood came out. "Move your ass, Garrett!" she ordered as she stepped forward, ducked under the Iron Guard's swing, and drove the bone shard into the sumo's vast belly.

Dan heard the Iron Guard gasp as the bones penetrated his body, but was too busy running for engineering to look back. A hand appeared over the edge of the railing. *Heinrich!* He was alive and pulling himself up. He didn't dare stop to help his friend. He could feel the air humming with the Tesla device's energy.

The lights were no longer red. He was in the engineering section. He jumped over the dead bodies of the Imperials he'd murdered and the pile of twisted bones and smoking fat that had been their Torch. There was a single man standing in his way, wearing the same red and black robes as the other Iron Guards, but this one wasn't nearly as physically intimidating. Skinny and ratlike, this had to be the Lazarus. He was blocking the steel door. Dan could *feel* the Geo-Tel on the other side.

But then the Lazarus moved a scabbard around in front of his body and drew a sword. His English was perfect. "I am not the warrior my brothers are, but I am more than a match for the likes of you." He tossed the scabbard away and lifted the blade in both hands. The eviscerated bodies were starting to move, groaning and whimpering on the floor as they came to. Even the ashen pile of bones was stirring. The dead soldiers began to cry out in agony.

The Lazarus hissed. "I am Hiroyasu of the Iron Guard, and my magic is based in *suffering*."

There was a grey flash as Heinrich surged past. Hiroyasu swung the sword through the blur. Heinrich rematerialized, blocking the weapon before it could come back up. "Suffering?" Heinrich asked, grabbing the surprised Iron Guard by the robe. "I'll show you suffering." Then the Fade spun him around, both of them going grey as they sailed into the wall.

Heinrich totally disappeared, but he must have let go of Hiroyasu partway through. The Iron Guard re-formed, solid, but his body had fused with the metal. The left half of his body and his head were still visible, but his flesh had become one with the bulkhead. Hiroyasu began to scream, incoherent with pain.

There was a clicking as the door unlocked from the other side. Heinrich held it open for Dan. The Fade saw the thrashing Iron Guard and admired his work. "That was for Delilah. Hurry." Dan stepped through after him, noticing that the Iron Guard's other arm and leg were flailing madly on this side. They ran down the hall. "Think we can use guns in here?" Heinrich asked.

They were surrounded by solid walls and away from the heaving bags. "Probably." Dan pulled the .45 from his belt.

"About damn time," Heinrich answered as a Luger appeared from inside his coat.

They reached the last door, both of them automatically taking up positions on either side. They'd worked together for a long time. There was a round glass window, and when he risked a glance through, he could see a strange device crackling with electricity sitting in the middle of a table. *That's it.* There were a bunch of men in long black coats surrounding it. He tried the latch. *Locked.*

Heinrich nodded, knowing what to do. He Faded, but as he did so, two Shadow Guard appeared, took the Geo-Tel between them, and Traveled it away.

Faye woke up, groaning. She felt nauseous.

"Hold still, you lost a lot of blood," Francis told her. She looked down. Her pant leg had been torn off, and her calf had been wrapped in a bandage. It really hurt.

There was more gunfire. She checked her head map. The *Tokugawa* was in chaos. Grimnoir and pirates were spread all over the big ship. The pirates were headed this way, being chased by Imperium. Some of her friends were in the middle of the ship, looking for the big, evil, magic superbomb, but it had just Traveled to the very bottom.

She was having a hard time seeing down there. At first she thought it was because of the blood loss making her silly-headed, but then she realized that the black fogginess came from the Chairman. His Power was so big that everything around it was cast in shadow, but the big, evil, magic superbomb was dragging so much Power up out of the middle of the world that it illuminated even him. Somehow she knew they only had minutes. The illumination showed that a couple of her friends were down there, surrounded by Iron Guards.

But there was something else. The Power wasn't just being attracted to Tesla's invention. There was another spot in the middle of the ship. It was glowing too. She concentrated harder, trying to figure out what was going on, and that's when she realized *exactly* what was happening.

She smacked her hands onto both sides of Francis' face. "We've got to get everyone out of here fast as we can!" She let go and tried to get up.

"Stay still, you're in no shape to move."

"No, you don't understand. It isn't what anyone thought it was! Everyone is wrong! The Chairman is wrong! We've got to *go*. I've got to bring everyone onto the *Tempest*."

"What? Don't move. You're still bleeding from—'

"Aarrggh! You are *such* a boy! You know I see the world different than everybody else. Listen, do you trust me or not?"

Francis was perplexed. "Yeah, I guess."

"Then get a bucket and fill it with nails and broken glass and anything else you can use to stab people with your brain, and get that blimp in the air. We've only got minutes."

He nodded. She could see it in his eyes. He didn't have a clue what she was talking about, but God bless him, Francis actually trusted her. She kissed him on the cheek and Traveled before she could see his reaction.

Chairman Okubo Tokugawa was sitting cross-legged on a simple mat, watching the brothers curiously. Jane was standing a few feet away in a white kimono, flanked between two robed Iron Guards. "Sullivan?" she asked in surprise.

"You okay, Jane?" he asked. She nodded. She sure didn't look okay. Poor thing was scared to death. "Don't worry. Dan's here. We'll get you home."

The Chairman spoke. "Rise, First Iron Guard." Madi jumped to his feet with superhuman speed.

"Sir, Grimnoir threaten the Geo-Tel," Madi said quickly, much more worried about that than the bullets lodged in his chest.

The Chairman nodded politely, as if to say, *tell me something I don't already know, stupid.* "I am aware. I have been watching. I dispatched Shadow Guards to retrieve it. They will Travel back here shortly."

"Well, if it ain't Mr. Fancy-Pants," Sullivan said. "What're you doing down here? Hiding?"

The Chairman studied him carefully. He was wearing a simple, comfortable robe, and his feet were bare. "As I said, I have been watching. This is a most interesting time for me, Mr. Sullivan. If I so desired I could send my personal bodyguard up and your friends would be dead in seconds, or perhaps I could just destroy you all myself."

"Then why don't you, big shot?"

"Because I am *bored*," he answered truthfully. "I have been alive for a very long time. I have lived for over a hundred years. I was born the youngest son of a minor samurai lord. My home was destroyed in a revolution, my family put to the sword, and I became ronin. I had seen my share of conflict by the time the Power came to me. Together we learned how magic could interact with mankind. Since that day I have traveled the world. I have learned its secrets. I have seen the heights and depths of magic. I have been to every land. Spoken every tongue. Learned everything. Fought every war. Led men into battle and killed legions with my own hands. I've lain with ten thousand women and sired a thousand sons. I sculpt nations as other men sculpt clay. I have traveled beyond our world and seen the others. I have spoken with the Power face to face as we speak now. I have seen the terrible being the Power fled from and I have protected our world from it in battle beyond your mortal comprehension. There is nothing truly new to me."

Sullivan could sense he was telling the truth. If the Chairman was anything, he was perfectly straightforward. "So, we're an interesting diversion?"

"Yes. I could kill you all with a thought. The Geo-Tel was never in danger. My plan will be fulfilled." As he said, that two black-clad ninjas Traveled in, holding a strange device between them. It sparked and buzzed with energy and Sullivan could feel the magic in the room distort toward it. "It was only a matter of time. But you and your people *interest* me, Mr. Sullivan. Your strengths, your flaws, your hates, your desires, your loves and dreams. You are one of the most powerful natural Actives ever born. Your young Traveling friend is even stronger, though she does not realize it yet. We should stand as one, united for what is to come, yet instead you will fight me to the end. Such purity of struggle is bitter, yet beautiful in its way. I wrote a poem about it. Would you like to hear it?"

"I'd rather slit my own wrists."

"Fair enough." The Chairman turned back to Madi. "I am

disappointed in you, First Iron Guard. Were it not for my preparation, the Geo-Tel would have been lost to the Grimnoir. And not only that, but it would have been lost to the forces of a man that you had thought you'd killed."

Madi bowed deeply. "Forgive me, Chairman. I can make it right."

Sullivan was surprised just how much genuine devotion there was in his brother's words. At least he'd finally found something that he could truly love.

"Very well. How much longer until the firing?" the Chairman asked absently.

A man in a long black coat answered. "Approximately ten minutes, sir."

The Chairman nodded. "Very well, First Iron Guard Madi. You may redeem yourself."

Madi bowed his head quickly, then moved to the side, shrugging out of his robe. All he was wearing now was a pair of very baggy black pants. Madi's torso was covered in kanji scars. Nearly every inch of him had been burned, and every one of those made him more dangerous. He shouted something in Japanese, and a moment later another Iron Guard hurried forward with two swords, one made of wood, and one made of killing steel.

Sullivan knew what was happening. He removed the tattered remains of his coat and canvas vest and tossed the rags on the floor.

Madi smiled. "Let's go then, little brother." He picked up the steel katana, swinging it back and forth so quickly that the air whistled, then he tossed it gently through the air. Sullivan caught it by the hilt. Madi grinned as he took up the wooden sword, testing its balance. "I'm literally *thirteen* times the man you are. Figure I'd keep it fair."

The Chairman nodded, appreciating this act of chivalry. Jane looked like she was about to puke. The Geo-Tel was steaming along behind five Iron Guards and two ninjas. The Chairman saw where Sullivan's eyes had wandered, and he shook his head softly. "I would not allow you to stop me . . . but I will not meddle in your family business. Carry on."

Madi was limbering up. His body was thick with muscle. Sullivan had seen him tear through hard men like they were nothing, and that was before he had been magically augmented and trained. Sullivan held up the unfamiliar sword. "I don't exactly know how to use one of these things . . ."

"You'll figure it out pretty quick," Madi said. "You always was the *smart* one."

"Not always," he muttered. Sullivan was the youngest. Jimmy had been the smart one growing up, until he'd been struck with a bad fever that had nearly killed him and had left his mind feeble. After their daddy had died, he'd stepped up, trying to take care of his mother and his dimwit brother, while the oldest, Matthew, had done nothing but cause trouble. He'd been a bully, a thief, a jerk, and was only happy when everyone else had been scared of him. Sullivan watched the light reflect down the razor edge of the sword. "Hell, we should've done this a long time ago."

"That's the spirit," Madi said.

Sullivan raised the sword. "I'm gonna cut you in half."

Madi grinned savagely. "Reckon you could try that and see how it works out for ya."

"Begin," the Chairman ordered.

They met in the middle. The Iron Guards formed a circle around them. Sullivan swung as fast as he could, the blade driven by his vast strength. Madi moved out of the way easily. He cracked Sullivan hard on the shoulder with the wooden sword. "Try harder," he said.

"Go to hell," Sullivan snarled, hurling his Power, trying to make Madi fall toward him. Their magic clashed, neutralizing each other's forces. The swords met, and then they were face to ruined face, and Sullivan was staring into that dead white eye. Madi grabbed him by the arm and used some movement to duck and hurl Sullivan over his hip. He hit the ground hard, but was already coming up when the wooden sword nailed him in the ribs. He gasped.

They went back and forth. Every time he tried his Power, Madi came back with an equal amount. The Iron Guard was stronger, faster, and had more skill. The wooden sword swept in low and hit him in the leg, and even with his long-magically-hardened bones, he felt the fracture. Distracted, he wasn't as fast, and Madi's Power dropped him backwards where he hit the floor and skidded away. On his knees, he swung the sword, but Madi easily leapt over it, and drove the wooden weapon *through* his shoulder.

Sullivan screamed, and Madi used one foot to shove him off the end of the wooden sword. Blood sprayed freely. He tried to rise, but Madi kicked him in the face. He rolled onto his back, and drove the sword upward, feeling it pierce flesh.

Madi paused, looking at the sword driven into his ribs. He stepped back as it slid cleanly out. "Nice shot, Jake." Then he shattered the wooden sword over Jake's skull.

Sullivan was crawling away, blood pouring out of his shoulder and head. The scar on his chest was channeling Healing magic, but not near fast enough to keep up with this. Madi tossed the broken hilt away and it clattered across the floor. "You idiot! You fucking idiot. I told you. I told you. I'm the strongest there is. I beat you with a bokken! You ain't done yet. Get up! Get *UP!*"

He rose, shaking. Madi punched him across the room. He collided with two Iron Guards, taking them all down in a heap.

Madi wasn't satisfied. He needed more. He looked to the Chairman, who was sitting there, showing no emotion. "This ain't good enough." Madi ran toward Jane, grabbed her by the hair and pulled her across the room. She cried out in pain. "Fix him! Now, damn it. I ain't done yet!"

Sullivan crawled off the Iron Guards. Madi shoved Jane down next to him. He could feel the warmth of her hands on his head. The hole in his shoulder closed. Somehow he knew that his skull was visible through the top of his head, but the skin pulled together and the blood quit flowing. He got back to his feet and picked up the sword.

Jane scrambled away. "Thanks," Sullivan said, tasting nothing but coppery blood.

Madi was pacing back and forth, unarmed, but deadly anyway. He saw his brother standing. "Again!"

They clashed. Sullivan feinted with the sword, and as Madi moved away from it, his boot collided with the Iron Guard's knee. It was like kicking a railroad tie. Madi punched him in the chest, breaking his sternum, then uppercut him so hard that he thought his face was going to come off. Sullivan landed on his back, but reversed gravity, and dropped himself into the air. He lashed out with the sword and caught Madi through the chest with the tip. Sullivan landed on his feet, and pushed the blade in deeper. Madi roared and grabbed onto the steel even as it sliced through his hands.

They were face to face again, with a foot of sword sticking out Madi's back. "You still don't get it. I'm the strongest there is!" Sullivan's nose broke as Madi's forehead slammed into it. Down was now up, and Sullivan fell ten feet into the air before the Power tapered off. He used his magic to cushion his fall, but by the time he hit the floor on hands and knees, Madi had already dragged the bloody sword from his torso. His brother raised it in both hands and bellowed. "Strongest THERE IS!" The sword cleaved through Sullivan's back, through one lung, out his chest, and dug deep into the floor. It was a brutal killing blow. Blood erupted like a geyser.

Sullivan fell facedown in a pool of his own blood.

Failure. He could see the Geo-Tel sparking, the Chairman watching curiously. All he could hear was a buzzing noise. As his vision darkened, he saw Madi's legs pass in those swishy samurai pants, and then he saw Jane being dragged across the floor by her hair again. Madi was screaming something, and then he felt the burn as his wounds were stretched tight and flesh was welded together again.

"Please, leave him alone," Jane was crying. "You've won. Quit torturing him."

Madi shoved her out of the way and grabbed Sullivan by the throat. "Last chance, Jake. Third strike and you're out." He shoved Sullivan back down and returned to the center of the room.

Sullivan climbed to his feet. It felt like there was a ball of molten lava in his chest. He didn't bother to pick up the sword. *Madi was the strongest.* But even the strongest can lose. He gathered all of the Power he had left. "No matter how tough you think you are, with all your Imperium bullshit, and all your fake magic, and all these punks looking up to you, you're still that same low-as-dirt bully you've always been, and I'll *never* be scared of you."

Madi watched him with his good eye. He was furious, the living half of his face red. Spittle flew from his lips as he screamed, "AGAIN!"

Sullivan threw every piece of magic he could. Gravity shifted ten times in as many seconds. Iron Guards fell up, down, and across the room. The Chairman, nonplussed, put out one hand to steady the Geo-Tel. Madi threw up his hands, countering magic with magic, every kanji on his chest glowing bright, burning so hot to keep up that the wood around his feet blackened and smoked. Every loose item in the room fell to the ceiling. Windows shattered. The light bulbs all exploded and dropped sparks until the room was lit only by glowing kanji and the pale blue light of the Geo-Tel.

And still, Madi kept getting closer, teeth ground together behind his destroyed lips, tears of blood leaking from his ruined eye. Sullivan stood his ground, feeling the pressure as Madi hammered him back. One of the bodyguards fell screaming out a broken window. Madi finally reached him and backhanded him across the face. It was the blow of the mightiest Iron Guard, and it shattered Sullivan's teeth and wrenched his neck around.

Sullivan landed on his back ten feet away. He started sliding away on his rear, crawling on his elbows, pushing himself back with his feet. Madi walked forward, following him, ready to finish it once and for all. They continued for several feet, Sullivan grasping along, desperate, while Madi took his time strolling after him, savoring the moment. Finally, Sullivan stopped, raised his trembling hands, and looked up at the killer towering over him.

"Why the sad face?" Madi asked sarcastically.

"Not sad," he spat around his broken teeth. "This is what I look like when I'm concentrating . . ." He cut his Power.

Madi's eye flicked up, realizing what was happening just as the katana dropped from where Sullivan had been holding it against the ceiling. The blade fell, the tanto tip piercing through Madi's skull, through his brain, down his throat, until it pierced his heart in two. Overloaded, the healing kanji exploded with the light of a bonfire.

Sullivan surged off the floor and grasped the hilt protruding from the top of Madi's head. He pulled his brother's face in close and whispered, "You're right. You always were the *strongest*." Madi's good eye was twitching madly in its socket, trying to focus. His hands came up, curled into useless, spasming claws. He was trying to say something, but the only thing coming from his mouth was foaming blood and a *gacking* noise. "But I'm the *smart* one, remember?"

With a roar, Sullivan pulled the blade toward him. The razor steel cut through the rest of Madi's skull, appearing right between his eyes, then through his nose and teeth. He wrenched the sword all the way out, opening him from top to belly button, and Madi's organs spilled out in a gushing heap. Somehow, he was still standing, the front of his head split in two. One side was the face of a human, while the other was the shredded white-eyed face of a monster.

No amount of healing magic could fix that. Sullivan raised his hand, palm open, and activated his Power.

“So long, Matty.”

Gravity changed direction and Madi plunged across the room, through the window, and out into the night.

Chapter 26

We have tried everything. Bullets bounce off. Bombs thrown under his carriage have turned it to splinters and killed the horses, but don't so much as muss the Chairman's hair. He does not sleep so we can't sneak up on him. He does not eat so we can't poison him. We've tried fire, ice, lightning, death magic, crushing gravity, bone shards, blood curses, all without effect. Decapitation might work, if you could come up with a blade sharp enough, but the finest steel simply dulls against his skin. Even if you were to wield this modern Excalibur the problem then would be that you can only touch Tokugawa if he lets you. He is all knowing, all seeing, moves faster than the wind, and can Travel in the blink of an eye. You don't touch the Chairman. The Chairman touches you, and as far as we've observed, that only happens when he's ripping the very soul from your body.

—Frank Baum,
knight of the Grimnoir,
testimony to the elders' council, 1911

San Francisco, California

IT WAS KRISTOPHER HARKENESS, elder of the Grimnoir, who responded to the call of his ring. The thin man came into the hospital room, locked the door behind him, and Browning wondered why he'd never seen it before. Plague lived in his flesh. This was an Angel of Death. This was the Pale Horse.

"You called?" Harkeness answered.

"I did." Browning pulled the Colt .45 out from under the blankets and leveled it at his fellow Grimnoir. "I'm surprised you came."

"I'm bound by a sacred oath. I had to come." He took a seat in one of the metal folding chairs next to the door. He did not look surprised to see the gun. "You are, after all, one of my brothers. Isn't that what the oath says? So I know you won't shoot me. I am still Grimnoir."

"I don't see a knight. I see a traitor."

Harkeness laughed. It was a hollow and joyless sound. "Allow me the chance to explain myself before you murder one of your fellows." His awkward accenting of random words grated on Browning's ears. He reached *very* slowly into his coat. "Mind if I smoke?"

"The man standing before the firing squad is always allowed one."

"Do I get a blindfold?"

"I'd prefer for you to see this coming, for I do believe you murdered John J. Pershing, and I would assume that even if they did not die by your hand, you are responsible for many other deaths."

The Pale Horse struck a match and lit his cigarette. He took a long drag and let it out in a cloud. "That would be correct. But not for the reasons you believe. You see, Mr. Browning, I am no traitor. I have accomplished that which has been considered impossible. I have accomplished the thing that has cost so many of our brothers' lives. I am the furthest thing from a traitor. I am a *hero*."

Browning decided to hear him out. Then he would shoot him in the heart.

Imperium flagship *Tokugawa*

FAYE COULDN'T WALK. Electrical shocks seemed to travel up her leg every time her foot touched the ground, but lucky for her, she didn't need to walk to Travel.

Time was short. Already the blue light was coming up out of the ocean. The magic jellyfish from the place with all the dreaming dead people was coming here, right now.

She appeared in the greenhouse where the surviving pirates had holed up. They were boxed in by two sets of Imperium marines, and they'd taken bad casualties. The woman that launched fire out of her hands was holding them back on one side, and the bald captain was shooting the soldiers that stuck their heads into the hallway, but they'd run out of bullets, fire, and luck before they'd run out of Imperium.

The Imperium didn't even see her arrive right behind them. They were too worried about the fireballs that kept squirting down the corridor. So she pulled the pins out of two grenades, then Traveled over to their friends on the other side, and did that to them too. She had appeared behind the pirates and had started talking before the soldiers had even exploded.

"Don't shoot!" Faye shouted. "I'm on your side." She glared at the fire lady. "And don't you *dare* set me on fire again or you'll be sorry." Several guns turned on her, but at least they were smart this time. There were several explosions, and then a moment later, more from the opposite corridor. "Okay, you're clear now."

The pirate captain used the lull to shove another magazine into his rifle. "Who're you?"

She waved her ring. "Sir Faye of the Grimnoir knights." She didn't know if she was technically a "sir," like the knights she'd seen in that one picture book, as none of the other Grimnoir ever called themselves "sir," but she thought Sir Faye had a nice ring to it, but then again she was a girl . . . She'd ask Lance. He'd know. "Never mind. You need to go down that way, up two flights of stairs, and then to the end of the boat. My friend Francis has a blimp waiting. You need to go now."

"What about the Geo-Tel?"

She rolled her eyes. "Oh, you people, always needing to know everything!" She was very frustrated. She didn't have time to explain this to every single person she had to go rescue. Why did people have to be so difficult? She grabbed the two closest pirates and Traveled. She dropped them at the rear end of the *Tempest* and then went back for more.

The captain must have figured she was a bad guy who had just evaporated his men or something, because he tried to shoot her, but she scooped him and a big fellow and dropped them with the others. Then she went back twice more. She was tempted to leave the fire lady. It'd serve her right for setting Faye on fire, but that was just the meanness talking, though Faye did leave her for last.

She found a young man next to a crashed biplane. It was sticking out the top of the tallest structure onboard. He'd crawled out, and was hiding behind one wing. He'd already used up all the ammo from the big machine gun he'd pulled off his plane, and was now shooting at Imperium with two fast-shooting pistols. His magic had something to do with changing how lucky stuff turned out, so he had shot bunches of them. She grabbed him by the back of the coat and dumped him with the other pirates, careful to point him out to sea, since bullets were still leaving his gun when they Traveled.

She found UBF people from the *Tempest* and scooped them up too.

Delilah was in the middle of a bridge in a place that was lit in red. She was curled up on her side, in terrible pain. Next to her was a big, dead Iron Guard. She'd pulled his arm off and beat him to death with it.

Faye landed nearby. She used the rail to steady herself. "Delilah?"

Delilah looked up. Half her pretty face was gone and Faye could see her skull. "Leave me alone. I'm almost out of Power, then I won't be able to stand it."

"I'm sorry, Delilah. This whole place is about to explode."

She put her face down so that Faye could only see the pretty side and smiled. "Good."

She understood. "Bye, Delilah." Faye Traveled.

Heinrich and Mr. Garrett were being chased by a bunch of zombies. At least they were smart enough not to argue when she showed up, and they'd be smart enough to explain to the others what was going on, so that gave her an idea.

The three of them landed deep in the steaming guts of the *Tokugawa*. An Imperium Torch took two steps toward them but Mr. Garrett shot him twice in the chest and once in the forehead. The thing she wanted to show them was behind a big, wheezing, stinky machine. "Where are we?" Heinrich asked.

"Look at this!" Faye cringed as she limped and led them behind the machine. A really complicated design had been engraved into the wall. She didn't think the others' eyes could see what her grey ones could, but she could see the energy connected from the big, evil, magic superbomb right to these markings.

"What strange geometries," Garrett said, running his hands over them. He pulled them away as if he'd been shocked. "It's from the

Rune Arcanium . . . It's a beacon! But that doesn't make any sense . . . I don't understand."

There wasn't time. "You'll figure it out!" She grabbed them both and took them up to the *Tempest.* There was a big crowd there now.

Mr. Garrett blinked in surprise, his hand still extended. He looked to Faye, biting his lip as the wheels turned. The entire night sky had turned a brilliant blue. Black storm clouds were boiling away around the energy. "The Geo-Tel!"

"About time somebody got it!" Faye shouted. "You're smart. You've got the words. I don't. Make them understand."

Mr. Garrett grabbed her by the arm. "I can't leave without Jane."

"I'll get her." She cried a little as her foot hit the ground. That's what she got for being in one place for too long. "Francis, are you ready yet?"

He came running, a metal pail in hand, filled to the brim with bits of metal and glass. "I did like you said."

"Good, listen, Mr. Garrett, tell Lance. He's smart too. Get in the air."

"We'll wait for you," Heinrich said.

"No! Get in the air." Since she was supposed to be the uneducated hick, it was frustrating how much slower everyone else's brain was. "We can catch up. But whoever put that mark down there didn't realize how smart the Chairman is. He'll figure out what's going on real soon if he hasn't already. I've got to stop him."

"From what?" Francis asked, confused. "Firing the Geo-Tel?"

"No! From shutting it off!" She grabbed Francis's shirt. "Let's go."

"What am I supposed to do with this junk?"

"You'll figure it out!"

Sullivan stood defiant in a vast puddle of blood, surrounded by deadly Iron Guards and the most dangerous man on Earth. Strong wind blew through the broken windows. The Geo-Tel was lighting the room in a stark cold blue, but it was no longer necessary, because the world outside had brightened considerably.

The Chairman stood. "It is done. A great man has been defeated. He will be missed. But the strongest survives."

"So that's what it comes down to? Survival of the fittest?"

The Chairman nodded. "As always. I would offer you a place in my service. It is my sincere belief that you could take more kanji upon you than even your brother. You could be the greatest wizard of all, perhaps come to rival even me. Together we could even defeat the ancient enemy, so that the Power could stay forever . . ." His face grew melancholy. "Yet, as I read your thoughts, you would fight me to the last."

Sullivan shrugged and spit half a tooth on the floor. "Whatever."

"You sum up so much philosophy in so few words. I wish that we could have been friends, Mr. Sullivan . . ." He walked over to the Geo-Tel, his bare feet crunching through the broken glass. "Would you at least watch the end of the old world and beginning of the new with me? I would very much like to share it with someone who can appreciate such things."

"You've got no right. No right at all to remake the world in your image. You're gonna kill millions."

"Millions is nothing. If only you could understand what is at stake . . . I thought you might, but I am disappointed." He was honestly saddened. Lonely. The Chairman watched the ocean. The night sky had turned an electric blue. The Iron Guards shifted nervously, all of them ready to kill Sullivan. "Interesting. When the pillar of fire appeared in Tunguska, did the air over Wardenclyffe also become so charged?"

"Unknown, Chairman," one of the Unit 731 Cogs answered. "The Geo-Tel is one end of the circuit, so perhaps. Our observers at Tesla's lab were murdered by the Grimnoir when they took the Geo-Tel, so we do not know."

"And the second time, when the Geo-Tel was almost fired, the sky over New York turned blue, but the Geo-Tel was close to the target geometry. It is possible that the sky is lightened both where the Power is provoked and where the Power is unleashed . . ." The Chairman nodded thoughtfully. "Yet, something feels . . . *wrong*. Has the energy gathered over the target in New York? Have we word from our spies in America?"

"No, Chairman," a different Cog responded. "I will prepare a mirror."

Okubo Tokugawa grasped his hands behind his back. Sullivan could tell he was using his Power to feel the surroundings, much like he did himself when the world faded into its component bits and their corresponding gravitational forces. The Chairman stepped away from the window. "I am too close to the device. It is disrupting my magic. I can't see anything."

"What do you wish us to do?" a Cog asked.

The sky had lightened even more. It was brighter than noon. The ocean below was glowing hideously. The Chairman scowled. "Shut it down," he ordered.

The Cog started to protest. "But Chairman, that could damage the sensitive—"

He held up one hand.

"Yes, Chairman," the Cog bowed, realizing that he'd gone too far in daring to disagree. He took a step toward the Geo-Tel, then froze, looking over Sullivan's shoulder. The Cog's mouth began to form a warning but then his head jerked violently to the side. Brains splattered the Chairman's simple robes.

Jane was holding up Sullivan's .45. The Chairman glanced over at the Healer. "I did not see that coming," he said as Jane shot him.

"Take that, you bastard!" She dumped the rest of the magazine into the grand leader of the Imperium. He appeared mildly amused as the bullets struck. Sullivan had nothing to lose. He surged forward as the Chairman raised his finger to blast Jane into oblivion. Three Iron Guards intercepted him, simultaneously buffeting his body with fire, ice, and electricity.

"Hey!" a voice cried from the other end of the great room. Every head turned, and Sullivan was surprised to see Faye and Francis. The girl hurled a bucket through the air, spilling tiny reflective bits behind it. Francis was concentrating hard. Sullivan instinctively threw himself to the ground.

The air hummed with movement as hundreds of fragments zipped through the room. Francis didn't just send them out. He whipped them back, using his Power to fling them at terrible speeds, around and again. Iron Guards screamed as bodies were pierced.

The Icebox at his right jerked as a piece of wire zipped through him and the Crackler at the left threw his hands to his neck to stop the spray of arterial blood. Then Sullivan was looking up into a pair of grey eyes as Faye dropped his missing BAR right into his lap. "This might help!" she shouted. "I'm gonna go protect the Geo-Tel!"

The crazy Traveler girl had gotten it backwards, but whatever. Sullivan rolled over and started shooting Iron Guards.

Faye landed right in front of the Chairman. Bits of shrapnel were flying around like crazy insects and the room was a really scary blue. The man she'd vowed to kill was there, brushing bullet fragments out of his hair. Francis was hitting him with all sorts of high speed projectiles but the Chairman didn't seem to notice. He held up one hand and every item in the room froze, then fell to the floor with a clatter.

"Now you—you are *strong*," the Chairman said. "Yet so unpredictable. Too unpredictable, and therefore you must die." His hands glowed like molten lava and he reached for her and somehow she knew that whatever spell he was using was going to rip the Power right out of her and pull her memories out of her head and yank her soul out of her body all so he could learn from it and then throw away the husk.

But he was right about one thing. She was *unpredictable.*

Faye grabbed the Chairman's glowing hands and felt a terrible surge of blood magic tear through her, but she only needed them for a second. Mr. Rawls had said that Travelers couldn't get close to the Chairman, unless he let them. She'd never done anything like this before, but she couldn't come up with any reason why it wouldn't work. *Probably* . . . She held on for dear life as terrible forces racked her body and Traveled.

She didn't go very far, just a little wrinkle in space. So she landed a mere five feet away, hopping on one foot, her injured leg bent. *It worked!* The Chairman was looking at her funny, not used to being surprised. She hadn't moved him, and he couldn't figure out what she'd just done, but then Faye held up the two cleanly severed hands. His eyes flickered down to the stumps his arms ended in, and realization dawned.

"Well, shoot! That worked real good," Faye squealed.

The Chairman was flabbergasted, offended, and then the pain hit. From the look on his face, Faye figured that it had probably been a real long time since he'd experienced that. Blood came squirting out both stumps. The Chairman opened his mouth and let out the most terrible yell she'd ever heard.

"GIVE ME MY HANDS!" he screamed, and she felt the voice inside her head, like Mr. Garrett could do, only ten thousand times bigger, but unfocused because she figured that she'd just messed up his concentration real good. Jane had once told her that she could Mend darn near any injury, but she couldn't make limbs grow back. Only some lizards could do that, but she could reattach parts that had been cut off, provided she got them fast enough, and that gave Faye an idea. So she Traveled to someplace that she'd been to very recently.

The rear end of the *Tokugawa* looked different because of all the bright blue light this time, but the big engine was still humming merrily along and the big terrible scary propellers were flying so fast that they were just a black blur and it was really super loud. *This should really make him mad,* she thought as she tossed the Chairman's still-convulsing hands right into the propeller. They exploded into a red mist.

She reappeared right off to the Chairman's side and grabbed Jane. "What have you done?" he shrieked.

"Threw 'em in the propellers," she answered as she fled, and the Chairman blasted half the bottom of the airship into pieces where she'd been standing.

Jane screamed as they appeared on the *Tempest*'s ramp. She was jumpy like that. Faye was glad to see that they'd done like she'd told them and taken off. Mr. Garrett cried out and swept Jane up in his arms and held her tight.

Faye Traveled back, knowing that the Chairman could Travel too, but for whatever reason, her head map seemed to still be working, while his was all jumbled up from being next to the big, evil, magic superbomb. It was probably because all she could do was Travel, where he could do about anything. It made sense that she'd learned to pay more attention, since she only had one tiny Power and he had so very many. Like who would be the better musician? The guy who tried to play a whole orchestra, or the girl who could only afford a banjo? It might not be pretty, but she could really play the hell out of that banjo!

She had to go fast. He didn't need hands to kill people, he could do it with his eyeballs or his brain or whatever else, and he was impossible to kill, except for one thing . . . Mr. Rawls had said that a direct hit from a Tesla weapon might do the trick, so she just needed to keep him distracted. She grabbed Francis next, since bunches of Iron Guards were trying to kill him. She was Traveling so fast now that she reached him before the bullets did.

There was no time for formality, so she dumped Francis in the center of the *Tempest,* and hurried back for Mr. Sullivan. He was the toughest, so he got to go last.

She had to hand it to Mr. Sullivan. He was stubborn. The fraction-of-a-second view her head map gave her when she hit showed three Iron Guards airborne, another one going out the window, and Sullivan was killing another with the big rifle extended in one hand while giving an Icebox a knuckle sandwich with his other hand. He'd made it to the Geo-Tel, and with a roar threw off the Iron Guards still clinging to him, raised his rifle to smash it, and she grabbed him by the back of the shirt and got them out of there as lightning from the Chairman's eyes consumed the Geo-Tel and the closest Iron Guards.

Mr. Sullivan brought down the big rifle and smashed the *Tempest*'s already damaged radio board in half. He was still roaring, but it tapered off, as he realized that he wasn't where he thought he was. They were in the cockpit of the UBF dirigible, and the *Tokugawa's* back deck was visible below them through the broken window. A blue pillar had come up out of the ocean and was shooting into the sky, right through the Imperium flagship. "The device!" he turned to Faye. "You ditz! You moron! I almost had it!"

"Good thing I stopped you then," Faye said simply.

He grabbed her by the shoulders and shook her hard. "Take me back," he ordered. His face was covered in splattered blood and he had the most desperate eyes she'd ever seen.

"Too late," she said. "The Chairman just blew it up, but he was too late. It's already clamped on. The Power is coming, no matter what. And if you don't let me go, it'll get us too."

He didn't get it. Sometimes she wished she was good with the fancy talk. "Take me back. *Now.*" There was a lot of danger in his voice. Mr. Sullivan could be scary when he was angry.

"Listen, Mr. Sullivan. I already cut the Chairman's arms off, so if you want to keep yours, I'd suggest you take them off me, right quick."

Sullivan let go.

"That's better . . ."

He was looking around, realizing that she must have Traveled all these folks here. "Delilah?"

It was a sin to lie, but maybe it was worse to make this man hate himself even more than he already did. "Delilah was dead when I found her. Sorry." She turned away so she wouldn't have to see his reaction, because she didn't have time to feel sad. Lance was behind the driver's controls. "Better go fast, Lance. It's on its way."

"We're going as fast as we can," he shouted. The *Tempest* rocked as Imperium biplanes flew past, shooting them.

She hopped over to the broken window and looked out. The Power was coming up out of the Pacific, aimed straight at the strange carvings she'd found hidden in the *Tokugawa,* instead of America, or wherever the Chairman had thought he'd been shooting it at. The other Japanese battleship was coming around, burning its hydrogen to power the Peace Ray on its front end, and it was aimed right at them. She wasn't sure which Tesla thingy was gonna kill them first, but they sure as hell weren't going to make it on this slow thing.

Traveling sure does spoil you.

Sullivan had joined her at the window. The blue light reflected on his face and the wind was blowing his tattered clothing. "The Geo-Tel is locked onto the *Tokugawa . . .*"

"About time somebody got it."

"We'll die too," he said. "We're too close . . ." He didn't sound too broken up about that, but she figured that Mr. Sullivan had lived with death so long that he wasn't rightly ever scared of it. "Well, at least we're taking the Chairman with us."

Faye looked around at all the people on the bridge. They were her friends. She kept losing families, and then making new ones, and then losing those too. She was sick and tired of that. She was just starting to have fun. Mr. Garrett was holding Jane and telling her that everything was going to be okay. Lance, who'd taught her so much and been as patient as Grandpa, was concentrating on not getting shot down. Heinrich was there, and he'd turned out to not be near as mean as she'd figured, and Francis, she'd never kissed a boy before, so she figured that Francis was her beau now, so it didn't seem fair that they'd get exploded before they'd ever gone on a date.

There was a roar of unbelievable thunder as the sky turned to fire, rolling over the *Tokugawa*, searing the giant vessel into a black shadow of ash and scattering its molecules on the winds.

Her head map was all frazzled. The magic was heading their way. The ocean had boiled away in a big circle and energy was crackling up the beam. The wave would hit in just over half a second and she knew that the explosion would be really huge and they'd die, skeletons visible through their bodies before being consumed. This was way bigger than the Peace Ray and everything for hundreds of miles would just be gone.

A tenth of a second later she'd taken inventory of the entire *Tempest.* She'd Traveled with two people a bunch of times now. She'd figured out how to do that. It just took more Power. She'd gone further than her head map could see, and that had just taken more Power and enough luck not to get something fused into her body. So how hard could it be to fling an entire blimp and thousands of pounds of people several hundred miles away?

Another tenth of a second passed while she measured her Power. Just like always, it was all still there. It never seemed to get smaller, just bigger and bigger, unlike everybody else. It must like her best. They were in the air, so it was pretty unlikely that she'd get foreign objects stuck into anyone, but even if she did, it beat getting exploded. She wasn't sure if she should use it all up at one time, because she didn't want to go too far and end up putting them on the moon or something.

Better safe than sorry. So she decided to use it all, even though she understood that using that much magic very well might destroy her. Ahead of the expanding ball of fire, the concussion bent the air and touched the very tip of the *Tempest.* For the first time in her life, Sally Faye Vierra gathered up every single last bit of magic she had . . .

And Traveled.

One.

Last.

Time.

Chapter 27

I swear before my God and these witnesses that I will stay true to the right and good, that my magic will be used to protect, not to enslave, that all my strength and wisdom must always shield the innocent. I swear to fight for liberty though it cost my life. The Society will be my blood and its knights my brothers, and that I will always heed the wisdom of the elders' council. I willingly pledge my magic, my knowledge, my resources, and my life to uphold these things.

—Oath of the Grimnoir Society,
original date unknown

San Francisco, California

THE PALE HORSE enjoyed his cigarette. It was a mild blend that soothed his nerves. He reasoned that it was more than likely his last. John Browning was watching him steadily and the .45 had not moved from his heart.

"You are a hero? For whom, the Imperium?"

"Oh, far from that, John. May I call you John?" He did not wait for a response. "I've been fighting the Imperium my entire life. I've sacrificed much to stop them and the others like them. I've stood with the Grimnoir since I was a child. My family were of the founders."

"Yet you betrayed them?"

"No. I stand by my oath to the end. Perhaps more than any other, for I was willing to go further than any knight before me."

The room shook slightly. Ripples appeared in the pitcher of water at the bedside. The glass in the window rattled. "Earthquake . . ." Browning said.

He could tell. It was done. "No. That was the firing of the Geo-Tel."

"Curse you," Browning said, lifting the gun.

"Save your bullet. America is safe," Harkeness said, tapping the ash from the end of his smoke. "What you just felt was the end of Okubo Tokugawa, and if Pershing's knights hadn't been so damn obstinate, then it would also have been the end of Japan as well, though with their leader vaporized, I imagine they won't be nearly the same threat anymore." He could see Browning was puzzled, but his finger was still on the trigger. "You are not convinced?"

"Please, go on." Browning was polite in his inquisition.

"I argued against Pershing in the councils. He wanted the Geo-Tel destroyed. I wanted to use it against Japan immediately. The elders were afraid to take so many lives. The Geo-Tel could have wiped the entire island from the map in one shot. As usual, the elders were cowards and took a middle way. They would not use the Geo-Tel *yet*, but they would hold it in reserve, entrusting it to the man who'd captured it, so that if that darkest day ever came, then we would have one final option . . . But even as our numbers dwindled, and we lost more brave knights every day, the elders were frightened. Pershing was calling for an all-out, open war, but even he was not willing to take the final step and use our ultimate weapon."

"Pershing was a solider. Soldiers fight against other soldiers. They do not kill an entire people."

"The Chairman would not hesitate. Why should we? Has he been right all along? Are we as weak as he says? Should we make way for the strong?" Harkeness asked. He'd had this same argument many times.

"Save your politics for the elders' council. My hand is getting tired and I intend to shoot you soon."

"Though the council was afraid, there was another one of the elders who had the will to do what needed to be done. We were tired of doing all the bleeding. It was time to end the secret war once and for all."

"So where is Isaiah?"

"On his way to Europe to face the other elders. We have some explaining to do . . . Our plan was simple. We could not just take the pieces of the Geo-Tel from Pershing. There were only two of us, and we'd be found and stopped. But if the Chairman were to find out where the pieces were . . ."

"Not shooting you down becomes more difficult by the second."

It felt good to talk about this, to get it off his chest. He'd dedicated years of his life to this mission. It was the culmination of his career. "We could not make it seem too easy. The Chairman was far too crafty for that. He'd smell the trap. We had to sell it. We had to make him believe. Isaiah is the finest wizard in the entire Society. He studied Tesla's notes until he was sure he'd mastered the targeting geometry. We just needed to make sure it would be hidden somewhere in the Imperium and the Chairman would kill himself and his entire country for us. When we found out that UBF was building a magnificent flagship for him we knew that we had been given the perfect opportunity."

Browning scowled. "You killed Francis's grandfather as well, I suppose."

"Yes. He knew too much. Originally I planned on just threatening old Cornelius into carving the target onto the *Tokugawa*. Sure, it was Isaiah who magically put the suggestion of cursing his greatest nemesis into his mind, but the murder is entirely on his head. Pershing had wronged him. It was your good general who exposed Cornelius's son's corruption and selling of secrets to the Imperium. Cursing your friend did two things for us. It secured the favor necessary to place the target and it removed the one Grimnoir who was most likely to thwart our plans."

"That's how I reasoned it was you. You were one of the few who helped us after the attack, you *Healed* Black Jack, and you were here again when Stuyvesant died of a Cursing. Tell me, was the attack on the mansion your fault too? Did you tell the Imperium we were stationed at the Talon home before that?"

"The latest, no. Three years ago, yes," he answered truthfully. "Though harbor no ill will toward my granddaughter. She was innocent. She only tagged along in the aftermath to try and help. Her volunteering to tend to Pershing only complicated things."

Browning nodded. "I'll not tell her of your plots. I'll tell her you died honorably."

"Thank you . . . But I'm afraid that she is gone as well. Just one more sacrifice among many. If fortune was smiling on us when she died, then the *Tokugawa* was sailing over Tokyo just now. I have no regrets. Stopping the Chairman was worth anything."

The other Grimnoir was completely calm. Harkeness knew Browning's reputation as a reasonable and level-headed man and now he too knew the whole truth. Sure, Harkeness had done many evil things, but he'd done them for the greater good. He could tell that Browning was pondering deeply on what was just said, and perhaps he too would come to see the inevitable wisdom in what Harkeness had done.

It did not take long for John Moses Browning to make his decision. "Any last words, oath-breaker?"

You never wanted to be judged by a man who was named after two biblical figures. Harkeness stabbed out his cigarette on the arm of the chair. There would be no begging. "I'd do it again."

"I know." John Moses Browning pulled the trigger and put a single .45 slug through the Pale Horse's heart.

UBF *Tempest*

THERE HAD BEEN an expanding wall of a world-consuming explosion and Jake Sullivan had blinked. When his eyes opened, the view out the front of the airship was entirely different. The sky was a gentle predawn grey instead of an evil cerulean blue. The ground far below was green, yellow, and brown, neatly blocked off into rectangular fields. In the distance, the sun was beginning to peek over purple mountains. It was the most beautiful sight he'd ever seen as they hung there, suspended.

And then the entire airship was spinning wildly out of control.

Wind slashed through the cabin. Someone was screaming, or maybe it was the aluminum airframe coming apart. He threw out one hand and caught a jagged edge of wall. A limp body tumbled past him, but he lashed out and caught an arm. It was Faye. She hung, either unconscious or dead. He couldn't tell, and he held onto her wrist with all his strength as her legs dangled out the front of the craft. He dragged her back inside.

They were rotating, faster and faster, as they corkscrewed toward the ground.

"Hull one compromised!" Lance bellowed. Every warning light in the cabin that hadn't been broken was flashing red. An alarm sounded. "Hull two bleeding helium fast."

Francis struggled over to the radio. He picked up the end of the horn and cranked the charge wheel. "Mayday! Mayday! This is airship UBF *Tempest.* We're going down. We're—" He stopped. "Where the hell are we?"

It didn't matter anyway. Francis just didn't realize that Sullivan had already smashed the radio. Dirigibles were not meant to go down this fast. They'd dig a pit at this speed.

Where were they? They sure as hell weren't in the middle of the Pacific. Which meant . . . He looked down at the skinny little Traveler in his arms. "Well, I'll be . . ." *Was that even possible?*

Barns Dalton shoved his way onto the deck, bouncing hard against a bulkhead. Sullivan was glad to see that at least some of the *Bulldog Marauder's* crew had been brought on board, not that it mattered much right now. The pilot managed to grab onto the back of the helmsman's chair and shouted in Lance's ear. "Let me drive!"

"Ain't nothing you can do."

"Scoot over, pops!" Barns shouted.

"Give him the stick, Lance," Sullivan stated. "He knows what he's doing."

Lance got out of the way, swaying with the blimp. "He'd better, or we're all dead."

Sullivan smiled. "Naw. I fall off blimps all the time. It ain't so bad."

Barns climbed into the chair and grabbed the controls. Sullivan could feel the magic thrumming through the ship. He didn't understand what kind of Active Barns was, but he was channeling a whole lot of Power. "Nice ride you got here," the pirate shouted. "Everybody grab hold of something. I'm taking her in."

El Nido, California

THE *TEMPEST* not only landed, it landed right side up, which wasn't bad, all things considered. Since there was only a single landing skid left, one bag was completely destroyed, and the other leaking and hissing, the airship looked drastically lopsided. It didn't help that Barns had landed them in a field filled with Holstein cows. Sullivan wondered idly if there had been any of the poor animals under the blimp when they'd hit. If so, that would be one unhappy cow.

There was a mess of wounded. Jane was running around tending to them. Even though she'd burned through most of her magic saving him from Madi a few times, she could still see right inside folks to tell exactly what was wrong with them. Dan was like her shadow. It would be awhile before the Mouth let her out of his sight.

He spit blood. Maybe if it wasn't too much trouble, and she'd taken care of everybody else first, he'd ask Jane to fix his teeth. They smarted something fierce.

Young Francis was talking to the UBF men. Apparently they were his employees now. Sullivan couldn't figure that one out, but his head hurt too bad to give it much thought. The kid was nervous, worried about the injured, and was taking the time to personally talk to every one of the company men. He'd make a good leader someday.

Some of the *Bulldog Marauder*'s crew had made it. Lady Origami had apparently never seen a cow before, and was trying to coax one close enough so she could touch its nose. He'd heard Parker had been lost, stabbed in the back by a ninja. Bob Southunder's baldness was hidden under a bandage, but he was still up, tending to his men. The old pirate saw Sullivan watching him and came over. "Mr. Sullivan," he said formally. Barns tailed along behind him.

He nodded. "Captain Southunder . . . Barns."

Southunder smiled when he looked down. This was another one who was surprised to be alive. "Guess I don't have to hide and protect the Geo-Tel anymore."

"So what's your plan?"

"Why, what I do best. I do believe I'm going to go speak to that young man who apparently owns UBF and try to convince him that he owes me a new dirigible. I was just going to ask you if you wanted a job. As you can see, I've had a few positions open up."

Sullivan gave him a broken-toothed smile. "I'll have to think on that one, Captain, but thank you."

Southunder patted him on the shoulder. "I should have listened to you sooner, Mr. Sullivan. Wherever the winds carry you, take care of yourself." He walked away, and within seconds was trying to coerce a blimp out of Francis, preferably something big, fast, and armored.

Barns looked him over. "You sure you don't want to go, Sullivan? It's a lot of fun."

"Maybe one of these days . . . I've got some things I need to figure out first. By the way, what the hell are you?"

Barns shrugged. "I don't know if it's got a name. I didn't know I was an Active until one time I crashed during a show and hit my head really bad . . . It still gives me wicked headaches. You got some pocket change?" Sullivan found seven pennies, a nickel, and two dimes, which was everything he had to his name, and passed them over. Barns took them all in his hand. "Heads or tails?"

"Heads."

Barns threw them all up, then swept his other hand across quickly, snagging every one out of the air. He slapped them down on his palm, and then held it out for Sullivan to see. All but one of them was heads. "Just lucky, I guess. I have a way of making things work out."

Sullivan pointed at the one penny showing tails. "What about that guy?"

The young man grinned. Southunder was calling for him. "I guess you can't win them all. It wouldn't be an adventure if you could . . . See you around, Sullivan."

There was still a lot to learn about magic.

After the pilot had left, Sullivan closed his eyes and went back to resting under the shade of the *Tempest*'s broken wing. Jane had Mended him, but he could still feel the wounds. Most men would still be incoherent with pain, but he was used to it. Him and pain were old pals.

He opened his eyes to see Lance Talon and Heinrich Koenig standing over him. Lance scratched his beard. "Just thought you'd want to know, Faye's still out."

Sullivan sat up, groaning. "Jane know what's wrong with her?"

"Nothing, far as she can tell. Nothing physical at least. I've heard of Actives putting themselves in a coma, using too much Power," Lance was concerned. He'd taken a real liking to that girl. "I'll let you know."

"I'd appreciate that. She saved my life."

"Saved us all," Lance said. "Hell, from what I heard, she maybe did in the Chairman. In that case that crazy Okie probably saved the whole world. Kill the Chairman . . ." He snorted. "I never figured she'd keep that promise!" Lance limped up the ramp, laughing as he went.

Heinrich was still there, not speaking. His face was nearly as grey as his ripped up coat. "Yeah? Spit it out, *Fritz*."

The Fade smiled as he sat down on the remains of the landing gear. "I am supposed to give you something. When we boarded the *Tokugawa*, Delilah knew she was not coming back." Heinrich held out a Grimnoir ring.

Sullivan didn't take it. "That her father's?"

"No. She kept that one. Said she was intending to earn it. This is Pershing's. I picked it up after you threw it down. When I'd told her what happened, she made me promise to make you take it back." He held it out. Sullivan took it slowly. "She was very adamant."

"Delilah and her promises . . ." he said softly as he curled his fingers around the little piece of black and gold. And Sullivan always kept his promises. He would not let her down this time. That was the end of it. "Sorry, got something in my eye."

Heinrich rose. "She was a remarkable woman. I've known thousands who shared her final curse, and only the very best of them were strong enough to think of anyone other than themselves . . . I offered to end her suffering, but she wanted her death to have meaning . . . I must go check on Faye."

Meaning. He'd survived Rockville. He could survive anything.

Sullivan shoved the ring back on his pinky.

Faye was in the place with the big glowing thing in the sky, which was apparently what the Power looked like in real life, two big shapes stuck together, all made of bunches of little complicated shapes, with dangling arms connecting to every Active in the world. It still reminded her of that drawing of a jellyfish that she'd seen in a book. Instead of Mr. Sullivan's wasteland from the big war, she was sitting on a haystack, watching the cows wander in on their own from the corral because they knew it was milking time. Crows were landing on the barn roof, and the air smelled like it had just rained, and above it all was the Power. Her place was a lot nicer than Mr. Sullivan's.

The last time she'd been here, in the dream world, not on the Vierra farm, she'd thought that this was hell, and she'd been condemned there for breaking the commandment about not killing folks. Well, since then, she'd killed so many people that she'd lost track, but they'd all been bad, and she'd done it all with her God-given abilities, so she figured her and God were square.

Her body was back in the real world, but she'd fried her brain map like an egg. She did not know if she would ever wake up. *Might as well get comfy.*

She watched the Power for a while, as it consumed the magic of the Actives who died. The Power had planted the seeds, the Actives had grown the crop, and now it was time to harvest. The Power wasn't scary. It was just a big critter. It wasn't good, or bad. It just wanted to live, same as anything else, and it did it through people like her. It was silly to be scared of the Power. In fact, it was scared itself. She could see that now. Something bad and hungry was hunting it, and the Power was afraid.

"You see it too, Traveler?"

The Chairman was sitting on another bale of hay, dressed in a robe just like when she'd seen him last, only he had his hands back. "No fair, I thought you was dead."

"I am." The Chairman turned his head, and she could see right through him. She should have been scared of ghosts, but she wasn't. Nothing could hurt her here, in the place where the dead came to dream. He bowed his head slightly. "Congratulations."

"You shouldn't have killed my Grandpa. Serves you right."

"Revenge is as good a motive as any. Nobler by far than most," the haunt said. He went back to the Power. "I tried to prepare the world, to create a society that would be ready. I failed. Now what will you do without me?"

Faye thought about it. She knew he was talking about the other thing, the hungry thing. "When it shows up . . . it'll get dealt with."

"You will need to be strong. Stronger than you are now. Perhaps in the future you will look back and regret your decisions, but I doubt that. May I leave you my final poem?"

"Sure."

"A second sun at night
from the ocean consuming
Life as oars to water
leaving no trace behind."

"Pretty," Faye said.

"Farewell, Traveler." The Chairman's form dissipated on the wind.

Epilogue

Now is not the end. It is not even the beginning of the end. But it is, perhaps, the end of the beginning.

—Winston Churchill,
longtime critic of the Imperium upon hearing of Chairman Okubo Tokugawa's demise, 1932

New York City, New York

3 MONTHS LATER

HE HAD TO ADMIT, this really was a pretty spectacular office. From the top of the Chrysler Building he could see the dirigibles docking at the Empire State Building, and every inch of the place was pure, polished opulence. "I've got to hand it to the old coot. He certainly knew how to live."

"Yes, Mr. Stuyvesant," the new UBF vice president of finance said as he flopped onto the overstuffed leather couch. "You know why your grandfather used to say that he liked this building the best?"

Francis Cornelius Stuyvesant II turned from the glass wall, picked up the bottle of fine wine from his marble desk, and walked over. "No, why is that, Mr. Chandler?"

The accountant laughed as he held out the empty glass. "He said it was because it was *pointy*." Francis poured him another refill. "Can you believe that?"

He sat on the couch, uncomfortable in his new tuxedo. He'd

inherited the most powerful company in the world. He'd gone toe to toe with the most dangerous wizard in history. He'd survived direct hits from two Tesla superweapons. He was a telekinetic and also happened to be a member of a magical secret society. "I can believe just about anything."

Chandler inhaled the drink in one gulp and gave a contented sigh. "Well, now that we've gotten the legal aspects taken care of, and all the papers are signed, UBF is all yours, Francis." The accountant usually only called him by his first name after he'd had a few too many. "What're you going to do now?"

Francis swirled the wine around but didn't really feel like drinking. "I don't know . . . I've got so much responsibility. I can run this company the way I always thought it should have been run."

The accountant shook his head. "I meant about the *other* thing."

The five UBF men who'd survived the *Tokugawa* had all been paid buckets of money and sworn to secrecy. "Well, in the papers I'm a famous billionaire playboy. I suppose it isn't really practical for the head of UBF to go out and battle evil . . . Hmmm . . . Maybe I could wear a *disguise* when I fulfill my Grimnoir duties . . . Like a mask or something."

"That is perhaps the stupidest thing I've ever heard." Chandler laughed. "You're a hoot."

Francis grinned sheepishly. "Yeah, that is pretty ridiculous. So, what are your plans now that everything is under control?"

"Me? I'm a bookkeeper who drinks too much, is always in a foul mood, and hates coming to work. But since you're paying me lots of money because of my refreshing honesty, I'm not going anywhere." He stood and walked to the door, but paused on his way out. "Though I have given some thought to trying my hand at writing . . ."

Francis chuckled. "Good night, Ray." The accountant gave a little salute with two fingers and closed the door behind him. It was a rare man you could trust with either a Thompson or a general ledger. Francis stayed on the couch, enjoying being alone and the quiet lights of the city. "It's been a long day . . ." he muttered to himself.

"No kidding!" Faye said as she appeared directly in front of him.

"Gah!" he spilled the wine all over his pants. "Don't *do* that!"

Faye clucked disapprovingly and put her hands on her hips. "It ain't my fault you don't have a head map. Sheesh. Look at that, you're gonna be all stained."

It was then that he realized Faye was wearing an honest-to-goodness evening dress. And her hair was done up. And she was wearing jewelry. And *lipstick*? *How scandalous.* "I . . . I . . ." He was speechless. "Well . . ."

"Yeah, I do clean up pretty good, huh?" Faye smiled. "Jane helped me." She twirled for him. "Not bad for a hick, huh?"

"Not bad at all," he answered truthfully.

She beamed at the compliment. "Like I was saying though, super long day. Rumor is that there's Iron Guards up to something in Alabama, and Lance is gonna go check it out, but then some Active kids got rounded up by a mob for nothing but being Active since folks are still all riled up at us, and they're having a sham trial, so Heinrich's going down there to help 'em, and Jane and Dan's wedding is coming up next week, and they said you have to come, don't care how busy you are, and Mr. Browning says hello from France, and his telegram said that he'd be honored to be in charge of the American knights, but the stupid elders still won't give up Mr. Rawls, and still nobody knows where Mr. Sullivan went off to but he said it was real important so it must be, and that reminds me, Mr. Southunder called and said thanks for the new fancy blimp, and—"

Francis put his finger on her lips. Nothing stopped Faye when her head got to spinning. "We're going to be late for the play."

"I can fix that real quick!"

He was hesitant. After she'd Traveled an entire dirigible, Faye had slept for a week straight. Her Power had been severely overtaxed, nearly burned out, and she was still recovering. It turned out that even Faye had limits. "Can't we take the elevator?"

Faye's grey eyes twinkled. The Traveler may only have worked her way back up to a small part of the magic she'd tapped during the battle, but nothing could keep Faye down for long. She took his hand. "Elevators are for chumps!"

END

Glossary of Magical Terms

From the notes of Jake Sullivan, 1932
Active Icons created by the Otis Institute for Magical Studies

A

Active—The catch-all term for people with magical abilities. Specifically those who have strong enough connections to the Power to utilize their ability at will and with a greater degree of control than a Passive. Actives vary in the amount of Power available to them, with some being more naturally gifted than others. The conventional wisdom has always been that Actives are only able to use one type of Power.

Actively Magical—Old-fashioned term for Active.

Angel of Death—(see Pale Horse)

B

Burner—(see Torch)

Beastie—Similar to Dolittle, but stronger, with the added ability to control animals telepathically. Extreme cases can actually put part of their consciousness into the creature and fully control it, including broadcasting the Beastie's speech, etc. There have been some rumors of Beasties capable of controlling human beings, but that may be antimagic propaganda.

Beastman—(see Beastie)

Boomer—Unknown type of Active. The Special Prisoners' Wing guards at Rockville mentioned holding one of these in solitary confinement in a special lead-lined chamber.

Brute—One of the most common of all Magicals. Brutes channel Power through their bodies, increasing their physical strength and toughness. They must work up to greater feats of strength. If too much Power is used too quickly, severe injuries or death can occur. They have been banned from professional sports in most countries, but there is always work available for a Brute.

C

Cog—The second most popular of all Actives. Cogs are able to tap their Power to fuel their intelligence, and to receive strokes of magical brilliance. They usually only have one area that they are gifted in, for example Ferdinand von Zeppelin was a Cog when it came to airships. If it weren't for his bursts of magical ideas, who knows what we would be riding. I do not know if all Cogs are already intelligent, but I've never heard of a dumb one.

Crackler—Capable of channeling, harnessing, and controlling electrical current. They are a relatively common type, and most make their living as electricians or in industry. The more powerful Cracklers can draw energy from the air and generate their own lightning.

demon—(see Summoned)

E

Edison—(see Crackler) I have been told this is considered the polite term now.

Beastie

Boomer

Brute

Cog

Crackler

elder—Member of the Grimnoir Society leadership.

Enemy—Unknown predatory creature that may be pursuing the Power, according to Chairman Okubo Tokugawa.

F

Fade—Capable of walking through solid objects. Perhaps they do this through modifying their density so that other matter fits between their molecules. They are the opposite of the Massive, yet both of them originate from the same Density related section of the Power. Fades are universally loathed for their reputation as thieves, cutthroats, and peeping toms.

Finder—Related to the Summoner, but dealing more with disembodied spirits rather than physical beings. Finders are primarily used as scouts, and their sensitivity varies greatly. It is possible that Finders and Summoners are using the same region of the Power, with Summoners simply being more powerful.

Fixer—(see Cog) Usually a term reserved for lower level Cogs, who are better at repairing than inventing.

Fortune Teller—Charlatans who pretend to have magic and know the future to rip off suckers. There is no proof of any precognitive Active.

G

Gravity Spiker—(see Heavy) The much more dignified term for an Active Heavy.

Grey Eye—(see Traveler) All known Travelers have strange grey eyes.

Grim Reaper—(see Pale Horse)

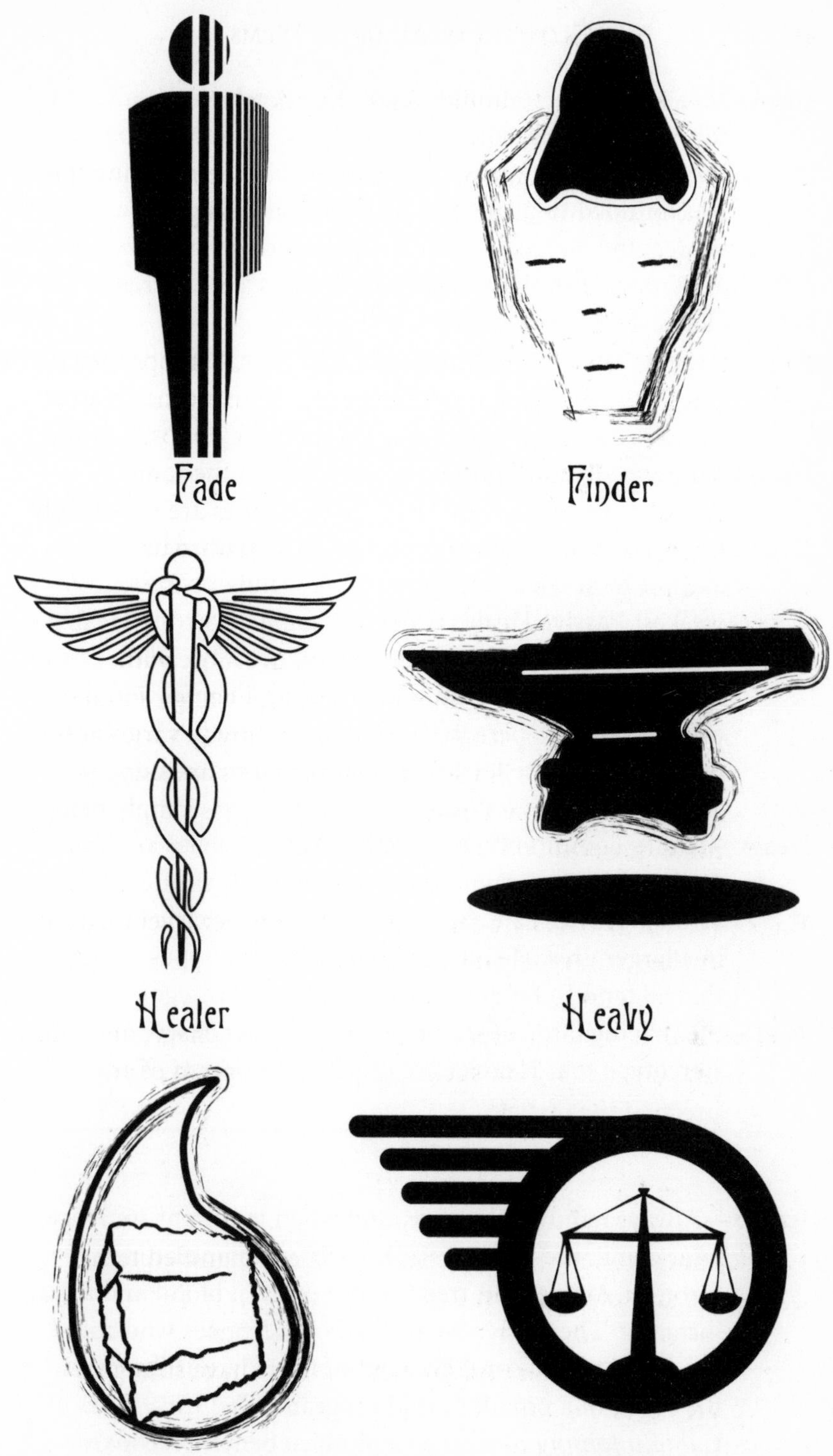
Fade
Finder
Healer
Heavy
Icebox
Justice

Grimnoir Society—A combination of the French words grimoire, for book of spells, and noir, for black, because at the time the origins of magic were shrouded in mystery. The Society was founded to protect Actives from the Normals and to protect the Normals from Actives. Their primary operatives are known as knights, and their leaders are referred to as elders. They work in secrecy.

H

Head Case—(see Reader)

Healer—The rarest and most popular of all Actives. They are capable of accelerating the natural healing process. Even the weakest Passive Healer is worth a fortune. Strong Healers can fix most wounds almost instantaneously. I have been led to understand that even without using their Power, they can always see a person's insides. I suppose it's a good thing they're paid so well, because that would make me ill.

Heavy—A very common type of Active. Most Heavies are limited to changing the gravitational pull in a very limited area. Strong Heavies can change the pull and also the direction in a larger area. Heavies are one of the few types of Actives that all tend to fall into the same physical category, most of them being large of stature. There is an undeserved stereotype that Heavies are dumb. (see Gravity Spiker)

I

Icebox—Always handy to have around when you want some ice in your drink, the Icebox is able to lower temperatures. Stronger Actives can freeze water or even blood and tissue instantly. There have been stories of Iceboxes who could produce ice walls or spikes out of thin air, but these may be the result of a popular radio program, *The Adventures of Captain Johnny Freeze.* As a physical benefit, Iceboxes cannot be harmed by frostbite or extreme cold.

J

Justice—This is a rumored type of Active. Supposedly, they can always tell truth from lies. Personally, I'll believe it when I meet one.

K

kanji—(see Spells) The Japanese term for physical spells. Their Kanji tends to be more stylized and artistic than the western European style markings of the Grimnoir, but is very effective at channeling Power.

knight—An operative of the Grimnoir Society.

L

Lazarus—An Active capable of chaining the spirits of the recently dead to their bodies, creating tortured undead. They are the worst of all, sheer magic scum, and the only good Lazarus is a dead Lazarus.

Lightning Bug—(see Crackler)

Lucky—I had heard about these for years, and thought they were a fairytale to explain people who cheated at cards. They use their magical ability to alter probability. The term used by Dr. Fort to explain this ability to influence chance was psychokinesis.

M

Machine Head—(see Cog) Usually a Cog who is in tune with physical machines rather than theory or science.

Magicals—A common term for people with Power, which can include both Actives and Passives.

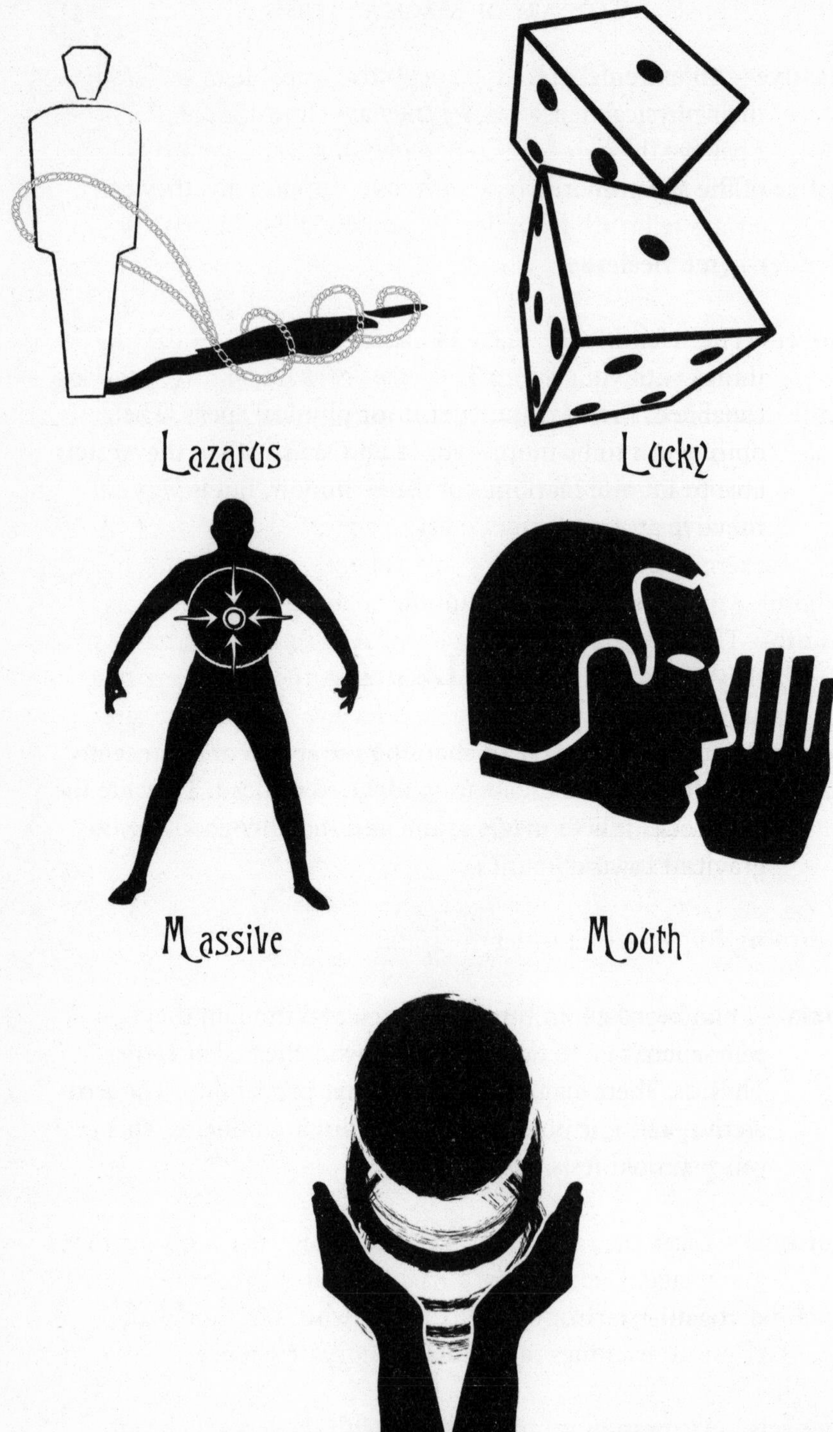
Lazarus
Lucky
Massive
Mouth
Mover

Massive—An extremely rare type of Active, capable of increasing their physical density, until they are almost invulnerable. I believe they are related to Fades, but in the opposite end of the spectrum.

Mender—(see Healer)

Mover—The scientific term is telekinetic, which means moving things with your mind. They are very rare, and very few are capable of moving more than a small number of small objects at a time. As a Mover's Power increases they are able to lift more weight, lift more individual items at once, move them to higher velocities, and most difficult of all, exercise a finer degree of control over the controlled objects.

Mouth—The most hated or most loved Actives, depending on if they are in charge or not. Mouths are able to influence anyone listening to their voice. Passive Mouths can alter moods and emotions, while a powerful Active can directly control your thoughts and feelings. The smarter you are, the harder it is for a Mouth to steer you. Mouths tend to gravitate toward politics.

N

Nixie—Unknown type of Active, cataloged by Dr. Spengler and referenced by Dr. Einstein's work relating to particle physics. There is no official documentation on this type of Active, and it is possible that this name is referring to some other known Active type.

Normals—Term used mostly by Actives to describe people without any magic. Depending on who is using it, it can be a derogatory term.

O

Opener—(see Lazarus) short for Grave Opener.

P

Pale Horse—The opposite of the Healer, the touch of the Pale Horse causes disease and sickness. No Active is more hated than these. Luckily for us, most Normals think that they are a story used to scare children.

Passive—A Magical who does not have active control over their Power. They usually have one small trick that they can do, but are unable for whatever reason to grow their ability. For example, Passive Heavies are instinctively able to pick up heavy things. Passive Healers can accelerate the natural healing process just by their presence but cannot target specific areas or wounds. Passive Readers can pick up snatches of other people's thoughts but often go insane from being unable to control the input.

Pipes—Unknown type of Active. Intelligence reports during the Great War showed that the Germans held one of these in reserve, but it is uncertain if we ever encountered him.

Power—1. The energy that all Magicals possess. As the energy is used, our reserves are depleted. The rate that it recharges and the total amount that can be stored depend on the individual's natural gifts and practice. It is currently unknown if a Magical is born connected to the Power, or if the connection forms at some point during their early life.

Power—2.The living being that all magical energy originates from. Its origin is a mystery. I believe it to be a symbiotic parasite. It grants magical abilities to some humans, and as we develop those abilities, the magical energy that we carry grows. When we die, the Power 'digests' this energy and feeds. The process is then repeated. The growth of the being explains the increase in our numbers over time.

Pale Horse

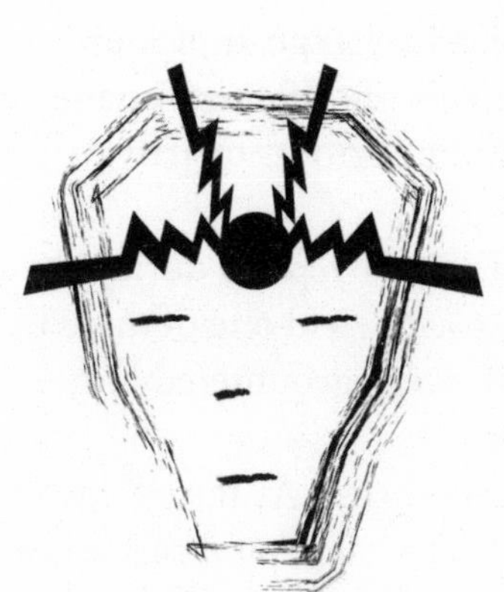

Reader

Ringer

Shard

R

Reader—Someone possessing the magical ability to read another's mind, sometimes called telepathy. Weak Readers can get general feelings from their target, while a strong Reader can crack your head open and watch your memories like a motion picture. Readers can also broadcast thoughts and memories. The stronger their target's will or intelligence, the more difficult they are to Read, and the more likely they are to sense the intrusion.

Ringer—An extremely rare type of Active who can change their appearance and voice to perfectly mimic another. It is unknown if they actually physically change, or if they just create the illusion in other people's minds. I met one once in Rockville but he escaped within 24 hours of arrival.

Rune Arcanium—A book of spells collected by the Grimnoir Society.

S

Scales—(see Justice)

Slinger (see Lucky)

Shadow Walker—(see Fade)

Shard—A rare type of Active that can modify their bone structure at will. I had one start a fight with me in Rockville. They still squish just like everyone else.

Shifter—(see Ringer) It is believed in some circles that there is a type of Active that can actually change their physical form, but my personal belief is that these are just talented Ringers.

Spells—Through creating a representation of one of the coordinate sections of the Power, specific magical energies can be channeled into, and connected to, those markings. Grimnoir-designed spells tend to look like old European-style writing, while Imperium Kanji are more artistic.

Summoned—A being brought into our reality by a Summoner. The strength of the creature is dependent upon the Summoner's skill. Summoned only communicate at a rudimentary level, though they do have some language. It is unknown where they originate from and they will never communicate on that subject except in the vaguest terms. Summoned remain in this world until destroyed or dismissed.

Summoner—An Active that can bring in creatures from another world to serve their bidding. It is unknown where these beings come from. The personal beliefs of the Summoner seem to affect what the Summoned looks like. Extremely powerful Summoners can bring in drastically strong creatures. The more forceful the creature, the more Power and attention it takes to keep it under control.

T

Teleporter (see Traveler)—A scientific term that has recently come into common usage.

Torch—The single most common type of magical ability, Torches control fire. Passives are usually limited to very small flames, while a powerful Active can put out a flaming hydrogen dirigible. Unlike the Icebox who can't be harmed by cold, Torches can still be burned just like any other human.

Trap—(see Mouth) Usually used with a dual meaning, as in "That politician is a Trap."

Traveler—One of the only Actives that can be spotted by a physical trait. All known Travelers have grey eyes. They are one of the rarest types, but not by birth, but rather because so few of them live long enough to control their ability. Travelers are able to move instantly between two places. The stronger the Traveler, the farther they can go, and the more they can carry.

U

Undead—A being created by a Lazarus. Physical death has occurred but the body remains animated. Consciousness and intelligence remains but so does the pain of whatever killed them. Undead possess no natural healing abilities and only continue to deteriorate. They cannot be magically Mended. Very few undead remain sane for any length of time and they tend to grow increasingly violent and erratic. They do not truly die until their body is utterly destroyed. There is a special place in hell for anyone who would curse someone to being Undead.

W

Weatherman—A Magical with the ability to influence the weather. Strong Actives can actually stop or start storms and change wind patterns, sometimes even up to hurricane force. Too harsh use of this skill can cause severe side effects, such as the Great Dust Bowl of 1927.

Words (see Mouth)

Z

Zombies—(see Undead) The first known Lazarus originated in Haiti. It is believed that is where the term Zombie originated from.

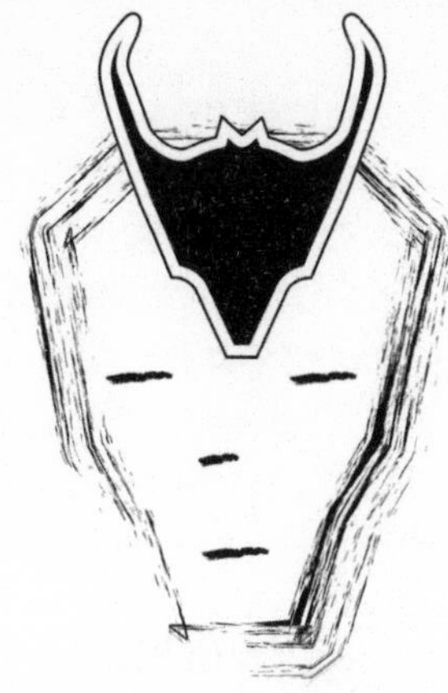

Summoner

Tinker

Torch

Traveler

Weatherman